Everyone stared around the arena and finally all eyes came to rest on the ring. The bloody Vorga, splashed red all over, and the mangled, chewed body of Brokk on the floor.

People started screaming and panicking, pushing and shoving each other to get away from the ring. In a mad rush of feet the crowd scrambled to get out of the slaughterhouse. They didn't want blood. They wanted to escape, to go back to their lives and forget what they'd seen. No matter how much he drank, or how hard he tried, Choss wasn't sure he'd ever forget and he doubted they would too.

By Stephen Aryan

Battlemage
Bloodmage
Chaosmage

BLOOD
MAGE

STEPHEN
ARYAN

www.orbitbooks.net

Orbit
Hachette Book Group
1290 Avenue of the Americas
New York, NY 10104
www.orbitbooks.net

Printed in the United States of America

RRD-C

First U.S. edition: April 2016
Simultaneously published in Great Britain and in the U.S. by Orbit in 2016

10 9 8 7 6 5 4 3 2 1

Orbit is an imprint of Hachette Book Group.
The Orbit name and logo are trademarks of Little, Brown Book Group Limited.

The Hachette Speakers Bureau provides a wide range of authors for speaking events.
To find out more, go to www.hachettespeakersbureau.com or call (866) 376-6591.

The publisher is not responsible for websites (or their content)
that are not owned by the publisher.

Library of Congress Control Number: 2015958533
ISBN: 978-0-316-29831-5

For my family

BLOOD
MAGE

CHAPTER 1

A large crowd had gathered on the street by the time Byrne arrived at the murder scene.

"Guardian of the Peace, let me through," he said, shoving people aside. "All right, fun's over. Go home."

He kept up the litany of platitudes, trying to get the obstinate crowd to move on even though he knew there was something to see. The people of Perizzi never passed up on a bit of street theatre.

Worried and scared faces surrounded him on all sides. People who'd spilled out of nearby taverns. A large group of fishermen on their way home after a long day at sea. A gaggle of drunk Morrin, their horned heads peeking over the crowd. A clutch of local merchants. A pair of tall Seve traders. A lesser noble flanked by two Drassi bodyguards and even a black-eyed Zecorran. He lurked on the fringe of onlookers, nervously dividing his attention between the crowd and the dead body. A few people glared but so far it had not come to anything more than dirty looks.

Just over a year had passed since the west, united under the Mad King of Zecorria, had surrendered to Seveldrom. Perizzi, the capital of Yerskania, had liberated itself in the final days, but the scars of the war still remained. In the days immediately afterwards, people went through the motions, pretending nothing had changed and that they could just go back to their old lives. Buying and selling, getting on with their jobs, drinking and gambling, loving and fighting. But it was just a sham. A shadow play where everyone knew their part.

No one had been unaffected. No one left without scars of some kind on the outside or within. After weeks and then months without a resurgence in violence the people in Perizzi finally started to relax. They stopped overreacting to small outbursts of hostility. Stopped staring at every stranger with suspicion and gradually a new rhythm started to emerge. People started paying attention to what needed rebuilding and what needed to change. When they realised another conflict wasn't around the corner they finally started to live again.

More than a year on and only now did Byrne think life had started to get back to a semblance of normality on the streets. That also meant a return to a certain volume of crimes being reported, but he'd been expecting that too.

Trade, the life-blood of the city, continued to flow. During the war it had stalled, but now it too had returned to a familiar level. In turn it generated noise, chaos, traffic and crime. The borders were open again and Yerskania traded with people from all nations, even the savage Vorga. But many still blamed Zecorria for letting a mad King take their throne and for dragging everyone into a pointless war. People needed someone to blame for everything that had happened and the Zecorrans drew the shortest straw.

When he reached the front Byrne gave the crowd another cursory glance. His instincts told him the killer had not come back to relive the moment or gloat at the inability of the Guardians to catch him.

Stood beside the body was another Guardian, Tammy Baker, a blonde who towered over everyone on the street. She and one member of the Watch were trying to keep the crowd back, but were having some difficulty as everyone wanted a look at the dead victim. Someone had covered the body with a cloak, but a shrunken claw poked out from underneath.

Byrne sighed. He'd seen two like it before. This wasn't a normal murder. It was something else, something messy and daring this time. The killer hadn't even bothered to try and hide the body this time. A squad of six members of the Watch turned up and they began to force the crowd away from the victim.

"All right, time to go home," said Byrne, facing the crowd. "Get moving. Go on."

The Watch started to chivvy the crowd and a few people began to disperse. Byrne pulled one of the Watch aside and pointed out the nervous Zecorran.

"Find out where he lives and walk him partway there. When you're sure no one is following, come back here."

"Yes, Sir."

The majority of onlookers were refusing to leave.

"Sergeant. Encourage them to disperse."

The Watch started turning people around, shoving them and forcing them backwards. Byrne stood with his arms crossed, doing nothing, simply watching the crowd. Eventually the onlookers realised nothing would happen while they lingered. All but the most stubborn took the hint and drifted away. Only when the majority were on their way did he turn back to the body and lift a corner of the cloak. Squatting down beside it Byrne tried to take in every detail and not think that it used to be a person. It was a lot easier to study if he made it into a thing in his head.

As far as dead bodies went, this one looked particularly unpleasant. Judging by the length of the corpse and size of the hands and feet, it had once been a man. Anything more than that was difficult to tell because of its condition. Although it had been lying on the ground for less than an hour, the body looked as if it had been decomposing for decades. All of its skin had been stretched tight over the bones. The eyes resembled two black raisins in cavernous sockets. The tongue was reduced to a shrivelled black lace. The mouth gaped open in a silent scream, but he was willing to bet no one had heard a thing.

Looking over the body Byrne saw no visible wounds or marks on the skin. No blood on the ground and the skull wasn't crushed or mangled in any way.

"Third one in three weeks," said Baker, clenching her jaw. Her fists were criss-crossed with old scars, the legacy of her former profession as an enforcer for one of the city's crime Families. Her unusual height was a gift from her Seve father, and if not for her pale skin, blonde hair and blue eyes, people wouldn't think her local. Byrne was constantly studying people and trying to unravel their stories. Today was no different, except he couldn't question his subject, so he'd have to find answers in a different way.

"Same story as before?" he asked, looking at their location and the surrounding buildings. The body lay in the middle of a fairly busy side street. Three roads connected at a junction less than half a dozen paces away. People regularly used this street as a shortcut down to the docks to visit the cheap taverns and seedier brothels that lined the waterfront. It wasn't exactly out of the way. The killer was becoming bold. Or desperate.

"No one saw or heard the murder," said Baker, shaking her head. "I spoke to a few drinkers dockside. They saw a bright light in the sky. Described it as orange or red. They thought a building had caught fire."

Byrne didn't comment because they all knew what that meant. Magic.

He stared at the body, trying to absorb everything about the scene before all the evidence was taken away. The victim had a silver ring on one finger and the coin purse in his pocket was half full. But it had never been about robbery.

The sound of marching feet intruded on Byrne's thoughts.

"What's he doing here?" asked Baker as the Watch snapped to attention.

"Three in three weeks," said the Khevassar, his shadow falling over Byrne.

"Yes, Sir."

Byrne stood up, towering over his superior. Unlike everyone else, the Khevassar's red uniform was edged with silver instead of black and he didn't carry any weapons. The Old Man wasn't much to look at, slightly built with white hair and blue eyes, but he was one of the most intelligent and dangerous men in Perizzi.

For as long as anyone could remember he'd used the honorary title and nothing else. Some Guardians believed him to be a distant heir to the throne who'd given up his position for a life of service. Others had more outlandish ideas, but having studied the man, Byrne knew they were nothing more than stories. There was no mystery. Whoever he'd been before wasn't important. He defined himself by what he did, not who he'd been.

Six more members of the Watch flanked the Khevassar and a rotund surgeon trailed after them, huffing at the Old Man's unforgiving pace.

"Same as the others?" asked the Khevassar.

"Sucked dry. Not a drop of moisture left," said Byrne, gesturing at the corpse and then the streets. "The killer could've come from one of six directions. Easy to disappear down here in the warren."

Centuries ago the city had been a fishing village, then a trading post. Over the years the ramshackle wooden buildings beside the docks had been rebuilt with stone. The village became a town as it spread, first along the mouth of the river, then further inland until it swelled and became a city. The oldest buildings were on the docks and they'd been rebuilt over and over, turning the area into a warren. Down here, no two buildings were alike, with old sat beside new as those in disrepair were torn down and rebuilt bigger and taller. There were many reasons the dealers and gangs frequented this area. You could always find a dark alley or a back door that led elsewhere if the Watch drifted too close.

"Witnesses?"

"None," said Baker.

The Khevassar pursed his lips and gestured for the two Guardians to follow him. They moved a short distance away, giving the surgeon space to inspect the body and record his findings. As per the other bodies, Byrne suspected there would be no clues to the killer's identity, but procedure had to be followed.

"What was the mood of the crowd?" asked the Old Man when he and the Guardians were out of earshot of the others.

"Anxious, scared," said Baker.

"Any violence?"

"No, but we know it won't last if this continues," she replied.

The Khevassar grunted. "We need to find this killer. Quickly and quietly."

"I know someone who could help with this sort of thing. A specialist," said Byrne.

"Outsider?"

"No, he's local, but he's not a Guardian or member of the Watch."

The Khevassar shook his head sadly. "Specialist, eh? Is that what we're calling them now?"

Baker shifted, clearly uncomfortable but didn't say anything.

Byrne shrugged. "People are scared of magic, and this sort of thing doesn't help," he said, gesturing at the body.

"How quickly people forget. It was magic that won the war."

"There are many people with dead relatives who would disagree," said Byrne.

"Then their memory is short."

Byrne didn't argue the point. Thousands of warriors had died on the battlefield in Seveldrom, hacked to pieces with sharpened steel or torn apart by devious traps. Magic had played a big part at the end, with the death of the Warlock at the hands of Balfruss, but no one liked to talk about it. Or him. That name had become something worse than a curse. No one dared say it out loud. They were scared he might hear them and come back.

Ever since that day the few remaining Seekers had stopped visiting towns and villages looking for children born with the ability to sense the Source. Those who showed any signs of magical ability were shunned, exiled and in extreme cases murdered. Byrne had heard one story about a girl being drowned in a river by a mob from her village which included her parents. People claimed to be more civilised in the cities, but out in the countryside, where the Watch didn't visit, anything could happen.

The Warlock had brought the world to the brink of destruction and anyone with magical ability was now seen as a threat. No one spoke about the Battlemages who'd died during the war, fighting to protect innocent lives.

Four foot of steel in the gut was deadly, but at least it was something people could understand. A sword was tangible and it had weight. Setting someone on fire just by staring at them wasn't natural. It couldn't be explained with logic.

"Who is this specialist?" asked the Khevassar, his mouth twisting on the last word. "Do I know them?"

"Yes, Sir."

The Old Man ran a hand through his thinning hair and sighed. "Can we trust them?"

Byrne hesitated, then said, "It's Fray."

Baker's eyes widened and the Khevassar raised an eyebrow. "Really?"

"He's the right man for the job."

"I've no doubt about that, but you'll have to do it officially. Enrol him as a Guardian of the Peace. Make him a novice in training, partnered to you."

"What about passing the entrance requirements and the paperwork?" asked Byrne.

The Khevassar waved it away. "I'll take care of it. That's the least of my worries. If this continues for much longer I'll be summoned to the palace."

"I don't envy you."

"I was about to say the same thing," said the Khevassar.

Thinking of the right person to solve a magic-related murder hadn't been difficult. Now all Byrne had to do was convince Fray to become a Guardian, the very job that had killed his father.

CHAPTER 2

"I'm very sorry about your father," said Katja, getting it out of the way. The Morrin couple were red-eyed and the wife kept wiping at her face with the back of a hand. It seemed as if her tears weren't welcome, or perhaps she didn't want to share them with strangers.

"Thank you . . . priestess."

The husband harrumphed. "She's not a priestess."

"You're right, I'm not. Katja is fine."

"Thank you for coming so quickly," said the wife, sniffing and trying to hoard her tears.

"Of course, although I was a little surprised by your message," said Katja, choosing her words carefully. "Do you not follow the Blessed Mother?"

A quick glance around the sitting room of their modest house suggested they were devout followers. From the roughly carved statue sat on the mantel above the fireplace to the three icons of the Blessed Mother on the walls.

"We do, but my father came to Yerskania many years ago because his views were different. He's been devoted to the Great Maker for over a hundred years."

"Is that going to be a problem? Are you asking for more money?" said the husband, determined to find fault. Katja couldn't really blame him for being cautious as the services she offered were unusual. Hers was the only business in the city that made arrangements for the deceased from all faiths. For now at least.

"No. It won't be a problem and it doesn't cost more. It's unusual for Morrin to follow the Maker, but not unheard of. I can make the arrangements at a nearby church of the Maker. The local Patriarch will stand watch over your father for three days, unless there's someone else you'd prefer?"

"That will be fine," said the wife. She managed a small smile and her eyes became distant. Looking into the past, no doubt to happier times when her father had been alive.

"Do you do this a lot?" asked the husband. Katja raised an eyebrow and he continued. "Deal with our people?"

"There are many Morrin in Perizzi," said Katja with a shrug. "The cities of Yerskania are open to all, and I'll help anyone who asks for my services."

"And no doubt charge more for foreigners."

"That's enough, Ton," snapped the wife, slamming her hand on the table. The husband withered under her glare and his shoulders slumped.

"I'm sorry. I just ... " Ton trailed off and bowed his head. "I don't know how to do this, yes?"

Katja inclined her head, offering a smile. "Once your father-in-law's watch is over, I'll arrange for his ashes to be brought here. The city permits you to scatter them from any of the bridges, or at the docks if you prefer."

"Thank you, I'll see you out," said the wife, leading her to the front door. As Katja stepped into the street the wife spoke again. "I'm sorry for my husband's behaviour."

"We all deal with grief in different ways."

She shook the wife's hand, pulled up the hood of her robe and set off towards her shop. As she walked along the winding streets, Katja studied the faces of those in the crowd. Just over a year ago when she'd arrived in the city, fear and suspicion of strangers had been apparent. Only now was it starting to fade and there was a better mix of people from abroad, including tall Seves and even dark-skinned merchants from the far east.

It had taken months of hard work to maintain a careful balance. The city authorities had done their best to stay visible without being seen as threatening. The number of patrols by the Watch were increased, especially in the popular areas frequented by foreigners, and gradually people had started to feel safe again. There were still areas of the city that no tourist or merchant ventured into, and the Watch only made brief sweeps, but it had always been that way.

As she passed a squad of the Watch, Katja noticed the sharp lines of their uniforms, the pride in their step and the keenness of the officer's gaze as she swept the street for trouble. The Yerskani Queen, Morganse, had brought in a number of new policies as soon as the war ended. Soldiers in the army and members of the Watch now received much better equipment. They also benefited from intensive weapons training in several disciplines and their wages had increased. As expected there had been a surge in the number of applications to join the army and the Watch, but only the best were accepted. And only the most capable and intelligent of those were able to apply to join the Guardians, the elite investigators.

Queen Morganse could not build walls around Perizzi, her capital city, which was renowned for being open to all, but she would not be caught unawares again. The visible changes on the street weren't subtle, but Katja knew there were a number of other less obvious policies being implemented.

As the busiest port in the world, a river of goods, and more importantly information, flowed from the docks throughout the city and beyond. There were now more spies of all nationalities spread out across the city, and the entire west, than ever before. The moment the war ended and the official documents were signed, merchants were keen to get on the road again. It had been the perfect disguise. Katja had been among the first group of agents to arrive in the newly liberated Perizzi with merchant wagons from Seveldrom.

As an agent for Seveldrom, all of Katja's information went directly to Roza, the local head of the network. Last time Seveldrom hadn't done enough to prevent the war. Roza had made it very clear it wouldn't happen again, and that those orders came directly from the top, from Queen Talandra.

This was Katja's first assignment and so far it had been uneventful. Most of her time had been taken up with establishing the business and convincing everyone that she was who she claimed to be.

As far as most people in the city knew, she was Perizzi's first religiously independent director of last rites. It was a position which gave the Seveldrom network a unique insight into any unusual deaths in the city. It also provided her with a good reason to travel anywhere in Perizzi without it looking suspicious.

Her pale skin and black hair marked her as Yerskani, which made it easier for locals to trust her. Only a few knew she'd been born and raised in Seveldrom. Her loyalty was to her Queen and the country of her birth.

As she turned the last corner and the shop came into view, Katja paused to look for observers, as a man had been following her a few nights ago. He always kept his distance and tried to stay out of sight, but she'd heard the scuff of his shoes and once caught a glimpse of his face from her eye corner. It suggested he'd received some training, or perhaps they were just skills learned on the streets. Whether innocent or otherwise it didn't matter, she'd managed to lose him in the warren down at the docks and had not seen him since. Even so it paid to be cautious and patient.

Once satisfied that the shop wasn't being watched, Katja crossed the street and went in through the front door. A small chime rang above her head as she opened and then closed the door. Summoned by the sound, a pale, gaunt man with wispy brown hair dressed in a hooded grey robe drifted out from the back room.

"Greetings," he said with a friendly yet sympathetic smile before he saw it was her. The smile slipped and his normal annoyed expression replaced it. She was sure that Gankle must question his decision on a daily basis about going into business where he had to deal with the living. He seemed much more comfortable with the dead. They didn't speak, or chew, or breathe, all of which annoyed him. "What took you so long?"

"They thought I was going to charge them extra."

"If they were expecting it then maybe you should."

Katja shrugged. "They want us to handle everything. Can you speak to the Patriarch at the Maker's church?"

Gankle's expression turned sour. It would mean leaving the shop and talking to someone other than her. Nevertheless he inclined his head. "I'll take care of it."

Katja followed him into the visitors' room and flopped down in one of the large comfy chairs, hooking a leg over the armrest. Gankle sat down opposite with practised grace, lifting the hem of his robe and brushing out the creases, as if they were at court and it was made from silk and not wool. Katja's bored eye roamed over the different religious symbols hung on the far wall, the shelves lined with sacred texts and books of poetry, the aromatic candles, charms and a hundred other bits of paraphernalia required for her role. The ritual was what really mattered to the bereaved. It gave them a path to follow amid the chaos. A raft to keep their head above water in the storm for which there didn't seem to be any end. Grief seemed to embarrass some people, as if crying and aching for those who were gone wasn't the most natural thing in the world.

"This came for you while you were out," said Gankle, handing her a folded note with a broken seal. "You need to see her immediately."

Katja pretended he hadn't spoken and took her time reading the note because she knew it annoyed him. Years ago Gankle had been an agent for Seveldrom, and although officially retired, he seemed to think his former status allowed him to get involved. His only jobs were to provide Katja with a place to live and to corroborate her position, but he often seemed to forget.

"The note sounds quite urgent. I should see her straight away," said Katja, struggling not to grin at his annoyance. She left Gankle grinding his teeth and went out the front door.

Following her training Katja took a slightly circuitous route, stopping occasionally to look in shop windows, checking her reflection for followers with the pretence of being interested in the goods behind the glass.

Stopping off at a bakery Katja went inside and bought a small fish pie then ate it on the curb outside where a few children lingered. They asked her a few questions about her grey robe and when her answers proved boring the children quickly lost interest. While they talked she scanned the crowd, looking for anyone familiar she'd already seen this morning. One or two people gave her a curious glance but no more than that. Satisfied that she wasn't being followed, Katja wasted no more time.

As she reached the spice shop the midday bell had just started to toll at a nearby church of the Maker. She pushed open the door and a woman with red hair behind the counter looked up, a friendly smile on her face. It didn't waver or change in any way, but Katja saw a slight tightening around her eyes.

"Welcome," said the spice merchant, gesturing at the racks of pungent herbs and spices arranged on the hive-like shelves. A heady scent of a hundred different perfumes raced up Katja's nose, making it twitch before she sneezed three times. She approached the counter and the shopkeeper shook her head slightly, gesturing towards the chairs by the window.

The spice merchant picked up a few items, incense and herbs often used in funeral rites, before going into the back room. Katja knew anyone could walk through the door at any time and she needed a valid reason for being here. The less she had to lie the more she could stretch the truth to make it convenient.

Katja sank into one of the chairs and stared out of the window. The spice merchant emerged a few minutes later with some pastries and a pot of tea. Only when the tea had been poured into two glasses and they had both nibbled at a spiced pastry did they speak.

"Your note said it was urgent," said Katja.

"I've received some distressing news from a reliable source," said Roza, blowing a loose strand of red hair away from her face. With a sigh she unfastened her hair before tying it back again in a tight pony-tail. Katja didn't think it suited her. It made her forehead too proud, but perhaps that was the point. In the right clothing Roza would turn heads, but dressed in an unflattering man's shirt and loose cotton trousers, with her hair scraped back and no make-up, it told a stranger everything they needed to know about her.

She had no time for frippery or decoration and her business came first. Katja knew Roza actually wore a thin layer of powder on her hands and face which paled her ruddy Seve skin, but no one ever got close enough to see it. There were other local girls far prettier, or at least more approachable, that men would pursue. It allowed Roza to be in plain sight and observe a great deal while going mostly unnoticed. Katja wondered if Roza was ever lonely, then realised her mind had been wandering.

Katja cleared her throat. "Can I ask where the news came from?"

Roza pursed her lips briefly before speaking. "It's reliable. It came from the Butcher."

Katja swallowed hard and drank a sip of tea which suddenly tasted bitter. There were many stories about him and all of them extremely brutal. A year ago no one had heard of the Butcher, but now he was well known in the underworld as a ruthless crime boss. No one dared cross him and any attempt to encroach on his territory was met with messy results. Sometimes he settled for chopping off both feet, but if he deemed the insult severe he took their hands as well. The victims were always still alive when people found them, screaming in pain or pleading for death.

When Katja had asked about him all Roza would say was that he was loyal to Queen Talandra. Any questions about his identity were met with a stony silence.

"How worried should I be?"

"Very," said Roza, letting her mask slip for a second to show Katja her level of concern. "There are rumours about a plot to murder Queen Talandra when she comes here on a state visit."

The words hung in the air between them, heavy with dread. Their Queen was still a relatively young woman, and new to the throne, having inherited from her father who was assassinated during the war. Despite that she had achieved much in a year. Ties between Seveldrom and the west were stronger than ever, particularly with Yerskania. Trade had increased to pre-war levels and she had worked hard to maintain peace through some difficult times. She'd negotiated several treaties, provided warriors and aid to Shael, and even reached out to the Morrin to try and help with their troubles.

The Queen had also survived two assassination attempts but had not publicly blamed anyone, despite rumours that the killers had been from Zecorria or Morrinow. Many in the west loved her for what she had done during the war and since. Anyone with a grain of humanity, or sanity at least, would be hard pressed to find a reason to hate her. Unfortunately there were many who lacked both.

There were a number of ridiculous stories floating around about Talandra. Tales of ritual murder, torture, corruption and blackmail to get people to do what she wanted. Someone in the west was intent on undermining Talandra and all of her good work. Part of Katja's job in the last year had been tracing the stories and passing the information to Roza. Someone was then dispatched to eliminate the story at its source. There had not been any stories for a while, but now a new threat had arisen.

"Do we have any idea who's behind it?" asked Katja.

"That's the problem. I've got everyone working on this, but the information is conflicted. One source claims it's a group of Morrin extremists, determined to destroy Seveldrom. They blame our Queen for their ongoing troubles at home. Civil war is still raging in Morrinow and many have died."

Katja grimaced. More nonsense intent on besmirching the Queen.

"A second source claims it was a group of Chosen from Zecorria who escaped the purge. Even though no one actually knows who did it, they believe Talandra killed their King."

Despite widespread persecution by every nation, a small contingent of Chosen still existed in Zecorria. The fanatical cult which had grown up during the war still believed their late King, Taikon, had been a prophet and living God who would rise again. On the surface, Zecorria seemed quiet, cautiously trading with its neighbours, but inside its borders the story was very different. There were still marches and people claiming to be Chosen speaking out in public against the new Regent, but so far the violence had been limited. Roza and other agents believed the most vocal were merely mouthpieces for the real Chosen who had been driven underground.

"If our Queen was murdered here, the dead would choke the streets," said Roza, gritting her teeth. "What happened to Shael would be nothing by comparison. The west would tear itself apart looking for the killer and every Seve would march to war, bent on revenge."

A year wasn't a long time. The fear of war had been buried, but it had not gone away. A tiny spark could easily turn the nations of the west against each other.

"What do you want me to do?" asked Katja.

"Find out if the rumours are true. Is there a plot, or is it just disgruntled people in the north? Call in every favour, speak to every contact, just find out."

"How long do I have?" asked Katja.

Roza shook her head, deep worry lines creasing her forehead. "I don't know. Maybe a few days. The date of the state visit hasn't been set, but it's a long trip from Seveldrom. So unless we can find some compelling evidence to dissuade her, the Queen will be setting off very soon."

"And if I find whoever is planning this, what then?"

"To accomplish something so big would require a lot of resources and money. If you find the group responsible, then keep digging until you find out who is funding them. We have to make sure we get the whole network before making a move."

"What kind of move?"

Roza's smile showed far too many teeth. "We kill every single one of them until the streets run red."

CHAPTER 3

A hundred familiar smells hit Choss as he stepped inside the converted warehouse. Stale sweat, spilled beer, and blood were the strongest. They mixed together to create something that felt like a homecoming. With them came a stream of memories. Countless hours of training, the crunch of bone on bone, the slap of meat hitting the canvas. Above and beyond them all was the roar of the crowd chanting his name. The sound used to fill him to the brim until he thought his ears would burst. Glory days.

A straggler on their way to the fight jostled him and the glow faded. He shook his head, cast off the memories and went deeper into the arena. That's what he called it. Most others just called it the ring, or the pit. But he'd been trying to get them to move away from that for a couple of years now. Away from the dark old days when two men would go into the ring and only one would come out on his feet. Even further back it had been worse. One came out bloody and the other a cold hunk of meat.

Choss walked down one of the narrow channels between the tiered seats and stopped short of the front. He didn't want to be seen. Even so a few people above his head spotted him and word began to spread. He reached up and shook hands, offered friendly smiles and turned his head slightly when one woman tried to kiss him on the mouth and had to settle for his cheek. A quick glance at the crowd showed there weren't many empty seats. The ring announcer was getting the crowd going and Choss could feel tension building in the air.

He melted away into the shadows and approached a door guarded by a thick-necked man called Jakka. With a big bald head like a melon and tiny ears that stuck out, some would think him a good target for jokes. Until they saw how broad he was across the arms and shoulders. Until they saw the size of his hands, the scars and sunken knuckles. Jakka might have a bit of a paunch, but even the most arrogant spoke with respect to the old fighter.

"Good crowd tonight, Champ," said Jakka without looking up from his book.

"I was just thinking that."

Jakka pulled the tiny pair of spectacles off his nose and offered a broken-toothed grin. "Bring back a lot of memories?" he asked and Choss just grunted. "Tempted to get back in there?"

Choss considered it, then shook his head. "I can do more out here. For all of us."

"I admire your spirit, boy, always have. It's what made you a champion. And I'll do what I can to help, but you know my thoughts. The aristocracy don't want us."

Choss had heard it from Jakka and plenty of others. Over and over again. It stung, but only a little. To show there were no hard feelings he gripped the big man on the shoulder as he went past into the back.

As Choss walked down the corridor his broad shoulders brushed the walls on either side. At the far end were two doors. Behind one he could hear a low rumble of conversation. Fighters getting ready for their time in the ring. Behind the other the sharp rasping voice of Vinneck as he lectured someone. A younger voice tried to speak but Vinneck cut them off. Choss knew that tone so he waited outside. A minute later the door flew open and a young man with red hair stomped away up the corridor.

"Who's next?" asked Vinneck.

Choss went inside and closed the door behind him. "Just me out here, Vinny."

"Thank the Maker," rasped Vinny, pouring himself another cup of foul herbal tea. They'd been partners in the business for two years now, but long before that Vinny had run the fights with other people. They'd all fallen away, some to drink, others to venthe, some just got tired or bored and wanted out of the business. One even tried to rob Vinny and the fighters of their money.

Choss had still been in the ring back then, a new face coming up through the ranks. Thankfully they'd caught up to the thief before he could get out of the city. They'd left him alive, but beyond that Choss didn't know what happened. Probably crippled for life or dead from the beating they'd given him.

The long years, or maybe the many back-stabbing deals, had taken their toll on Vinny. He looked old and worn out. He was thin as a broom handle with skin like old leather. What little hair he had was ash grey, clinging around the back. The top of his head was bald and mottled with brown spots. He looked weak until you saw his eyes. Any fighter could break him physically, it wouldn't be worth calling it a fight, but none of them had a tenth of his brains.

"Those boys, they want more for doing less," said Vinny, jerking his head towards the changing room.

"Is that why you showed Lostram the door?"

"He showed all the signs," said Vinny as he added two lumps of sugar to his tea. He took an experimental sip and grimaced, then added another lump. A few doctors and even a couple of expensive surgeons had taken a look at his stomach.

At first they thought it was something he'd eaten, or maybe the creep that made people waste away in months or sometimes even days. But Vinny had kept living, so in the end they'd shaken their heads and sent him away. An old herbalist had given him the recipe for the tea and it seemed to help with the pain for a while.

"The boy has talent, but he's impatient. He wants riches and women. Wants to travel the world."

"About that—"

"Don't," said Vinny, holding up a claw-like hand. "I know what you're going to say. Please, don't."

Choss felt his temper flare but gritted his teeth and waited for the fire to fade. He counted in his head until he felt calm. "I won't leave it alone."

"I know, and neither will I."

"It's been a year."

Vinny sighed. "It might seem like a long time to you, but people are still scared. You've seen how they react to black-eyed Zecorrans on the street. Even some Morrin are given a wide berth. It's going to be years before we could look at arranging fights elsewhere, or bringing in champions from abroad."

"All right, then what about moving it out of the shadows? What about a proper arena?"

Vinny offered a rare smile. "Don't get too excited, but Doña Jarrow has been charming all sorts of people. A few have said they'll come to a fight."

"What sort of people?"

"People with money, but more importantly, influence. Those who can whisper in the right ears. Maybe even get a whisper into the palace."

Choss felt his chest swell. It's what he'd always hoped would happen. Some people thought fighters were just butchers and thugs, pounding each other until they were bloody. They weren't interested in talk of skill and stamina, the years of train-ing and dedication, the sacrifices made. They thought the fights were low entertainment and should be kept in the shadows. But at every fight he'd see people from all areas of the city. The rich rubbing shoulders with the poor, and once or twice people in hoods surrounded by soldiers out of uniform. The Prince had also been semi-regular, maybe five or six times a year, until the war. Until they cut off his balls, to punish Queen Morganse for her rebellion.

Sometimes women sought out the fighters because they wanted to touch them and be part of it, if only for a moment. The touching sometimes led to more, but it was freely given. Others just wanted to give them gifts, money or their favour, usually a piece of cloth to wear during the fight. There were many deals to be made, under the table and above. All they needed to take the fights further was a chance.

"Just imagine if we could get one big sponsor. Someone with a name in the city," said Choss.

"Feet on the ground, Choss," said Vinny with a hint of reproach. "We're not there yet."

"Fair enough."

"We just need to keep it clean. That's another reason I sent Lostram away. He'd been using venthe to numb himself before a fight."

Choss grimaced. "I'll check on the other lads and look for the signs." Using drugs to cheat wasn't new, but Vinny had managed to keep the business clean for years.

"Send anyone you suspect my way. I'll get to the truth." Vinny drained the last of his tea, swallowing the little bits at the bottom with a grimace. Even so, the lines of pain on his face eased a little. "Speaking of clean, will you have a word with Gorrax? He won't listen to anyone else."

"I'll do it now," said Choss, heading out the door.

He crossed the hall and entered the changing room. Several large, well-built men were preparing for their fights, having a wash or getting dressed. Choss received more smiles of camaraderie from the fighters, as it wasn't that long ago he'd been one of them. One or two called him champion or gave him a brief salute of respect, touching their heart with a fist. He wasn't really a champion, since they'd not hosted fights from other countries yet, but he remained undefeated in Yerskania and they used the title just for him.

The room wasn't big, but all of the fighters stayed away from the figure sat at the far end of the room. As Choss approached Gorrax, the green-skinned Vorga stood up, putting them at eye level. Gorrax was the average height for a green Vorga, at just under six and a half feet. Although there were faster men in the room, few could match the Vorga's raw power and instincts in the ring.

"Good to see you," said Gorrax, opening his mouth wide and giving Choss a clear view of his sharp teeth. It had taken Choss a while to realise it wasn't a yawn or a smile. The Vorga had tried to explain it, but couldn't find the right words. Choss had gathered that it was a sign of respect and a form of greeting between equals. It was also something the Vorga never did with anyone but him. Although it felt peculiar, Choss did the same, showing Gorrax his teeth.

"And you, my friend. Are you ready for your fight?"

Gorrax looked himself up and down, flexing his massive hands then shifting his neck left and right, making it crack. A network of pale scars covered his face and arms, chunks were missing from one wide ear and a few of the bony nodules around his jaw had been broken off. It meant nothing to him. Like scratches on the face of a blade. Vorga were born knowing how to fight and nothing short of death would stop Gorrax.

Dressed in a knee-length leather kilt and a loose vest over his bulky torso, Gorrax had everything he needed. His hands were his most dangerous weapons.

"Two arms, two legs, one head. Ready to fight," said the Vorga. Choss smiled, knowing it was Gorrax's attempt at humour. "What about you? Will you fight again?"

He always asked the same question. No one else had ever beaten the Vorga in the ring. Not since Choss had retired two years ago.

To lose, for a normal Vorga, went beyond shame, beyond embarrassment. Gorrax had once told him they didn't have a word for defeat in his language. Vorga fought to win and the alternative was death. Fighting for money or the entertainment of others were alien ideas. But that was one of the things which made Gorrax an outcast from his people.

Choss didn't know why the Vorga had come to Perizzi, but he was glad. No one had challenged him or fought as hard as Gorrax.

"Maybe one day, but not tonight."

"I will be ready for you when the day comes," promised Gorrax.

"Hear me," said Choss, choosing his words carefully. "I need you to repeat the promise you made."

Gorrax hissed through his teeth, the equivalent of a wince. "I do not need to say it."

"Please Gorrax. For me."

Gorrax remained silent for several long breaths before speaking. "Only for you," he said, staring Choss in the eye. He maintained eye contact, knowing it mattered to the Vorga. "I promise I will not kill my opponent."

"If you do, you won't get paid." The moment he said it Choss regretted the poor choice of words. Gorrax clacked his teeth and shook his head.

"Money doesn't matter."

"If you kill him, they'll put you in a cold cell."

"Cold is fine for me," said Gorrax with a shrug of his broad shoulders. "No lock or door can hold me."

"A cell in the east then, in the desert. Many long days far away from the sea, or even a river. Somewhere with no water."

Gorrax hissed so loudly all other conversation stopped. Choss ignored the other fighters, keeping his eyes locked on Gorrax's face. Being so far away from water horrified green Vorga. All of their cities, towns and villages were built along the coast and on the banks of the wide rivers that criss-crossed the west of their country. Only the blue Vorga wouldn't care, as they came from the mountains, but they were least respected and smallest of the clans. As far as threats went it was the worst he could conjure up for Gorrax.

"I will not kill him," spat Gorrax, looking away first and bowing his head. Guilt burned in Choss's stomach, but it was the only way he knew. He laid a hand on Gorrax's shoulder and after a moment the Vorga put one of his big hands on top, giving it a squeeze. Many times Choss had wondered why Gorrax had been cast out. Living in Perizzi couldn't be easy for him. Surrounded by humans and Morrin. Being seen as the monster from children's stories. Being feared by everyone and hated for what his people had done during the war.

"Thank you, Gorrax."

"Yes, yes. Enough talk and touching," said Gorrax, lifting his head. "More of this and I will think you want to sex me."

Choss tried not to wince at the idea. Instead he laughed and withdrew his hand. Gorrax didn't laugh but he did show his teeth again and Choss mirrored the gesture.

As he headed towards the door Choss noticed one of the fighters, Brokk, wiping his nose and sniffing. As Choss walked past, their eyes met and Brokk quickly turned away. Choss crossed the hall and mentioned his suspicions to Vinny.

"Maker's balls," cursed Vinny. "Sounds like he's on venthe. He's next in the ring as well with Gorrax."

"Do you want me to pull him from the fight?"

Vinny sighed. "No. We don't have anyone else to take his place. I'll speak to him after."

"Are you sure?"

"It took me weeks to persuade him to fight the Vorga. It's getting harder every time, but the crowds love it." Vinny shook his head. "He's a good kid, lots of potential. It's a shame this'll be his last fight for us."

"We're not turning away a lot of new fighters. Maybe we should give him a second chance?"

"We'll see. Send him to my office after the bout," said Vinny, getting to his feet. Choss followed his partner along the narrow corridors towards the ring and then up a set of stairs to the viewing platform.

The noise from the crowd started to build. A chorus of boos and hisses meant Gorrax had just stepped into the ring. As Choss walked onto the raised area above the crowd, people began to cheer as Brokk stepped between the ropes. He waved and blew kisses to women, flexed and danced about. Normally he wasn't a showman and didn't like to show off. Vinny had spotted it too and shook his head.

"This might be more serious than we thought," Choss shouted over the noise of the crowd.

Gorrax didn't move, barely seemed to breathe. He ignored the crowd and the noise. Choss could see his eyes on Brokk, following him as he played to the crowd. The referee brought them together in the centre of the ring, but neither man was really paying attention. Brokk seemed unable to stand still whereas Gorrax resembled a statue. The referee made a show of checking the wrappings on the hands of both opponents, but the real checks had been done earlier.

The referee gave up trying to engage them, quickly ran through the rules and then gestured to the side. As the bell rang, the crowd fell silent, waiting for the first punch.

Much to Choss's surprise, Brokk attacked, laying into Gorrax with a series of jabs to the face. Maybe the venthe had given him a dose of courage. It wouldn't last, especially against such an implacable opponent. Gorrax soaked up the blows like they were nothing, then retaliated with a cross that sent Brokk reeling. The crowd went wild, shouting and calling out a hundred insults and curses at the Vorga.

The cross had opened a cut above Brokk's left eye. He angrily wiped at it then came forward again. He didn't hesitate, didn't take a moment to study his opponent. He just charged, lashing out with a blurring combination.

"Something's wrong," said Choss, but the noise swallowed his voice and Vinny didn't hear.

Gorrax didn't seem to feel any of the punches as he barely covered up. He took several on the chin, even a sharp uppercut from Brokk's heavy right. The Vorga's feet didn't move and his head barely lifted. Instead of pulling back or working the body, Brokk went berserk, pounding the Vorga's face as if he wanted to knock him down. Blood began to soak through the coverings on Brokk's hands as his skin split on the Vorga's bony face.

Gorrax let it continue for another minute without retaliating, then he responded, sending Brokk across the ring and against the ropes.

Before it could devolve any further the bell rang and the two fighters reluctantly separated, going to their corners.

Choss pulled Vinny close so he didn't have to shout. "There's something wrong with Brokk. He's not just being reckless, he's angry."

Vinny's eyes were wide. "It's like he's forgotten all his training."

"I'm going down there," said Choss, racing down the stairs. Vinny called something after him, but he didn't hear. He had to do something. Speak to Brokk, maybe even stop the fight.

Brokk didn't understand Gorrax and the Vorga. They were born to fight. It was in their blood and in their bones, going back hundreds of generations. Trying to bully Gorrax wouldn't work. The only way to beat him wasn't to match his strength but to outsmart him. To take him apart, like a butcher breaking down a carcass into different cuts of meat. It wasn't that easy. It required giving something more, but Choss shied away from the thought. Away from what he'd done to win on that day two years ago.

The crowd began cheering and stomping their feet as he ran down one of the aisles towards the ring. It was getting worse. Brokk came out of his corner punching wild and reckless, going for dangerous shots, illegal low blows and even an elbow. The referee got up onto the edge of the ring to object but Brokk sent him tumbling away with the back of his hand. The crowd loved it. They seemed to think it was part of the show and not something to worry about.

By the time Choss had reached ringside Gorrax was under attack again. Brokk laid into his body, pounding him over and over again, trying to crack a rib or wind him. More blood had seeped through the wrappings on his hands. He left red splashes which stood out against the green of the Vorga's skin. Gorrax clicked his tongue and Brokk misunderstood the sound. Choss remembered but even as he opened his mouth to warn Brokk it was too late.

It didn't mean pain. It meant Gorrax was finally ready for battle. He had warmed up and would now get into the fight. Two lefts and a right sent Brokk back and three jabs cracked his nose. Gorrax pressed his advantage, dodged around a clumsy swing and drove two hard jabs into Brokk's side. He gasped and stumbled, barely holding himself up, only managing it by resting a hand on the ropes. To his credit Gorrax stepped back.

The bell rang, marking the end of the second round, but Brokk ignored it. Instead he charged at Gorrax, lashing out wildly, catching the Vorga on the side of the face, finally splitting the skin.

The crowd shouted and screamed, so loud it made Choss's ears ring. It seemed as if this was why they had really come. Not for sport, but to see two men beat each other to death. He felt something in the air. A strange prickling against his skin. A desperate hunger flowing towards the ring from every raised voice. He remembered that feeling but didn't want to. The last time was when he'd been in the ring with Gorrax. People screaming for blood, desperate to see him break the Vorga into pieces. Smash him into a pulp, hear him beg and cry out in pain.

It had gone far enough. Choss started to climb onto the edge of the ring to stop the fight, but someone grabbed him from behind. He shook them off and tried to move forward again, but more hands pulled him back. To his surprise the hands belonged to people in the crowd, half a dozen men and women. More put their hands on him, locking him in place, weighing him down until sheer numbers stopped him from moving.

"What are you doing?" he shouted but they didn't respond, didn't seem to hear him. Looking in their eyes his heart skipped a beat. They were open and blinking, but they looked straight through him, as if they weren't seeing him at all. As if none of them knew where they were or what was happening.

Looking at the crowd Choss saw the same distant expression over and over, even on the faces of those cheering. In the ring Brokk had become desperate. Blood ran from his hands, his elbows and even his knees were red. There were a few cuts on

Gorrax, but not many. Something metal landed in the middle of the ring, glinting in the light. Brokk scooped it up and slashed at Gorrax's arm.

This time the clacking sound he made with his tongue was one of pain. For a few seconds both fighters stopped and just stared at each other. Gorrax looked at the knife in Brokk's hand, then the green blood dripping to the floor.

Something started to push its way forward from the back of Choss's mind. Strong emotions he'd buried and dark thoughts that he'd never dare mention to anyone. With them came a terrible rage and inside his chest his heart began to race. Calling out for blood, calling out for the feeling of something breaking beneath his power. A sacrifice to his might.

Closing his eyes Choss blotted out the noise and went down into himself. Into the cool and calm place he lived in during a fight. It was the only way to win. By staying calm and letting his instincts guide him. Anger would only get you so far. It might even help you to win a few fights, until you met someone with more stamina. He'd come too far to go back to that. He wasn't that boy any more, trying to provoke his dad to hit him so that no one else got hurt.

With a roar that was lost in the crowd, Choss thrashed about, shaking off many hands, but more grabbed him. Brokk had cut Gorrax in half a dozen places and finally the Vorga started to let go. He'd made a promise, but it wouldn't hold him indefinitely. Choss was actually surprised he'd lasted this long. Gorrax grabbed Brokk by the shoulders, lifted him off the ground and bit into his shoulder. The crowd cheered wildly at the sight of more blood splashing across the ring. Women were shrieking so much they sounded like birds and the men were growling like wild animals. As Choss's heart thumped in his chest he heard a louder echo flowing around the arena. Something bigger and primal, like he'd rested his head against the chest of a ragged horse. A monstrous heartbeat filled the arena. A drumbeat so deep he felt it in his bones.

Brokk continued to slash at Gorrax and he retaliated in kind, biting chunks of flesh, ripping muscle and then finally snapping bone. One of Brokk's arms came off, torn away at the shoulder, but he didn't fall and blue foam bubbled from his mouth like a rabid dog. Brokk stabbed Gorrax in the stomach and with a shrill cry the Vorga grabbed his opponent by the neck and snapped it like a twig.

As the dead body hit the ring Choss heard a loud crack, like a tree breaking in a storm. But it was more than that. He felt it, as if someone had broken one of his bones deep inside, then snapped it back into place. The crowd fell silent. People began to shake, coming awake from a dark and terrible nightmare. A dream of blood and violence. A dream of slaughter.

Those holding Choss let go and stepped back, embarrassed and making apologies. No one seemed to know what they'd been doing or why. Everyone stared around the arena and finally all eyes came to rest on the ring. The bloody Vorga, splashed red all over, and the mangled, chewed body of Brokk on the floor.

People started screaming and panicking, pushing and shoving each other to get away from the ring. In a mad rush of feet the crowd scrambled to get out of the slaughterhouse. They didn't want blood. They wanted to escape, to go back to their lives and forget what they'd seen. No matter how much he drank, or how hard he tried, Choss wasn't sure he'd ever forget and he doubted they would too.

CHAPTER 4

Vargus stared into his mug of ale, careful not to look at the man sat opposite. He didn't need to see the fear, or the lies.

Vargus appeared to be just a grizzled warrior, battle-scarred with a sword on his back, but he was so much more than that. Neither of them was what they appeared to be at first glance.

The tavern, humble by the most generous of standards, was empty apart from the owner behind the bar and an old man dozing in the corner. The rest of the villagers were out working in the fields or the forests. Flimsy walls barely held the building upright and the wind found its way through gaps in the window frames. The gloom inside was chased back with worn nubs of candles, their flames wobbling in the breeze.

The room was so quiet the silence hummed in the ears.

"I heard a story recently," said Vargus, wetting his lips with a taste of ale. It was light, crisp and there was a hint of something citrus. "It was about the Brotherhood."

The man sat opposite said nothing. He just swallowed nervously, making no move to pick up his mug of ale. He'd asked for wine but they didn't have the money to grow grapes out here.

"I followed the rumours and they led me to Yerskania. There I found a group who'd been calling themselves the Brotherhood.

It was a twisted version of what came before, based on ritual sacrifice. It was almost as if someone was trying to poison the Brotherhood, perhaps in the hope that it would die. That my legacy might die."

"I had nothing to do with that," protested the Lord of Light.

"Sadly, all of those involved were killed," said the Weaver.

"Good. Then that's the end of it." The Lord of Light offered a tight smile and raised his mug, then changed his mind, setting it down on the table.

"Not quite," said Vargus. "You see, the group was being funded by someone abroad. Someone who wanted to start another war. I found out the money came from Zecorria."

"Ah. Then you want me to find this person?" said the Lord of Light. After all, his was the dominant religion in Zecorria. He was smiling, suddenly happy to help, and yet sweat trickled down the sides of his face.

"No, I found him too. It turned out to be a priest," said Vargus. His hand tightened on his mug and the clay started to crack, ale seeping onto the table. After finding out what kind of a man the priest was he'd found it difficult to repress the urge to crush his skull like the mug. Vargus eased his grip and took another sip before it was all gone. The golden liquid ran across the table and started to drip onto the floor.

Vargus raised his mug towards the owner for another.

"Here, have mine," said the Lord of Light, pushing his full mug across the table. "I can't drink this swill."

"Imagine my surprise when I discovered the money came from High Priest Filbin, Most Holy, most beloved of the Lord of Light," said Vargus, raising his eyes to stare at the boy.

"You didn't—"

"Oh no, he's alive. If he were to die horribly then the blame could fall on one of his many enemies. And who knows what might follow. Probably more violence."

"What did you do to him?" asked the boy.

"Nothing. Filbin and I just talked. We talked for a long time about everything. In fact when I left he couldn't stop talking," said Vargus, watching as the blood drained from the boy's face. "He had an urgent need to tell people the truth. I heard he filled the cathedral and then gave a powerful sermon about receiving divine instruction. He spoke about how his God told him to start another war. About how he'd molested dozens of children and that he'd been stealing money from the church for years."

"What have you done?" asked the Lord of Light, utterly aghast.

"I hear Filbin had to step down from his role as High Priest. He's currently being cared for in a safe and secure place, somewhere in the country."

The Lord of Light started to get to his feet. "I have to go. I must fix this."

Vargus grabbed him by the wrist and pulled him back into his seat. His fingers tightened around the boy's arm until he looked him in the eye.

"I warned you," said Vargus. "I told you not to interfere, that *we don't* interfere, but you didn't listen. You thought you were being clever, that I wouldn't find out."

Reaching over his shoulder with his free hand Vargus drew his sword. The boy's eyes widened in alarm and he desperately looked around the room for some help. That was when he noticed they were alone. The landlord and the old man were gone. He tried to pull his hand free but Vargus didn't move.

"Have mercy, Weaver!" wailed the boy. Vargus stood up, dragging the Lord of Light to his feet. "What about my followers? How will they cope without my guidance?"

"What about the Lady of Light? I'm sure she can guide them in your absence."

Despite the circumstances the Lord of Light sneered. "She's an idiot. My people need a strong hand to guide them."

"You mean interfere with their lives."

"Wait, wait!" said the boy as Vargus raised his sword. "The entire religion will fade without me."

Vargus briefly lowered his sword and laughed. "The Maker has been absent for a thousand years and there are more of his churches than ever before. If the faith of your followers is strong then it will endure, and so will you."

"You can't do this. You have no right!"

"No more words," said Vargus, swinging his sword. The boy raised a hand to ward off the blow but the sword cut cleanly through his fingers and then his neck. Four fingers tumbled to the floor alongside the boy's head. It rolled across the ground and came to rest in front of the empty fireplace. His gaping mouth continued to scream and his eyes rolled around frantically.

The boy's body remained standing upright but as Vargus reached into the Lord of Light's chest it started to convulse. Vargus dug deeper with his fingers until he found the boy's essence. He pulled it free and the body dropped to the floor, a lifeless sack of meat. The head died and fell silent, but in his mind Vargus could still hear the boy screaming. Now the sound came from the purple and black swirling orb sat on the table.

Vargus brought his blade down on the orb and it cracked. Energy exploded as the orb shattered, blowing the walls of the tavern apart, blasting off the roof and turning every piece of furniture into kindling. Power continued to seep out of the core, flying to the four winds, scattering the Lord of Light across the world. After a few seconds it was done and silence returned. The screaming inside faded away and Vargus stood up in the ruins of the tavern. Nothing remained except tumbled stone.

After a short walk Vargus stopped in front of a horse and cart laden with belongings. He passed the tavern owner a bag of gold to help him rebuild, shook his hand and watched him ride away.

"You heard everything?" asked Vargus.

"Yes," said the Lady of Light, stepping out of the trees. "Will he come back?"

"Eventually, if their faith in him endures." Vargus turned his steely gaze on the girl. "I hope you'll be smarter than he was."

"I had nothing to do with any of it."

"I know, otherwise you'd be sharing his fate. Just remember, I'll be watching."

Vargus left her alone by the side of the road in the pouring rain.

The lifeless banqueting hall echoed with the sound of Vargus's breathing as he walked towards the head of the table. As the first to arrive he took a moment to study the black wooden edifice and run his fingers across the grain. It revealed a landscape of tiny mountains and valleys, rivers and streams. The table had been here for as long as he could remember, which was a very long time, and yet in all those years he'd never seen the like before in the world. It was made of a single piece of wood, which seemed impossible. Perhaps once, when the world had been young, giant trees such as this had covered the land.

Other furnishings started to appear around Vargus. Huge marble fireplaces tall enough to walk into. Tapestries from nations long dead and forgotten, but he barely paid them any attention. Everything was an illusion tailored to his mind. A world within a world that best suited his memories. Nothing really existed except the table and chairs. Every person that stepped into the hall would see something different, something comforting and familiar.

The others started to arrive shortly after, in pairs and groups. Kai, the Eater of Souls, approached him, looking to be in good health, and a quick check told Vargus it wasn't bluster. Something had changed and Kai was doing well, quite a turnaround from a year ago during the war. Vargus heard Nethun before he saw him, bellowing and laughing as he greeted others, relentless and eternal as the oceans.

With a broad smile Vargus clasped his hand and they exchanged a few words while waiting for the rest to arrive.

One or two faces were missing, but no one said anything about them. The Lord of Light's chair also remained empty, and although one or two glanced at it, no one said anything out loud.

Towards the far end of the table Vargus spotted a new face, a young man with red hair, but he didn't go over and introduce himself. Many had come and gone over the years. If the young man survived and flourished, then eventually they would meet and become familiar with one another, either here or out in the world.

Normally Vargus found his eyes drawn to the Blessed Mother, but today all eyes were pulled towards Summer. She was at the height of her power and the air around her stirred with musk, an earthy smell that spoke of tasty food and sex. Staring at her voluptuous curves Vargus felt his mouth go dry and his imagination began to wander in an obvious direction. He forced his attention away and the feelings began to subside.

The Lady of Light appeared but hardly anyone noticed as she didn't attempt to make an entrance. When everyone had finally arrived, Nethun, as one of the eldest, took his seat and the rest followed suit.

"Several people asked for this meeting and if they hadn't I would've," said Nethun in his usual brusque manner. "There were rumours and now it's been confirmed. Someone is killing people in Perizzi using magic. While not unusual in itself, the method is familiar. Every victim is being drained of all energy. The last time something like this happened was five years ago, and we all know what nearly happened then."

A rumble of conversation flowed up and down the table and Nethun allowed it to continue for a minute before banging his meaty hand on the table for silence. "Our rule, passed down from the Maker, is that we don't interfere in the course of world events. The mortals must be free to make their own decisions. However, what transpired was not natural and if left unchecked it would have destroyed the world. Back then we all agreed that if it became necessary, we would step in. Through great sacrifice the mortals succeeded without our help. Now, I'm calling for a vote again. We need to stand ready."

Vargus took a moment to look down the full length of the table. He saw a lot of scared and worried faces, for their followers and themselves. What lived beyond the Veil was not like them and yet sometimes it pretended to be. Whispering secrets, sharing pieces of knowledge and promising great rewards that some mortals could not resist.

They only had one rule, which had rarely been broken, and now Nethun was asking them to do it again.

"All those in favour, raise your hand," said Nethun. A few followed his lead, immediately raising their hand, while others deliberated a little while before deciding. One or two crossed their arms, stubbornly refusing to even consider going against the rule, while others eventually went with the majority. The Lady of Light took a moment before slowly raising her hand. Halfway down the table Kai met Vargus's eyes and winked, his hand firmly aloft.

Nethun looked up and down the table, counting the number for and against. Apart from half a dozen everyone had voted in favour of action.

"It's decided," said Nethun. "One of us will travel to Perizzi and remain in the shadows until such a time as they are needed. I nominate Vargus. Does anyone object?"

Nethun looked down the table but only four raised their hands. All of them were known to Vargus. Two had grudges against him and the other two were new and probably trying to get noticed by opposing him. As before, Nethun gave everyone another minute to decide, but no one else raised their hand.

"Done and done," said Nethun, running a hand over his big bald head. "Is there anything else?"

"Since no one else has asked the obvious, I will," said Winter, tapping her blue fingernails on the table. "Balfruss killed the Warlock. The Red Tower is broken and supposedly no students are being trained there. So where did this magical killer come from? Who taught him such a black art?"

No one had an answer, or at least no one was willing to volunteer one. Vargus knew something like this could not go unnoticed. Someone knew who was responsible.

"What about Balfruss?" asked someone new from further down the table. "Where is he?"

Many looked towards Vargus, hoping he had an answer. Most around the table knew that he'd been there on the front line and fought beside the now infamous Battlemage. Those who didn't were at least familiar with his name and many were afraid. For as dangerous as the Warlock had been, ultimately he'd been defeated and Balfruss was still out there.

"Could he be responsible for this? Is he still alive?" asked the Blessed Mother.

"He was," said Vargus. "When the war ended he went to live with the First People. After that I lost track of him."

All eyes turned towards Elwei, Lord of the First People and the northern tribes. Most forgot Elwei was there during their meetings as he remained silent unless called upon. Even though he was in the room with them, Vargus always had the impression part of him was elsewhere, listening and watching.

Elwei's face was partly hidden by a dusty grey headscarf, but Vargus could see the stark lines of his lean face, his crooked nose, one glinting eye. A loose grey garment covered his lean body but his arms were bare, his black skin decorated with faded blue tattoos. Sat down he seemed no taller than anyone else, but on his feet he towered over everyone.

Elwei didn't move, and if being the focus of everyone's attention bothered him it didn't show.

"Is he asleep?" someone asked, one of the youngest.

"You have a question?" asked Elwei, his sonorous voice startling a few. They'd probably never heard him speak before.

Nethun grinned at their discomfort. "Yes brother, did Balfruss stay with the First People?"

"He did, for a time."

"And where did he go after that?"

"He crossed the Dead Sea and travelled north into the endless jungle. He's there among my people even now. He is becoming."

More than a few were baffled by the old pilgrim's words. Vargus had not believed Balfruss was involved with the murders. When they'd met during the fighting last year the mage had seemed a good, if serious sort of man, but at least this ruled him out in the minds of others.

"Becoming what?" asked one of the newcomers, a boy with red hair. His words echoed around the hall in the silence that followed.

Slowly, as if the movement were difficult, Elwei turned his head towards the boy who paled under the intensity of Elwei's stare.

"Yes, that is the right question," said Elwei.

Nethun hid a smile behind his hand and Vargus turned his face away until he'd smothered his grin. The youngster looked even more confused and he wasn't the only one. Elwei seemed inscrutable to most, but Vargus had known him long enough to unravel his sense of humour. He knew Elwei wouldn't volunteer any information unless he thought it was the right time or the person was worthy of having such knowledge.

"If there's nothing else," said Nethun, once he'd stopped grinning. No one raised their voice, so he stood, signalling the meeting was over. The Lady of Light left immediately, disappearing in the blink of an eye. A few stayed to chat and exchange information and the rest started to drift away.

Nethun approached Vargus and they moved a short distance away from the others.

"How long will it take you to reach Perizzi?" asked the sailor.

"I'm already there," said Vargus. Nethun raised an eyebrow in question.

"I've been in the west for the last year, keeping an eye on things. Some people here are keen to see things stirred up again, start a new war," he said, glancing over the sailor's shoulder at a few faces. "And I won't let that happen."

"No, we won't," promised Nethun. "Not again."

CHAPTER 5

When the front door of his shop opened Fray tried to hide his surprise with a smile. The woman shuffled in, stared at the bare stained walls, the battered table and mismatched chairs before turning her gaze on him. As their eyes met he barely held on to the smile, but then it softened, becoming something sympathetic and genuine.

"Hello mother," he said, since she looked old enough to be his mother. The tight grey hair in a bun, the stoop of her back, the cracked skin on her hands and the lines around her mouth spoke of a hard life. A life spent scrubbing floors, or gutting fish, not laughing and carousing, drinking and gambling. Her clothes were modest and practical, warm and well-used, which told him she didn't have money to spare, or that she spent it on someone else. Even the basket she carried was battered and had seen better days, but she continued to use it.

He took several cushions from under the table and added them to the chair on her side of the table to make it more comfortable. Taking her hand, as if she were a member of the aristocracy, he guided her to the chair, waiting until she had sat down and looked comfortable, before taking a seat opposite.

A little smile touched her face but then she sighed and it faded. He knew that sound. It came from the bottom of her soul and was a sound he'd heard many times. It couldn't be faked. And from that single exhalation of breath he knew the shape and the weight of her loss. Fray wasn't quite ready to wade in, so he stalled and mentally began to prepare for what would be needed.

"Would you like some tea?" he asked.

"Yes, thank you."

He ducked into the small room at the back, set the kettle over the fire and they chatted idly about the weather as they waited for it to boil. The glasses were old and battered and the pot didn't match, but she didn't care. He set the pot on the table to steep, put out a few withered slices of lemon and even the pastry he'd been saving for later. She accepted the tea and lemon, but refused the pastry, for which he was grateful as hunger already gnawed at him.

"I'm Fray."

"Sanna."

"Tell me about yourself, Sanna," he said, sitting back and waiting for his tea to cool.

"Not much to tell," she said in a firm voice. He raised an eyebrow and Sanna relented, shaking her head slightly. "I used to be a dancer, not a gaudy titty-flasher. A proper one you only saw in theatres. Things were going well, but I was young and stupid. I trusted the wrong man, someone with money. Then I ended up with a child, no husband and no money. After that I took work where I could find it, and we got by. We did all right, me and my boy."

Despite the tragic turn of events she'd described there wasn't any resentment in her voice. But then her bottom lip began to wobble. Before it went any further Sanna took a loud slurp of her tea and cursed that it was too hot. Fray looked away, giving her time. When she spoke again her voice didn't waver.

"My boy, Jerrum, grew up to be a good man. He made me

proud when he joined the Queen's army. Then the war came along."

Fray didn't need to hear the rest. She wasn't the first and wouldn't be the last person who'd lost someone in the war to set foot in his shop.

"Do you have something that belonged to him?"

Sanna reached into her basket and brought out a blue shirt, a pair of trousers and even a battered hat. She set them on the table and Fray lightly ran his hands over the items, feeling the fabric and stretching his senses, waiting for the familiar prickle across his scalp. He tapped the shirt with two fingers and with some reluctance she let him pull it to his side of the table.

From under the table he produced a blindfold, but before she put it on, her expression became sheepish. It couldn't be about the blindfold. If she knew where to find him then she would already be aware of his rules. Everyone believed it was necessary to protect them from the spirits and Fray did nothing to correct this misconception.

"Is something wrong?" he asked.

"I don't have much money to spare."

"That's fine."

"I heard you took goods in trade," she said, reaching into her basket again. Fray touched her hand and she stopped cold, as if he were holding a knife to her throat. He quickly withdrew his hand and she relaxed, but then had the grace to look guilty. But she didn't apologise. He swallowed the bitterness and felt it pass through him. It was just how things were at the moment.

"We'll sort it out after," he said, filling the awkward silence that threatened to swallow them both. Pointing at the blindfold again he settled back, taking the shirt in both hands and waiting until her eyes were covered.

Fray took a few deep breaths to calm himself and then stared down at the shirt. Reaching out with his mind he stretched towards the sound of the sea at the edges of his perception. It was always there, almost out of reach. All he had to do was concentrate on it. The world around Fray juddered slightly and a ripple spread out with him at its centre, as if the air was made of water.

Everything around Fray shifted slightly, becoming brighter, the colours deeper, the smells richer. Staring at the shirt he could see the weave of the material, smell the faintest whiff of leather and feel the coarseness against his fingertips. Pulling his focus away from the shirt he searched the air around him for a faint thread. Something to indicate the connection that he'd felt earlier.

After a few seconds he could see it. A faint red wire that sparkled like a string of pearls dipped in blood. It stretched away from the shirt across the room, disappearing through the wall on his right. Although it didn't have any physical weight Fray imagined himself pulling on it and his hands involuntarily made a beckoning gesture. To his surprise the shade responded quickly, appearing in the room as if he'd been waiting to be summoned.

"I see him," said Fray, staring at the broad-shouldered man who had Sanna's eyes and smile. For some reason Jerrum wore his Yerskani uniform, suggesting his devotion to the army. He didn't show any of the fatal wounds he must have suffered, for which Fray was grateful. Being told how someone had died was bad enough; he didn't need to see it. Most didn't show any injuries, but some shades were so shocked by the moment of their death it imprinted itself upon the fragment that remained.

"How does he look?" asked Sanna.

"He's wearing his uniform. He looks ... happy," said Fray, knowing how strange that sounded, but it was the truth. He felt some sadness from Jerrum, no doubt at being separated from his devoted mother, but mostly Fray felt his sense of pride. Jerrum gestured towards his mother and Fray heard the corresponding words in his mind. "He said to mention the red brooch he gave you for your birthday when he was a boy. The one he stole from the fat jeweller with the wooden leg."

"Blessed Mother," wept Sanna, dabbing at her eyes as a sob escaped her lips.

Fray offered her a wry smile, even though she couldn't see it. "He said to tell you that so you'd know I wasn't tricking you."

"What else?" she asked and Fray cocked his head to one side, listening as Jerrum made a complex series of gestures.

"He misses you and he's sorry to leave you alone. He hopes you can forgive him."

Sanna sobbed and laughed at the same time. "Tell him there's nothing to forgive."

Jerrum turned away from his mother and stared at Fray, his expression turning serious. His mouth moved silently and Fray's eyebrows arched in surprise.

"Is he still there? What's he saying?" asked Sanna.

"A minute, please," said Fray, his attention still focused on the shade. "You can trust me. I swear it by the Maker."

"I know I can trust you," said Sanna, thinking he was speaking to her. Jerrum nodded gravely and then made another series of gestures, pointing at his mother several times.

"He wants you to know that he's still going to take care of you." Fray saw Sanna shift in her chair, suddenly uncomfortable despite the cushions. This wasn't what she'd expected to happen. A few personal anecdotes, a message of love and something to help her move on with the rest of her life. That's all they wanted and what most needed to hear.

"He saved a portion of his monthly wages after he joined the army. It was supposed to be money to set up a brewery when he got out. He wants you to have it."

Despite knowing the rules, Sanna started to reach towards the blindfold. She needed to see his face and look at his eyes to make sure he was telling the truth. Fray put his hand over hers, bringing it back to the table before she did something she would regret. Knowing this had already gone on too long he scribbled the address Jerrum had given him.

"Do you want to ask him anything else?"

"Why did he linger? Why is he still here?"

Fray smiled. If he had a coin for every time someone asked that question he would be richer than the Queen's first cousin, the Duchess. "For you. He stayed because he wanted to make sure you'd be looked after."

Sanna began to weep quietly as Jerrum looked on benevolently. Fray let go of the thread and his connection to the spirit slowly faded away. The world around him rippled again, becoming smaller and quieter, dull and washed-out by comparison. He went into the back room, taking his pastry with him and giving Sanna some time alone. When he returned a few minutes later she'd stopped crying, but her eyes were red rimmed. There would be more tears to come, but hopefully they would be those that healed instead of driving the pain deeper into the heart where it could fester.

Sanna set her basket on the table and took out several items. Three loaves of bread, half a dozen apples, two pairs of black trousers, a sturdy pair of boots and a slightly worn leather belt.

"I was going to ask you what you wanted, but you should have all of it. You look about the right size. It's the least I can do." She put everything back in the basket and pushed it across the table.

Fray gave her the piece of paper with the address, shook her offered hand and was pleased to see she didn't cringe this time.

A familiar middle-aged man with touches of grey in his wavy brown hair and moustache stepped into the shop as Sanna approached the door. As he held the door open for Sanna, he locked eyes with Fray, which made a flurry of emotions roll through his stomach. They both waited until the sound of Sanna's footsteps had receded before moving.

Fray gestured at the chair opposite, resuming his own seat. His visitor paused on the threshold, his eyes sweeping the shop and no doubt recording every detail in his analytical mind.

"How long has it been, Byrne?" said Fray, running it through in his head.

"About five years," said Byrne, his eyes finally coming to rest on Fray's face. Byrne had visibly aged since Fray had seen him last. There were bags under his eyes, more lines around his mouth and Byrne's moustache now had flecks of grey running through it. There was only ten years difference in age between them but Byrne looked a lot older. "Since just after the funeral."

"You're not here for personal reasons," said Fray and Byrne shook his head.

"I need your help."

"You're just going to plough straight in?" said Fray, raising an eyebrow. "Not even one question about how I've been, or what I've been doing since he died."

At first Byrne said nothing and his expression remained unreadable. But then he sighed, blinked and his intense stare faded, which was a surprise. Perhaps he'd softened a little in the years since they'd last been face to face.

"I made a promise to your father. Several actually," said Byrne, correcting himself. It was an annoying habit Fray hadn't missed. Byrne was always so precise and rigid that he not only corrected everyone else, but also himself. "But this promise concerned you. Right before the end, he asked me to watch over you."

Fray was stunned. "Why am I only hearing about this now?"

Byrne scratched his moustache. Fray knew it was a mannerism Byrne used to buy himself some time when he didn't have the right words. "You made it very clear that you wanted nothing to do with the Watch or the Guardians. After your father died, I thought I'd be the last person you'd want to see, so I stayed away."

"Byrne, you're an idiot." The Guardian blinked a few times, but said nothing. Fray suspected it had been many years since someone had said anything like that to his face.

"I was in pain after he died," said Fray, clutching his chest where a ghost of the agony remained. "You were the only person I could've talked to, who would have understood, and you weren't there."

Byrne sat back in his chair, utterly speechless as a mixture of emotions passed across his face. Fray took a minute to try and settle himself, but old feelings he'd buried were rising to the surface.

Finally Byrne's expression settled into one of regret. "There's nothing I can say to make it right. I never meant to hurt you and I certainly didn't abandon you."

Fray waved it away, pretending it didn't hurt. "It doesn't matter. Why are you here now?"

"There's been a string of unusual murders in the city. The Khevassar needs it to go away as soon as possible before it attracts more attention."

"Unusual?"

"Magic is involved. More than that I can't say," said Byrne.

"Why me?"

Byrne raised an eyebrow in surprise. Fray needed to hear it.

"Because I trust you, and so does the Old Man, which is amazing because he doesn't trust anyone. Because you were born here and know this city better than almost anyone. And because your father was the best Guardian of the Peace I've ever known."

"That doesn't mean I'll be half as good as him."

"Don't play coy with me, Fray," said Byrne. "We both watched him on the job. I was his partner for only ten years, but you saw him every day of your life. I also know you've got his journals, and I doubt you threw them on the fire. How many times have you read them?"

Fray didn't answer, especially as he didn't want to admit Byrne was right. Those journals were priceless. Not because they detailed every case his father had ever worked on, the victories and the failures. The journals were his one remaining link to his father. Every time he read them Fray felt as if he understood the man a little better. He could hear his father's voice in his head and smell him on the pages.

Byrne cleared his throat, interrupting Fray's thoughts. "We could try to find someone else, but it won't be easy. Besides, I think you need this," he said not unkindly, gesturing at the shop.

Before the war Fray's shop had been in a good part of the city and his customers had included some wealthy and well-connected people. Business had been good, the money paid for a comfortable lifestyle, and he'd been happy. Now he had to hide his ability and had relocated to a fairly seedy part of the city, and most of his customers traded goods or a hot meal as they couldn't afford much else.

These days anyone with any magical ability or a Talent didn't announce it. Those who'd previously made their living using magic either did something else or customers had to seek them out in dark corners like this one. People still wanted closure, still wanted to speak to the lingering dead, but most were too afraid to visit him.

The irony of the situation wasn't lost on Fray that someone with magic was needed to solve the murder case.

"I don't want your charity," said Fray, clinging to the remaining shreds of his pride.

Byrne ignored him. "You can help people. You can save lives."

"But only by hiding what I really am," he said.

Byrne's expression turned grim. "If you say yes we'll start tomorrow. You'll be a novice Guardian, partnered with me, and you'll receive on-the-job training. We can't afford any more delays. The Khevassar will take care of the rest, paperwork, a uniform and so on. Given your history, and your name, no one will question it."

Normally someone had to serve five years in the Watch before they'd even be considered for the Guardians. If he jumped straight to being a Guardian it would put a few noses out of joint.

Fray sat back in his chair, looking around at the bare walls of the dingy little shop. It had been a while since he'd eaten three good meals a day and been warm at night. All he had to do was break a promise he'd made to himself not to follow in his father's footsteps. But it had been made in a moment of anger by a young and naïve boy. That boy had grown up into a realistic man who'd faced hardship and disappointment many times. Ultimately he knew there were many worse things he could become than his father's son.

Byrne sat quietly and let him work it out for himself. He'd always been patient. Fray remembered countless nights where Byrne and his father had sat up late discussing various cases. Byrne never seemed to raise his voice or lose his temper.

"All right, I'll do it."

"You don't have to decide now. If you need more time—"

"I'm ready," said Fray. Byrne stared deep into his eyes, weighing him up, before a broad smile stretched across his face.

"I thought it was going to be more difficult to convince you."

"I might be my father's son, but I also have my mother's common sense."

"For which I'm enormously grateful," admitted Byrne with a grin.

CHAPTER 6

For the last two nights Katja had been calling in every favour and speaking to every contact. Unfortunately she was no closer to finding any real information about the plot to assassinate the Queen. There were rumours, but that was all it amounted to. The lack of solid leads was frustrating, but a little reassuring too, as it suggested the plot was nothing more than gossip. However, she would keep digging until the truth came out.

From what Roza had told her last night the rest of her network in Yerskania was faring no better. This only made them angrier and led to even more drying blood under fingernails. Someone had to know something and they were determined to find out. The network was stretched thin and no one was getting much sleep.

Every lead was being chased, every avenue explored, which led Katja to her next appointment. Roza stood waiting for her a couple of streets away from the Blacksmith's Arms.

"Remember, he's not someone we can put any pressure on," said Roza without preamble as they set off. "Let me do most of the talking. Listen carefully to what he says, and if he gives his word, don't question it."

Katja could see the tension in Roza's shoulders by the way

they were bunched up. Setting up this meeting had taken a lot of careful negotiation and delicate work. All they had been given was a place, a name, which was probably fake, and a time.

"Why am I here?" asked Katja.

"Because I don't feel safe going to this meeting alone, and I'm told you're good at reading people. Be polite, but also be ready for anything." Roza stopped her on the corner, scanning the street and buildings neighbouring the Blacksmith's Arms. "Are you armed?" she asked, her eyes still watching the people.

"Yes."

Roza had told her to come prepared. A hole in the pocket of her trousers gave her access to a long narrow blade strapped to the outside of her left thigh. The dagger tucked into her right boot and the knotted leather cord, acting as a belt, were there as backup weapons, just in case.

"Keep a weapon handy, just in case. If I give you the signal I want you to run, and don't stop, even if I fall behind."

Katja knew Roza had been doing this for a long time. She had a reputation and had earned her promotion to head of the Yerskani network. Trying to swallow the huge lump in her throat Katja checked she could easily get to her hidden blade.

"Who is he?" Katja managed to ask.

"A speaker for the Silent Order," whispered Roza, as if she feared that even saying their name too loudly would attract unwanted attention. The Silent Order was a league of assassins which some claimed to be as old as mankind. They had toppled rulers, started wars and changed the fate of nations, always carrying out their missions from the shadows.

"Let's go," said Roza, squaring her shoulders, one hand resting on the dagger at her belt. Katja followed closely behind her and they crossed the street and entered the Blacksmith's Arms.

Roza went to the bar and ordered them drinks before carefully scanning the room. Her eyes settled on a lean man with grey hair sat with a petite brunette woman at a table in the corner. The woman was talking quietly but her hands were very animated, as if she were trying to restrain her anger.

Roza approached and sat down opposite without invitation. The man offered them a warm smile while the young woman glared. Katja had the impression her annoyance was more to do with being interrupted than anything else.

"Ben," hissed the woman.

"We'll talk about it later, Munroe," said Ben, cutting her off with a sharp one-handed gesture. She closed her mouth, crossed her arms and fumed in silence.

"Thank you for coming," said Roza, trying to give the impression that she was at ease, but Katja could see one hand still rested on her dagger.

Studying the mismatched pair across the table Katja didn't think Munroe looked particularly dangerous. Her companion was a different matter. Ben had an unnatural stillness to him, and although he smiled Katja could see that it was only skin deep.

"You wanted to ask us something?" said Ben. He was speaking for the Order, not just himself.

Roza took a sip of her drink first, perhaps to try and get rid of the same dry mouth Katja was experiencing. "Do you have any information, that you'd be willing to share, about Queen Talandra?"

Roza didn't need to say anything more. Munroe stopped sulking and was suddenly paying attention. Ben sat forward and Katja had the impression they were balanced on a knife-edge. At the slightest provocation he could erupt into violence.

"I may have something," said Ben.

"Name your price," said Roza.

Ben laughed and sat back in his chair. The tension faded and the air of impending violence eased. Katja saw both Roza and Munroe visibly relax at the change in Ben's attitude.

"Even with your resources, I doubt you could afford it," said Ben. He knew exactly who they were and who they worked for. "No, on this rare occasion I'm going to give you the information for free."

Katja wasn't sure who was more surprised, her or Munroe. She was staring at Ben as if he'd just offered to strip and dance naked on the table. Roza looked sceptical but gestured for Ben to continue.

"A few weeks ago someone approached the Order, via a third party of course, about a job that involved Queen Morganse."

Katja opened her mouth but Roza beat her to it. "I'm here about Queen Talandra."

Ben's smile was chilling. "Removing your Queen was the second part of the job."

Katja's hand tightened on her glass until her fingers turned white. Killing one Queen was unthinkable. The chaos it would unleash could reignite the simmering tensions in the west and start a new war. Killing Morganse, the Yerskani Queen, as well would be even worse. The rebellion which had driven the Chosen out of Perizzi had inspired others to fight back and reclaim their towns and cities from the zealots. Once all of Yerskania was free Morganse had turned her attention to her neighbours, helping them rebuild after the war. She was a hero to her people and many others across the west for her efforts.

"Removing both Queens would unleash horrors I can barely imagine," said Ben. "Despite the money offered we turned down the job. As did several people in the Families," he said. Katja knew he meant the crime Families who ran the city's underworld.

Roza carefully wet her lips before asking her next question. They were getting into a very grey area and she didn't know how much she could push, despite her own warning earlier about not pressuring Ben. "Can I ask who wanted to hire you?"

"You can ask," said Ben, smiling at them like a cat looking at a very small mouse. "Unfortunately I don't know. The person who met with our contact didn't know either."

"How can you be sure?" asked Katja. Ben turned his gaze on her and she felt pinned to her chair.

"Because we asked him, very thoroughly," he replied, offering her a wintry smile. "Whoever is behind it was very careful to insulate themselves. And that's all I can tell you, except for one other detail. Whoever wanted to hire us has a lot of money. We always set the price, but their starting bid was significant."

"We'd hoped it was just a rumour," muttered Roza.

"Oh no, it's real," said Ben. "Someone is going to try and kill both Queens here in Perizzi."

Katja walked quickly along the streets, doing her best to burn off some of the excess energy currently making her hands and feet tingle. The threat against the Queen had her tied in knots. It was real. It was going to happen unless they could find out who was behind it. The anger bubbling up inside needed a release.

Taking streets at random she went deeper into the seediest part of the city, moving with purpose. Despite the hour and being on her own, no one approached her. She passed through without incident and emerged beside the River Kalmei.

Halfway across one of the narrow footbridges she paused, staring down into the murky brown water. A cool wind coming in from the sea cut through her clothes, sending a chill across her skin.

Not far away Katja heard a brief scream. Common sense told her to ignore it, to go home or call the Watch. Instead she went towards the noise, following the muffled whimpers until she found two burly men robbing a third dark-skinned man, who looked like a merchant from the desert. One thug held the merchant from behind, a hand over his mouth and a knife at his throat, while the other searched him for valuables.

"Is that any way to treat a visitor?" asked Katja, startling the thugs. The first span around with a blade in his hand while the other tightened his grip on the merchant. When they saw she was alone and wasn't a member of the Watch they visibly relaxed, surprise changing to annoyance.

"You should start running," said one of the men with a wicked grin. "Because when we're done with him, you're next."

"I don't have any money," said Katja.

"I'm sure you've got something I'll like."

Fencing with words was clearly going to be of little use. Both of them looked witless, so she resorted to the direct approach. Katja lashed out with her belt, wrapping the knotted leather around the outstretched arm of the man nearest. With a twist and a yank the blade flew out of his grip, skittering away across the ground. Predictably he reached towards her with his other hand so she twisted the knotted leather tight, swivelled her hips and yanked as hard as she could, as if she were trying to pull him towards her. The thug was at least three times her weight, his stance was wide and she didn't have any leverage. From her current position, Katja didn't have the slightest chance of moving him.

When he saw what she was attempting he instinctively pulled away. With a snapping sound his shoulder popped out of joint. The thug screamed and dropped to the ground, his arm bent at an unnatural angle. The other thug shoved the merchant away and moved towards her, knife held low.

Katja stuffed the belt in one pocket and pulled out the long narrow blade from the other. The thug paused for a couple of seconds, reassessing her before starting forward again with a shrug. He moved well for a man of his size, but she could read every attack from his body language before he moved. Katja swayed to one side and sliced him across the stomach, the tip of her blade drawing a line of red on his skin. It also cut his belt and a heavy pouch of money hit the floor with a metallic thump.

The thug ignored it, his eyes never moving away from her face, even when the merchant scrambled to his feet and ran away down the street.

"Now you owe us double," he said.

Katja waited, poised on the balls of her feet for his next attack. He feinted high with his dagger then tried to kick her legs out, but she saw it coming. Turning sideways on the spot she avoided the blade and lashed out with her heel, slamming it into a kneecap. With a hiss of pain the thug stumbled and then fell to one side, dropping his weapon. As he reached for it Katja cut him across the back of his hand.

Pressing the blade against his throat she took his money pouch, before taking every coin from the other man as well.

"We'll find you," one of the men called after her as she casually strolled away. "You're dead. Dead!" he shouted. Katja didn't turn around but gave him a dismissive wave over her shoulder, which only incensed him further. As he cursed her and promised bloody retribution the pace of the last few days and long nights finally started to catch up with her. By the time Katja reached her rooms her limbs felt heavy and she barely made it into bed before she collapsed.

CHAPTER 7

Talandra stared out the window of her office, ignoring for a few minutes the difficult decisions that needed to be made. A year had passed since she'd taken the throne of Seveldrom, but at times it felt as if it were only a few days. She'd spent more hours than she could count in this room, sat behind her desk, reading and signing bits of paper. Even as she thought about paperwork her mind tallied up what still needed to be done today.

She also had several appeals from local people to deal with and then a formal dinner with the new ambassador from Shael. The country was still a smouldering ruin, free from the invaders that had occupied it during the war, but it would be a long time before any real sense of law and order returned.

The capital city of Shael and surrounding areas were secure and free of bandits, policed by a combination of her warriors and local soldiers in training, but it would be years before they could free the other territories from the lawlessness that had overrun them. At the moment the country didn't have enough food to feed all of its people and resources were scarce. She was helping with that too, shipping food west at the same time as trying to help the people become self-sufficient again, but progress was slow. Everything was currently piecemeal.

She'd coordinated with nations in the west to liberate Shael at the end of the war, keeping the promise her father had made, but it was an ongoing problem. The country was broad and her resources finite. Talandra knew she could only do so much to help, but it didn't stop her feeling that she'd failed Sandan Thule, the Shael Battlemage, who'd given his life to protect her city and its people.

"I can hear you brooding about Shael from here," said a voice from the other side of the room. "You're doing all you can, but it won't get better overnight."

She didn't turn around. Her brother, Hyram, had become her constant shadow. After the first assassination attempt, which hadn't come close at all, she had refused all suggestions about having a bodyguard. When the second attempt came two months after the first, and the assassin had made it onto the palace grounds, nothing she said made any difference. Hyram had taken on the responsibility and would not be turned aside.

Shanimel, the head of her intelligence network, had been livid about the assassin getting so close and had gone to ground for two weeks to personally uncover those responsible. Talandra heard stories and saw two reports about a trail of bodies in the city. After that Shani had returned to her post and would only say that she had taken care of the problem. There hadn't been an attempt on her life since, or if there had been any Talandra never knew about them.

She heard a faint rustle and clink of metal. Glancing over her shoulder Talandra caught sight of a blur of black as Hyram shifted at his post. In a way some things had come full circle. Graegor had been an old friend of her father who had eventually become his bodyguard after an assassination attempt on his life. After her father was murdered by the Warlock, Graegor had protected and mentored her for a time. Although her brother was not nearly as foul-mouthed as the old General, the two men had many things in common.

Against all sense Hyram had waded into the front-line fighting during the siege of her city. Mercifully his injuries had been mild, but the deep wound on his face had resulted in a nasty scar, turning his beard grey around it.

Once again she had a tall, scarred and dangerous warrior, who wasn't afraid to share his opinion, watching her back at all hours of the day. The only concession she'd insisted on was to have a second bodyguard of her choosing, as Hyram needed to sleep and attend to his other duties.

Before she became Queen, women had not been allowed to join the army. She didn't blame her father for this, it was an old tradition that had served her country and its people well for centuries, but the world had changed since the law had been written.

Her people were known for being tall and strong, so it made little sense that a Seve woman couldn't train and serve in the army. Both Morrin and Vorga had male and female warriors, but she had not used that as part of her argument to make the change. Many still hated both races for what their people had done during the war. The hard truth was that she had lost many warriors and needed more bodies to replace them. Halving the number of potential applicants made no sense.

Once the law had changed many women had applied to serve. As she'd expected, many were already experts with a blade. Alexis was the best of them, a blonde who stood eye to eye with Hyram.

The door to her office opened but Talandra didn't turn around to see who had entered without knocking. That meant it was midday. Hyram and Alexis swapped over at exactly the same time every day.

"You look like crap. You should get some rest," said Alexis.

Hyram grunted, but didn't immediately leave. A strained silence settled on the room. Talandra could feel him staring at her back.

"I'm fine, Hyram," she said, watching a grey bird wheel about in the clouds above the city. It seemed to drift without effort on the thermals rising up from the streets far below. At times like these she envied the bird's freedom.

The door closed and a more comfortable and less tense silence returned. Alexis didn't offer her opinion unless asked, whereas Hyram was never shy about saying what he thought. Some days she wasn't sure who she preferred.

Talandra had a few minutes of peace to sort through what she wanted to say, absently rubbing her stomach and thinking about the future.

The door slammed open and her older brother Thias marched in waving a piece of paper.

"What in the name of the Maker's cock is this?" he demanded. Thias almost never cursed. Alexis wisely stepped outside again, quietly closing the door behind her. Thias continued to rage, pacing back and forth in front of Talandra's desk. He rarely lost his temper and it never lasted long, so she let him run out of steam. Talandra made noises in all the right places and maintained eye contact, but her mind remained elsewhere.

After a couple of minutes Thias had exhausted himself and flopped into a chair.

"Well? What do you have to say?" he asked.

"This isn't a decision I came to quickly, Thias. Several times I've asked your opinion about the situation in Shael and each time you agreed that something more permanent needed to be done. All the help we've given to Shael is uncoordinated. There needs to be someone with vision we can trust to help them in the short term, and plan for the future."

"Yes, but I didn't think we were talking about me."

Talandra moved from behind her desk and sat down beside her brother. "Do you remember what you said to me when you gave up the throne?" asked Talandra. Thias had been first in line when their father had died but had given up his right to the throne.

Thias brooded for a minute before answering. "I wasn't ready."

"In the last year you've been a much needed cool head and wise counsel. But recently it's been clear to me that you've outgrown the position. You're ready, and Shael needs you more than I do. There's so much work to do and it will take years. In some ways I envy you and the challenges ahead."

"Why? Aren't you happy here?"

Talandra considered her words carefully before answering. Thias had a sharp eye and missed very little. "I am, but I'm living in father's shadow. Whenever they talk about the war, they speak of him. Our victory will be his greatest legacy. Mine will hopefully be one of lasting peace and prosperity."

"That's not an easy challenge in itself. But I didn't think you were so vain as to worry about what they'll write in the history books."

Talandra laughed in spite of herself. "You're right, I don't care. But where you're going, you'll have a chance to make widespread and lasting changes."

"You have repaid the blood debt, Tala," said Thias, taking one of her hands in his. The skin on his fingers was callused but his hands were warm. "Father would be proud."

"I hope so, but some days I don't think we've done enough. They lost everything. Everything, Thias."

Her brother sighed and then nervously cleared his throat. "There's also the other matter. The Princess."

"She's the last surviving member of the royal family in Shael. She's young and headstrong. People will try to take advantage of her, exploit her lack of experience and control her. You need to be there from the first day she takes the throne. She will need your support and guidance."

"She's just a girl," said Thias, pulling his hands away.

Eighteen was young to sit on the throne and rule a nation, but historically others had done it before.

"I hear she's very pretty," said Talandra.

Thias frowned at her. "You know me better than that."

Every day he looked more like their father. Even his expressions and mannerisms were the same. As painful as it would be to send her brother away, it would make things a little easier. At times it felt as if she was living with a ghost.

"I'm sorry, that was callous."

Thias stared at the ceiling for a minute, his eyes sad and distant. "I don't know a single thing about her."

"We all have to make sacrifices," said Talandra. She hated to sound so cold, and although Thias said nothing, she saw his frown deepen. "Feelings may come in time. That's all you can hope for. It's all any of us can hope for."

She hadn't told Thias much but everyone knew her relationship with her husband had not started on the friendliest of terms. They were in a much better place now than a year ago at their first meeting, which had been horrible. She'd loathed him on sight and thought him ignorant and vulgar. He'd had similar feelings about her but slowly their relationship was improving.

Thias remained silent for a long time before speaking. "All right. I'll do it."

"If there were any other way, I'd suggest it. It's not as if I can send Hyram."

Thias laughed, a little guiltily, but his mirth was genuine nonetheless. She wondered when she would next hear him laugh in the same room as her.

She pulled Thias to his feet and embraced him, taking a deep breath and trying to lock the smell of him in her mind.

"I'm going to miss you, so much."

"I'll miss you too," said Thias, his voice thick with emotion.

"There's one more thing I need you to do for me, before you go."

Thias stood back and made a formal bow. "Command me, my Queen."

"You have to tell Hyram the bad news."

Thias's good humour quickly evaporated and she laughed at his expression. Talandra kissed his grizzled cheek then saw him to the door. She watched him march down the corridor and noticed Alexis's gaze lingering on her brother.

"Please tell the kitchens I'm ready for my lunch."

"The usual?" asked Alexis.

"Yes, but tell them to make it a large portion."

Alexis didn't ask, for which she was grateful. It was only right that she told her husband first that she was now eating for two.

Talandra had barely finished her lunch, with Alexis hovering over her the entire time like a mother hen, when there was a frantic knocking at the door. She took a few deep breaths to settle herself and then gestured for Alexis to open it.

Shani gave Alexis a curious look, probably wondering about why she had taken so long to open the door, but her bodyguard's expression gave nothing away.

"Your Highness," said Shani, sketching a bow before stalking towards the desk. Talandra had always thought red and black suited Shani. Her black trousers and jacket were cut in the latest style, with a tight red shirt open at the throat, revealing a hint of cleavage. Talandra made sure her eyes didn't linger and quickly searched her desk for a relevant report from her network in Yerskania.

"I've read the report," she said, holding up a hand to stall Shani. "I haven't changed my mind about visiting Yerskania."

"May I?" asked Shani, gesturing at the chair, and Talandra

gave her a curt nod, bracing herself for a tirade. "Did you actually bother to read all of the report, your Highness?"

Talandra didn't bother to answer and just crossed her arms.

"I'm going to wait outside," said Alexis, moving towards the door. "My ears are still ringing from your last argument."

The door closed with a dull boom and the echo drifted around the room. She and Shani stared at one another. Talandra noticed that Shani looked tired and she wondered if it was the work that kept her up late or maybe someone else. Talandra had no right to ask any more and had to work hard to keep her expression neutral.

"Roza has confirmed that the rumours are true. There is a plot to kill you, and Queen Morganse," said Shani, eventually breaking the silence.

"I saw that in her report."

"Then you also saw there's more to it than we thought. Whoever is behind this has money and they're being extremely careful to conceal their identity. It's going to take time to identify who is pulling the strings."

"You want me to postpone my trip," said Talandra.

"Unofficially, yes. Pass word to Queen Morganse through channels, but maintain the appearance of the visit going ahead as planned. It will help to draw them out."

Talandra pursed her lips and considered the advice. Her stomach rumbled and she tried to ignore it, but recently she was always hungry.

"And how long should I, unofficially, delay the trip?"

Shani started to answer and then saw the hook. "I'm only trying to protect you."

"Which I appreciate, but what sort of a message does it send to others if I cower behind my walls every time someone threatens to kill me?"

"Is your reputation more important than your life?" asked Shani.

Talandra ignored the question. "We've been vague about the date of my state visit to Yerskania. It's time to make it public knowledge."

"You're taking a huge risk," said Shani, struggling to control her temper.

"I won't give in to intimidation and threats," said Talandra, forcing herself to breathe slowly. Shani always managed to get under her skin.

"If you're going to go ahead with this, against my advice, then at least take your body-double with you."

"I'll consider it," said Talandra.

Shani threw up her hands in despair. "You're being stubborn, yes?" said the Morrin, slipping back into her old speech pattern. "Do you do this with everyone, or just me?"

"This isn't the first group that's threatened my life and I'm sure it won't be the last."

Shani tilted her head to one side. "When does your husband return from his diplomatic trip?"

The question caught Talandra off guard. She paused, trying to see why Shani was asking but couldn't find the angle.

"He said in his last letter that it would be at least another week before they leave the capital city. I get the impression that the Desert King is not a man who likes to be rushed. Why do you ask?"

Shani shrugged. "I was just curious."

"Normally he's the last person you want to talk about."

"True, but he's probably the one person you'll actually listen to when you're in one of your moods. I hoped he might be able to talk some sense into you."

Talandra shook her head, relaxing her shoulders and trying to maintain a semblance of calm. "I won't let you bait me. I've made up my mind and we leave tomorrow as planned."

"You were always so damn stubborn," said Shani. "You had to

have everything your way. It's why I always came to your rooms and we never stayed at my house."

"That's not true," said Talandra, but Shani was just getting started.

"We always ate where you wanted to as well. It was simpler to say yes than argue every time. It made life much easier and a lot more fun."

Shani bit her lip to stop herself from saying any more. Her face was flushed and she sat back, refusing to look at Talandra. They stayed like that for a while, each listening to an uncomfortable silence that had once been something else. Something more than formality, duty and an imitation of friendship. They couldn't go back, the present remained unstable and the future looked bleak and untenable. Talandra wanted to say something, to try and bridge the widening gap between them, but couldn't find the words.

"And now? If I'm so stubborn, why do you argue every point?"

Shani finally looked at her. "Because things are different. Sometimes you're wrong and my job is to protect you, not . . ." She trailed off and took a deep breath before trying again. "Your father wasn't an arrogant man. He listened to all opinions and considered them, before making up his mind."

Talandra heaved a long sigh. "You're right. I'll think about what you've said."

"That's all I ask, your Highness," said Shani.

CHAPTER 8

Choss shuffled into Don Jarrow's theatre behind his six Gold jackals, Captains in the crime Family. In front of them were a dozen Silver, thirty or so Brass, street bosses for the gangs, and a scattering of other people without any distinct rank. Normally while they waited the Gold and Silver talked and made jokes with each other. Not tonight. Instead they kept to the back of the large round room, never straying far from the door. Everyone knew what was coming. They were nervous and no one knew where the blame would fall.

Choss leaned against the back wall and stared at the seats above his head. From his position he could only see two balconies, but he knew there was a third at the top near the domed glass ceiling.

A long time ago the building had been a theatre where small groups of actors had shouted to be heard at the top, up in the cheap seats. The tiny conical building looked more like a grain silo than the broad theatres he normally saw dotted around the city. The story he'd heard was that the style had fallen out of fashion and been abandoned decades ago. No one had bought the building, leaving it to fall into disrepair and then ruin.

When the Jarrow Family took over the area the Don had made the old theatre his centre of power. He'd restored the tiered seating, replaced the carved wood panelling on the walls and hired the best glassmakers to fix the shattered roof. The stage had not been restored, but a raised wooden platform covered half of the floor. Sat on top were two massive chairs positioned side by side like thrones. Everyone had to look up to them when they came for an audience, except for Choss and one or two others. Being tall had its advantages.

The room fell silent as four people entered the theatre from the back door. The Don and his wife, the Doña, and their two Naib, their bodyguards. The Naib saw and heard everything and were among the most trusted people in the Family. Two years ago Choss had been offered a position as the Doña's Naib when he'd stepped away from the ring. He took the appropriate amount of time to consider it and then very politely had turned it down.The Naib on the right was a reed-thin man with golden skin from Shael. He wore hard leathers, two swords crossed on his back and two daggers at his belt. His cold blue eyes swept over the room and everyone made sure they were looking elsewhere. Tough as they were, dangerous as they were with reputations to match, by comparison Pietr Daxx was a bastard.

During the war when the Morrin and Vorga had invaded his homeland of Shael, he'd fought with one group of rebels after another. Eventually Shael was liberated and stories began to emerge of atrocities, but not all were at the hands of the invaders. For all the cruel and merciless things Daxx had done to the enemy, his own people had cast him out in revulsion.

The other Naib was a grizzled Seve with deep blue eyes and a shaven head. His chest and arms were covered with faded scars and Choss suspected he was a veteran of several wars. Long before he'd even heard of the Families, Choss knew of Vargus. Over the decades he'd built up a fearsome reputation as an implacable warrior and discreet problem solver for different Families. Some people thought him to be nothing more than an urban legend as he'd not been seen in public for years. That had all changed when he'd returned last year.

Where Daxx was cold and cruel, Vargus was warm and friendly, appearing at first glance to be nothing more than a kindly uncle or big brother. But the sword on his back and the daggers at his belt had tasted more blood than every Gold jackal combined.

"Stop lurking," said Don Jarrow, gesturing for his people to move closer. The Don waited until his wife had sat down before taking his own seat. Some men thought the Don had earned his position because of his size. In his youth he'd been a wrestler and Choss could see he still had powerful shoulders and arms. The Don could easily snap a few bones with those massive hands if he wanted to, not that he got his hands dirty these days. Don Jarrow ruled this part of the city not because of his muscle, or even because of the number of people that worked for him. His cunning mind kept him in power.

He often ranted and lost his temper, but would soon cool down and spend time thinking on what had been said. He was also known to take the long view on a situation, which some-times made him unpredictable and very dangerous.

The Doña could not have been more different from her hus-band. She never raised her voice, never swore and barely showed any emotion, which was often worse. No one ever knew which way she'd go. At any moment someone could be rewarded for their efforts or chopped up and fed to the hogs for not doing enough.

At least with the Don you always knew where you stood. At least with him you saw the bear pit before you were pushed in.

"Now, can someone tell me what happened last night?" said Don Jarrow, his voice unusually calm. Choss braced himself. The Gold and Silver looked around at each other, hoping someone would answer. "What the fuck happened?" roared Don Jarrow, his voice echoing around the wooden walls. Despite all of the restoration there were no soft surfaces. Even the wooden chairs had no cushions to muffle the sound. Maybe he'd planned it that way.

Don Jarrow sat back in his chair, running a hand through his thick black beard. His green eyes raked the crowd like a lash and none of them dared meet his gaze.

Choss heard someone slip into the room and take up a position beside him against the back wall. The familiar rasping sound told him it was Vinny.

"Do I have to explain this? Do I really need to spell it out?" asked Don Jarrow.

The Doña placed a hand on her husband's arm and sat forward, giving everyone a view of her cleavage. Not that Choss was looking. Everyone could see she was a beautiful woman, with cocoa skin from the desert, and a body that curved in all the right places. But even if she hadn't been married to the Don, he'd rather take a viper to bed. She terrified people even more than her husband did.

"We sell venthe. It's nasty stuff and I don't like it," said the Doña. Choss didn't think she cared what it did to people, but he kept his mouth shut. "If we didn't, someone else would, and we can't have that on our turf. Even so, if our customers keep dying, they can't buy more next week, and every week after that."

Every man and woman here had earned their position. They weren't slow, but they were being spoken to like dim children or Paper jackals, the lowest on the ladder. But they took it in silence, because they were loyal and because someone here was to blame. Someone had bought the stuff, probably on the cheap, and just passed it on to their dealers, no questions asked.

"Do you know how many addicts we lost?" asked Don Jarrow. "Thirty-three. I wouldn't give a shit, but even I can't make that many bodies disappear in one night without someone noticing.

Everyone is asking questions. Families, friends, the fucking Guardians!"

The last word rang out and the Doña waited until the echoes had faded.

"We also lost four fighters in one night," she said, glancing briefly at Choss. His heart skipped a beat as their eyes met.

"I've had Guardians of the Peace and the Watch all over my streets," spat the Don. "My streets!" he bellowed and the words went around and around, spiralling up the building then coming down again. Choss wondered if an actor had shouted so loud one night that the glass dome had shattered. If this went on any longer it might happen again.

"Vinny, did you know about this?" asked the Doña, glancing at the slight figure stood beside Choss.

"No. Last night we let one fighter go because we suspected he'd been using. They must have been taking it away from the arena."

"And Brokk?"

Her question was directed at both of them, but Vinny answered. "By the time we realised, it was already too late."

The Doña's eyes rested on him and Choss had to work hard not to squirm under their intensity. Her blue eyes bored into him, as if she could read his mind and was listening to his thoughts. Eventually she looked elsewhere and he let out a long slow breath, giving Vinny a nod of thanks. If the truth came out that they'd known and still let Brokk fight, they'd be in trouble.

Don Jarrow had calmed down a bit as he'd stopped shouting, but he still looked angry. "Find out where it came from. Speak to our usual suppliers and then talk to everyone else. I'm also talking to the other Families about this."

A strange tremor ran through the crowd at that. The Families didn't work together. That was the story for those outside the business. The truth of the situation was far more complicated.

The Families had been cooperating with one another since the beginning, but only when common interests aligned. Uniting to ease out unwanted newcomers, freelancers and utterly destroy problems that arose from time to time. The exception to the rule seemed to be the Butcher. No one knew what to do about him.

Venthe was highly addictive, but it didn't kill an addict outright. It gradually rotted away their body and mind over many years, but no one benefited from dead addicts. So the Families would talk, dig out the lethal batch of poison, and make an example of whoever had supplied it.

Normally the arena was the perfect place for such uncomfortable Family business. Neutral ground where all of the Families could meet in private. Many of them sponsored a fighter, so they all had a stake in ensuring that the arena stayed in business.

The Jarrow Family had sponsored Brokk. The other three fighters who had died from the bad batch of venthe had belonged to other Families. With four dead bodies and the madness that had swallowed the crowd, Vinny had been forced to close the arena until further notice. Guardians and the Watch were still there now, desperately searching for something to explain what had happened. Choss and Vinny hadn't talked about it, what they'd seen and felt, but they'd heard stories from other people who'd been there. About the hunger and the awful desires. Choss shook his head, focusing on the Doña.

"Apply as much pressure as needed," she said, showing her white teeth in an approximation of a smile. "Find out where it came from, but more importantly, who supplied it. Whoever finds those responsible will receive my personal thanks. Do not disappoint us."

She dismissed the crowd with a flick of her hand. Like scolded children they began to shuffle out, but Choss stayed behind with Vinny.

"Idiots," said Don Jarrow as he and Vinny approached. "I'm

surrounded by fucking idiots. I should have Vargus kill every single one and start over."

The Naib looked towards the door expectantly, waiting for the signal. He'd race out and cut off all of their heads if Don Jarrow gave the order. He'd probably be able to do it as well.

"Perhaps," mused the Doña. "But it would take a while to find so many replacements. Besides, it's going to get messy before it gets better, and some of them will not survive. We can recruit more competent people afterwards."

It sounded like a veiled form of mercy, but he suspected she was merely being practical. Choss doubted she knew anything personal about any of their senior jackals. To her they were tiles on a Stones board, nothing more.

"You're right," said Don Jarrow, shaking his head. "So, Vinny, how much did we win?"

"A lot," said Vinny, handing over a red notebook. It contained a list of the bets from last night. As owners of the arena Choss and Vinny couldn't place bets, but they could advise others. Of course the house took a small cut of all bets made on the night, so it was in their best interest to give solid tips. Vinny dealt with the money and Choss told them who would win. They made a good team.

Choss never bet against Gorrax and had told Don Jarrow to bet heavily against his own man. He'd been reluctant, but had finally agreed, bowing to Choss's superior knowledge of the fighters. Despite the grisly end, the Vorga had been the last one standing, so all bets were still valid. A lot of people had not even bothered to claim their winnings. Maybe they couldn't stomach the idea and didn't want the money. Maybe they just wanted to forget everything about that night.

"That's good," said Don Jarrow. "It will help cover some of the cost of the clean-up."

"When can we reopen the arena?" asked Choss.

Don Jarrow shook his head. "Not for a while. The stink of this will hang around. We can't just brush it under the rug. Four dead fighters is one thing, but with so many other dead bodies, everyone is watching. I also heard what happened to the crowd." The Don didn't ask for more details, which was just as well, because Choss didn't have any answers. Even so, that it had been noted meant Don Jarrow was thinking about it. It would come up again in the future.

"I need a drink," said Don Jarrow, heading for the back door with Vargus in tow. "I'll send someone when there's news," he added, dismissing them. Vinny walked towards the front door but turned around when he saw Choss hadn't moved.

"I'll catch up," he said, keeping his eyes on the Doña. Daxx glanced at him briefly, and Choss felt the Naib's eyes take in every detail, weighing him up. Fighters did it all the time when stepping into the ring. They tried to absorb everything about their opponent. They made a big list in their head, adding up all the good points and bad, and marked it against themselves. Sometimes the score came out low and the fight was very short. Other times the score was even and the outcome came down to grit and most often luck. The outcome was normally decided before the first punch landed.

Daxx didn't like the tally in his head as he tensed and reached for one of his swords, but the Doña waved him back. "There's no need. Choss and I are old friends," she said, which wasn't even slightly true. They'd never had one personal conversation in all of the years he'd known her. "Call me Sabina," she said, but he didn't and never would.

"How bad is it? The situation with the other Families?" he asked, knowing that acting so friendly was dangerous, but he'd nearly been where Daxx was standing, acting as her Naib. If she said they were friends he'd play along and use it to his advantage.

The Doña tapped her blood-red lips with an emerald fingernail. He idly noticed it matched the colour of her silk dress. "It's not good. Despite losing one of our fighters, many think we were responsible. They don't trust us to resolve the situation."

"So they'll send their own people," he guessed and she inclined her head. "Is there anything I can do to help?" he said, not caring that he sounded desperate.

The Doña cocked her head to one side. "You're very single-minded." She knew he only cared about the arena.

"We were so close. The fights were bigger than they'd been in years. You said it yourself. You said we were ready to step out of the shadows."

"I did. People with real wealth in the city were paying attention, mostly because they saw the potential profit, but they were interested. It would've been good business for everyone," admitted the Doña.

"If I solve this problem with the venthe, will you try again? Will you speak to the right people?"

The slight edge to her voice told him she was losing patience. "As I said, whoever solves this problem, before it escalates into something with the other Families, would have my personal thanks."

"Your word on that, Doña Jarrow?" asked Choss. He knew he was pushing it, and Daxx bristled, but the Doña ignored her Naib. A ghost of a smile briefly touched her lips. Choss hoped that meant she liked him being forthright and wasn't about to give Daxx the order to cut off his head for overstepping a boundary. Finally she spoke.

"You have my word. I will do everything in my power to restore the arena to its previous glory."

He extended his hand and she stared at it for a moment before shaking it. Her grip was surprisingly gentle but it felt as if he were holding on to a block of ice. Choss quickly let go and turned to leave but then remembered something.

"What happened to Gorrax?"

Even though the Doña's expression didn't change, he saw a subtle shift behind her eyes.

"I like you, Choss, and I like that you're bold, but don't push it. The Vorga is gone and he won't be coming back."

He wanted to say more, to ask her to show mercy or to bargain for his friend's life. But he'd already tried her patience. To try again would be pointless and might anger her further. He had no way of knowing what she would do to Gorrax or if he was even still alive. So he said nothing, promised to say a prayer to Nethun for his friend, and walked away with guilt burning in the pit of his stomach.

CHAPTER 9

Munroe stared at her victim in horror. His head dipped towards his chest and a thin trail of blood trickled from one corner of his mouth. She heard a final gasp of breath, then silence returned, engulfing the bedroom as if her ears had been wrapped in a blanket. Her nose detected something unpleasant and she quickly realised the smell was coming from the recently deceased.

Trying not to gag she stumbled away, her legs colliding with the back of a table. With arms whirling through the air she toppled backwards, knocking something onto the floor that shattered with a crash of breaking glass. Munroe scrambled to her feet, but stayed in a crouch, eyes darting between the closed door and the open window.

Somehow the sound of her fall hadn't drawn any attention from the rest of the house. Just to be sure, she stayed frozen in place, head tilted to one side, listening for even the slightest sound that was out of place. The creaking of the old wooden house seemed very loud. Somewhere nearby, liquid dripped onto a hard surface and outside she heard an owl on the hunt, but nothing else.

With a relieved sigh she straightened up, dusted herself off and looked around the room. Apart from the dead body pinned to the wall, and the shattered lamp beside the table, nothing looked out of place. Using a shirt from her victim's chest of drawers, she soaked up the oil, swept the glass into a cupboard and dried the soles of her boots until everything looked perfect. Apart from the farting corpse.

Given that her night had not gone according to plan, she considered just leaving through the bedroom door. She could creep through the silent house and use the front door like a normal person. In the end she decided it was too risky. It would be better to bravely grasp the remaining shreds of her plan in the vain hope that it could be salvaged. As she climbed out the window Munroe remembered the wet shirt and threw it back into the room towards the bed.

It was only later, when she'd had time to think it through, that Munroe came up with half a dozen other things she could have done with the shirt.

Unfortunately it landed on a small table beside the bed where another lamp burned. With a faint whoosh the shirt ignited and oily black smoke began to curl up towards the ceiling. At this point she considered climbing back in and trying to put out the fire, but as she gripped the window ledge with both hands the lace curtains surrounding the bed ignited. The fire ran along all four sides of the bed and then the second lamp cracked, spilling more oil.

"Maker's ballsack!" she said, slipping down the tiled roof. She nearly fell off into the garden but managed to dig her fingers at the edge. Eventually her dangling legs found the top of the narrow ladder she'd left resting there.

Wasting no time Munroe slid down the ladder, her hands and toes gripping the outside. She heard a faint crackling from above and warm orange light filled the window as the curtains caught fire. A small cloud of black smoke drifted out of the window, growing thicker by the second.

Scurrying with the ladder under one arm she ran across the open lawn, not even trying to hide. All eyes would be on the house soon enough and it was the last place she needed to be seen leaving in a hurry. Even as the ladder was settling against the outer wall Munroe scrambled up, pivoted on top and threw it into the street. She jumped down, tucking and rolling before coming to her feet, a little muddy but without injury.

With a quick twist and a few subtle shifts of her wrists the ladder broke into two pieces, which she then pulled apart until a dozen pieces of hollow timber littered the ground like a child's puzzle. Munroe scooped them up into a cloth sack she'd left in the shadows, then pulled on a felt cap and musty red coat. Taking a bottle from the sack she splashed a generous amount of cheap ale onto the front of her jacket, threw the sack over her shoulder and set off down the street, swaying and pretending to drink from the bottle.

Sounds of panic and alarm reached her ears and as she turned a corner Munroe risked a glance back at the house. The window and now part of the roof had caught fire, with more flames running along the edge of the building. Cursing her luck she continued on her way, pretending to be drunk and completely ignorant of what had happened.

Over the course of her life Munroe had come to realise that while some women drew more attention, she still received a fair number of admiring looks from strangers. Going against what her mother had wanted she'd not gone into the trade, despite assurances that men would be queuing up, day and night, to bed her. The idea of dealing with that many cocks every day had the opposite effect than her mother intended, contributing to Munroe's aversion to earning money by lying on her back.

Unfortunately Munroe still hadn't quite worked out what she

did want to do with her life. Her current employer treated her well, her accommodation was comfortable and she could buy whatever she wanted within reason, but she was trapped. Just because there weren't any bars on her windows, it didn't mean it wasn't a prison.

This latest endeavour to create a new life certainly made people pay attention. As soon as Munroe walked through the front door of the Hangman's Noose every person in the room stopped what they were doing and stared at her. As she crossed the room towards the door at the back any jeers or catcalls died on the lips of even the drunkest sailor.

Once she'd closed the back door behind her, the familiar hum of conversation resumed. With a sigh, she slowly walked towards the door at the end of the corridor, dragging her feet and delaying what was about to happen just a little longer.

She knocked loudly three times, paused, then knocked twice. It wasn't code, just another small delay.

"Come in," said a muffled voice.

The room beyond had previously been used to store barrels of beer, but many years ago it had been converted into a temporary office. Those in the know came back here when they wanted to speak to a representative of the Silent Order, the league of assassins.

The man normally found behind the plain desk was a scribe. He recorded the details of clients' grievances and then dropped them off at a secret location. The Order would then assess the requests and if any were to their liking the client would receive a note with a price, a location to drop the money and a date. Sometimes it was only days away, other times it could be weeks or even months ahead. But the Order's reputation guaranteed that by the given date the target would be dead.

As far as anyone in the front of the tavern knew, Munroe had replaced the former scribe. The truth was more complex.

"Please sit," said the grey-haired man, gesturing at the chair in front of the desk. Munroe knew he wasn't a scribe, but beyond a first name, which was probably a fake, she knew very little about him. He terrified her slightly, well actually quite a lot, but she did her best to hide it.

The only thing that mattered was he'd given her details of the three trials she needed to pass before the Order would consider taking her on as an initiate. Last night had been the final and most difficult test.

Munroe slumped into the chair, her face crinkling up into a pained expression. "Ben, before you start, let me just say, it wasn't my fault."

"Really? Then whose fault was it?"

Munroe shrugged. "I did finish the job."

The lines on Ben's face deepened as his expression became incredulous. "You were supposed to kill him and make it look like an accident!"

"Maybe he burned down his own room."

"House, Munroe. You burned down his whole damn house!"

"Oh."

"Yes, oh." Ben settled back in his chair, shaking his head sadly. "What's even worse are the statements his servants gave to the Guardians."

Munroe winced and didn't want to ask, but Ben folded his arms and waited. "What did they say?" she finally asked.

"As soon as one of them smelled smoke they raced upstairs to rescue their master. With great effort they broke down his bedroom door to find him impaled against the wall."

"I can explain that. He fell," said Munroe.

"Really?"

"Yes, I swear."

Ben wasn't convinced. "Onto the horns of a Sorenson bust, in his own bedroom."

"It was just bad luck. I startled him and he tripped and fell. Besides, who keeps a bull's head on their bedroom wall?"

"Oh, so it was his fault. Is that what you're telling me?"

"Well, no. But he was already dying at that point."

Ben raised an eyebrow. "What?"

"It was his heart."

"I thought I'd made it clear you couldn't poison him."

Munroe bit her lip. "I didn't. I crept into the room but the floor creaked. I startled him and he was so surprised he started clutching his chest and wheezing. Then he tripped and impaled himself."

Ben winced and rubbed at his eyes. He seemed unable to look at her. "And the fire?"

Munroe carefully considered her answer. "All right, I'll admit to that, but it was an accident. I broke an oil lamp and then accidentally started a fire. I was going to try and put it out, but then it spread quickly, so I ran."

Ben shook his head sadly and Munroe desperately tried to think of something to say in her defence. In the end she settled for knowing the truth. "How bad is it?"

Ben raised one eyebrow again. "How bad do you think?"

"Well, I passed the other tests, right?" she asked.

Ben was slow to respond. "Yes, but I'd be willing to bet gold against copper that accidents were also partially responsible for your success."

Munroe ignored the barb. "Two out of three isn't too bad," she said, hoping he'd see her side of the situation.

Ben rolled his eyes. "We're called the Silent Order for a reason. Most of the time when we carry out a job, no one knows if we've really been there. We're just a shadow on the wall, a whisper on the wind. We're not con-men, cutthroats or penny-pinchers. Most of the time, people think our marks died of natural causes. Our reputation is one of the reasons we can demand any price. Your final test was to kill a difficult target and leave no trace."

"But you told me that sometimes you leave a calling card. So people know it was the Order when a message needs to be delivered."

"That's true," said Ben, reluctantly conceding the point.

"And those are always elaborate kills, that leave no doubt that it was murder." Ben made a noncommittal noise, but Munroe took it as assent. "Then surely we could just say this was one of those."

Ben shook his head. "No, we can't."

"Why not?"

"Anyone can burn down a house, Munroe. Even when we tell others we've been there, we're always subtle about it. The other members of the inner circle had doubts about you from the start, but I told them to give you a chance."

"Which I appreciate—"

"This time we all voted no."

"Ah. Cock."

Munroe slumped down even further in her chair feeling utterly defeated. Months of training had been wasted. Countless hours of exercise to tone the muscles in her arms and legs she hadn't known were even there. Endless days of running, stretching, climbing and learning how to fight in close quarters. Long tiring nights crawling over rooftops, tiptoeing across bridges and learning how to move without making a sound. All of it meant nothing now. She would never become a member of the Silent Order. She would have to go back to her old life at the Emerald Dragon and accept her place in the world.

"So, what happens now?" she asked.

"Tomorrow the old scribe will come back. We'll let it be known that you displeased the Order, so we let you go. You're never to return here. Ever. And don't try to hire us in the future, because we won't take the job."

"What am I supposed to do now?"

"I don't know, but maybe you should think about a job that doesn't rely on subtlety or luck," suggested Ben.

Munroe started to laugh. At first it was just a giggle, but soon she was laughing so hard tears streamed from her eyes and her stomach ached. She was still laughing as she walked out of the Hangman's Noose.

CHAPTER 10

As the cobwebs of sleep started to fall away, memories of last night began to resurface. Standing up made the room spin for a moment but it quickly faded. Fray splashed cold water on his face and drank deeply, which settled his queasy stomach. What he really needed was something greasy and dripping with fat.

Throwing on some clothes, he ran a comb through his straggly hair and pulled on his boots. They were wearing thin and come winter would be useless, but it didn't matter now. Soon he'd have a uniform, a job and enough money to buy new clothes. But he didn't have the money yet.

There were a few people about whom he recognised but they didn't stop or even acknowledge his presence beyond brief eye contact. In this neighbourhood the only people awake at such an hour were either on their way to work, or were at the end of a very long night out. Normally neither group would be looking for trouble, but there was always someone determined to be the exception.

The baker had already been up for hours and his shop smelled of fresh bread and delicious pistachio cakes made by his wife. Fray ordered two meat-and-egg-filled pasties and managed to eat one before making it back to his room.

Last night had begun as if they were just old friends meeting up after a long time apart. They had talked about the past and their shared memories from the days when Byrne had been the apprentice and Fray's father the teacher. After several drinks the walls inside each of them had started to crumble and then came the guilt. Fray felt guilty for not being there when his father had died. Byrne for not being able to do something to prevent it.

As the night progressed Byrne divulged a few small details, but not as many as Fray had hoped about his father's last case. It was the one Fray knew very little about as it wasn't in his private journals. After a few more drinks Byrne let slip that Fray's father had fought a terrible enemy and won, but the victory had not been without cost. All he would say is that Fray's father had died in his arms before any help could arrive.

The more they talked about the past the more it brought old wounds to the surface. Buried deep was an old pain that still had the power to hurt him. Fray knew his father had been disappointed by his choices. Everyone had expected him to follow in his father's footsteps and become a Guardian of the Peace. But he'd rebelled and decided he wanted something different. The only problem was he'd no idea what to do instead.

For a time he tried being an actor, even managing to appear in a few plays, but the money wasn't steady and his commitment wavered in the face of poor reviews. To earn some money he worked on the docks, loading crates and from there continued to move from one job to another to make ends meet. It had taken his father's death to lift him out of his rut and finally start using his Talent, his magic. But he'd not been ready to take up the job that had finally killed his father.

Last night Byrne had reassured him that his father had always loved him and been proud, but Fray still had his doubts. After many drinks Byrne had helped him home and promised to come by in the morning for the first day of his new life.

Still feeling hungry Fray ate the second pasty before it went cold, savouring the hot bread and greasy meat. While he waited for Byrne to return he started to gather together his meagre belongings. As soon as he got a little money he'd move out of the one-room hovel and find somewhere clean and safe. It didn't take long to collect his possessions, and all of them together amounted to a mere two small piles. The only things of real value lay hidden beneath one of the floorboards, wrapped in old blankets, sealed in greased paper, secured inside wooden boxes. His father's journals. At night he would often take out one thick volume and read it by candlelight until he fell asleep. Fray contemplated digging one out while he waited, but then he heard the thump of boots on the steps.

Byrne strode into the room dressed once more in his red and black Guardian uniform, and the walls were back in place. His expression gave little away and he looked ready for the worst, armoured and carrying a sword. The deep worry lines etched in his forehead stood out, a testament to many years of policing the streets of Perizzi.

"This is for you," said Byrne, handing over a large bundle and a pair of black boots.

"I've always liked a man in uniform," said Fray with a grin.

Byrne's expression didn't change. "They're expecting us to solve this case very soon. It was good to talk last night. Hopefully we'll do it again soon but—"

"Right now we have to focus on the job," said Fray.

"That's right."

"I know," said Fray, slipping off his shirt and trousers. "I remember how Dad used to separate the different parts of his life. He didn't want work intruding at home. He thought he could leave it all at the front door. I think that's why he kept a journal. Maybe he hoped that by writing it all down, he could forget and move on."

"Did it work?" asked Byrne, although Fray suspected he already knew the answer.

Fray shook his head. "A part of the job always came home with him and I'm sure he sometimes took us with him onto the streets. At some point the edges blurred together. I think it's inevitable."

"Then you're already ahead of most novices. A year from now, you'll be a different person."

Fray pulled on the black trousers, running a hand down the familiar red line on the outside. The red cotton shirt smelled of lavender and fitted him perfectly across the chest but the sleeves were a little long.

"He often talked about you and your mother," admitted Byrne, watching as Fray pulled on the thick black belt. He handed Fray a short sword with a worn grip and leather scabbard. A quick peek at the blade showed him sharp edges. Finally he pulled on the heavy red and black jacket, its weight settling on his shoulders. A thick layer of leather lined the inside, made from the famous Sorenson cows from Seveldrom. From the outside the jacket looked fairly ordinary, but it would stop a blade and sometimes an arrow.

"You look good," said Byrne as Fray shrugged his shoulders, trying to get used to the weight. He leaned close and tightened Fray's belt one notch, helping him settle the blade on his left hip. Finally, after looking him up and down once more, a smile briefly touched Byrne's face. "Are you ready?"

"I think so."

As soon as they left his building Fray noticed people looked at him differently. The Guardian uniform had always been associated with justice, but now both the Watch and the Guardians had been elevated in the eyes of the people. The Queen only recruited the best, which made people feel safe. Fray saw a lot more smiles from strangers as they walked past.

When his father had first joined their ranks there had been rumours of corruption and bribery. Criminals paying Guardians to look the other way. Money changing hands for the release of certain goods or prisoners. Byrne assured him it didn't happen now, as they'd rooted out the bad seeds and gutted the entire network.

Byrne led the way towards the docks, but stopped at a junction of several alleyways before they reached the waterfront.

"The body was—" he started to say but Fray cut him off.

"Don't tell me. I need to see it for myself. Can you make sure no one is watching? Using my magic always unnerves people."

Byrne moved a short distance away to stand at the junction of streets leading to the docks. Hopefully Byrne would be able to intercept anyone who came this way before they saw Fray's eyes.

The location wasn't ideal and he was in a hurry, but the more frequently Fray used his Talent, the easier it became. He reached out with his mind towards the sound of the waves at the edge of his senses. To an observer very little would've changed, except his posture became more relaxed. But looking closer they would have seen the colour of his eyes shift from green to pale yellow and finally rich amber.

Stories of demons and monsters from beyond the Veil with glowing eyes had persisted in myth and folklore for centuries. The blindfold meant he could earn a living without angry crowds trying to drive him out of the city or drown him in the river.

As Fray's vision shifted, everything in the world became more vibrant and full of life, right down to the rats scurrying through the rotting food. Moving his head slowly from one side of the street to the other Fray's eyes showed him a rich history of information. Even though he couldn't see or hear any of the bars down on the docks, he could feel the buildings on that side of the crossroads. They held echoes of music, laughter and layer upon layer of conversation. They were not remnants of people, merely stray words, song lyrics spoken in unison by dozens of voices over and over again until he could hear the chorus from an old song 'The One-Eyed Witch'. Echoes of more intimate noises drifted towards him from the brothels but Fray quickly moved his attention elsewhere.

On the other side of the crossroads the buildings were very different. They were mostly places of work for merchants, traders and warehousemen. The buildings were quiet but he could feel a low hum of energy from where feet hurried back and forth all day.

At the centre of the three narrow roads all colour had been leached out of the world leaving only a black crater. Squatting down beside it Fray reached out with one hand towards a minor depression in the ground.

"The body lay here," he said, just loud enough for Byrne to hear. "It was utterly drained of all life. Even the ground is show-ing signs of ageing. The whole place has been leached clean." Fray poked the paved road with the toe of a boot and some of the stone crumbled like slate.

"The corpse was barely human. He'd been dead only minutes, but it looked like a body decades old," said Byrne.

"I'm guessing no one heard anything."

Byrne shook his head. "No, but they saw a flash of light."

Fray studied the ground trying to find some clue to help him identify the killer but there wasn't anything to find. He stood up and moved around the junction in a slow circle, one hand held out in front of him like a blind man searching for obstacles. Even to his attuned senses, the air felt exactly the same and there wasn't even a hint of unusual energy. He'd left it too long. If he'd visited the murder scene immediately after it happened, he might have been able to follow the killer. Absorbing that much energy would have made the killer glow like the sun and left a trail of energy in his wake, but now it had dispersed.

Fray thought about asking to see the body, in the hope that it might reveal a few clues, but changed his mind. He knew there would be nothing to find, just an empty shell. It looked as if for now they would have to rely on more traditional methods of finding the killer.

Fray let go of his Talent and the world around him shifted. Colour leached from his vision until he found he was standing at the centre of a grimy crossroads that stank of piss and rotting food.

"There's very little here."

"I was afraid you were going to say that," said Byrne, leading the way down a narrow street, moving away from the docks.

"Were the other bodies exactly the same?"

"Just dry husks," said Byrne. "Three in three weeks."

As they moved through the streets Fray noticed people glancing in their direction. At first he was suspicious and found it uncomfortable, but then he saw the expression on people's faces. The Guardians had become a symbol people associated with the liberation of Perizzi. Many Guardians had led units of Drassi and the Watch in the final confrontation with the zealots who had called themselves the Chosen. The uniform had come to mean so much more than when his father had worn it. Fray was saddened that his father had not lived to see it, and to see him take up the mantle.

"Do you know why the killer is draining all life and moisture out of his victims?" asked Byrne, bringing him back to the present.

"What makes you think it's a man?"

"Experience. So, why drain the bodies?" said Byrne, unwilling to be derailed from his line of questions. Fray had the impression this was part of his first lesson as a novice.

"If a person were very unwell, this would be one way to cure something like the creep or the red pox."

"Permanently?"

"Yes."

"Then it's not that," said Byrne, sounding confident. "Otherwise why would he kill three people?"

"Perhaps the technique takes practice?"

Byrne considered it. "Maybe, but I think it's something else. I think the killer is getting a rush from it, like an addict."

"Murder is the killer's drug?"

"I've seen it a few times before," said Byrne, his expression turning grim.

"Did you catch them?"

"Yes, but don't ask me for details. The things they did to their victims were unspeakable."

Fray dealt with the bereaved, but that was a long way from seeing, first-hand, some of the horrible things that went on in the city every day. Fray tried not to dwell on it too much. He would face that part of the job when it happened.

"You said this was the third victim in three weeks. So we still have some time before it happens again," said Fray, hoping for a little good news.

"Perhaps," said Byrne. "This last murder was in a very public place. The killer took a big risk, so either he's becoming more desperate, or the rush isn't lasting as long. If it's the latter then he could kill again very soon."

Fray had been a Guardian for less than a day and already he felt as if a great weight had settled on his shoulders.

"The Old Man can only keep this secret for so long before word gets out. No one saw any of the murders, but all three ended the same way: with a crowd of people staring at a peculiar corpse, and all of them wondering if magic was involved."

It all came back to the war. Fear of another conflict lurked in the minds of many and fear of magic was palpable. People were not only nervous of foreigners, now they were also afraid of their neighbours. If more deformed bodies turned up on the street, it would be harder to deny that magic was involved. Once rumours began they were more difficult to smother than a forest fire. He didn't want to think about what would happen if people began to panic.

A week had seemed liked a reasonable amount of time to find some clues. Now they didn't even have that. The friendly smiles that greeted Fray on the street suddenly seemed paper thin. They would soon fade if they knew magic was involved or that he was hiding his own magical Talent. Maybe he'd end up face down in the river at the hands of an angry mob or driven out of the city. Guardian or not, it wouldn't make a difference if they knew the truth.

Byrne glanced over. Noticing Fray's grimace he clapped him on the shoulder. "It's not too late yet."

Fray tried to smile but didn't quite manage it. "We're running out of time," he muttered.

CHAPTER 11

Despite having been very busy for the last few days, Katja felt unspent energy coursing through her. She was distracted and went through the motions of her day in a daze. If Gankle noticed she was acting differently he didn't say.

Finally the last of the weeping and sobbing relatives left the building after making arrangements for their dearly departed. She helped Gankle tidy up and then went to her room upstairs.

She changed out of her formal robes into something more comfortable, a white shirt and loose pleated skirt. She tied back her hair to keep it out of her face, checked her weapons and put a few coins in her pouch, mostly copper and a few silver. Any gold would be suspicious and attract the wrong kind of attention.

Checking herself in the mirror Katja spotted the pile of gold and silver she'd stolen the night before. A smile touched her lips and a spasm of unspent energy ran through her body. She took one gold coin from the pile and tucked it inside her clothes, just in case.

When Katja arrived at the bar Roza was already waiting with two drinks. Now that they knew the threat was real the network of spies in Perizzi had redoubled their efforts. The Silent Order had refused the job, and if their information was to be trusted, the Families had turned it down as well. Katja had been told that left two possibilities. There were independents, mercenaries who were only as loyal as the gold kept flowing, and then there were those even more dangerous. True believers. People who felt what they were doing would serve the greater good and that any action was justified.

"Why are we here?" asked Katja, glancing around the bar as they moved towards a table.

"I've got people in the low dives, dockside bars, the high-end boutiques and the aristocracy's drinking clubs. That leaves a lot of middle ground to cover." Roza already looked tired and the night was still young. "We have to comb as many bars as we can. Look at the crowd, tell me what you see."

Katja sat back in her chair and let her eyes roam over the room. Her left foot tapped an endless rhythm on the floor and she could feel the blade shifting slightly against her thigh. Taking a deep breath she stopped her foot and tried to calm her thoughts.

"I see a man surrounded by people looking to him for affirmation," said Katja, flicking her eyes towards a broad-shouldered local man with a thick black beard.

The group sat with him were an unusual mix, which is what had also drawn Katja's attention. A couple of the men looked like merchants. Others sat as if they had an iron bar for a spine, which meant they'd been in the army. A few others had money, but were trying to hide it. The women were equally diverse. A Drassi merchant in a flowing silk gown, one rich local who looked very uncomfortable in such a low dive, and two bruisers who were hired muscle.

"I don't think they're the ones we're interested in," said Roza.

"Why not?"

"It's the way they're all looking at him. He's not the leader, he's something else. A figurehead. Maybe a smuggler of something unusual. A new drug perhaps?"

None of the people seemed to be burning with rage or struggling to control their temper. Belief fired the blood and made people very passionate and animated.

As Katja watched, one of the women hurried to the bar to fetch the bearded man a drink. The huge smile on her face showed how much pleasure she took from serving him in this simple act. As soon as she moved away others rushed to catch his attention, hanging on his every word when he spoke.

"Maybe a sex cult," muttered Katja, gesturing with her chin towards the woman and man sat on either side of the bearded man. Both were stroking a leg and trying to attract his attention while he spoke to someone else. Whatever the group was involved with, it all centred around one individual.

She and Roza finished their drinks and left, making sure they weren't followed before continuing to the next place on the list.

In the next bar Katja saw another mixed group of people who were doing a bad job of being inconspicuous. The rich at the table had thrown ragged cloaks over expensive silk and richly dyed wool that she knew was the latest fashion in the city. They had made a small effort and removed any jewellery, but pale bands showed on the fingers of three men, indicating they normally had several rings on each hand. Then there were their weapons, which shone so brightly they created reflective circles on the walls that danced whenever one of them moved.

The group were huddled together, revealing their inexperience in such establishments as the room had been carefully laid out to facilitate private conversation. Whenever someone strayed even slightly close to their part of the room, the whole group fell silent, tracking the individual with their eyes. Only when they were sure the person was out of earshot would their frantic whispering recommence.

They were thrill-seekers. Rich sons and daughters of wealthy families who were roughing it. Pretending to being bad boys and girls to show they were tough and could drink in some of the worst bars in the city. Katja thought it possible they were planning something, but it would be a petty and childish prank. Perhaps painting a rude phrase on the side of a building or even something as depraved as killing someone, just to see if they could get away with it.

If that was the case it would be something for the Watch or the Guardians to deal with, not her.

Studying their faces she saw no indications of panic or genuine fear. So far no one had crossed any lines. She and Roza finished their drinks and left them to their games.

As the night wore on, frustration caused energy to build up inside her, making Katja's skin itch. She was desperate to act, to do something physical, but this search required a level of stillness that made her increasingly uncomfortable.

They went to yet another bar that seemed like a dead-end for the first hour. Just as Katja was starting to despair she saw an odd group of people drinking together.

At first glance they didn't look too unusual. But from looking at their clothes, their manners and even the way they sat, Katja could see they came from different backgrounds. By itself that wasn't uncommon but their conversation was full of tense silences, holes in the natural rhythm that told her they were newly acquainted. Nevertheless a common purpose had brought them together.

Even though she couldn't hear what was being said, Katja picked up a great deal about the mood from their body language and gestures. Most were anxious, but all were clearly irate about something. They were passionate and focused on a united purpose. One would speak and the others would keenly listen, nodding in agreement and making encouraging gestures. The only exception at the table was a tall Seve woman wearing a sword on her back. She never said a word. Her face showed no emotion and her eyes constantly scanned the room. When their eyes met Katja didn't look away, instead she offered a friendly smile. The Seve woman held her gaze for a few seconds then resumed looking around, clearly finding nothing of interest in her and seeing no sort of a threat.

"They might be the ones. They're planning something," said Katja.

"The man with the red beard. Did you notice his hand?" asked Roza.

"No."

"His fingers drum the table when someone gets too close, but the conversation never stops, it just changes. It's getting late," said Roza, draining the last of her ale with a grimace. "We should leave before they do."

As Katja followed her out the front door she felt someone's eyes boring into her back. Her instincts told her to turn around and see who it was, but she ignored it and tried not to tense up.

Once they were a few streets away she and Roza ducked into an alley, moving deep into the shadows, weapons at the ready. A few tense minutes passed in silence with Katja's heart pounding loudly in her ears. The two of them stayed like that for a long time, listening and waiting. Eventually Roza signalled they were not being followed and Katja relaxed. They retraced their steps until they were standing in an alley down the street from the tavern.

"What do we do?"

"Find out where red beard and the big woman are staying and who else they've spoken to. The group tonight could be their first batch of recruits or their fifth."

"Couldn't we just take them off the street and press them for answers?" suggested Katja, one hand moving towards her concealed blade.

Roza shook her head. "We could, but remember what the Silent Order told us? Even they couldn't find out who was behind it all.

These two are most likely just the latest pawns in someone else's game. We need to infiltrate the group and find out what they're planning."

"How?"

Roza bit her lip. "I'm working on it."

They didn't have to wait too long until the bar closed and the owner, apparently keen for his bed, started urging people out of the door. Individuals from the group they'd been observing left first and then red beard and the big swordswoman last, going in separate directions.

They waited a minute and then followed the swordswoman, keeping her just in sight ahead of them on the street.

After a while Katja realised they didn't need to be so cautious as the swordswoman never once checked to see if she was being followed. She strode with purpose, never wavering from her path, and people moved out of her way or crossed the street as she approached. Katja suspected she was taking the most direct route simply because it was the quickest.

The swordswoman was exactly what she appeared to be. A blunt implement used to bludgeon people. The only mystery would be her reason for getting involved, not her role. Katja looked forward to hearing her twisted justification for conspiring to murder not one but two Queens.

Half an hour later the woman marched into a slightly run-down inn called the Pear and Partridge. The sign was battered, the windows grimy, but someone had made an effort to make it look nice by adding hanging baskets. These couldn't disguise the worn nature of the building and modest accommodation it offered.

They waited a few minutes, giving the swordswoman time to settle, and then Roza circled around the back while Katja kept watch. A few minutes later Roza reappeared and Katja fell in beside her as they walked away from the tavern.

"I spoke to the owner. He didn't want to talk at first, but I loosened his tongue. Our friend, the big swordswoman, is supposed to be staying in room five. Apparently the owner accidentally stumbled into her room one night and found it deserted. She's paying for a room here and sleeping elsewhere."

It was beginning to sound as though this group, whether paranoid or just cautious, was more than amateurs or thrill-seekers.

"What do we do?" asked Katja when they were a few streets away.

"Go back to the inn tomorrow and hope they return," said Roza. "In the meantime I'll get some more bodies to follow other members of the group. Be careful and take precautions on your way home. Someone could be watching us." Katja couldn't see anyone, but that didn't mean they weren't being watched.

Taking the long route home, Katja walked fast, hoping to burn off some of her energy. It was no good. She needed something else and ignoring it wouldn't make it go away.

Changing her route again Katja took a side street and went deeper into the dark heart of the city. She walked briskly while letting her hair down and unfastening the top buttons on her shirt, exposing the tops of her breasts. Without her really thinking about where she was going her feet took her away from the main streets, down winding alleys and up narrow lanes. Not once did she look behind her to check if she was being followed. Her mind had become focused only on what lay ahead.

Katja felt the music before she found the place. A low thrum deep in her chest that vibrated through her bones. Her pace quickened as she went down the grimy set of stairs to a thick door set below street level.

She knocked and waited, anxiously hopping from foot to foot. On the other side of the door she could hear the music, an insistent beat that called to her.

Eventually a slot at eye level slid back to reveal the bald head of a big man. The black door opened to reveal a dirty and smelly corridor, the floor sticky and daubed with muddy footprints.

The doorman was a massive slab of meat, covered with faded blue tattoos on his thick arms and up one side of his pockmarked face. He was so tall that he barely fitted in the corridor and the top of his head brushed the ceiling. He jerked a thumb towards a doorway to his left and locked the door again.

"That must be really annoying," she said, gesturing at the ceiling then his head. His impassive face regarded her carefully, perhaps to see if she was making fun of him.

"Is that someone coming or going, Marrow?" said a rasping voice from the doorway. Marrow guided her towards the door, lightly resting one hand on the small of her back.

Through the doorway sat a grey-haired Zecorran woman whose black eyes were utterly without pity. A permanent sneer curled the corners of her mouth and she looked at Katja as if she were a maggot that had just crawled out of an apple she'd bitten into.

"The price is eight," she said, stabbing the scarred surface of the table with two black fingernails.

"Eight? Last time it cost five."

The sneer stretched even wider, exposing yellow and black teeth. "You pay eight or Marrow will throw you into the street. Don't think flashing your tits will change the price."

The music was much louder now and she could feel it passing through her body in waves, over and over like the tide. Gritting her teeth she counted out eight silver bits onto the table, making sure no part of her skin touched its surface.

The gatekeeper's hand snapped out and scooped up the coins. "Have fun," she said, offering another sickening smile.

Turning her back on the wretched woman Katja went into the

corridor and headed towards the music. It pulled her forward, calling to her in ways she couldn't put into words. She pushed open the thick door at the end of the corridor, and passed through a set of heavy black curtains.

The first thing to hit her was the insistent drumbeat and then the heat from all the bodies, dancing and writhing together. Katja immediately began to sweat and her body swayed in time to the music.

The large oval room had a low ceiling and the dancers had their hands extended towards it. At the far side of the room several musicians performed on a raised stage. Lighting came from flickering alchemical lamps set into glass-fronted alcoves along the walls, but the dull green glow did little except show her the outline of many sweaty bodies. Around the edge of the room were several short corridors where people could find dark corners and continue enjoying themselves in other ways.

The tempo of the endless drums increased, and with it the sea of bodies started to writhe more quickly, each in time with one another, as if they had become one monstrous creature with hundreds of arms and legs. A screeching fiddle scratched at her eardrums, seemingly at random. Somewhere in the chaos lay a pattern that slowly started to emerge.

As Katja moved through the crowd, bodies pressed on all sides and she merged with them, becoming one, moving in time. A woman with red hair laughed and threw her arms around Katja's neck, kissed her on the cheek and then span away. As the music passed into her being, filling the void and easing the terrible ache deep inside, she closed her eyes. Strong hands wrapped around her waist, lifting her off the floor and Katja laughed and felt herself raised above the crowd. A sea of hands passed beneath her and she floated, drifting for a time, losing herself in the beat, swallowed by the music. When her feet finally touched the ground again a smile would not leave her face.

Across the room she saw a familiar Morrin man disappear into one of the shadowy alcoves with a local woman with red hair. By the time Katja cut through the crowd the woman was already walking away and chewing something.

"What have you got?" she shouted, trying to compete with the music and noise from the crowd.

The Morrin's horns emerged from the shadows first, making him look demonic. The image was intensified by the feral grin and wicked twinkle in his eyes.

"Whatever you want, pretty lady," he said, launching into his spiel. "Something to make you float, something to bring you back down, something to make you cry like a little girl, or smile because life is beautiful. Or maybe you just want to forget everything for a night?"

"I'll take a blue button," said Katja, fishing out the gold coin from underneath her clothing. He bit the coin before handing her what resembled a small blue pebble. She let it dissolve on her tongue and merged back into the group of dancers.

A second fiddle began to weave in and out of the first, as if they were duelling. The sounds blended together into something indescribable, as the drumming increased in tempo again.

Her heart began to beat faster. The room span and Katja felt her arms reaching towards the ceiling with everyone else. But now she could see through the wet stones to the street above, and beyond that to the sky filled with stars. She felt part of her mind leave the room, passing over fields and farms, mountains and rivers, caves and forests. Leaving her flesh behind was so simple. She wondered why she'd never done it before.

Somewhere she felt hands on her hips and then a hungry mouth pressed into hers. Even as she continued to travel, her eyes found an unfamiliar face and she felt something hard pressing into her hip. She led him by the hand to an alcove where the shadows were deep and no one was watching. His mouth explored her neck and she wrapped her legs around his waist, pulling up her skirt then guiding him into her.

With the music pounding and her heart racing, her skin tingling and face on fire, she ground her hips against him, building towards a climax. Time had no meaning and she stayed in that perfect moment, suspended in time, feeling nothing, until suddenly the music had changed and the man had gone.

Katja rejoined the crowd and danced until all colour bled from the world and the sun touched the sky. Eventually she found her way home and collapsed on her bed fully clothed.

CHAPTER 12

The silence inside a church of the Maker always filled Choss with a sense of peace. As a boy he'd often just listened to the silence, soaking it up as if he were a dry sponge. The house was always busy and full of noise. His mother tirelessly working in the kitchen. His father talking loudly. His sister and her friends cackling at play. It made it hard for him to think or rest. At home he'd always felt on edge, waiting for the door to bang open, for the shouting to begin, for the screaming to start.

At first he'd always chosen one of the seats near the back, in case the priest tried to chase him out, but he never did. The old man had just smiled and left him alone for the first couple of weeks. Later they'd talked and Choss had told him about his mother and sister, the bruises and his drunken father.

They were all gone now. The drunk burned up into ash. His sister living a new life in Seveldrom. His mother dead ten years from the creep.

The silence in the church felt different now, lighter somehow. It also felt as if it was waiting for something, but Choss didn't know what for.

At the front of the church a pale-faced woman stood beside the attending priest. The old man he'd known as a boy was long gone, but the new priest had a similar look. World weary and stooped, with a lined face and eyes that seemed to know many things.

On the other side of the priest was a young man, proud and angry with tight shoulders. Laid out on a plinth at the front was what remained of Brokk. Normally a body sat in plain view so that people could see the face, preserved somehow with alchemical liquids so it didn't droop or smell. Since bits of Brokk were missing, chewed up and spat out by Gorrax, a heavy grey sheet lay over the body, covering it from head to toe. No one wanted to be reminded of how he'd died, but they all knew. The Patriarch, a local man with a ruddy complexion, stood watch over the remains, already into his second day. His eyes never moved. His face never changed. He stared into the long distance.

Once the woman had finished her business with the priest she turned around and Choss saw the red around her eyes. Fresh tears ran down her face unnoticed, but she'd stopped making any noise when she cried. Now the tears had become a reflex. Her body's way of trying to expunge the pain in the only way it knew. Although he'd not met her before, Choss knew she was Brokk's widow and the other man his brother.

Despite being hunched over they easily spotted him sat in the back row.

"I'm very sorry," said Choss as they approached, not knowing what else to say. The words felt small against their pain. He'd been in the same position as them after the death of his mother. He knew the words didn't really matter, as long as the sentiment was honest. "He had a lot of talent."

The wife, whose name he couldn't remember, wiped at her cheeks and her expression turned angry. "They're saying my Brokk was using venthe. He'd never do that. He was a good man. A good husband."

She didn't want to hear anything he had to say, especially now. So Choss just waited in silence, but over her shoulder he could see Brokk's brother looked uncomfortable. As if he knew more about it than she did.

"It was that filthy Vorga. Why did Vinny let it into the ring with my Brokk?"

"I don't know," said Choss, trying to catch the brother's eye, but he kept looking away, maybe on purpose.

"The Vorga hate us. They're nothing more than vicious monsters. It should be strung up by its neck. We beat them in the war, but they're too stupid to know it's over. All they want to do is kill people."

Choss let her words roll over him as he knew they weren't true. He heard enough to nod in the right places, but his attention stayed focused on the brother. They both knew the truth wasn't what the wife claimed. One day she might accept her husband had been less than perfect, but not today.

The priest approached them, taking the wife aside where they spoke in hushed tones. Choss took advantage of the distraction to step close to the brother.

"I'm Choss," he said, offering his hand, which the other man accepted.

"Tarnus."

"Have you ever been to the Jolly Crispin, down on the waterfront?"

"With the brewery out back?" asked Tarnus.

"That's it."

"I know where it is, why?"

"We should meet there later for a drink," said Choss.

Tarnus glanced over his shoulder at the widow. "I'm not one for drinking."

"I'm not asking," said Choss, trying to smile to soften his words, but it still came out as a threat.

The priest moved away and Choss took a step back as the widow turned around.

"I have to go," said Choss, before she could offer more advice on what should happen to all Vorga. "I just wanted to pay my respects."

"Thank you for coming."

He waited a moment, locking eyes with Tarnus, then turned and walked out of the church.

One of the jolly Crispin brothers was serving drinks behind the bar when Choss pushed open the front door. The big bearded man looked up but didn't smile. In fact his was a face that looked as if it never smiled. Choss wondered if the bar had been named after someone else.

Even this early there were a few people drinking. Sailors just come off the water or those preparing to go back out. Dock workers on a break, and a few lounging merchants. Six big tables sat in the middle of the room, huge oak things with scarred surfaces. An assortment of mismatched chairs and stools sat around each. All of the drinkers ignored the tables and were standing around the edge of the room, leaning against the wooden rail at waist height.

The decoration in the room was minimal, bare walls and a simple but sturdy bar. At first glance the floor looked unusually fancy, made of heavy black stone tiles, until you noticed the channel around the edges of the room that ran straight into the drains. A lot of beer and spilled blood had been washed off those tiles, night after night.

As a young man with more fire in his belly than common sense, Choss had come here a few times for a fight. To get back at his old man. To break faces and release some of his pent-up anger. The fights didn't happen every night, but the owners and the room were always ready, just in case.

To his surprise the bar smelled of fresh bread and bacon. There wasn't even a hint of old blood in the air. It had been a long time since his last visit. Perhaps the fights happened less often these days.

Even here, one or two people recognised Choss, but after a nod or a wave they left him alone. Choss bought a drink from one of the dour-faced owners then found a space against the wall. He'd nearly finished his ale, and was about to order another, when Tarnus finally showed up. Tarnus bought a drink and leaned back against the rail, facing into the room. He'd been here before then. You didn't show your back to anyone in the room.

Choss waited, giving Tarnus time to think, sipping the last of his ale. It was dark and rich, with a hint of liquorice. The smell of bread and bacon made his stomach rumble.

"My brother was in pain," said Tarnus. A catch in his voice made him stop, so Choss waited again. Being in the ring had taught him patience. Rushing in headfirst was stupid. Amateurs and those whose anger ruled their heads did that. You watched, you listened, you waited and then you attacked. "About six months ago he had a bad fight."

"In the arena?" asked Choss, thinking back to that time.

Tarnus shook his head. "He needed some extra money so he took a turn in one of the pit fights. One of those one-night things in the warehouse district."

Choss bit his lip and said nothing. The Watch stamped down hard on pit fights and were becoming better at finding them. Illegal rings could spring up at any time, but they never stayed in the same place as it was too risky. Pit fights meant there were no rules, high stakes, quite often bad injuries and sometimes dead fighters.

"Something felt wrong in his left arm after the fight. There was a bruise for a few days, but then it faded. Brokk thought it had mended, but then it kept hurting even though there wasn't a mark. He took some snuff for the pain and rested for a few days."

"He said something about your mother being sick," remembered Choss.

"She's been dead for years. He just needed a rest." Tarnus shrugged by way of an apology. "But it didn't help. He tried a couple of surgeons, but there was nothing to see so they couldn't help. The snuff stopped working so he got something else for the pain."

Choss leaned closer. "Where did he get it?"

Tarnus glanced up at him and then away. "He knew if Don Jarrow found out he'd be in trouble. So he went into the west end."

"Where?" asked Choss, forcing himself to breathe slowly and stay calm. If he frightened Tarnus now he'd run and probably never talk to him again.

Tarnus took a long drink before answering. "From one of Don Kalbensham's dealers, in the meat district. He thought if he got the venthe outside of Don Jarrow's turf, it wouldn't get back to him."

Don Kalbensham ran another of the crime Families in the city and he controlled one of the worst areas. No one ever went into the meat district unless they worked in the meat trade, worked for Don Kal, or were searching for something special on an evening. Gambling, drink, drugs and prostitution came as standard, but there were also a few other things that happened in the area that city officials didn't know about.

There were also lots of slaughterhouses in the west end, which meant a lot of screaming animals and trickling blood. A few human screams amid the noise and the occasional odd-shaped carcass hung on a hook was easy to miss.

Choss knew the Watch had recently started patrolling the area, but so far their incursions had been small. They always happened during the day, were always in big numbers and heavily armed. The pain must have been bad if Brokk had been desperate enough to go into the west end.

"Are you going to tell Don Jarrow?" asked Tarnus.

Choss shook his head. "It wouldn't help. I'll keep it a secret."

Tarnus looked relieved. Perhaps he'd thought there'd be some repercussion against him. He finished up his drink in three long gulps and left without another word. Choss lingered, bought another drink and something to eat, while he thought it through.

Doña Jarrow had said she would use her influence to help the arena if he solved the venthe problem. Going into the meat district wouldn't be easy, but he didn't know what else to do. He'd have to be cautious in another Family's territory. If Don Kal found out he'd been there, he'd accuse Don Jarrow of spying. Then the Family feud that threatened to blow up would happen that much sooner.

The front door opened and a group of sweaty labourers came in, calling for drinks and food. One of the burly men nudged his friend and they all turned and smiled or called out in his direction. Choss lifted his mug and smiled. Not for the first time he wasn't happy to have such a recognisable face. It made him realise that if he did go into the meat district, he'd have to wear a disguise.

CHAPTER 13

It still felt strange to be dressed as a Guardian of the Peace, but if anyone noticed Fray's nervousness they didn't mention it. As Fray waited with two other novices outside the Khevassar's office his eyes began to wander.

The Khevassar's outer office, much like the rest of Unity Hall, was sparsely furnished with heavy wooden furniture stained with black lacquer. The polished wooden floors were painted a deep red, the colour of fresh blood, and yet more red and black dominated the rooms and corridors. A Guardian had adopted the style two hundred years ago and no one had bothered to change it. The consistency was reassuring in some ways. It reinforced the idea of dependability and the unwavering arm of the law in Yerskania.

From floor to ceiling the office walls were lined with shelves filled with hundreds of identical books with red spines. A Guardian's history of the city over the last thirty years, written by the Old Man himself. Fray suspected his view of the events in Perizzi would bear little resemblance to that of other people's. The journals recorded crimes and their investigations, the victims and the horrors people inflicted upon one another. Miserable reading to be sure, and there were tens of thousands more just like these in the vaults, written by other Guardians going back several centuries.

Rummpoe, the Old Man's fussy assistant, hadn't acknowledged Fray and the other novices, as if they were beneath his
attention. He'd also given no indication that he remembered
Fray or recognised his name, which struck him as odd but he'd
said nothing. Today he wasn't here as the son of a former
Guardian, a witness or victim of a crime. This formal interview
with the Khevassar marked the official start of his apprenticeship
with the Guardians of the Peace.

The other two novices were very nervous. One kept biting his
nails and the other couldn't sit still, as if there were ants crawling inside his clothes. The Old Man had a fearsome reputation,
and although they'd earned the right to be here, some more than
others Fray realised, no one wanted to be in a locked room with
the most intelligent man in the city.

The office door opened and the Old Man stepped out. It had
been a few years since Fray had seen him, but the leader of the
Guardians looked almost exactly the same. A small old man with
wavy white hair and dazzling blue eyes that moved slowly but
missed nothing. He glanced briefly around the room before turning to his aide.

"I'm feeling a little parched," said the Khevassar, smacking
his lips.

Rummpoe carefully cleaned the ink from his pen and set it
down before looking up. "I'll have a pot of tea sent along."

"Thank you," said the Old Man, going back into his office,
but he left the door open. "And send in the first novice."

Rummpoe glanced across at Fray and gestured towards the
open door with two fingers.

"Close the door," said the Khevassar as Fray stepped into his
office. His most recent journals lined the walls and there was yet
more black painted furniture, red books, red curtains and grey
stone walls. The Old Man gestured at one of the two seats in
front of his desk and Fray sat down.

"How are you?"

"I'm well, Sir. Thank you."

The Old Man's smile was wolfish. "No need to be so formal, boy. I've known you since you were born. This isn't an interview like the others."

"I didn't want to assume."

"Which speaks well of you. If anyone asks, we spoke about why you want to be a Guardian. I also asked you some difficult questions that made you feel uncomfortable. Understood?"

"Yes, Sir. I mean, yes."

"Good. I actually asked you here to talk about the case. What did you find?"

Fray told him what they'd discovered at the most recent crime scene. Despite his magical Talent they were no further forward on the case. The Old Man's expression became thoughtful for a few seconds, but he didn't react like Byrne.

"I don't think my help was all that Byrne had hoped for. Perhaps he'd thought I'd be able to find the killer immediately."

"How did he take the news?"

"Not well."

"Hmm," said the Khevassar, and his eyes became distant. With someone of a similar age it would have been reasonable to assume his mind had wandered. Fray knew from his father's stories it meant the Old Man was working something through in his head, weighing various options and running scenarios. He said nothing and waited. A few seconds later blue eyes found green.

"I want you to do a favour for me."

"Of course, Sir."

"Keep an eye on Byrne." It was the last thing he'd been expecting to hear.

"What am I looking for, Sir?"

The Khevassar cocked his head to one side. "How much do

you know? About what really happened with your father at the end?"

"Not much," said Fray. The Old Man's raised eyebrow formed a question. "I have his journals, but the last few pages were torn out. Anything about his final case is missing."

"Have you asked Byrne about what happened?"

"Yes, but he didn't tell me very much. I don't think he really knows either."

The Khevassar grunted. "No one really knows what happened, only that something was averted at great cost. Byrne took your father's death very hard as they were closer than brothers. I thought he'd recovered, but he became a different man afterwards. Cold, more reserved. Then the war started, there was that business with the Queen abdicating, and we had Chosen flooding the streets."

"I remember their brutality."

The Khevassar grimaced. "We became prisoners in our own city. They left us to investigate crimes, but they were always there, watching for signs of sedition. Byrne felt as if he were the one that had been neutered, not the Prince."

Fray winced and tried not to squirm in his chair. Once the Chosen had been driven out of the city the Queen had resumed her rightful place on the throne. But now there were many questions about who would wear the crown when she stepped down. Some had suggested she would break with centuries of tradition and stay on the throne until death instead of retiring like her ancestors. Others thought the crown might skip a generation and pass to one of her grandchildren or a blood relative instead.

There were many rumours and wild stories about what had happened to the Prince, which Fray discounted as nothing more than gossip and fantasy, but there was one detail on which they all agreed. Once Perizzi had been liberated the Prince rode out of the city and had not been seen since.

"We started resistance groups," said the Khevassar with a short barking laugh. "Held clandestine meetings and whispered in dark corners. We spread rumours and finally a real rebellion began in earnest. Byrne led one of the squads that destroyed the Chosen's temple. A year on and the streets are still not as they once were. And neither is he."

"Should I send you reports?"

"No. We won't be able to speak in private like this unless it's an emergency. If you see any unusual behaviour just leave a note with Rummpoe. He's been briefed but there's no official record of this. Are we clear, Novice Fray?"

"Yes, Sir," said Fray, knowing that erratic or unusual behaviour would mean an internal investigation of Byrne's activities, and no one wanted that. Even the Guardians had their own internal investigators, who everyone loathed, but they were a necessary evil.

"We've been in here too long. I'm going to shout at you now, but don't take it personally."

"Sir?"

"No one likes favouritism, Fray. You bypassed serving in the Watch and immediately became a Guardian. This is the only way to stop you being an outcast. You can't afford it. Some jobs are just too big. You'll need help from other Guardians in the days to come. It will be hard at first, but give them time to come around."

As usual the Old Man was five steps ahead of everyone else. The Khevassar cleared his throat and gave Fray a cheeky wink.

"I don't care what you heard, or who your friends are," he bellowed, directing his voice towards the door. His voice was so loud and there were so many hard surfaces in the room it made Fray's ears ring. "Your father earned his position and you'll do the same. Now you listen to me, boy, I don't want to hear one more word about this, or I'll cut off your balls and shove them down your throat. Now get out of my sight!"

Fray adopted a shamed expression, yanked open the door and stormed down the corridor, avoiding all eye contact. The other two novices were sweating profusely and they made a point of not looking at him.

"Send in the next one and where is my damn tea, Rummpoe?" Fray heard the Khevassar yell just before he turned the corner.

Fray spent the rest of the afternoon training with the other novices in a seemingly endless series of drills. Somehow word had already reached the other novices about what had happened and they did their best to avoid him, as if the wrath of the Khevassar had become contagious. Fray had been an outsider all his life, so it wasn't new. For the time being he decided to grin and bear it and trust the Old Man's judgement that it would eventually get better.

He spent hours running, swimming in a narrow and freezing cold tributary of the river, then more running and climbing ropes. After that came a test to measure the novices' proficiency with a blade and many sparring sessions. It quickly became clear to Fray just how far behind the others he was in terms of physical fitness. He struggled to run very far without wheezing, barely clawed his way up the ropes using both his legs and arms, and managed to come last during the swimming. A few months of good food and doing this every day would soon change that, but for now the distance between them was obvious.

The only time he excelled was during the sparring sessions where he bested seven of his ten opponents. What he lacked in style and grace he made up for in brutal efficiency, making him unpredictable and dangerous. All afternoon their grizzled training instructor had mocked his physical fitness, but as Fray pinned his last opponent to the floor he received a grunt of approval.

Every week, from the age of eight when he'd been strong

enough to lift a sword, until the day he'd stormed out of the house, Fray's father had trained him to fight with a sword. Over the years the lessons had paid off when he'd found himself in trouble and they were proving useful again.

By the time he'd washed the sweat from his skin and sat down to eat in the mess, Fray's stomach was growling. The cook took sympathy on him, perhaps because he too had heard the news, or maybe he just thought Fray was skinny and needed fattening up. Either way he didn't complain about the double portion of roast sandfish with black beans, carrots and buttery potatoes.

As Fray mopped up the last of the tangy cheese sauce with a slab of rye bread, Byrne sat down opposite.

"Ready?"

"Yes. Where are we going?" asked Fray.

"Someone reported a missing person. We've identified him as our third victim from the silver ring found on the body."

"So who was he?"

"He's called Rann. He was a labourer down at the docks. The others in his crew will be coming off shift in a little while."

"I've been thinking about the bodies," said Fray. "They reminded me of something from a previous case in my father's journals." Byrne didn't react so he pressed on. "I checked last night and this has happened before. Bodies being drained of all energy."

At first he thought Byrne wasn't going to answer. He kept staring around the mess hall, scanning the room but not really looking at anything in particular. Fray didn't remember him being so distant.

"It was similar," Byrne responded at last. "A woman was killing people and assuming their identities. This is different though. It's the beginning of something much larger."

"Why do you say that?" asked Fray. "Does it have anything to do with my father's last case?"

"We need to get down to the docks," said Byrne, getting to his feet. "Let's go."

Fray wanted to ask him more about what had killed his father but Byrne's expression told him the conversation was over.

The Guardians had told Fray very little, but he heard a number of rumours. Dozens of dead bodies, a strange cult and even weird coloured lightning seen over the city. No one he spoke to had actually seen what had happened. Only Byrne and the Old Man knew the truth and neither of them was talking. It was almost as if they were afraid, but of what Fray didn't know.

By the time they'd walked down to the docks all ships coming in were tied up for the night. A few were still unloading goods but almost everyone had stopped working. The waterfront bars and taverns were already swarming with people eating and drinking, and the main street was crowded with faces from all over the world.

Fray spotted several men who'd probably been at sea for days. They were rushing into the cheap brothels as fast as their bandy legs could carry them. Those less desperate and with more money casually strolled along with working girls or boys on their arm to find somewhere a little more refined. Merchants, soldiers, warriors, sailors, dock workers and a hundred different craftsmen all drank beside each other without incident. It reminded Fray of what it used to be like before the war, although there were some noticeable differences.

There were few black-eyed Zecorrans in the crowd. Any Zecorran merchants he spotted were surrounded by well-armed bodyguards or Drassi warriors. Vorga hated crowds, and people as a general rule, so they never drank at the seafront bars. Fray also didn't spot a single golden-skinned face from Shael.

Although no one said anything or stared at him and Byrne, Fray felt a ripple pass through the crowd in their wake. Some of the looks were hostile, some curious but mostly people just noticed the uniform. They passed a squad of the Watch and Byrne exchanged a nod with their leader but didn't stop to talk.

"Every night we station squads all along the waterfront to keep the peace," said Byrne, pointing at another squad a little further ahead. "It's quiet at the moment, but they'll be busy later tonight. Helping to turf out the drunks and rowdies, breaking up fights before anyone gets killed."

"Did you ever work the docks?"

"When I first started in the Watch," said Byrne. "It's brutal and it can be dangerous. You learn to trust your squad mates and grow eyes in the back of your head."

Not for the first time Fray wondered if the other novices would come around, or if he would forever remain an outsider.

"I want you to listen but also to study the men when I ask them questions," said Byrne. "Since you can't always use your Talent, and shouldn't rely on it, you'll have to develop more traditional ways of reading people. Look for signs that they're lying, nervous, hiding something. Listen to how they say something as well as what they say. We'll talk after."

"I understand," said Fray.

They passed two more squads of the Watch before Byrne pointed at a third group stood beside a group of four burly men. The men were sat drinking at a table outside a tavern called The Fierce Fowl. The unusual wooden sign showed a chicken attacking a dog.

"Guardian Byrne," said the squad leader, a lean-faced man with a long T-shaped white scar on his right cheek. "These are the men."

Fray did as instructed and studied the four men carefully. Three were locals, with light brown or blond hair. The fourth man had mixed blood, being much taller than the rest, but with the pale hair and eyes of a Yerskani. All four were dressed in steel-toed boots, worn but tough-looking leather trousers and leather vests with padded shoulders. Fray noticed that all had broad shoulders, arms corded with muscle from handling goods all day, and that their fair skin had tanned from a life spent working outdoors. Caps and bandannas poked out of pockets and their hands were scarred and callused from their work.

"I'm sorry about your friend," said Byrne. "And I'll try to catch the person who killed him, but I need your help."

"What do you want to know?" said the tallest man, sipping his ale. Fray noticed the others didn't look annoyed that he'd spoken up first, suggesting they were happy to defer to him.

"What's your name?" said Byrne.

"Lorgan."

"Had you known Rann for very long?"

Lorgan took another drink while he fished for the answer. "About five years now, sound right boys?" he asked and the others agreed.

"Had you noticed anything unusual in the last few days? Had he been moody, or upset, or did he seem worried about anything?"

"No, mostly the opposite. His bastard of a father died a couple of weeks back and he was due a share of money. Split three ways between him and his two sisters. Still, it was enough to keep him happy for a while."

"Where do his sisters live?"

"Somewhere just over the border in Morrinow. They've got a bakery, I think. Guess all the money will go to them now."

"Was Rann married?"

"Nah," said Lorgan. "He visited a friend's widow from time to time, but it wasn't serious. Mostly he paid for it when he had the urge."

"It can get pretty lively down here at night," said Byrne, gesturing at the crowds. "Rann ever get into any trouble?"

"I won't claim we're priests of the Blessed Mother," said Lorgan, choosing his words carefully. "We don't go looking for trouble, but if someone spills our beer, we're likely to talk to them about it. At length."

"That's understandable," said Byrne. "Did Rann ever upset anyone who's likely to hold a grudge?"

"Not that I can remember."

"What was he like when he'd had a few too many drinks?"

Lorgan grinned, showing a set of surprisingly even white teeth. "Rann didn't drink. His bastard of an old man was a drunk, so he swore off it for life. Never touched a drop."

Byrne raised an eyebrow. "Good for him. So what did he spend his money on? Food? Buying gifts for the widow?"

"He and Bav liked to spend some on the fights, down at the arena. The rest he sent to his sisters."

"Who's Bav?" asked Byrne.

"We were a six-man team. Bavram's been in bed the last two days with a dodgy gut. Probably something he ate."

"Where does Bav live?" asked Byrne, taking out a notebook for the first time. He wrote down the address and then put it away again. "So what happened that night? Anything different?"

Lorgan finished the last of his beer but Fray noticed Byrne didn't offer to buy him another or let him go and buy one. "Same as always. We had something to eat, a couple of the lads went to see local girls, and we stayed dockside all night. Rann and Bav left together for their beds, 'cos they live close by, and that was it."

Fray watched the other men as Lorgan spoke, studying their expressions and body language. They looked tired, saddened by the loss of their friend, and he didn't believe they were trying to deceive Byrne.

Byrne asked Lorgan a few more questions, going over some of the details, but nothing significant emerged.

"I won't keep you any longer," said Byrne, gesturing at Lorgan's empty glass. "Thank you for the help."

"What will happen when you catch who done it?" asked Lorgan.

"The final decision for a crime like this is up to the judge," said Byrne, "but most of the time it means beheading."

"Sounds fair to me," said Lorgan before he and the others went inside for fresh drinks. Fray hurried to follow Byrne as he strode away from the docks and the Watch returned to their post.

"Tell me what you thought of them," said Byrne over his shoulder. "Lorgan and the others."

"My instincts tell me they are what they appear to be. Honest men, a little rough around the edges, but I didn't sense any deception. They weren't nervous or worried, none of them fidgeted and they were all focused, despite the drink. They want us to catch the killer."

"Agreed. They want to help and cared about their friend. Lorgan's a straightforward man and he didn't ramble, despite the beer."

Byrne ducked around a swaying pair of sailors, who tripped and collapsed on top of each other laughing all the while. They must have started drinking very early. Fray hurdled the pair, who cheered, but he didn't stop to take a bow. The Watch would pick them up soon enough.

"I made sure they'd started drinking before we spoke to them. It's an old trick, but it works."

"It makes them talkative," surmised Fray and Byrne favoured him with a brief smile.

"But you have to get there early. Arrive too late and they'll ramble on. If you time it just right the drink will loosen their tongues. It means we don't have to drag the answers out of them."

"But they wanted to help."

"Even so, this way they're more likely to tell me all the details, not just the ones they think we want to hear."

"What happens now?" asked Fray.

"Now, we look for a connection between the three victims. Speak to their friends and family again, speak to Bav. He was probably the last person to see his friend Rann alive."

"Is there any chance I could see the other bodies?" asked Fray. "I might be able to see something you missed," he continued, tapping the side of his head.

Byrne shook his head. "One's been given to the Maker and is a pile of ashes, and the other one's been buried. We can't hold on to bodies for long before crying relatives and priests start showing up."

On the one hand Fray could sympathise. The thought of delaying a final goodbye or performing last rites for several days would be unbearable. On the other hand he could see how useful it would be for the Guardians to be able to study a victim's body for clues. For the first time since putting on the uniform Fray felt what would no doubt be one of many moments of frustration about being a Guardian.

"So what do we do now?" asked Fray.

"See if any of the relatives will talk to us. Try to find Bav and hope that we catch him at home."

"You don't think his illness is genuine?"

Byrne's laugh was more than a little cynical. "Don't be naïve. There's no such thing as coincidence."

"Are you saying he's involved?"

Byrne shrugged. "Either that or he's another victim, and so far no one has found the body. We need to find him."

Glancing up at the darkening sky Fray realised another day

was almost over. If Byrne's theory was true, the killer could strike again any day now. It felt as if they were stumbling along, but Byrne didn't look too worried. Fray's instincts told him there was much Byrne and the Old Man weren't telling him about this case. He didn't know if it was somehow connected to what had happened to his father, but he was determined to find out.

CHAPTER 14

After another emotionally tiring day Katja decided to treat herself to a steak from Seveldrom. It was possible to buy beef raised here in the west, but the quality wasn't as good, and she needed a reminder of home.

She had enough time to get something to eat and then meet Roza for another night of watching the most suspicious group they'd seen. The big swordswoman had proven to be more elusive than anticipated. They would have to keep a close eye on her, as well as on the man with the red beard, who appeared to be the leader.

There were several taverns more luxurious than the Golden Goose, but as somewhere to eat, Katja knew it was one of the best places in the city.

The chef, a portly man in his fifties, had lived an extraordinary life, criss-crossing the entire continent for years. In every place he'd taken away something from the local cuisine. All of his experience, combined with thirty years to hone his craft, resulted in some delicious creations.

The chef emerged from the kitchen to present Katja with her meal. With a flourish he whipped the white cloth off the plate and set it down. A juicy steak, small but the height of four fingers, sat on a plate of yellow rice mixed with red berries. A moat of thick black gravy surrounded it and the dish was finished with a spicy green relish on the side. The combined aromas made her stomach growl and the chef grinned at the sound.

"Enjoy," he said, backing away as she dug in with vigour.

Just as Katja was mopping up the last of the rich gravy with some bread, a shadow fell across her table. She ignored it, hoping that whoever it was would go away and leave her in peace to savour the tastes swirling around her mouth.

Two people sat down opposite and it took her considerable effort to keep chewing and not choke on her food.

"My name is Rodann," said the man with the red beard. He gestured at his companion, the tall Seve swordswoman Katja had been following. "This is Teigan."

Katja took her time, washing down the last of the gravy with a mouthful of red wine. She wiped her mouth and then sat back, resting one hand lightly on the hilt of the blade strapped to her thigh. This couldn't be a coincidence, which made her wonder how much Rodann knew. Had he or Teigan seen her and Roza following them?

"What do you want?" asked Katja.

Rodann's smile reminded Katja of a generous merchant she'd seen giving away sugared almonds to street urchins in northern Yerskania. The poisoned nuts had killed seventeen children before they managed to stop him.

"That is what I was going to ask you," said Rodann, "because I know you're not going to find it in the places you've been looking."

Katja looked at Teigan who met her gaze but didn't react. Her expression could have been carved from stone. The spark of life behind her blue eyes was the only indication that she was alive. While Rodann looked soft, with plump cheeks and woollen clothing, Teigan dressed in leathers, cut her brown hair short and her face was lean and angular.

"What does that mean?" asked Katja.

"We know all about you."

Katja laughed and gestured with her free hand. "Tell me. I want to hear this."

Rodann opened his mouth but then frowned and gestured at the bar. "Give me a moment. Another?" he said, gesturing at her glass of wine, but Katja declined.

She and Teigan sat in silence while Rodann waited at the bar to order a drink from the barman.

"So if he's the talker, what do you do?" she asked.

Teigan glanced briefly at her and then away, studying the room and the crowd. "Negotiate," she said, tapping the hilt of her sword.

Rodann returned a couple of minutes later with two mugs of ale and a glass of wine for Katja. Both she and Teigan didn't touch their drink but Rodann took a few large gulps before settling himself.

"I know that you came to this city with an idea," said Rodann, gripping his mug with both hands as he stared into its black murky depths. "And you've done something remarkable. Others will copy, but you were the first. I also know that despite being immersed in so many religions, it's left you feeling hollow and unfulfilled."

Katja stifled her anxiety, carefully schooling her features and keeping her breathing slow and even. She was right. Someone had been following her. She thought she'd lost them, but perhaps they'd just been more careful. It would explain how they knew so much. However, so far Rodann showed no indication that he knew she had been following him and Teigan.

Instead of showing concern she simply raised an eyebrow. "Why do you say that?"

Rodann's brown eyes were sympathetic. "Why else would you go to places like the Cave? Or drink in one low-down bar after another with your friend. What's her name?"

"Roza," said Teigan. Katja stared at her in shock, but Teigan's attention remained elsewhere. At the moment it was on two merchants in the far corner conducting business in hushed whispers.

"Ah yes, Roza. A sad story," said Rodann. "Forced to give up her old life and take over the spice shop when her poor uncle died. She's just as lost as you."

Katja eased the blade out of her pocket but kept it pressed against her leg. As clever as he thought he was Rodann had no idea that she and Roza were anything other than what they appeared. However, it was possible Rodann was simply playing with her. Katja tightened her grip on the blade.

"You're searching for something," said Rodann and Katja heard the first stirrings of passion in his voice. "But you won't find it in oblivion, however you get there."

"And I suppose you have all the answers," said Katja, not bothering to hide her sarcasm.

"No, I don't. But I believe you're concerned with more than your own gratification. You're not the only one who's lost. Many of us are feeling disconnected and betrayed."

Rodann spoke as if his betrayal was very personal.

"Betrayed by who?"

"Everyone," said Rodann taking another long drink. Katja noticed Teigan had still not touched her ale. "The world has changed and we need to change with it. Look at Queen Morganse. She gave the throne away and then reclaimed it, just like that." Rodann snapped his fingers and a flush started to creep into his cheeks. "What about the line of succession? What about the laws of the land? She serves the people and yet we weren't involved in her decision to reclaim the throne. We had no voice."

"You want to get rid of the Queen?"

Rodann shrugged, perhaps unwilling to show his cards so quickly. "Let me give you another example. Most people follow scripture that is thousands of years old. The scribes had no way of knowing what life would be like when they wrote those holy books. So why do we hold to them so tightly?"

"Only idiots follow scripture to the letter. It's about the spirit of the text," said Katja, spitting her words out sharply enough to earn a frown from Teigan.

"Ah, but mostly we just do as we're told," said Rodann. "The priests guide us, often interpreting complex and conflicting passages, but they're no better than us. Most of them are corrupt and unworthy. In the old days priests earned their position through sacrifice, through blood or celibacy, through the Iron Challenge or the Long Walk. Now they're just people in silk robes spouting old words."

"You're not here for a religious debate. So what do you want?" asked Katja, starting to lose patience despite her best attempts. Her knuckles turned white on the handle of her blade. Katja knew she could slit his throat before Teigan drew her sword. Maybe she could even bury the dagger in the big woman's chest if she moved quickly enough.

"To help bring about change," said Rodann with passion. "And I think you want the same thing. I'd like you to meet with some of the others, just to listen to our ideas. After that, if you don't agree, we'll part ways as friends and you'll never see me again."

Katja eased her grip and considered her options. It was starting to sound as if Rodann and his group were involved in something far more complex than just an assassination. It sounded as if he wanted to start a revolution. On the surface his goal of challenging the status quo sounded like a heartfelt cause, but there was obviously more to it. Otherwise, why the need for secrecy and the obvious paranoia?

So far he'd not even mentioned Queen Talandra or blamed her for anything. Most of Rodann's ire seemed to be directed towards Morganse, Queen of Yerskania. Katja doubted his anger would solely be directed at one person.

Putting the plot to one side a single question loomed large in her mind. Why her? Why had he specifically chosen her? There were many disheartened people in the city.

Katja considered killing them both and just walking away. Perhaps if they died the others would just fade away into the shadows.

She took a few deep breaths, pushed the impulse away and slipped the blade through the hole in her pocket and refastened it to her leg. Katja placed both hands on the table, considered the wine and took a drink. If they wanted her dead there were easier ways.

"I will listen, but I make no promises about anything else," said Katja.

"We're meeting tomorrow night. Just come with an open mind, that's all I ask," said Rodann, grinning like they were old friends. His smile still made a shiver run down her spine.

He gave her an address and a few landmarks to find the right door. While they'd been speaking Teigan had remained silent. She'd not reacted to anything they'd said, which made it difficult to read her. Katja would have to watch her closely to find out her role and why she'd become part of the conspiracy.

Rodann finished the last of his ale in two big gulps, glanced at his companion and gestured at her untouched ale. Teigan downed the whole mug in one long breath and moved towards the door, leaving Rodann to hurry after her. It left Katja wondering if perhaps she'd misjudged their relationship and in fact Teigan was in charge.

There would be time to think it over more thoroughly once she'd attended their meeting the following night. After paying and sending her compliments to the chef, Katja left to meet with Roza. They went to another tavern out of the way to talk, sitting in a quiet corner.

"Why did they choose you?" was the first thing Roza asked once Katja had explained what happened.

"I don't know."

"You should assume you're being followed from now on," said Roza. "Go about your duties as normal and if you need to talk, visit me at the shop during the day. They know we're friends, so it won't look suspicious."

"What do they want with me?" asked Katja.

Roza shook her head, unable to provide an answer. "I'll see what our people can find out about Rodann and Teigan. In the meantime be careful, and don't take any risks."

Roza left first and Katja considered going out again and losing herself in the music. Part of her wanted to just forget everything for a few hours, but paranoia, or caution now that she knew someone had been following her, won out.

Taking a roundabout path, regularly stopping to check for signs of pursuit, Katja gradually made her way home. If Rodann's people had been following her they'd been very discreet.

Part of her mind kept track of her route and the people, but the rest remained focused on her conversation with Rodann. She kept turning it over and over in her head, thinking back to the other people she'd seen with him and Teigan the previous night, looking for a connection. There were too many possibilities to even try and form a plan. She needed more information.

Even as she ducked into a side street that led back the way she'd just come, Katja knew it would be prudent to be more vigilant than usual, especially as she went about her day job.

She crossed one of the main bridges, feeling a gentle wind

from the sea against her skin like a caress. The tang of the salty water filled her nostrils, helped to clear her head a little.

She skirted the edge of several lively streets, packed with people drinking and wandering about in a haze, before heading north. A few more turns and then she could cut back across the river again and be at her front door in another half-hour.

As she turned a corner onto a narrow lane between rows of houses she spotted two men at the other end. They were deep in the shadows, studying the street and balanced on their haunches with their backs to her. Something about them seemed vaguely familiar and it took her a couple of seconds to remember. They were the two thugs who had been trying to rob the merchant a few nights ago.

Just as Katja started to back away one of them glanced around nervously. His mouth fell open and she put a finger to her lips, hoping he'd take her advice.

"You bitch!" he shouted, springing to his feet. His shout drew the attention of his friend, whose surprise quickly turned to rage.

"Don't be stupid. Remember how this turned out last time?" said Katja, trying to keep them calm. "Just walk away."

Both men drew daggers and slowly came towards her. Katja risked a glance over her shoulder, then turned and sprinted away, skidding around a few corners until she found what she needed. Several alleys crossed, creating an open area, which gave her some space to move.

One of the men had a bandage around his right hand, which meant the other one had the dislocated shoulder. Seeing them again up close she noticed the men had similar features, suggesting they were related. Both were armed with a dagger and they approached her cautiously this time, taking nothing for granted. To even the odds a little Katja drew the long blade from her pocket and the dagger from her boot.

The two men glanced at each other and nodded. Moving

slowly they started to creep towards her from two different directions.

"Last chance to walk away," said Katja, but they ignored her.

Taking a deep breath Katja tried to calm her nerves and slow the frantic beating of her heart. She waited as the men edged forward, watching both of them from her eye corners. When they were just out of her reach she feigned an attack towards one then launched herself at the other. Using both blades in wide circles she drove him back, making him focus on defending himself against her weapons. Which meant he completely missed her kick against the same knee she'd injured last time. With a howl he stumbled and then fell backwards onto his arse. Katja rushed forward and darted around behind him.

A blade whistled through the air behind her and the man on the ground tipped backwards to avoid being sliced by his friend. To make sure he stayed there Katja jabbed him three times in his right arm with the tip of her dagger. The wounds weren't deep, but they made him howl and bled enough to keep him busy for a while.

The other thug rushed forward but she kept him back with her long blade.

"Kill her!" screamed the man on the ground, trying to stem the bleeding. Katja moved away, giving herself plenty of room. The thug started making threats about what he'd do to her, but she ignored him. Soon he resembled a gaping fish dying on the riverbank, his mouth flapping open and closed. Katja sniggered at the mental image and the thug flew into a rage. He charged and she ducked and span away. He came forward again and she danced away once more, mindful of the man on the ground. He might not be able to fight, but he could grab her legs.

The thug attacked, slashing left to right. She didn't try to block, just kept moving away and to the side. He kept trying to corner her. In close quarters she wouldn't be able to move or match his strength, so her best chance was to watch and wait. She didn't have to wait long.

He lunged, trying to jab her with his dagger, but overextended. Instead of moving away she stepped forward, ducking under his arm. The thug hissed and span around, his hand coming away red from where she had cut him across the ribs.

"I could've killed you," she told him. "Take your friend and go home."

Stubbornness, or maybe pride, wouldn't let him leave. He attacked again with a howl and when she tried to dart away his other hand snaked out, grabbing her by the shoulder. She flicked the blade towards his arm, scoring a long gash on his forearm. He screamed but held on and shoved her backwards.

Katja stumbled, dropped her dagger, but didn't fall to the ground. She regained her balance in time for his shoulder to collide with her chest. Her back and head slammed into a wall, driving the air from her lungs, making stars dance in front of her eyes. One meaty fist closed around her throat and she gasped for air. With his other hand he pinned her knife hand to the wall.

A nasty grin stretched across the thug's face. She cut it short, ignoring the hand on her throat and her weapon. Her free hand slammed into the shoulder she'd recently dislocated and the pressure eased on her wrist. She pulled her hand free then buried her long blade in the thug's stomach. Both of his hands dropped to his sides and they stood face to face in silence. His face went slack and his eyes bulged in terror.

With a vicious twist she turned the blade, making him wheeze. Something hot and wet gushed over Katja's hand, spattering loudly against the stones beneath her feet. His dagger dropped from loose fingers, clattering to the ground. After a few seconds his knees buckled and when his weight threatened to snap her wrist she let go and he collapsed.

A long L-shaped hole ran across his stomach. Red and blue ropey innards spilled out. Black blood spurted and gushed, soaking into the thug's clothing before spreading out and forming a red pool around his body. It ran between the paving stones, giving the street a network of veins written in blood.

The other man was screaming, struggling to his feet. The noise would draw unwanted attention if it hadn't done so already. Katja swept up the thug's fallen dagger, stalked across the rotunda and buried it in his throat. Hot arterial blood splashed over her face and arms, in her eyes and mouth. Gagging and choking the thug fell back, both hands against his neck, vainly trying to stop the flow.

Katja sank to the ground, dripping with gore and blood. Both men gasped their final breaths and silence returned. Not far away she heard a faint trickling as blood found its way down the drains, mixing with filth in the sewers.

The adrenaline faded leaving Katja feeling hollow and exhausted. For some reason her teeth ached. She started to shiver and became aware of the cuts and bruises from the fight. Moving like an old woman, she retrieved her weapons, tried to wipe the blood from her clothes but only made it worse. She spat the blood from her mouth and stumbled home, sticking to back alleys and side streets. It took a long time, as several times she was forced to hide in order to avoid other people and squads of the Watch. At one point her exhaustion was so great she nearly fell asleep, her head dipping towards her chest, but fear of being caught woke her up.

Eventually she came to the right street but couldn't go through the front door as every part of her clothing was soaked with blood. She darted into the alley behind the shops, counting the buildings until she found the right one. Thankfully she could see a light and as she approached the back door she heard movement inside.

Gankle opened the door slightly then threw it open, his mouth stretching wide in shock. Katja stumbled inside before he could ask his questions, her hip collided with the kitchen table and she fell onto the floor.

All remaining energy seemed to drain from her body and she lay there with her face pressed against the cool stone. Just before she fell into the black she felt strong hands lifting her and she stopped fighting, sinking into oblivion.

CHAPTER 15

Choss turned the mask over in his hands, carefully checking it for any spots he'd missed. The masquerade for the summer solstice wasn't for over a month, but lots of people were already buying costumes, so he'd not looked suspicious. It would help for what came next. He'd picked up the black paint at a different shop and the wooden file from a carpenter. He'd widened the eye holes, smoothed off all the rough edges, the spiny ridge on the nose, the nodules on the cheeks. Now the garish pheasant mask had been reduced to a bone white oval which he'd painted black. It left his chin and mouth free, but everything else was concealed behind the mask.

It wasn't quite a Drassi mask, but getting hold of one of those was impossible. None of the costume shops dared copy the distinctive teardrop style, a decision which had been mandated by the Queen. The Drassi were easy people to get along with, and trade with them was good, as long as you didn't piss them off.

Every Drassi man had only one mask and they guarded it more closely than their money. The only way to get one would be to take it off a dead body, and that was extremely difficult.

Black trousers and steel-toed black boots, a black padded leather vest that left his arms bare, and long metal bracers on his forearms, finished his outfit. Choss pulled down the mask and stared at himself in the mirror. The perfect outfit for a bit of thieving or sneaking about. He knew he couldn't move very quietly compared to some, being big had its disadvantages, but with the borders open again for trade, large men from Seveldrom were common in the city. If anyone saw him, all they'd remember was someone tall, dressed in black.

Choss tucked two punching daggers into his belt, their handles and his belt buckle blackened as well. He wasn't used to hiding in the shadows, but he'd been around enough people who did it regularly to know the basics. He pulled on a grey baggy shirt over the top of his vest and weapons so it didn't look completely obvious what he was about.

A little before midnight he followed groups of people heading towards the west end and Don Kalbensham's turf. At this time of night plenty of people had already drunk a fair bit and were in search of other forms of entertainment. Although no one stopped and searched him, Choss knew when he crossed into the meat district. He could feel people watching and weighing him up for signs of being a potential troublemaker.

Choss merged with one group, sang along with them and swayed in time. Just another drunken reveller seeking a bit of a thrill, or maybe some company for an hour or two.

A few streets into the district he peeled off from the group, sprinted down a narrow lane between two of the long flat warehouses and found a shadowy corner. He stripped off the shirt, shifted the daggers around from the small of his back to the front of his belt and pulled on the mask.

Bracing his legs and arms against walls on either side, he slowly inched his way up the walls, finding footholds in the pitted stones. Choss rolled onto the roof and stayed low, looking out across the city. Only a couple of buildings stood higher than the warehouses in the meat district, and none of those were nearby. Beyond those he could see a good portion of the local area, including a couple of bridges in the district, and hear the hush of the River Kalmei. Up here the air was hot and sticky, but it would be a lot worse inside the warehouses, pressed up against people or herds of animals waiting for slaughter. From above the streets he studied the layout of the area, noting the streets full of light and loud with music. Just beyond them was a ring of silence. The streets away from the busy areas, the bars, the brothels and gambling houses, would be his best place to find corners where people bought their fix. Nearby would be derelict and shoddy hovels, dens full of half-conscious bodies piled on top of each other like kindling, oblivious to the world beyond their rush.

Choss carefully manoeuvred down to street level again and headed for these silent streets. His breathing sounded unnaturally loud in his ears, but he knew it was only his nerves. As the warehouses became less frequent he passed into an area once used to house slaughtermen. They still housed people who dealt in flesh, but now it was work of a different kind. Moans of pain and pleasure mixed together into one huge chorus until he couldn't tell one from the other. The slapping of flesh on flesh and rhythmic creaking and grinding called out to him. It reminded Choss of how long it had been. How long since he'd been able to relax in a woman's company and just be himself, not the fighter, not the Champ. The only exception was Munroe and theirs was a complex relationship. Everyone else looked at him in a certain way. He'd never be able to live up to their expectations.

With a shake of his head Choss pushed away his loneliness and focused on the task at hand. Turning his back on the brothels he went deeper into the dark heart of the district, where the lights inside the buildings were dim and more windows were covered or boarded up.

Even so he caught glimpses of horrific sights through shuttered windows. Outside one grimy building, with bars on every window, Choss saw a long queue of men waiting in the street. He circled around the back to avoid the crowd and as he passed a window risked a glance inside. A burly local man stood around a huddle of scantily dressed skinny women who all reached out towards him with greedy, desperate hands. Choss couldn't see what the man passed out to each, probably black crystal, but the women all gobbled it up. Their eyes glazed over, a few just fell to the floor and the rest stumbled away. More jackals came in, took the women away over their shoulders like sacks of grain, shoving others who could walk ahead of them. He heard the front door open and the customers come inside. The clink of money followed and the whimpering and rhythmic grunting began soon after.

A few street away Choss paused, leaning against a wall to catch his breath and swallow the burning coal of rage. Every fibre of his being told him to go back, to rush in there and do something to help. He had no illusions. Don Jarrow wasn't a good man, but there were lines he wouldn't cross. You could buy company for an hour in his district, but the Jarrows didn't enslave anyone or get them hooked on crystal or venthe. He'd heard stories about it being worse in other areas, but hadn't seen it with his own eyes until now.

It took a while but eventually he calmed himself down. One thing at a time. As he turned a corner he stumbled into a teenage boy, sending him flying. A gang of six more youths laughed at their friend's misfortune until they saw Choss's mask.

"Who are you supposed to be?" asked one.

"Do you work for Don Kal?" asked another and Choss shook his head slowly. "That's good news for us then," said the chatty lad, pulling a narrow shiv from his pocket. The others copied him, drawing out sharp spikes of metal. "'Cos we do, and he don't like outsiders. So give us your money and maybe we won't cut off your balls."

If they really did work for Don Kal they would be Paper jack-als, the lowest on the ladder in the organisation. They were just the eyes and ears for a Family on the street. It would have to do for now. Choss loosened his shoulders, cricked his neck from side to side and sank down in the cool and calm place in his mind. He shut out all emotion, ignoring the coal of anger that permanently burned in his gut. It was an eternal flame of rage that had never gone out. But he could control it. He was the better man and had proven it many times over. Instinct and experience would guide him, blind rage would only cripple his talent. Gesturing with one hand he beckoned for the boys to approach.

"All right, big man, we'll do it the hard way. Fuck him up!" screamed the youth, before he charged. Choss pulled his punches but still broke the first lad's nose, smashing it across his face with a hard left jab. A right backhand sent the boy spinning into the wall. He deflected a clumsy stab on a bracer and kicked a second boy in the chest, breaking ribs and knocking him into two more bodies. Choss broke the leg of another lad, shattering his shin with a vicious kick, threw another headfirst into a wall, and snapped the forearm of the next boy. They had the numbers and crude weapons, but were untrained opportunists. Choss had been street fighting against bigger opponents since his tenth birthday. After that came years of training and countless professional fights. Over the years he'd lost many times, and had learned more about himself from those beatings than from any victory. The outcome today had never been in doubt.

The fight lasted less than a minute and soon the ground was littered with crying teenage boys. Their bravado and arrogance had evaporated. Terror replaced it as Choss approached, lifting one boy off the ground until his feet dangled in the air. A bit of drama always helped at times like these. Suddenly his mask and black clothing weren't funny. A wet patch spread across the front of the boy's breeches as he pissed himself.

"Where do I find the venthe dealers?" he asked. The boy hurried to answer so Choss grabbed one wrist, bending it backwards until the boy screamed. "Look at your friends and think carefully before you lie," he said.

In between cries for his mother, with snot bubbling out of his nose, the boy gave him directions. Choss dropped him to the ground, then moving slowly and calmly, he walked away and didn't look back. Mercy in this place was worthless and it would be exploited. He couldn't afford to show any weakness.

He followed the boy's directions and a few minutes later saw two people shuffling along the street. They were twitchy, one muttering to himself, and Choss recognised the tell-tale blue stains at the corners of their mouths. Venthe addicts. He trailed after them and soon saw the dealer, a Zecorran man wearing a red bandanna. When the last addict had shuffled away Choss approached. The man knew how to handle himself but even so he didn't last much longer than the boys.

The left side of his face was a bloody pulp, one eye swelling closed, and both lips were split. His collar bone was broken on the left and the arm dislocated from a hard collision with a stone wall. Choss held the man upright against a wall, casually leaning his forearm across the dealer's throat.

"Tell me about your new supplier."

"Same one. Hasn't changed," gasped the dealer. Choss shook his head sadly and delivered a hard punch to the man's gut. The dealer fell to the ground, wheezing and gasping for air. Choss took the venthe powder from the dealer's pocket, tipped it out of the little paper bags and ground it into the mud.

He stalked the darkest streets of the meat district for the next hour and took out three more dealers. Each time they gave him the same answer. Nothing had changed. Same supplier, same routine. As doubt crept in, a new line of worry began to furrow the creases between Choss's eyebrows.

As he approached yet another dealer the inevitable happened. As soon as the dealer caught sight of his black mask he ran, but Choss didn't chase him. Instead he followed at a slow walk and around the next corner he found five thugs waiting for him. All of them were armed, and stood in front of them with his arm in a sling was one of the boys from earlier.

"That's him!" he screamed. The biggest man, tall enough to be a Seve except for the pale colour of his skin, shoved the boy away, his eyes never leaving Choss. The others were two local men and two Morrin women who watched him with merciless amber eyes.

"You work for Don Kal?" asked Choss and the big man inclined his head. That meant he was probably a Brass jackal. A street boss who ran one of the gangs. None of the thugs made any threats. They held themselves well and their weapons looked worn but sharp. A different sort of fight then.

Choss drew both punching daggers from his belt and waited. The boy turned and ran. As the five came towards him Choss quickly studied his surroundings before focusing on the way his opponents moved. The big man held back, letting the others go first, probably to wear him down.

One man on the left swung at Choss with a short-handled mace. The other on his right came at him with a sword. Choss dodged the mace and jabbed the man in the shoulder, his punching dagger biting into flesh, then he elbowed the man in the face. Deflecting the sword on his right bracer, he quickly jabbed the other man twice in the stomach with his left hand. Both men fell back, howling in pain and clutching their bleeding wounds. The others clambered over them never taking their eyes off Choss.

He gave ground, moving his feet carefully to avoid tripping. The two Morrin came forward. One held a short sword and the other a local Yerskani cleaver blade. With a roar that startled them both, Choss charged, feinting at one and then ducking and sweeping the legs of the other. As the Morrin's head struck the ground it bounced, but the Morrin rolled away before Choss could finish her. They had thick skulls which made it very difficult to knock them out.

With both arms crossed Choss blocked a lethal blow from a short sword that would have split his head in two. Sparks rained down from where the blade struck his bracers. Morrin had sensitive eyes, which bought him a second as she fell back.

The other came forward again. Instead of trying to block the blow Choss lashed out at the same time towards her arm. His blade bit clean through the Morrin's forearm, stopping her attack cold. As her cleaver started to fall from useless fingers, Choss grabbed it and threw it at the other Morrin. It was badly timed and the weapon wasn't made for throwing, but it bought him a couple more seconds. He sawed the blade back and forth in the Morrin's arm as she screamed and tried to shove him away. With his right fist he jabbed the Morrin hard in the thigh, then stepped back, leaving her bleeding on the ground in two places.

The other swung at him wildly, enraged and determined to finish the fight quickly. Emotion had fired her up and made her clumsy. Perhaps the other Morrin was a relative or close friend. He ducked one blow, sliced off one of her ears and punched her low in the back. Such a blow would normally kill, but Morrin didn't have kidneys in the same place. They did, though, have a thick nerve cluster there, which made her drop to the ground, twitching like a puppet with cut strings, head and ankles rattling on the ground.

Choss waited for the big man to attack but instead he turned and ran. It was only when the adrenaline faded that Choss become aware of his heavy breathing and the sweat trickling down his sides. More ran inside the mask, making his face itch, but he didn't dare take it off. Being this deep in another Family's territory made him very nervous. It would be extremely dangerous for someone to discover his identity.

Leaving the bleeding jackals behind, Choss went into the next street before finding what he needed. Someone had illegally dug out the basement of their house, creating the perfect place to grow venthe in dark wet soil. It didn't happen in areas of the city where the Watch regularly patrolled, but out here it was common.

Choss descended the three steps to the low door, but didn't try to open it and force his way inside. He hunkered down and waited. A short time later his breathing had returned to normal and the sweat cooled on his body. A wave of fatigue ran through him, but adrenaline kept him awake and alert. The thump of many feet made him lean deeper into the shadows but no one was looking for him. They wouldn't expect him to linger nearby.

Ten more armed toughs, led by the tall Brass jackal from earlier, went past him and around the corner towards their fallen friends. He couldn't hear what was being said, but the conversations were angry and short. The thugs stumbled past him in the other direction, taking their injured friends with them.

Choss waited until they were out of sight before following at a discreet distance. The Brass had no need to move quietly. They ruled these streets, which made them easy to follow. Instead of moving towards the more populated area, they went further out, towards the edge of the district.

About half an hour later Choss watched the jackals approach an old run-down warehouse. All of the immediate buildings surrounding it were nothing more than ruins, shells with gaping roofs and missing walls, tumbled stones and one or two wooden frames of projects half built. It created a lot of empty space around the warehouse and few shadows, which meant he had to watch from a distance. Even from his position Choss could see that several men armed with crossbows were patrolling outside the warehouse. There were a couple more on the roof and when the main door slid open to admit the Brass, four more armed thugs stood waiting.

He only had a brief glimpse inside the warehouse, but saw a big table covered with a network of glass tubes and bubbling cauldrons manned by people with bandannas over the lower half of their faces. The injured thugs stumbled inside and the door slid closed.

It didn't make sense. Choss turned the puzzle over in his head but only came away with more questions. Either this was one of Don Kal's farms, where they cooked up the venthe, or his Brass were secretly working for someone else. If they were loyal, then did the Don know about the lethal version of venthe? Had he been producing it in secret? Perhaps he'd been trying to make something more addictive and it had gone wrong.

Or someone else had managed to turn some of his people and they were muscling in on Don Kal's turf. It seemed unlikely, but none of the Brass had reported back about what had happened. If Choss had been in their position he or one of the Brass would have gone directly to the Gold or the Don himself.

He needed more information and to get inside the warehouse, but couldn't do it by himself. Choss desperately needed help and he knew exactly where to get it from.

CHAPTER 16

Talandra stared around at her rustic surroundings and smiled at its simplicity.

All of the furniture, the two chairs, the table, the wardrobe, even the bed, had been handmade. If she was honest Talandra would've said the workmanship was fairly poor. Some pieces of wood didn't quite fit together, and the head of a couple of nails stuck out from the top of an armrest on one chair. Talandra loved it all the more.

Every piece was made by the same pair of hands. Every bit of wood sawed, varnished and put together over countless hours with one person in mind. Ursel had lost his daughter at sea when she was twenty-one. Since then no one had entered the small apartment above his tailoring shop. He could've sold it, or rented it out many times over the last ten years, but he couldn't bear the thought of that. Talandra felt blessed to be sitting in Munlala's chair. The amount of love Ursel still had for his daughter was a pleasant reminder of her own father. Many years ago the tailor had been a spy for her father. After hearing his story Talandra had been unable to refuse his generous hospitality.

Alexis bustled into the room with another armful of cushions and, without being asked, Talandra stood up so that the taller woman could add them to both chairs. It was strange to see her out of uniform, but the sword on her hip was still there. Another of her royal guard came into the room bearing a tray loaded with bread and a huge bowl of steaming soup.

"Alexis, could you—"

"After the soup," said the big blonde. "Whatever it is will wait until after you've eaten."

Both women hurried out of the room, leaving her to eat. Talandra could hear the other woman going back down the steps to resume her post while Alexis stood outside her door.

The most difficult part of Talandra's secret journey to Perizzi had not been the miles on horseback, but persuading other people to let her travel. After listening carefully to Shani and reading the latest intelligence report she had agreed to a body-double and the need for extreme caution.

However, a formal visit required a lengthy caravan including a contingent of royal guards, wagons full of supplies so that her journey could be made in comfort. Then there were the people to look after the animals pulling her carriage, people to prepare her meals, scouts to check the roads ahead, and before long the number in her entourage had swelled to more than fifty.

The pace at which such a large group could move each day, including time to break camp each morning and set it up each night, was incredibly slow. After a lengthy discussion and heated debate with her brother, Hyram, he'd eventually agreed to let her travel ahead of the official caravan with six of her royal guards. He'd wanted to send a dozen, but the larger the group the more difficult it became to go unnoticed. Perizzi had several gates into the city and all of them were being watched for the unusual, which someone could sell for a profit.

While the royal caravan slowly crawled its way towards Perizzi, with her body-double doing a convincing job of pretending to be her, Talandra had ridden ahead. For the next few days she would be able to move around the city without her every move and word being reported and studied. For the first time in a year Talandra felt an easing of the weight of her responsibilities.

As she absently rubbed her swelling stomach Talandra read the latest report from Roza. She was glad they had already set off before this information became available. Now that the plot had been confirmed Shani would never have let her travel, adding her voice to the others about it being too dangerous. So far the implied threats had only been directed towards Queen Morganse, but Talandra didn't believe the danger for her had passed.

A sharp double rap at the door announced the first of her guests. She took a moment to compose herself and adopt a carefully neutral expression.

Alexis stepped into the room first and behind her came a short, spindly Zecorran man with thinning grey hair and a haughty expression. Valkrish was the Zecorran Minister of State and not someone Talandra would normally have the misfortune of meeting, let alone being forced to deal with. A wave of annoyance ran through her merely from the way he held his nose aloft while looking at the room.

"Majesty," he said, not bothering to bow or even incline his head. Over his shoulder Alexis frowned but left the room without incident. Talandra didn't bother to stand up or greet him. Instead she merely gestured towards the other chair. Valkrish slowly lowered himself into it, as if afraid it might hurt him or break under his weight. "Very . . . rustic."

"Isn't it charming," said Talandra with a smile, ignoring the sneer in his voice. "Thank you for agreeing to this meeting, Minister."

Minister Valkrish finally looked her in the eye. "This is highly irregular, but the messenger indicated it was important."

"It is."

"Important enough to disrupt my usual schedule. I had other appointments."

She'd tried to be polite and treat him with a certain level of respect but he was showing her none in return. Talandra decided to get straight to the matter at hand.

"It involves the Chosen and the recent surge in their popularity in Zecorria."

Valkrish was taken aback but quickly covered his surprise. "I'm not sure I know what you're talking about."

"Play coy if you want, but we both know the Chosen weren't eliminated in Zecorria. Every other nation in the west managed it, but they've grown in the shadows of your country like a fungus."

It was a petty dig, but Talandra was annoyed by his arrogance.

"I'm not sure what you've been told—"

"I've read first-hand reports of the recent problems in the capital. It started a few weeks ago with the tragic events surrounding the former High Priest Filbin," said Talandra, barely managing to keep the contempt from her voice. Filbin was a cunning and power-hungry deviant who she'd wanted to see deposed for years. Surprisingly he'd done it to himself in the end, having some sort of breakdown whereby he confessed all of his darkest sins to a cathedral full of people. This, combined with proclaiming to have received divine, and very specific instructions, from his God, earned him an early retirement to a special facility in the country.

"The church of the Holy Light will recover," said the Minister. "But I don't see what that has to do with the Chosen uprising."

"So you admit they're becoming a problem," said Talandra. The Minister spluttered and looked around for a distraction, perhaps something to drink and buy himself some time, but she'd not offered him anything. "Filbin's sins have smeared the church of the Holy Light in Zecorria, and around the world."

"The new High Priestess Robella is pure of spirit and without sin. People will return to the church."

"Perhaps," admitted Talandra. "But in the meantime they're looking for an alternative and the Chosen are very outspoken. They don't deal in vague scripture or centuries-old myths. Their God was a living, breathing person."

"Who is dead," snapped Valkrish.

Talandra shrugged. "All the old religions have something about resurrection and rebirth. The Chosen are no different."

"Did you ask me here so that you could gloat?" asked Valkrish.

"Far from it, Minister," said Talandra, offering him a gentle smile and using his title again to massage his bruised ego. "I'm here to offer you some help."

Valkrish smacked his lips and glanced around for a drink, but the room was bare of any bottles or decanters. A jug of water sat on the table between them and she poured him a glass, which he accepted with a gracious nod.

"What sort of help?" he asked, after a long silence.

"My people have some experience of rooting out the Chosen," said Talandra. "They're devious, and very clever people who hide in plain sight. But if you get too close they disappear."

"They're like rats," admitted Valkrish. "Every time we find one of them and eliminate it, two more take its place. Either that or they scuttle away and hide in a dark hole."

"I understand your frustration. It took my people months of patient work to gather all the names before we made a move and eliminated them in Charas."

Valkrish raised an eyebrow. "They'd made it all the way to your country?"

"Right up to my doorstep. In my capital city."

"But you've dealt with them?"

"Yes. They will not return," said Talandra, feigning confidence. Shani had reassured her of this, but even so she still had a nagging feeling at the back of her mind.

The Minister processed this for a minute, carefully sipping his water. Talandra poured herself a glass and mirrored the gesture. Somehow, despite a huge bowl of soup and bread, her stomach was still rumbling and she felt the first stirrings of hunger. It wouldn't be long before she started to show and would need some larger dresses.

"What are you offering?" said the Minister, bringing her back to the present.

"A list of names. Not only key figures in the Chosen network in Zecorria, but also a list of locations. You said it yourself, Minister. They scuttle back to their holes, but if you already know where they're going, it doesn't matter. They'll have nowhere to hide. My people have over two dozen names, which includes several recruiters who have been trying to increase their numbers."

"And what are you asking for in return for helping us with the Chosen?" asked Valkrish.

"I don't want anything," said Talandra, twisting her mouth into a snarl that she hoped was convincing. "They're parasites and their twisted beliefs are an abomination. Their crimes during the war were horrific. Seeing them eliminated is enough of a reward."

Valkrish didn't seem moved by her passionate display. In fact it seemed to have the opposite effect she'd hoped for as Talandra sensed him withdrawing into himself. She'd been told he was a devoted patriot and had hoped to appeal to his national pride, but it hadn't worked. Either Valkrish was more astute than people realised or he was more paranoid.

"If I were to ask how you obtained these names, would you tell me?" he asked, but before Talandra could answer Valkrish pressed on. "What else are your spies feeding you? Perhaps the names of Ministers with secrets? Those with debts or mistakes they'd rather remain buried?"

"Of course not," Talandra managed to say, but he was just getting started and would not be stopped.

"How could I possibly trust your information? For all I know you're making the Chosen a similar offer! To sow seeds of despair in my country and keep it off balance."

"Don't be ridiculous, Minister."

Valkrish slowly rose to his feet, the haughty sneer returning. "I will not be manipulated or led around by the nose. We will take care of our own problems, without outside interference. I will not be beholden to you."

With that he stormed out, but the display was spoiled when he yanked open the door and walked headfirst into Alexis. The little man rebounded off her chest and would have fallen if she'd not caught him by the arm.

"Get your hands off me, you great oaf!" Valkrish snapped, yanking himself free before stomping away down the stairs.

"Should I even ask?" said Alexis, and Talandra shook her head. "Your next visitor is here. Do you want a minute?"

"No, send him in," said Talandra, standing up to greet her guest.

It had been over a year since she'd last seen Ambassador Mabon from Zecorria and the plump man had changed little during that time. Even so it took Talandra a moment to recognise him as she wasn't used to seeing him with his clothes on. Last time they'd met, in a rather special boudoir in her capital city, he'd been hanging naked from a cross while a madame whipped him across the buttocks. A little colour crept into Mabon's cheeks as they shook hands. Clearly he'd also not forgotten about their previous encounter.

"Ambassador," said Talandra, offering him a warm smile, which he mirrored.

"Your Highness," he said, bowing over her hand.

"How are you? How is the family?" she asked, taking her seat.

Talandra was pleased to see that Mabon waited until she'd settled before sitting down opposite.

"We're all in good health, thank you. I believe congratulations are in order." For a second Talandra thought he was referring to her pregnancy. "How is your husband?"

"He's fine, thank you," said Talandra, taking a breath to calm herself. She would have to be careful about that in the future. "I just had the distinct pleasure of meeting the Zecorran Minister of State."

"Ah. Him," said Mabon. "A prickly and annoying man at the best of times."

"Arrogant and paranoid too, it seems. I'd heard he was a loyal patriot."

"I take it your meeting didn't go well."

Talandra sighed. "No. I made him an offer, which he refused. Now I'm going to make you the same offer."

She repeated what she knew about the Chosen and their growing popularity in Zecorria. Mabon didn't deny their existence, which was a good start, and he took a moment to consider his reply when she'd finished speaking.

"You're right about Valkrish. Despite his brusque manner, he is a patriot. He just won't accept help from outsiders."

"How about from one of his own ambassadors?" asked Talandra.

"It will take some convincing, but it's possible," conceded Mabon.

"Do you remember what happened in Charas, Ambassador? Do you remember the favour I did for you?"

Mabon swallowed hard and braced himself. "I remember."

"I'm collecting on your debt. I want you to make sure either the Minister, or someone else with equal influence in your government, uses the information I've supplied. I want to see the Chosen eliminated from Zecorria."

From his surprised expression Mabon had been expecting her

to ask him to do something dangerous, disloyal or even commit a crime to clear his debt.

"Why? What do you get out of it?"

"Do you remember how the war started?" asked Talandra.

"It was Taikon and his black wizard."

"They came later. Long before people flocked to Taikon's banner, the seeds of chaos were being planted. People whispered in corners about getting rid of his father, the old King, and nothing was done. A cult, based on a twisted reading of scripture, began to flourish, and nothing was done. Dozens of people in your capital city went missing and then turned up dead, their bodies misshapen and blighted by dark magic."

"Who?" asked Mabon.

"The Warlock, conducting his experiments." Getting detailed information out of Zecorria had been difficult during the war, but since then Talandra had read dozens of reports from her people. "Those murders, and a dozen other threads, were ignored long before Taikon killed his father and took the throne. If we do nothing about the Chosen they could fade away in time, or they could fester and infect more people. You asked me what I want," said Talandra, sitting forward and pinning him in place with her stare. "I want to prevent another war. The people here in Yerskania are nervous and jump at their own shadows. A violent outbreak seems unavoidable. Civil war still rages in Morrinow and Shael is a wild land, without law and order."

"And my country is being poisoned from within," added Mabon.

"The war may be over, but we've not even begun to heal. It feels as if the west is covered with kindling and a spark could set it all alight," said Talandra. "You're a moderate at home. People will listen to you. Will you do this?"

"Yes, your Highness," said Mabon, giving her a seated bow. "I will see that it is done."

CHAPTER 17

Sweat trickled down Fray's face, making him itch, but he didn't try to wipe it away. Drauk, his red-faced opponent, was also suffering in the summer sun. It wasn't even noon and the heat was already unbearable. The air was sticky and there wasn't a whisper of a breeze to give the city some relief.

Despite their discomfort neither of them looked away, both doing their best to ignore their surroundings and focus only on each other. Fray had to work very hard to ignore the way Drauk's sweaty shirt stuck to his chest and arms.

He'd heard the other novices mocking Drauk for his dedication to the rules, but as three generations of his family had been Guardians, a great deal was expected from him. Fray could understand the pressure of not wanting to sully the family name. They both had a lot to live up to.

Drauk would do well in the Guardians. Apart from being clever and driven to succeed he was also handsome, which wouldn't hurt.

A smile tugged at the corners of Fray's mouth. Drauk frowned, over-thinking the situation, and quickly took a step back. When Fray didn't attack he came forward, striking with precision towards Fray's shoulder. Fray sidestepped the attack and his riposte flicked towards Drauk's face, forcing him to sway backwards. They moved back and forth, their wooden blades clacking together. Drauk fought with superb control. Fray knew his own style was far less elegant, more duck than swan, but he still kept Drauk's blade at bay.

Finally he saw his chance when Drauk overextended. Perhaps he was tired from a long morning of training, or maybe he wasn't as good as Fray thought. With a flick of his wrist Fray knocked the point of Drauk's blade aside, slid inside his reach and jabbed the point of his sword into his opponent's armpit.

"Point," shouted Kenzo, their instructor. "You're dead, Drauk."

Their gruff trainer's voice snapped Fray out of his trance and he became aware of his surroundings again. The other novices were still half-heartedly practising, but many had been watching their bout. Drauk wiped the sweat from his face, saluted Fray with his blade and stomped away to get a drink.

The others watched him go, glanced at Fray and then went back to work. All of them had heard about his run-in with the Khevassar. Apparently no one had seen the Old Man that angry in years. His plan was starting to work as Fray had been met with sympathy from most of the other novices. A few still thought he'd achieved his position as a novice Guardian because of his name, but he suspected that would fade over time.

"You fight like a horse with three legs," said Kenzo, a short, bald and barrel-chested Drassi with grey hair. His legs were a little stiff and his body bore many old scars from years of wearing the mask in service, but his skill with a sword had not diminished. When he held a blade and moved from one form to the next his body flowed like water.

"But I still won," said Fray.

Kenzo grunted. "Ugly, dirty, but effective," he said, conceding the point. "I will teach you to forget all of the bad habits you have picked up. From tomorrow you will practise without a blade. I will teach you how to stand and walk. When you have mastered those, I will return your weapon."

Fray wanted to argue but knew better, so he just smiled and nodded. Kenzo glared, perhaps thinking Fray mocked him, then grunted and moved away. Despite sharing a common language Drassi people sometimes had difficulty understanding their neighbours.

Fray moved into the shade and took the offered cup of water from Drauk. His opponent said nothing but that was just his way. He'd talk when he had something to say. Instead they stood together in companionable silence and watched the others spar.

"I'm ready to lie down and sleep until tomorrow," muttered Fray, more to himself than Drauk. The other man glanced at him and slightly inclined his head. It was good to know others were equally tired from their gruelling schedule.

"Stop, stop, stop," shouted Kenzo and the sparring pairs quickly stepped away from one another. "That's enough for today. You can all go and get some rest. But first, one small task that remains."

"The Bridge of Tears," whispered Drauk and Fray groaned.

"You must run to the nearest bridge at the edge of the district and back. Whoever arrives last will receive a special task."

While the others quickly moved to put their weapons away in the racks, as failing to do so would earn them an even worse task from Kenzo, Fray and Drauk set off at a fast jog. The novices had nicknamed the innocuous footbridge over the river the Bridge of Tears, since many were often close to crying by the time they made it back.

Fray knew that unless he had a good head start he would be among the last to return to the barracks. All of the other novices had gone through years of service as members of the Watch before applying to become a Guardian. None were seriously overweight, but a few had become a bit soft and indulged a little too much while in the Watch. Nevertheless they were used to discipline and their bodies had gone through an extensive period of conditioning. Fray didn't have the same experience and his exercise had consisted of walking around the city. The gap between them was slowly decreasing, but he wasn't at the same level of fitness yet.

Drauk didn't wait for him and soon disappeared around a corner. By the time Fray reached the bridge Drauk had already gone past him in the other direction. Several others had also caught up and passed Fray as well. A pack of seven novices reached the bridge at the same time. They all touched the iron post and then span on their heels and set off again in the baking summer sun.

There was still a month until the summer solstice and then the blissful slide into the cool air of autumn. Fray tried to imagine it as itchy sweat soaked into his clothes.

Thankfully he wasn't the last to make it back to the barracks. His knees were shaking so badly he almost collapsed, but managed to stay on his feet. Kenzo made sure everyone drank two cups of water before letting them leave the training grounds.

After a quick shower alongside the other novices, men and women, he slipped into his clean uniform. Mixing the sexes didn't bother him but he could see it made some novices uncomfortable. They showered quickly and covered their nakedness as best as they could while getting dressed. He'd known about it from his father and Byrne, but even so experiencing it first-hand was different.

Over the years his father had told him many things about the Guardians, no doubt in the hope that one day Fray would join the Watch and then progress up the ranks. His father had also spoken about his magic and how he used it, but Fray had rarely seen him doing so. As with everything else, poring over his father's journals would only teach him so much.

Fray had been using his power more frequently in recent years, to contact the lingering dead, but it was always with a very specific purpose in mind. His father had done all sorts of things with his magic, but now he wasn't around to explain how. Fray was a beginner in every way. With practice and training he would get fitter and better with a sword, but who would teach him how to use his magic?

Taking a deep breath Fray focused on the immediate problem. First things first, his dad always said. Break down the problem. Solve it in small pieces one at a time. First they had to find the killer and he wasn't doing this alone. Byrne had years of experience and Fray couldn't think of anyone better to teach him how to be a Guardian.

As before Byrne came to collect Fray as he was finishing the last mouthful of his lunch. He followed the older man out of the barracks and they walked for a few minutes in silence. Fray could see Byrne was turning things over in his mind, so he left him alone. The cries of seagulls tugged at Fray's ears and somewhere in the distance he could hear the sound of the waves. They passed along a busy road laden with street merchants offering a range of wares to cool you down in the summer heat. Chunks of fruit chilled on icy stone slabs. Fans and brightly coloured parasols and wide-brimmed hats woven from riverbank reeds. Some people had even adopted a version of Drassi trousers, baggy cotton garments which were much more comfortable and less restrictive. Fray's uniform chafed a little, but it was nothing in comparison to the aching muscles in his tired legs and arms.

A hundred conversations flowed around Fray and he picked up a tentative atmosphere of happiness and hope. Recent events were troubling some, and many were still nervous of anything to do with magic, but so far stories about the murderer hadn't become public knowledge. Many people were still worried, but the city had been without trouble long enough that they were willing to entertain the idea this was the norm again. He hoped he wouldn't disappoint them.

Finally Byrne came back to the present. "While you were learning about the Bridge of Tears, I spent the morning speaking to the families of the first two victims. I also called in on Bav, our missing dock worker. Once again he wasn't at home."

They'd visited his house the previous day but no one had been there. Questioning the neighbours had revealed very little, so they'd been forced to leave empty handed.

"We'll go back later today."

Despite Bav's continued absence, which played into Byrne's theory about him being involved in the murders, Byrne didn't seem pleased. He continually scanned the streets, one hand resting on his sword, and barely acknowledged Fray was even there.

"Where are we going?" asked Fray, hoping Byrne would at least look at him, but he never made eye contact.

"I found something the first two victims had in common with both dock workers. They were also regulars at the arena."

"Sounds promising."

Byrne grunted. "Then you're an idiot."

"What?" said Fray, pausing in the street. Byrne had gone a dozen paces before he noticed Fray was not beside him. Slowly he came back and spoke in a low, harsh voice, glancing suspiciously at people who came too close.

"This is your first case. Reading about them in your dad's journals doesn't make you an expert. Remember that."

Fray was stunned. "What are you saying?"

"You need to prepare yourself for failure. Cases are never straightforward. They twist and turn like a maze before we find the right path. The arena could be a coincidence. Is that understood?"

Byrne didn't even wait for him to reply. He turned his back on Fray and set off towards the arena. Fray took a minute to calm himself down and then caught up.

The Old Man had been right about Byrne. Whether it was the loss of his partner and closest friend, or what had happened during the war, Byrne had become brusque and indifferent to other people. Fray hadn't wanted to believe it, as the person he remembered had been friendly and generous, but the stone-faced man beside him was starting to feel like a total stranger.

A few minutes later they arrived at one of the many footbridges that spanned the river. Another Guardian, a tall blonde woman, had just finished speaking to a young couple.

"Baker. Is everything all right?" asked Byrne, scanning the area for signs of trouble. Baker towered above Fray and he had to crane his neck to look at her face.

"This must be your novice," said Baker, offering Fray a hand, which he shook. "I had the pleasure of working with your father. He was a good man."

"Thank you," said Fray, feeling slightly taken aback by Baker's warmth. He'd known his father had been respected but thought it would have faded in the intervening years.

"Did you lose something?" asked Byrne, looking past Baker into the churning waters of the River Kalmei.

"Maybe. I've been given a missing persons case. The one you dodged."

"It was a waste of my time, and yours," said Byrne with venom.

Baker looked surprised at Byrne's attitude. "The parents of both boys are very worried. They've been missing for three days."

"They're dead. It's that simple. And the only reason we've been given the case, instead of the Watch, is because they're sons of rich nobles."

"The Khevassar—"

"Is a powerful man," said Byrne, cutting her off, "but even he has masters that must be obeyed. The nobles complained to their powerful friends, who told their friends, and soon they'd created enough noise that someone in the palace heard about it. They bent the Queen's ear and now she wants it to go away. So she bends the Old Man's ear and he dumps it on us."

Fray had never seen Byrne like this before, agitated and so bitter.

"So where are they then?" asked Baker, unwilling to be put off from the problem at hand.

"They drowned. He and a friend were last seen stumbling home late at night. They'd been at a party, they got drunk, they fell in. I'd look at the bottom of the river. Given that it's been three days, I'd look a mile or so downriver. If the bodies aren't snagged on anything they will soon bloat and rise to the surface."

Baker looked as if she would argue further, but Byrne marched away before she had a chance to reply. Fray raised an eyebrow but Baker just shook her head. From her puzzled expression Fray wasn't the only one who thought Byrne was acting peculiar. He would have to send a note to the Old Man very soon.

Fray left the Guardian on the bridge and jogged after Byrne to catch up. The aching muscles in his legs screamed at him as he put them under even more pressure, so he quickly slowed to a fast walk instead.

"What was all that about?" asked Fray, hoping to see a glimmer of the man he remembered.

Byrne looked annoyed but he quickly shook it off. His expression became neutral as he ticked items off on the fingers of his right hand. "There's a magical serial killer in the city, dozens of unsolved murders, a lethal version of venthe on the streets, and rumours of a feud brewing between the crime Families. And that's just the beginning."

"But you're not tackling all of those cases by yourself," said Fray.

"No, I'm not. But do you think I should drop any of them for a pair of drunken teenagers?"

Fray didn't have an answer and an uncomfortable silence settled between them. Twenty minutes later they arrived at the arena. Fray was disappointed to see a large poster on the double doors. It was a city proclamation from the Watch about an indefinite closure due to an ongoing investigation. Byrne didn't look surprised.

"You knew about this?"

"I'd heard a rumour so I asked one of the other Guardians. There was an incident," said Byrne, rather vaguely. "It might have been drugs or something else. They're still investigating."

Staring up at the outside of the building made Fray's skin prickle and he began to feel uneasy.

"You're not telling me something," said Fray.

"I need your first impression, untainted by my ideas. Your father and I would do this and then discuss it after."

Fray had more questions but decided to play along for now. Byrne knocked loudly on a small side door and a short time later Fray heard bolts being drawn back. A huge bald-headed man with arms as thick as Fray's legs answered the door. He didn't look surprised to see two Guardians at the door, merely puzzled.

"I thought you lot were done for now," he rumbled.

"This is about something else. Are you Vinneck?"

"No, Jakka. Vinny's in his office," he said, stepping aside to let them in. The second he stepped over the threshold Fray felt as if someone had punched him in the stomach. He stumbled and would have fallen if Byrne hadn't caught him and kept him upright. All of his skin itched and the air felt tight and dry in his lungs. Every breath brought a wave of pain and sweat burst from his pores.

His nose filled with the smell of salty old blood, fear, sweat and a rancid stench of decay. Looking around he expected to see a rotting corpse, but there was nothing except bare stone walls. When he tried to swallow it felt as if there was a lump of food stuck in his throat and he started to choke. As his face turned red Fray reached out with his hands in desperation. Byrne and Jakka were trying to help, one slapping him on the back, the other trying to wrestle open his mouth, thinking he'd swallowed his tongue. As Fray fell to his hands and knees he reached out with his other senses, the world rippled and a flood of new feelings rushed in.

Suddenly he could breathe again, but now he could hear the distant cry of many voices as if the arena were full of people. Behind the chanting and cheering was a loud and steady heartbeat, as if the building itself were the body of a great beast and they were standing inside its chest. The building wasn't alive, but it had been a focal point for so many strong emotions they had left an indelible mark. An old scar that had never quite healed. But the old emotions were only a background whisper in comparison to what Fray now felt. Something terrible had happened more recently and the wound it had left was still fresh.

Staring down at the stone and sawdust, Fray could see lines of power running through it, deep beneath the surface, like a hidden river of molten lava. The glowing red and yellow threads coursed with energy. Staring towards the ring at the centre of the arena, he could see a giant network of lines criss-crossing each other like a spider's web. All of them twisted and angled towards one spot among the seats.

Slowly Fray became aware of Byrne squatting down beside him, telling him to focus on his voice. Byrne told him to push aside all emotions from the past and concentrate on the present. That was a lot easier said than done, but he desperately clung to the idea that the raw feelings were only a memory of what had happened. Fray held on to another truth. The building was mostly empty, and by extending his senses further he found only four people. After a few minutes he was gradually able to suppress the past and slowly withdraw his magic.

When Fray's eyesight returned to normal he still felt a slight catch in his throat, but could breathe normally. He stood up and dusted himself off.

"Where can we find Vinny?" asked Byrne, as if nothing had happened.

"Down the corridor, office on the right," said Jakka, giving Fray a puzzled look. They left the big man behind and Fray followed Byrne down a narrow corridor that ran along the outside wall of the arena.

Byrne knocked and went inside without waiting for an answer.

A thin balding man sat behind a battered old desk in a cramped office filled with neat stacks of paper and books. As they entered he was adding to a page of neat tallies and scores which Fray guessed had something to do with gambling. Byrne didn't introduce himself and Vinny didn't ask. The uniforms were enough.

At the edges of his perception Fray could still feel the echo of what he'd experienced. The distant murmur of a monstrous heart. He tried to force it away and focus on the conversation.

"I wanted to ask you about some of your regulars," said Byrne, and Vinny raised an eyebrow.

"You're not here about the other night?"

"No," said Byrne, taking out a notebook and flipping through it. He rattled off the names and descriptions of the three victims, then looked at Vinny expectantly.

"They don't sound familiar, but we have a lot of regulars."

"Which means what?"

Vinny mulled it over for a minute. "They never did anything

to get themselves noticed, never got into any trouble, and their bets were modest."

"Do any of them owe any money?" asked Byrne.

Vinny twisted around and pulled a slim blue book from the nearest shelf. He flipped to a page halfway through and quickly scanned what looked to Fray like a random list of numbers and initials.

"Hmm, no. They're all square with the house."

It was just what Byrne had warned him might happen. Although all three victims had attended fights at the arena, there didn't seem to be anything else that connected them. No reason they had been chosen by the killer. None that they knew of yet.

"Tell me about the other night," said Byrne. "I've heard about it from others, but not from anyone who was here."

Vinny didn't say anything for a long time and at first Fray thought he wouldn't answer. Byrne seemed willing to wait and eventually Fray realised Vinny was summoning his courage.

"There was something in the air," said Vinny in a quiet voice. "I've seen all kind of crowds, but nothing like this before. They were hungry."

Fray couldn't help himself. "Hungry for what?"

Vinny's eyes locked onto his but then drifted away into the past. "Blood. When the fight started to go wrong, they revelled in it."

"I heard the fighters were on drugs," said Byrne but Vinny shook his head.

"No, it was something else. The fighters ripped each other to pieces and every single person enjoyed it. The carnage, the brutality. They loved it. Men and women, young and old, screaming for more."

The echo at the edge of Fray's senses seemed to grow louder in response to his growing sense of unease.

"You can still feel it, can't you?" said Vinny, staring at Fray, who could only nod, his throat tight and uncomfortable. "It's worse near the ring."

Byrne seemed calm and unaffected, but Fray noticed he kept smoothing out his moustache, which he only did when anxious.

"We'd like to speak to someone who was here that night. Do you have a list of names?"

"Only those who placed bets."

Something occurred to Fray. "Did anyone called Bav place a bet that night? He's a dock worker, so it was probably modest."

Vinny consulted his notebook again, running his finger down the list of figures. "Hmm, yes actually. He placed a small wager on an early bout, but hasn't been to collect his winnings."

Byrne and Fray exchanged a knowing glance, which Vinny saw but didn't ask what it meant.

"Thank you for your help," said Byrne, turning towards the door. Fray offered a smile of thanks and together they hurried out of the building. Jakka let them out without asking what had happened earlier but Fray knew he was curious.

When they were a few streets away from the arena the sound of the monstrous heartbeat faded and Fray started to relax.

"It was him. The killer. He was at the arena, and did something terrible with his magic," said Fray before something else occurred to him. "You already knew that, didn't you?"

"I suspected."

"Did you know what it might do to me?" he asked, hoping Byrne would deny it but he didn't.

Byrne's expression turned hard. "I'm not here to be your mother. If you want to be a Guardian then you need to get used to unpleasant situations. They happen every day in this city. People die all the time. Our job is to make sure that justice is served."

Fray was speechless, but either Byrne didn't notice or didn't care.

"We need to find the killer, before he strikes again."

"How?" Fray managed to ask.

"We start with finding Bav. He's involved somehow, I just know it."

"What do we do?"

"Put a watch on his house and hope that we find him before the killer strikes again."

It was clear from Byrne's dour expression he didn't think they would succeed. Someone else was going to die and there was nothing they could do to stop it.

CHAPTER 18

An hour before midday Katja finally managed to drag herself out of bed. When she'd dressed and brushed the knots out of her long dark hair, she found herself staring at the kitchen and back door. The entire area had been scrubbed clean and she couldn't see a single drop of blood anywhere.

"Your clothes couldn't be salvaged," said Gankle. "I had to destroy them."

The only proof that she'd killed two men last night was in her memories. She made herself a promise not to spend too much time thinking about them. They'd left her with no choice and had not been good men.

"Are you hungry?" asked Gankle from the doorway, snapping Katja out of her reverie. "Thirsty?"

Gankle chattered on as he brewed the tea, telling her about recent clients and what had been going on in the city, starting with the Guardians investigating the fighting arena. She'd heard from Roza about a weird event that had closed it, but oddly no one had any details. The fights were very popular and yet no one who'd attended that night was willing to talk. The truth would come out eventually.

"I have to go out shortly for a visit," said Gankle, staring out the window at the street with some discomfort. "It's for a new client. They've paid a substantial amount in advance, so we can't really refuse."

It would mean speaking to other people, on purpose, interacting with strangers in an unfamiliar space that hadn't been properly washed, swept or dusted. Gankle started biting his lip and scrubbing the palms of his hands with his fingernails, no doubt imagining the dirt.

"I'll go," said Katja, since it was her job.

"I don't think that would be a good idea," said Gankle, choosing his words carefully. "We know that people could be watching."

"It would be more suspicious if I didn't go. I have to pretend nothing has changed. Besides, I always visit the clients."

Gankle relented and passed her the address. "I'll stay here and watch the shop, for any drop-ins."

The back door opened and Roza came into the kitchen. Her expression was grim and the deep shadows under her eyes suggested she'd not had much sleep.

"Sit down," she said to Katja, pulling up a seat.

"A client is waiting."

Roza didn't repeat herself. She just stared at Katja and waited.

"I know what else happened last night," said Roza.

"It wasn't my fault," said Katja. "I ran but they followed me. I had to defend myself."

Roza shook her head. "You're not ready. You lack control and take unnecessary risks. You should be sent back home for more training."

Katja tried another approach. "What should I have done? Run? Reported it to the Watch?"

Roza didn't respond. Any sort of attention, especially from the Watch or the Guardians, would be unwelcome. The first lesson Katja had been taught back in Seveldrom was about blending in and not being noticed in a crowd.

"Hopefully no one saw you last night," said Roza. "If I were in Rodann's position, I would have someone watching you at all times."

"I'll be more careful," said Katja, getting to her feet.

"And no more trips to the Cave," said Roza, catching her by surprise. "I know you went there the other night."

"How did you—"

"You're putting everyone at risk, not just yourself," warned Roza. "If you can't see that, then you shouldn't be doing this job."

Katja pulled on the grey robe over her clothes and quickly went out the front door of the shop. She needed to focus on something else. She didn't want to think about what Roza had said.

Gankle had told her the new clients were grieving parents who had lost a child. The address indicated they were wealthy, but little else. In fact they'd given no hint about the type of service they wanted or their religion. No doubt the people she was on the way to visit would require something extravagant.

The streets were busy and crowded despite the midday heat that made her sweat and start to itch. Almost everyone wore a hat or headscarf to ward off the worst of the heat, and many had pulled up the hoods on their robes. Katja left hers down, as she spent too much time indoors and her skin needed some colour. Fresh sweat beaded in her hairline but it dried out before it reached the bottom of her face.

A light breeze blew in from the river, bringing with it a faint smell of the sea, but it wasn't enough to cool anyone down. The fruit and ale vendors were selling as fast as they could pull a pint or chop up melons and spiny apples into manageable chunks. Katja bought two fat slices of red melon and slurped along with everyone else, spitting out the seeds with casual abandon. Daring seagulls came down onto the streets, fighting over scraps and scuttling out of the way of the many busy feet.

By the time she reached the front gates of the large manor house she felt more alert, but no less empty. But it wasn't hunger that gnawed away at her, it was guilt. Roza's words rang in her ears and the possibility that she'd put others at risk burned her.

Trying to keep her mind on the present Katja gave her name to the armed guard at the gate and was immediately shown inside.

The guard led her along a winding path through a lush tropical garden sheltered by tall trees, creating delicious pools of cool shade and deep shadows. Bright flowers in every shade of red, yellow and purple lined the path on both sides, and the air hummed with a low buzz of insects and clusters of bees. Here in the garden, behind the stone walls, Katja could almost forget she was still in the city. The whole neighbourhood seemed quiet, although on reflection she realised only those who had to be out in the midday heat would venture outdoors. If the wealthy homeowners in this neighbourhood needed something they would simply send out a servant.

Another servant, dressed in grey livery with a purple and red crest over the heart, met her at the door. Brief introductions were made and she was shown to a sitting room dominated by a large marble-fronted fireplace. Katja didn't know a lot about art, but even she recognised the style of the landscape painting above the fire. Jade figurines, crystal glasses on a beautifully carved wooden table and other signs of wealth dotted the room. Ornaments and strange items, both familiar and foreign, probably gathered over many decades filled a cabinet to bursting against the back wall. A small portrait, presumably of the owners, hung on the wall, showing two adults and two small children. Even the painting was extravagant and very detailed, but it also looked old as the paint was starting to crack in places.

The owners had a lot of money, but didn't seem to know what to do with it except buy more curios from their travels.

The silence of the house seemed absolute, which would normally have relaxed Katja, but now it bred thoughts she wanted to avoid. She rested both hands and then her forehead on the cold mantelpiece above the fireplace, cooling her flushed skin.

The clicking of heels on the tiled floor brought her back to the present. Her eyes snapped open in time to see a couple in their late fifties approaching, shadowed by a servant carrying a glass tray with a jug of some sort of fruit juice.

"Leave the tray, I'll pour our guest a drink," said the man, a local with a weather-beaten face, grey hair and matching beard. His wife looked only slightly younger, but her skin was equally weathered, suggesting she'd spent as much time working outdoors as her husband. Katja recognised them both from the painting, but it must have been commissioned many years ago as their hair was dark in the portrait.

The servant raised an eyebrow at his owner's unusual order, but said nothing and quickly withdrew, closing the doors firmly behind him.

"Please, take a seat," said the husband with a gesture at the red and yellow chairs set around a low metal table with a glass top. Katja settled herself and tried to wait patiently as cool drinks were poured by hands that shook.

"Thank you," said Katja, accepting a glass, noting the old calluses on the husband's hands. A life spent at sea then. He probably owned a shipping business with a fleet of vessels.

"I'm Sim, this is my wife, Belle," said the man, keeping it very informal, which only made her more nervous. At their lowest moment, most people were desperate to hang on to their full names and titles, rank and merit, to show they'd achieved and accomplished something. They hadn't beaten death, hadn't stopped the sand falling through the hourglass, but they mattered. But here, they were talking and treating Katja as if they were ordinary clients who had walked in from the street with only a few coins to their name.

"How can I help?" asked Katja, addressing the question at both.

Sim licked his lips nervously. "Can we rely on you to be discreet?"

"Anything you tell me will only be shared with those who absolutely have to know. The priest we involve and my business partner. No one else. If the manner in which your ..." Katja trailed off, suddenly aware she didn't know if their child had been the boy or the girl from the painting.

"Our son," said Belle in a quivering voice. She fiddled with the lace on the front of her dress and wouldn't meet Katja's eye.

"If he died in a manner you'd rather not have others know about, there are ways to obscure it." Katja waved a hand vaguely, certain they wouldn't want to know about the heavy make-up and materials that were sometimes stuffed inside a body to pad it out and make it look more normal.

The couple shared a look that she didn't fully understand, but they weren't appeased by her assurances. Katja took a sip of her drink, a cocktail of wine mixed with chilled fruit juice.

Belle tried a different approach, forcing a smile. "Is it true you're the only one of your kind?"

"Yes, at the moment, but I'm sure that will change."

"You're a leader," said Sim. "Whatever others do after, you were there first." It sounded as if he spoke from personal experience.

"Are you personally tied to any particular faith?" asked Belle. Katja had been asked the question dozens of times. Normally people wanted to know if she was truly independent or if she favoured some religious customs.

"I deal with people from all faiths, and I've come to respect them all equally. I have no personal affinity to one faith," she told them carefully.

Sim tried to ask a question but nothing came out. He looked to his wife for support but she just gulped down her drink, leaving him trying to find the right words.

"Are you familiar with . . . old religions?" he finally asked.

"Not personally, but I have contacts who can carry out last rites for all faiths."

"All?" pressed Sim and a growing suspicion in Katja's mind started to take shape.

"I have a friend who runs a farm, a few miles outside the city," said Katja, almost casually as if the subject wasn't related. "He has a hundred head of beef and about forty pigs. They're always hungry. In fact they'll eat almost anything."

Sim heaved a long sigh while Belle looked as if she would faint, but both were visibly relieved. They were Eaters. Followers of Khai'yegha, the Pestilent Watcher, the Eater of Souls. They practised an old faith that had supposedly been wiped out during the war when mad King Taikon had razed every temple and murdered all of the priests. Apparently some of his people had not lost their faith.

Although their religion wasn't illegal, people did find it distasteful and would often distance themselves from its followers. It had become much worse since the war when the Mad King, Taikon, had tried to create his own religion with him as the central deity and prophet. Now anyone who deviated from one of the main religions was treated with disdain and people who followed the old faiths were seen as deviants.

Eaters were not ashamed of their faith, but they were now wise enough never to declare it in public in case they were shunned. From the size of their house Sim and Belle were obviously people of significant wealth and standing in the city. If people found out it could have a significant impact on their life and business.

Sim produced another heavy purse which he put down on the table.

"You can collect him whenever you like. We've said our good-byes."

The money they'd already paid would cover her expenses five times over, but she took the heavy purse anyway. It wasn't for the service, but to ensure her silence.

They led her to the front door where they shook hands and Belle quickly hurried away, no doubt keen to forget about such unpleasant business. Sim took a more stoic approach, gritted his teeth and was determined to look her in the eye and get through it.

As she stepped outside again the heat hit Katja like a wave, making fresh sweat bead at her brow. She wanted nothing more than to linger in the garden and enjoy the shade but knew she couldn't. She had an appointment with Rodann in a few hours and needed to be ready.

CHAPTER 19

The Emerald Dragon sat in the heart of the Jarrows' territory, a gambling den for those with an excessive amount of money to waste on cards, dice and other games of chance. The buy-in for some of the tables was more money than Choss had ever seen in his life. Normally it wasn't a place he'd visit but he'd been told by a Silver jackal that the owners would be visiting tonight.

The thick-shouldered man at the door looked him up and down, sneering slightly at his clothes, but eventually agreed to pass a message to someone inside. In some ways it was refreshing to be treated exactly the same as everyone else and Choss unnerved the doorman by smiling at him.

A few minutes later the front door opened and Vargus came out. The doorman looked extremely uncomfortable at the Naib's presence.

"Come in," he said. "I'm sorry you were stuck out here." Vargus glared at the doorman who, despite towering over the older man, leaned away in alarm.

From outside, the Emerald looked like every other building on the street, slightly shabby and in need of repair. Inside, it had been completely gutted and rebuilt by expert craftsmen to make it appeal to the rich clientele.

The main room was a large oval with tables in the centre and booths around the edge for onlookers and drinkers. The top stakes games were held in one of the private rooms on the first floor, where players were waited on by a famous chef from Morrinow and a local vintner who offered only the best wines from around the world.

The atmosphere in the main room was one of constant celebration, with some in the crowd crying out at their victories, while others laughed at their appalling losses because, after all, it was only money. The clink of coins and rattle of dice mixed with a loud hum of conversation. Men and women dressed in green and white livery moved through the room with trays of free drinks.

Stationed around the room at regular intervals, looking very uncomfortable in tight and expensive clothing, were several enforcers. Customers at the Emerald required a velvet glove instead of the iron fist which Don Jarrow preferred, but deterrents were sometimes necessary.

Choss followed Vargus to the bar at the back of the room and took a seat, resting his forearms on the cool marble surface. He didn't want to guess how much the bar top alone had cost.

"The Don and Doña are greeting some new customers," said Vargus, gesturing towards the rooms upstairs. "They shouldn't be long."

"Thank you."

Vargus nodded and walked towards the crowd, which parted as he approached and closed in his wake.

"Hello sweetheart," said a slurred and husky voice to his left.

"Hello Munroe," said Choss. Tonight the petite brunette was dressed in an elegant black dress and elbow-length gloves. She tried to lean against the bar, missed and would have fallen if Choss hadn't caught her. He held her gently by the elbow until she managed to pull herself onto a high stool. Glancing over his shoulder Choss noticed a lean-faced Morrin woman watching them from nearby. A Naib for Munroe in all but name, and one of the few people openly armed in the room.

"My hero," said Munroe, trying to blow a strand of her curly hair out of her eyes. It persisted in being an annoyance until she tucked it behind an ear in a way he found endearing.

"Another of my usual, Col," she said, gesturing at the barman, who looked at Choss expectantly.

"Nothing for me."

"Come on, drink with me. It's a party," said Munroe, gesturing expansively, wobbling and nearly falling off her stool.

"It's not my kind of party," said Choss, feeling more than a little out of place.

"Me neither, but here we are." Munroe squinted at him. "Why are you here?"

"Business."

"Ahhh." She touched the side of her nose with one finger in a conspiratorial manner, nearly poking herself in the eye. "Business, good. Because I never get tired of that."

"You could leave," suggested Choss. It was a conversation they'd had many times.

Munroe threw back her head and laughed. It was a rich sound that made the hairs stand up on the back of his arms until it changed in tone, becoming something cynical and mocking.

"Maker's balls. I needed that," she said, leaning over and kissing him on the cheek. "I love you, Choss. You're so naïve."

Choss said nothing, one eye on Munroe in case she fell off her chair, the other on the closed door upstairs.

"Don't sulk," said Munroe, winking salaciously at the barman, who swapped her empty glass for a full one. Col hurried away and Munroe sighed dramatically.

"I'm not sulking. I'm worried."

"Business, right?" said Munroe, taking a big gulp of her

drink. "Something dangerous, I assume? Putting your life at risk?"

"Something like that."

"Then why don't you enjoy yourself a little before getting to that. We could go upstairs," she said, running a hand up his arm, making his skin tingle. "I have a key to the Don's private suite. No one would disturb us, all night long."

Choss felt her hot breath on his ear as she leaned over, pressing her body against his arm. A shiver ran down his back at her touch and Choss felt his body start to respond.

Munroe was clever, beautiful and she had a wicked sense of humour. She didn't care about his celebrity status and wasn't trying to get close to him to curry favour with someone in power. She had plenty of her own. In the last few years she was the only woman who'd shown any interest in him for who he actually was beyond his reputation. They'd been friends and sometimes a little more, but her unusual circumstances prevented them from being completely intimate.

Several times they'd come close to doing something drastic, they'd even joked about running away together, but each time one of them had faltered because the risk was too great.

"Sadly, I'll have to say no," said Choss.

Although Munroe had no official rank in the Jarrow Family, she was the most valuable member of their organisation. She was worth more than ten times her weight in gold to them. The Morrin warrior breathing down Choss's neck was there to ensure no one so much as looked at Munroe in an unpleasant manner. The bodyguard also prevented Munroe from taking any risks, which he knew rankled her.

"Not even tempted a little?" said Munroe, leaning forward to give him a generous view of her cleavage. "I promise, it would be a night you'd never forget."

"I'm very tempted, believe me," said Choss, taking the time

to glance at her assets with an appreciative eye. "But you know we can't."

"Your loss," said Munroe, shrugging as if it didn't matter before slumping back in her chair and rearranging her dress. She recovered quickly and the hurt look faded in her eyes. "Did I tell you I recently tried to join the Silent Order?"

Choss's jaw fell open. "The assassins' league?"

"That's the one," said Munroe, slurping her drink. "They said I was too dangerous. Me!" This time her laugh started out bitter and only went downhill from there.

She had a lot of stories about things that had happened to her, most of which he didn't believe, but her latest had a desperate ring of truth.

The last three men to have sex with Munroe had died during the act. The first could have been caused by any number of things and ignored. Perhaps the second could've been attributed to bad luck, but by the time the third turned up cold, people realised it was more than a string of unfortunate events.

She'd been given many unpleasant nicknames but Widowmaker seemed the most accurate, not that Choss ever used it. A lot of dangerous people were very afraid of her, but she didn't worry him. Munroe presented one face to the world to protect herself, but he knew the real person behind the mask.

For the last four years she'd been working for Don Jarrow, bringing her bad luck to those doing a little too well at cards or dice. The tables were straight and the dice clean, but the house didn't want to lose too much money and Munroe ensured that it never happened. Unfortunately her bad luck meant she couldn't get too close to anyone in case she hurt or killed them.

"We're alike, you and I," said Munroe.

"We're outsiders. We don't belong here." Neither of them were officially part of the Family, and yet both were caught up in the business for different reasons.

"There is that, but I meant the other thing," said Munroe. For the first time since she'd sat down Choss looked at her properly. He knew that part of the loneliness he saw in her brown eyes was reflected. "We're untouchable."

He reached across the bar and gave her right hand a squeeze. Someone cheered loudly in the crowd, but their joy was distant and didn't affect either of them.

"I'm curious, how long has it been?"

"Since what?" he asked but Munroe just raised one eyebrow. "Ah, that."

"Four years for me," said Munroe, not bothering to hide her bitterness. "Four long, long years."

Choss had to think, which told him it must have been a while. "A long time."

"This dangerous business you're involved with. Is it something you enjoy doing?"

"No, but it's a means to an end. If it all works out, something good might happen."

"I'm jealous," said Munroe, letting go of his hand so she could finish her drink. "At least you're working towards something. I just go around and around."

Someone cleared their throat loudly behind Choss. He and Munroe turned to see a nervous-looking enforcer, sweating into his expensive clothing. "Miss Munroe, if you wouldn't mind, we could use you at the tables. Please."

"Duty calls," she said, slipping off her stool and nearly falling onto her face. Both Choss and the enforcer moved to catch her, but Munroe righted herself at the last second. "I'm fine. I'm fine," she said.

The enforcer heaved a sigh of relief and hurried after Munroe, staying two steps behind, poised to catch her again. The Morrin bodyguard followed her as well, muttering under her breath about her own bad luck at being stuck with looking after Munroe.

Finally the door upstairs opened and Don and Doña Jarrow emerged, followed closely by Vargus and Daxx. The Doña sat down beside him at the bar while the Don and Vargus went out the front door. Daxx glared at Choss, then took up his position a short distance away. Despite being in the heart of their territory, surrounded by a dozen armed enforcers and two hundred witnesses, Daxx wasn't taking any chances. He endlessly scanned the crowd for signs of trouble.

"I've never met a more serious man in my life," said the Doña, catching his eye. "He's good at what he does, but not really one for conversation. I think you would've been a much better match for me."

Choss shifted uncomfortably on his chair, not sure if he should answer or not. He hoped she wasn't thinking of getting rid of Daxx and asking him again. Turning her down once had been a risk, twice would not be acceptable.

"Enough about the past. I take it you're here with some news?" she asked, smiling at the barman, who'd brought her a drink without being asked.

"I found something in the meat district. I think Don Kalbensham is responsible for the new lethal venthe, or someone in his Family knows about it."

Doña Jarrow put down her drink and turned towards him. "That's a very serious accusation. One that could start a war. Tell me exactly what you saw."

Choss told her everything, from the second he'd stepped into the meat district, to the moment he saw the injured Brass go into the warehouse. The Doña said nothing throughout and only clicked her tongue when he mentioned the drug-addled prostitutes. When he'd finished she made him repeat everything again and this time asked him questions all the way through.

For a time afterwards she said nothing, just pursed her lips in thought, but eventually she spoke. "I can see it in your face. You know it's not enough. We've no idea if Don Kal is behind this or someone else."

"I need to get inside that warehouse, but I can't do it by myself."

"You'd need a lot of warm bodies," said Doña Jarrow, shaking her head. "And I can't loan you any of our people. One person can go undetected. Twenty is a different story. And what happens if one of them is caught in his territory? They'd be put to the question and it would lead back to us. No, you'll have to do this by yourself."

"I can't," said Choss, hating her for forcing him to admit it. She knew it was impossible. She just wanted to hear him admit to being incapable.

"I could give you some new faces. Paper jackals with no official ties to us. They're always desperate to prove themselves. Of course you'd need to make sure none of them survived."

The casual manner in which she talked about killing people gave him a chill. There wasn't even a spark of warmth in her gaze. Suddenly he found himself missing Munroe.

"I have one idea," said Choss nervously, hoping this wouldn't cross one of her invisible lines. "But I don't think you're going to like it."

Something that was almost a smile touched her face. "Tell me."

"I think I can get in and out with one other."

One of Doña Jarrow's eyebrows quirked slightly. "Who?"

"Gorrax the Vorga, if he's still alive."

He did his best to keep looking straight ahead and not stare at her. All he could see from his eye corner was a flash of red and black from her dress. Although the room continued to be noisy, a peculiar silence settled over them. Her breathing seemed loud and fast, but he didn't know if that meant she was excited or angry.

"Why? Why him?" she asked in a cool voice.

"Everyone knows the Vorga are only loyal to themselves, so no one would ever think he was working for you. Most people can't tell them apart anyway."

"That isn't what I asked."

Choss thought for a moment and tried again, not sure what she wanted to hear. "The odds will be still heavily stacked against us, but there's a small chance we can do it. He's stronger than anyone I've ever met and is a vicious fighter. We have to hold him back in the arena, but not this time."

Doña Jarrow touched him on the arm and he turned to look at her. Her calm expression had cracked a little and behind it he saw a flicker of rage. She raised one arm, pointing at Daxx across the room, who instantly tensed, one hand on a sword.

"With one small gesture, I can order him to kill you. He would do it without question, and no one in here would stop him. I could walk through the streets of this city splashed in your blood and no one would come after me for vengeance."

The room had fallen silent and he felt every eye on him, but when he looked around nothing had changed. People continued to gamble and drink as before. A few glanced curiously in their direction, but Choss felt as if he'd been struck deaf. He tried to speak a few times, unsure of what to say, but eventually managed the truth.

"I don't understand."

"Never tell me what you think I want to hear," hissed Doña Jarrow, her expression calm but her knuckles had turned white around her glass. "I will ask you one final time. Why do you want the Vorga?"

Choss was left with the truth. "Because I trust him. Because he's loyal to me, and because he's my friend."

Doña Jarrow stared at him and Choss didn't turn away from her piercing gaze. He wondered what she saw when she looked in his eyes, because all he saw in hers was ambition and a beautiful exterior that hid a cold and merciless heart. She was a cruel killer, far worse than Daxx.

Eventually she lowered her arm and Daxx sneered, disappointed at not getting the chance to kill him. Choss sighed in relief, trying to slow the frantic beating of his desperate heart. Touching a hand to his forehead it came away damp. It had been a long time since he'd been that close to death.

"You'll find the Vorga in the tombs. He will be released into your care on one condition."

"Thank you, Doña Jarrow," said Choss. He dreaded finding out what had been done to his friend in those dank cells, but made no comment and waited in silence for her stipulation.

"When this mess with the venthe is resolved, you will give up the arena and serve as a full member of the Family."

Half a dozen responses ran through his mind, but only one question mattered. "Why?"

"Because you need to understand your place, Champ," she said, using his title like an insult. "You belong to us, and you're nothing more than a Paper jackal."

She left her drink and went out the front door. Despite the friendly atmosphere and noisy crowd, Choss had never felt so alone in his life.

CHAPTER 20

Fray came awake with a start. For a time he just lay there in the dark, listening to the silence. In another two weeks, when he and the other novices received their monthly stipend, he would be able to move out of this grimy hole and never come back. He certainly wouldn't miss it. The vermin, the chill and the constant threat of catching damp lung. He had no fond memories on which he might look back in years to come. But today it was still his home and now he wasn't alone.

Turning his head very slightly Fray looked over towards the window. The thin curtains were full of holes from hungry moths and they didn't fill the space. Light leaked in from around the edges, but even so the room was almost completely black. There was just enough light from outside for him to see shapes and contours. Sat on his chair beside the window was a figure, their hooded face turned towards the meagre light.

Moving one hand very slowly, his fingers crept towards his sword which he'd stashed beside his bed.

"If I wanted you dead we wouldn't be talking." The raspy voice made it difficult to tell if it was a man's or woman's. "Cover your eyes."

A second later something bright flashed in the room. Fray had shielded his eyes too late. He had a brief glimpse of something gold and black before spots danced in front of his face.

Shuffling back he sat up in bed, pulling the thin blanket to his chest. Now that he was awake his body had begun to cool down and he felt a chill. Slowly his eyes adjusted to the gloom. Looking around he realised the stranger had simultaneously lit all the candle stubs dotted around the room without moving.

"You already know how," wheezed the stranger, whose breathing sounded incredibly loud, hissing in and out of tired, old lungs. Fray didn't understand why he hadn't heard someone breathing earlier.

Staring closely at the stranger Fray tried to determine something about them, but there were few clues to unravel. A loose black ankle-length robe with a deep hood, and a stylised gold mask, gave very little away. The mask had only a slit for the mouth so he couldn't see the shape of his visitor's lips, or if they had stubble on their chin. A bisecting line ran down the centre from forehead to chin and a symbol he didn't recognise was painted on the right cheek.

The person's posture gave little away, even their hands were covered with black gloves, but some instinct told him the stranger was female.

"What do you want?" said Fray.

"Don't you want to know who I am?"

"If you wanted me to know, you wouldn't be wearing such an elaborate disguise. And as you pointed out, you could have killed me while I slept. So you want something from me. So what is it, Milady?"

The woman chortled, another dry sound. "I'm no Lady, but you can call me Eloise."

Fray didn't know if it was her real name or not, but at the moment it didn't matter. "Why are you here, Eloise?"

"I need your help."

"I'm only a novice Guardian."

Eloise waved that away. "Not that sort of help, although your position may be useful later on."

Fray ignored the new questions that came into his head and focused on the first mystery. "What do you want?"

"I've been told that your father died five years ago saving the lives of everyone in this city. There are many rumours and all of them mention he fought against someone with magic," said Eloise. Fray was still trying to piece together what had happened and he still had so many questions. "Your father was a hero, but now people have conveniently forgotten he used his own magic to do it."

"The war has made people afraid. They think anyone with magic could be the next Warlock."

"And yet it was a Battlemage who killed the Warlock and turned the tide. And now here you are, protecting the people of Perizzi like your father before you, using the same magic as him. But you have to lie about who you really are."

"I know magic isn't evil, but I can't change the past. All I can do is try to earn people's trust, and hope one day they'll change their minds."

"A noble idea. Naïve, but noble. One day it may happen, but in the meantime people are needlessly suffering and dying," said Eloise, shaking her head. "We both know magic cannot be ignored and it's not going away. A time will come when people will need powerful magic again. When their steel will not be enough. We need to be ready for that day."

Fray had to ask. "Who are you?"

The mask moved and he sensed Eloise was smiling behind it. "The gates of the Red Tower have been reopened. A new Grey Council has been formed."

"You're a Seeker," said Fray.

They'd been common in his early childhood, people who criss-crossed the world as part of their work for the Red Tower, testing children to see if they had any sensitivity to magic. Those with any ability were taught how to control and master their power at the Red Tower in Shael.

Without training, children could die unexpectedly or trigger unusual accidents, often killing themselves and other people in the process. After the Grey Council had abandoned their posts sixteen years ago, the Red Tower became disorganised and the number of Seekers dwindled.

Since the end of the war no Seekers had been seen anywhere in Yerskania and Fray knew it would be the same in every other country. People were trying to pretend the problem didn't exist in the hope that it would just go away.

"You've heard the stories," said Eloise. "Children dying in bizarre accidents. Parents casting out, or even killing their own children, if they show a hint of magical ability. Some of them might survive on their own and become adults, but then what? They'd be outcasts, forced to live on the fringes in places like this," she said, gesturing at the room around them. The words stung a little, but they were true. Once he had lived well, but those days were over and he'd been forced to adapt. He wouldn't wish this life on anyone where he was always hungry and afraid of strangers. For the first time in many years Fray saw that he had a future.

"I'd like to help, but I don't know what I can do."

Eloise reached into her robe and held out a small pot of red paint. "When you find someone with the ability, mark your window with this. A Seeker will find you and we'll take care of the child."

"I don't know how to sense magic in others."

Eloise picked up the chair, moved it closer and sat down beside him. "It's easy. I will show you how. Open your senses to me."

For the first time in many years when using his magic, Fray

didn't have to worry about upsetting the person sat opposite. Eloise's lips moved behind the mask and he guessed it was a smile of encouragement.

The world rippled around him as Fray embraced his magic. Suddenly the room became much brighter and it teemed with colours where before there had been only grey and black. When he looked at Eloise his mouth fell open in shock. It took him a moment to understand what his eyes were showing him.

She was glowing from head to toe. Waves of orange and yellow energy spread out through the air in time with a new pulse he felt in his mind. The light faded a little until just the outline of Eloise glowed, but still he could feel a connection to her that had been absent before.

"That link between us is our connection to the Source. You can sense it in others, even without doing that," said Eloise, gesturing towards his face and glowing amber eyes.

She guided Fray through a series of simple exercises and gradually he learned how to sense Eloise's magical ability without embracing his own. A couple of hours passed without Fray noticing, but fatigue began to set in.

"It will become easier with practice," said Eloise, moving towards the window.

"If I asked who you are under that mask, would you tell me?"

She paused with her back to him. "As you said, the past is lost and we cannot change it. The person I used to be died in a fire."

With that she launched herself out of the window and all of the candles were snuffed out, plunging the room into darkness. He heard nothing outside on the street, but sensed an echo of Eloise moving away and then it vanished.

As his eyes adjusted to the gloom, Fray stared at the pot of paint she'd left him. He wondered how differently his life would have turned out if his father hadn't hidden him from the Seekers.

*

After another gruelling morning of training Byrne came for Fray after lunch. They set off for Bav's house in silence, each wrapped up in their own thoughts. He could see Byrne's eyes were distant and apparently he'd forgotten what he'd said yesterday. Either that or it didn't register as important enough to bring up again. That draconian and callous attitude was at odds with the man Fray had known. It wasn't the man he thought he'd been reunited with a few days ago.

Turning his thoughts away from his problems Fray studied the people on the street. Eloise's words from earlier in the night echoed in his mind and more than once he saw fear etched into faces. Mostly it was around the eyes, and although many seemed happy at first glance, their smiles were only on the surface. The war had broken many families, but it had also left an invisible mark on everyone that would not be easily removed.

Just as Eloise had shown him, Fray extended his senses without using his magic. As he passed people in the street he briefly touched them with an extended net of awareness, but nothing happened. He felt no echo as he'd done with Eloise. After feeling nothing for the twentieth time he began to wonder if he was doing it right.

"Someone has been watching the house all morning," said Byrne, breaking the silence. "We'll take over until he shows his face."

"Do you think he will?"

"Maybe," said Byrne. He didn't say what they would do if Bav failed to turn up or how they'd move forward with the case.

With questions swirling in his head Fray felt his pace and heart quicken. They passed over the river and people stepped aside to make room for them on the narrow footbridge. Byrne didn't seem to notice or acknowledge the courtesy, but Fray smiled at or thanked each person.

When they reached the end of the street where Bav lived, Fray felt something prickle at the edges of his perception. A tight ball of tension formed in his stomach. His skin began to itch and he absently rubbed his forearms before he realised what he was doing.

"Byrne," he said, and the tone of his voice made the Guardian stop.

"What is it?"

He'd felt something like this yesterday. "He's been here. The killer."

Some of the colour drained from Byrne's face. "Shit."

Byrne marched up the street, Fray a second behind him. Halfway down the road two Guardians stepped out of a doorway.

"Anything?" asked Byrne and they shook their heads.

"Who's that?" said Fray, pointing at the elderly woman going into the house.

"Bav is supposed to live with his mother," said Byrne. "It's time to get some answers." He marched down the street and hammered on the front door. "Guardian of the Peace. Open up!" shouted Byrne.

Fray scanned the street for signs of trouble or someone that might be the killer. He only saw surprised faces and ordinary people going about their business. It now felt as if a colony of ants were crawling across his skin. The prickle at the edges of his senses had become a sharp jabbing pain in the back of his mind, making Fray afraid to embrace his magic. The arena had nearly killed him and this felt just as bad, if not worse.

Byrne thumped on the door again and finally they heard someone shuffling behind it. It opened slightly to reveal a thin grey-haired old woman with a stooped back and rheumy eyes.

"Is your son at home?" asked Byrne.

"He's not here. You should go away," she said, trying to close the door.

"Are you sure?"

The old woman gave Byrne a withering look. "I'm old, not stupid."

"Perhaps we could come in and wait for him," said Byrne. The old woman shook her head and started to close the door. "We don't have time for this," said Byrne, sticking his foot in the door. He shoved it open, knocking the old woman backwards. She would have fallen if she'd not collided with the back of a chair.

Fray paused on the threshold while Byrne went inside without being invited. "Where is he?" he yelled at the woman, but Fray was only partially listening. The crawling sensation across his skin was even worse.

"He's been in this house," he whispered.

Byrne turned to Fray. "Do what you need to do. Find me something."

With that, Byrne grabbed the old woman by the elbow and pulled her out of her house onto the street. Fray could only stare at Byrne in horror.

"Get on with it," said Byrne, gesturing at Fray's eyes. The old woman glared at them both, but didn't struggle or say anything else, which only made Fray more nervous. He stepped across the threshold, descending three steps into a small kitchen.

It reminded him of his mother's kitchen, with dry herbs hanging from the ceiling, an old black kettle over the fire on a hook and a worn table covered with flour and dough. Coals in the fireplace took the chill off the stone walls but Fray felt a different kind of cold in his bones. Bracing himself against the inevitable rush, he slowly embraced his magic.

Despite his preparation Fray stumbled backwards and fell to one knee as his senses were flooded, the world exploding in a variety of new colours and feelings. Power throbbed all around him, from the stones beneath his feet to the grub-infested ceiling beams above his head. Slowly he adjusted to the wash of feelings that filled his senses, keeping them at a distance so they didn't overwhelm him.

When he looked around the room it seemed as if every surface had been covered with a thin layer of red and black paint. It was the only way his eyes could process it, layer upon layer of tainted magical residue from the killer's passing. As he'd seen at the arena it was an echo from the past, days old, but also he sensed fresh layers.

"He's been here recently," said Fray over his shoulder. "But I don't think he's here now."

"Make sure. Check every room," said Byrne.

With his sword held ready, Fray moved into the narrow corridor that led to two small bedrooms. The first showed very few signs of being touched by the killer. A narrow bed, a small wardrobe and chest of drawers glowed with echoes of old memories and strong emotions, but no real magic. Even before he set foot in the other room Fray felt waves of power pulsing towards him like ripples on a pond. As he pushed open the door with one hand he expected to find something grisly inside, but at first glance it was much the same. A small room with a few pieces of worn furniture, a narrow bed, a table, a wardrobe and a set of drawers. When he looked again he noticed a black stain on the floor that echoed with fear and pain. Bending down he briefly touched it with his fingers but pulled them back as if burned. Someone had recently been murdered here.

A quick search of the room revealed very little of worth, but Fray felt as if he were only scraping the surface. Opening his senses a little more he stared around the room again, his breath whistling through clenched teeth.

The wardrobe caught his attention, but he found nothing inside apart from worn clothing and a few mementos. Bending down again Fray noticed marks on the stone floor. He tried to shove the wardrobe to one side but it was well built and he could barely move it. Putting his back against it and bracing his feet against the wall he managed to move it just enough to see behind.

Someone had carved an opening in the wall and a narrow set of steps led down into the earth. Basements were illegal in the city for many reasons, but the primary one was to stop people growing venthe, which thrived in dark, damp conditions. But the smell coming out of the hole wasn't earth, but a dry rot of old bones and musty paper. There wasn't enough light to see inside the hole and Fray didn't want to go in there while using his magic.

"Fray!" shouted Byrne. Fray raced back through the house to the front door to where Byrne stood pointing up the street. He heard the old woman's gasp as she caught sight of his glowing eyes.

"It's Bav," said Byrne, pointing at a figure that had stopped in the street.

Instead of the normal mix of bright colours that infused every other person on the street, all Fray could see was an absence of light. A black pit that absorbed the energy that drifted past from other people. Tiny red sparks danced like crazed fireflies in the abyss, but they did nothing to fill it with any semblance of life.

"It's him. It's the killer," said Fray.

Bav dropped his bag and sprinted away down the street, Fray and Byrne a few seconds behind. Fray withdrew his magic, reducing his senses to normal, which came as a relief. The flood of emotions from the city around him was too much to process at once. Besides, he didn't want anyone else staring at his eyes.

Bav was heavy set and middle-aged, but he ran like a much younger man, flying along the streets, widening the gap between them. He collided with several people but every time they were knocked aside and he didn't lose any momentum. Fray and Byrne were left to dodge around obstacles and jump over bodies in the street, but they managed to keep him in sight.

As they chased him along curving streets and down narrow alleys Fray's lungs began to burn, his sword heavy in one hand. He managed to sheathe it without tripping over, but fell a few steps behind Byrne. Despite his training Fray was already beginning to tire and he could hear Byrne's breathing getting louder and more laboured. He knew Bav must be feeling it as well, which was probably why their quarry shoved his way into a tavern, taking the chase off the street.

Screams followed and a few seconds later Byrne burst through the front door, Fray a few steps behind. People pointed towards the back of the room and the two men skirted around tables and chairs, jumped over a fallen woman, raced through the kitchen and flew into a paved backyard with a closed gate. Byrne didn't hesitate. He leapt for the top of the wall, caught it with both hands and scrambled up, before disappearing over the other side. Fray mistimed his jump and slipped down to the ground. He took another run-up and managed to clasp the top, pull himself up and drop into the narrow alley on the other side. At several intervals along the alley clothes had been hung up to dry on lines between the buildings. But it wasn't that which drew his attention.

To his surprise Byrne stood a short distance away looking at something on the ground by his feet. Fray drew his sword and approached, scanning the alley for signs of Bav, but there was no one in sight, just clothes flapping in the breeze.

"What is it? Where's he gone?" asked Fray.

Instead of answering, Byrne moved to one side, letting Fray see what sat on the ground beside his feet.

At first Fray didn't understand what he was seeing. It looked like the spilled innards of something from an abattoir, red and fleshy with bits of hair and bone clinging to it. He watched in morbid fascination as Byrne lifted one section of the pink lump with the tip of his sword to reveal the full horror.

It was a whole human skin, the face staring back at him, complete with a beard and eyebrows.

"By the Maker," hissed Fray.

"I know what he is," said Byrne. "I've seen this before."

CHAPTER 21

The directions Rodann had given Katja took her to a run-down part of the city. The people who lived here had fallen on hard times and never managed to claw their way back to a better standard of living.

The buildings reflected their tenants, structures that had once been grand with beautiful carved figures on odd-shaped asymmetrical ledges, delicate iron scrollwork railings around tidy gardens, decorative fountains and even a few trees. Now hordes of squawking seagulls nested in the crumbling ledges of every building. Their fronts were smeared with a frozen river of bird shit which had turned them grey and black. The iron railings had been stolen or rusted, leaving behind only jagged spears that no one wanted. The gardens had been paved and the rare trees cut down and burned for firewood.

No one came here unless they had to. Katja could see why they'd decided to hold their meetings here. The locals were dejected, lost and in desperate need of change. Rodann and his talk of revolution would fire them up, for a time at least. If he didn't produce results they'd slit his throat and throw him in the river.

Katja knocked on the warped wooden door before glancing

around the empty street. She couldn't see anyone but the cold prickle along the back of her neck told her someone was staring.

She'd taken precautions to make sure she'd not been followed, and would do the same when she left. If she left. Rodann had said they would part ways as friends if she didn't want to join his crusade, but she doubted it would be that simple. There would be a complication, a wrinkle he'd forgotten to mention previously, and seconds later Teigan would try to cut off her head.

Katja patted her thigh, double-checking that the blade was still there. She had a dagger tucked into the front of her belt and another hidden in the top of her left boot. She wasn't going to make it easy for them.

The door opened a little and someone in the shadows peered out at her. A second later it was thrown wide and Teigan gestured for her to enter, her eyes on the street. In her other hand she held her sword at the ready.

"Expecting trouble?" asked Katja as Teigan closed and then locked and barred the door. From the outside it looked feeble, but it would take someone a long time to get into the building.

Teigan didn't answer, just sheathed her sword and set off down the dusty corridor. Katja followed although part of her was tempted to stab Teigan in the back and then kill anyone else she could find in the building. That might end the assassination plot before it went anywhere.

Through open doors on either side Katja saw dusty storerooms full of old furniture, discarded chairs, plates, tables covered in sheets, a few worn religious statues and even an old fountain. The tail of the fish at its centre scraped the ceiling, and stood all around it, like silent witnesses, were more battered old statues of men and women.

"Through here," said Teigan from the far end of the corridor. Katja didn't realise she'd stopped. Taking a deep breath she tried to keep her mind in the present and focus on the immediate danger. Part of her struggled to care but she shoved that voice to one side, smothered it and did her best to pretend it wasn't there.

All of the other rooms were covered with dust. The air was heavy with regret. Katja followed Teigan into a room that was noticeably different, full of bright candles, a roaring fire to chase off the chill and lots of comfy chairs stuffed with brightly coloured cushions. There were so many in fact that the floor was littered with them and some of the people there were lounging on the pile.

Everyone's attention was focused on Rodann, his face lit up with intense passion as he spoke. Katja only caught the end of what he'd been saying to the half-dozen people gathered there, but it was more of the same. Talk of change, of making things better for everyone, creating a better future.

She didn't recognise anyone in the group, but despite big differences in appearance, Katja could see they were all of like minds. All were nodding along to Rodann, swept up in his story, rapt and focused to the point that they barely noticed her and Teigan's arrival. It was only when Rodann stopped talking suddenly that they looked around for the cause of the disturbance.

"Ah, we have a guest," said Rodann, gesturing for Katja to approach. With all eyes on her she moved to stand beside him with her back to the fire. She noticed Teigan close the door and then lean against it. There were no other ways in or out of the room. She would have to go through the swordswoman.

"Everyone, this is Katja. She hasn't decided if she's going to join us, so I invited her here tonight to listen. Hopefully we can win her over." Rodann oozed confidence and the tone of his words suggested it was a foregone conclusion. She would join them, or else. Dancing with Teigan was the alternative.

Rodann made the introductions and Katja carefully studied every face, making a mental note of small details to help her identify them. One woman, Lizbeth, had chapped red hands and the hair on her head seemed strangely flattened and misshapen. It was common with servants who wore livery that included a tight bonnet. That meant either Lizbeth worked at the palace or for a rich noble, one of the old families, not the recently appointed nobility who didn't bother with such old-fashioned traditions.

The couple in the corner, Lord and Lady Kallan, had done their best to show off their wealth, but there was something peculiar about them. They were both dressed impeccably, with perfect hair, nails and teeth, but they seemed nervous. It took Katja a moment to realise that while their clothes were expensive they were old and not the latest fashion. They wore very little jewellery and what they had was silver. All of which made them minor nobles, probably with a grudge, or perhaps they were greedy individuals who just wanted more.

She would have said the big man with broad shoulders and thick arms was a thug or a mercenary, except for the way he held himself. He looked uncomfortable at being at the meeting, in this company, but the shrew-faced woman beside him was full of venom. To her surprise, Rodann introduced Marcella and Borren as a married couple.

The last woman was the easiest to identify. Her clothing was ridiculously expensive and seemed risqué, yet she showed off very little bare flesh. She was utterly stunning with huge brown eyes, luxurious black hair and features from a sculptor's dream. Katja also had no doubt that the egg-sized red jewel hung around her neck on a gold chain was real and not coloured glass. An escort for the rich who probably had more money at her disposal than Lord and Lady Kallan. For some reason Rodann didn't introduce the escort by name, perhaps because in her line of work names and identities were easily changed and cast off like clothing.

They were an eclectic group of strangers with nothing to connect them to one another. Except for Rodann and this meeting. Katja felt relief that she'd not followed through on her earlier impulse and tried to kill everyone. This group wasn't all of those involved. She recognised none of them from Rodann's previous meetings in the tavern.

Rodann guided her to an empty chair, then resumed his place by the fire. She listened to him talk for a while, absorbing the words, but most of her attention stayed on the others. All but Borren, the big timid man, were true believers. Some more than others and one or two had the gleam of a zealot in their eyes.

"So, that brings us to our guest," said Rodann and Katja felt all eyes settle on her. "She's here because, like us, she's disillusioned with how things are. Something must change. Do you agree?"

Katja considered her words carefully. "Yes, but so far all I've heard is no different to any sermon given in a temple or church. What makes you different?"

One or two people started to grumble but Rodann held up a hand and they fell silent. "It's a fair question. We're not a religious group. We don't believe sinners and wrongdoers need to be cleansed with fire. Lack of faith isn't what led to the downfall of this city, or our country."

"Then what did?"

"The Queen. She failed us," said Rodann, his voice getting louder and more passionate. He hated her and the more he spoke about the Queen the more Katja thought his grievance was personal. "In our darkest hour, when this city and the entire country was in danger from the Mad King, she abandoned us and abdicated. Every man, woman and child was put at risk because of her. And then the situation only became worse. We had gangs of armed zealots patrolling the streets, imprisoning people for no reason. It was the people of this city who rose up and saved it.

We need to take back our city again from a Queen who doesn't care about us. Someone worthy of governing us should be sitting on the throne."

So far Rodann had not mentioned Talandra, but Katja had the impression he wasn't telling her everything, not just yet anyway. He wanted to see if she was interested and would commit, because once she was in there would not be any half-measures. Anyone who changed their mind or lost their nerve would be found floating face down in the river.

"I can already see the scepticism on your face," he said to Katja. "You think I'm mad."

"I'm not sure," said Katja, playing along, although in truth she thought him very sane but extremely dangerous.

"Such a big change sounds impossible, but it's achievable. It will not be easy and it won't happen overnight. But . . . " and here Rodann paused, holding up one finger, showing it to all in the room as if the answers were written on his fingertip. "A fire is lit with a single spark. We can be that single candle burning in the darkness. We can show the others. I don't need you to believe. All I require is your commitment to the idea of change."

Pretty words from a bold man. While it sounded like a noble idea in principle they were still holding a clandestine meeting in an abandoned building.

"That is all I have to say," said Rodann, his voice settling as he calmed down. "You can take some time to think about it if you want."

"No. I've made my decision," said Katja, carefully looking at each person in the room. Only the timid man wouldn't meet her gaze. "I want to help you."

"Wonderful!" said Rodann, clapping his hands together. He made a strange gesture at Teigan, who briefly left the room and then returned dragging a blindfolded man behind her. She shoved the man down on his knees, where he stayed, sobbing around the gag in his mouth. His hands were tied behind his back and Katja could see blood on the front of his shirt.

"Who's this?"

"Who he is doesn't matter," said Rodann. "All you need to know is that he is an obstacle that needs to be removed. I won't lie to you. The way forward will not be easy and there will be bloodshed. We want to keep it to a minimum, but sometimes it's the only way. This man could not be bought, blackmailed and he wouldn't join us. He gave us no choice."

"Then kill him," said Katja. "If that's the only way."

"Ah," said Rodann, holding up a finger again. She was tempted to cut it off, just to stop him doing it. Even before he said it she knew. Here it was. The wrinkle in the plan. "We need a sign of your commitment. We need you to do this."

"With a few exceptions, no one else in this room has killed before," said Katja. Teigan had the look of a killer, and Rodann obviously had no compunctions about gutting those who opposed him. Katja's instincts also told her the escort had killed before. Beneath the make-up, expensive clothing and jewellery lurked a vicious serpent, cold and cruel.

"They have shown their commitment in other ways. This is your task. It will also show me that you can follow orders, even if you don't understand them."

Katja mulled it over. "I could kill one of them, or you," she said to Rodann, but he didn't look worried and Teigan didn't stir from her post by the door. The others were less comfortable. "It wouldn't prove anything. This man has done nothing to me. I don't know who he is or anything about his crimes."

Rodann gritted his teeth, finally starting to lose his patience. "Nevertheless, you must do this if you want to join us."

Katja noticed he no longer offered her the option to walk away if she said no. She sensed Teigan tensing by the door. She'd always known that becoming a spy would require her to kill, but this was something else.

Katja stared at the man, carefully studying his face, his clothes, trying to pick out any clues that might give her an idea of who he was and why he might be dangerous. He didn't look like any kind of a threat to anyone, bound and gagged, kneeling on the floor in front of her.

If she didn't do this they would kill her. There was a slim possibility she might escape, but then what? This group was involved in a conspiracy against Queen Morganse and was her best chance to find out more about the attack on Queen Talandra.

No matter how she tried to justify it in her mind, killing this man was a coward's act. It was murder, plain and simple. Katja knew that by doing it she would be damning herself.

The room fell silent. She couldn't hear the fire or the others breathing, just the weeping man, praying around the gag in his mouth. The rasp of metal as she drew the dagger from her belt made him flinch but he didn't stop praying. She moved to stand behind him, then knelt down and whispered a prayer in his ear as a small act of mercy. When she'd finished speaking he let out one long, final shuddering breath.

Wrapping her arms around him from behind as if embracing a lover, she rammed the dagger home into his heart. The wound was small and bled little, but her aim true. He wheezed a few times and then stopped breathing. She pulled out and let him fall forward onto his face.

The air of tension eased and Katja saw some of the others staring at her with a mix of emotions – fear, respect, awe even – but only Rodann dared smile.

"Welcome, sister," he said, moving to embrace her but then changed his mind when he noticed the bloody dagger still clutched in her hand. "Together, we're going to change the world."

CHAPTER 22

Centuries ago when people had first settled in Perizzi, they'd built huts along the banks of the River Kalmei. Over time they'd spread further inland and those first wooden huts were replaced with stone. But even then, when people had very little, greed thrived in the hearts of men. Which meant there was crime and a need for law and order. So in some ways, the Watch and the Guardians had always existed.

This was the story Choss had been told by a member of the Watch as a boy when he'd been caught stealing. All these years later he still remembered the man's red beard and the weight of his meaty hand as it had clipped him around the back of the head. After that, Choss changed his ways. He ran faster and for longer before stopping with his pilfered goods.

Down here by the river, away from the port and its bustle, the buildings had seen many owners. Ten years ago there had been a fashion for riverside bars, but that had eventually passed, giving way to an army of scribes and merchants renting offices because the rent was cheap.

Choss made his way to one of the older buildings on the waterfront. Its grey and yellow stone façade was black in places from an old fire and the name above the door had been removed long ago, but one or two battered letters remained.

He rapped on the old iron door and waited, scanning the street out of habit, but there wasn't anything to see out of the ordinary. Just a few scribes going about their business, satchels bulging with papers and merchants sat drinking at a tea shop. The atmosphere was relaxed but Choss felt tense, the muscles in his shoulders pulled tight.

The door opened to reveal a tall Morrin, his horns polished until they gleamed, much like the short blade in his right hand. Scars covered the Morrin's face and arms, one of his ears was missing and he held himself ready for a fight. His amber eyes regarded Choss carefully before flicking around the street.

"Come," he said, stepping back into the hallway, keeping himself out of sight from people passing by. Choss closed the door and followed him down a long stone corridor with bare walls and a rough wooden floor. The rooms on either side were bare of any furniture and were mostly being used for storage. Crates and boxes were stacked to the ceiling. Goods obtained by the Jarrow Family or one of its associates.

The Morrin led him down an old set of wooden stairs to the basement and from there through a trapdoor into the tombs. Just as the old Watchman had said, back when the city was first being built, people still needed to be punished. Their techniques had been a lot more inventive, or barbaric, depending on which side of the bars you stood.

Choss had to slouch to avoid scraping his head on the low stone ceiling that had been carved into the bedrock. The walls were a dull grey with veins of black, and set in the walls at regular intervals were black iron frames. Torches chased away the gloom, but not the stench of filth or decay that came from unwashed bodies and rotting corpses. Voices murmured and whimpered in the dark cells and Choss felt grateful that he couldn't see the prisoners inside.

Don Jarrow had inherited the tombs with the building and

only his most hated enemies or the worst offenders were sent here to die. They were tortured first of course, and no one who went in ever came out alive. What made it even more interesting for prisoners was that at high tide the cells would flood with sea water.

In the last cell at the end of the corridor a man stuck his hands out between the bars, desperately grabbing at Choss's clothes.

"Help me! I'll make you rich! Anything, whatever you want. Just help me!"

With a snarl the Morrin lashed out with a boot, snapping one of the man's arms against the bars. He squealed in pain and fell back, weeping and making wordless pleading sounds.

Beyond the cells was a large open area where several more armed jailors sat playing dice around a table. The room reeked of the sea and the bottom half of the walls were smooth from high tide.

The jailors were a mix of locals, Morrin and a couple of Seves, but all were battered and scarred from years of fighting on the streets. They wore their brutality proudly, like a badge of honour, and here it could be unleashed without fear of reprisal. Choss didn't care. He just wanted to find Gorrax and get out.

"Where's the Vorga?" he asked. The Morrin smiled and pointed at a set of iron grates set in the floor on the far side of the room. Choss crossed the room and peered down into the black. The smell of the sea was even stronger here and he could hear faint sloshing as if someone was treading water. The grates led to the river and were always at least half full of sea water, even at low tide.

"Why did you put him in there?" asked Choss.

The Morrin shrugged. "The boss told me to make him suffer, yes? So we beat him and dumped him in there. No one ever leaves this place, so what's it matter?"

He seemed baffled by Choss's concern for the Vorga. Choss

took a deep steadying breath, forcing himself to remain calm. The Morrin hadn't noticed but the others were alert, their game forgotten as they stared at Choss, suddenly aware of his size.

"Get him out. Now!" snapped Choss.

"You do it," said the Morrin, turning towards the table. Choss grabbed him by the back of his neck and ran him across the room before smashing his face into the wall. He slammed the Morrin's head against the stone six times before letting him fall. It would have pulped a normal man's skull, but it merely left the Morrin bruised and unconscious. Choss followed up with a sharp kick to the Morrin's lower back. The jailor began to thrash and twitch on the floor, blood running from his nose and mouth.

Choss pointed at the next man. "You get him out."

He jumped up from the table, quickly unlocked the largest grate and then stepped back. Choss glared at the other men, expecting trouble, but none of them made a move for their weapons. Keeping one eye on them Choss knelt down by the grate.

"Gorrax, it's Choss. Can you climb out?"

He heard more sloshing of water and then Gorrax's face appeared at the bottom of the narrow stone shaft. Gorrax showed his teeth, something approximating a smile, and then braced his long arms against the walls on either side. He spider-climbed his way up the stone chute until Choss was close enough to grab one hand and haul him out, heaving with his arms and legs. The Vorga weighed at least as much as him and by the time Choss pulled Gorrax out of the hole he was red faced and short of breath.

The jailors had all drawn their weapons and were watching Gorrax closely in case he sought revenge for the beatings. Gorrax wore only a kilt and white vest and his bare green skin was mottled with white lines and pale blue patches which Choss knew were fading bruises. He started to stand up but Choss stepped in front of the Vorga, obscuring his view of the room.

"Lean on me," said Choss, throwing one of Gorrax's arms over his shoulder.

"But, friend Choss, I'm—" he started to say, before Choss cut him off.

"It's all right. Let me help you."

Gorrax stared at him for a moment and then over Choss's shoulder at the nervous men, carefully keeping their distance.

"Yes, I need your help," he said finally, letting Choss carry some of his weight. They shuffled past the jailors then down the corridor, which had now fallen silent. The prisoners watched in shock as one of their condemned brethren left with a pulse.

Choss kept his mouth shut and Gorrax did the same until they were a few streets away. Only then, when he was sure no one would see them, did Choss let go of Gorrax, who stood up under his own power. Choss started to laugh and Gorrax made strange clicking and hooting sounds which indicated his own mirth.

Vorga were children of Nethun, creatures of the sea who longed for the ocean and the healing power of salt water. The strongest and biggest tribe of Vorga, like Gorrax, were green skinned who built their cities on the coast, as close to the sea as possible. They spent hours every day in the water, fishing, farming, and plumbing its murky depths for pearls and other riches they could trade with the land dwellers. Brown Vorga lived in the marshes and the smaller blue-skinned tribes lived in the hills. Gorrax had said they were the least favoured of Nethun, but others claimed them to be the most intelligent. It would explain why all Vorga merchants that visited the cities of the land dwellers to trade were blue skinned.

Instead of punishing Gorrax, the jailors had done the exact opposite. He'd spent days in a regenerative bath and now most of his wounds had completely healed.

"I am grateful, but why are you here?" asked Gorrax.

Choss's good humour drained away as he remembered what lay ahead for them. "I made a deal with Doña Jarrow. In return for your freedom we need to do something for her. It's going to be dangerous and we may die."

"This is a real fight? We can kill?" asked Gorrax.

"Yes, if we have to."

Gorrax considered it for a moment. "Dying in that cell would have taken a long time and been very small," he said, making a circling gesture with both hands. "I prefer to be here. I'm very happy to see you and to have this chance. I am yours."

The Vorga inclined his head and seemed to be waiting for something. His eyes stayed on the ground in a subservient manner that Choss had never seen before from him.

"I can't do this without you. I need you," he said. Gorrax lifted his head and showed Choss all of his teeth, which he imitated in turn.

"I'm ready. When do we begin?"

Choss had given Gorrax very clear instructions. To take out the sentries without making a sound. The Vorga had looked at the building, stared at the open space between their position and the sentries, and declared it easy. All he needed was a slow count of two hundred.

Choss had nearly reached the end of his count, with no sight of Gorrax, when he noticed the sentries outside Don Kal's warehouse were missing. The men on the roof with crossbows were still patrolling, moving in a slow circuit.

A shadow rose up against the front of the warehouse, to the left of the main door. Choss didn't know how the Vorga had reached the warehouse without being seen as there was nowhere to hide. It felt a little peculiar to be wearing the mask and black clothes again, but he didn't have Gorrax's stealth and he needed every advantage. Strength, a constant companion for his entire life, would not be enough to see him through.

Gorrax gave him a brief wave and Choss waved back, watching the sentries on the roof to time his approach. As they moved out of sight he sprinted across the open ground, doing his best to avoid tripping over rubble, broken bits of timber and loose cobbles. More than once he had to vault over something but managed to maintain his stride.

Choss slammed into the warehouse wall and spent the next minute catching his breath. For the first time since he'd retired from the ring, he was glad that he'd maintained his fitness regime. There were mornings when he considered just sleeping in and forgoing exercise, but it had been such a big part of his life for so many years he couldn't break the habit. He wouldn't know who he was if he didn't hold on to some part of his old life. In his mind he was still a fighter. Now that was about to be put to the test.

He stood up, signalled to Gorrax he was ready and the Vorga gestured to follow him around the side of the building. Choss spotted three bodies piled on top of each other in the shadows, the sentries' faces pointing in the wrong direction. Gorrax must have snapped their necks before they'd had a chance to scream.

At the back of the building they found a tall ladder leaning against the wall. The bodies of the other three sentries stared at Choss with unblinking eyes. He stepped over them and started to climb the ladder, which creaked alarmingly at his weight. Gorrax remained on the ground, melting into the shadows and keeping an eye out for any signs of trouble.

Peering over the edge of the roof Choss could see another sentry to his left, making a vague attempt at a patrol. He looked bored and distracted, while three others were playing cards, sat at a makeshift table made of an old crate. They each sat on an upturned box, their crossbows by their feet but still within arm's reach. Their backs were towards Choss and the third man was partially hidden from view behind one of the chimneys. Six chimneys broke up a flat roof, providing some cover, otherwise this would have been impossible.

"Come on, it's got to be my turn soon," complained the sentry still on duty.

"I've almost wiped out these two jokers. You'll get your chance to lose soon enough," promised one of the sentries and the others grumbled.

Moving as quietly as possible Choss climbed over the lip of the roof and scuttled on all fours behind the nearest chimney. Pale grey smoke drifted up from inside and he smelled something earthy and acrid, a mix of damp soil and an alchemist's shop.

With slow precise movements Choss pulled on the punching daggers and took a long slow breath to centre himself. He risked a couple of quick glances around the corner and saw that the fourth sentry had now given up any pretence of work and stood watching the game. The other three spoke in low voices, trying to avoid being noticed by anyone inside.

Moving as quietly as possible, Choss snuck up behind the fourth sentry. The other three only knew something was amiss when warm arterial blood splashed onto them from the dead man's throat. Thoughts of the game were forgotten as they saw his black mask. Lashing out with both blades together he punched two of the men in their throats and kicked the last man in the face a second later. As the first two started to choke and gag he dived at the last sentry, who fell backwards off his seat. He scrambled for his weapon and frantically tried to aim his crossbow.

When he saw Choss bearing down on him the sentry opened his mouth to scream. Choss landed on the man's chest and punched him in the face, his blade biting through his skull. The sentry twitched once and the roof fell silent.

Now came the difficult part.

When Choss reached the bottom of the ladder Gorrax gestured for him to lean close so he could whisper.

"There are many people inside, all digging and working in the black soil. They are not warriors. Four men in masks are cooking with coloured liquids. They are also not opponents."

"Is there anyone else?"

Gorrax nodded. "Two more. Everyone is afraid of them. One is a Morrin, maybe Don Kal. One is white everywhere," said the Vorga, touching Choss's skin and then pointing to his hair.

"He's a local. A Yerskani," said Choss, trying to clarify.

"No, no. Not a pale man. He is not short. He is big like you, a cow man, but white. With red eyes and no smell."

He knew that Gorrax separated people into different groups in a way he didn't understand, but he didn't know what to make of his description.

"Show me."

Gorrax led him to a wide set of grime-encrusted windows, so layered with filth that Choss had assumed they were just another section of wall. Gorrax had scraped the black and grey crud off two small panes, giving him a good view inside the warehouse. The interior was gloomy with deep shadows around the walls, but the rest of it was bathed in a pale blue light from peculiar-shaped lanterns.

Below the window were stacks of supplies, boxes and tools more suited to tending crops on a farm than something used inside a city. However, the stone floor of the warehouse had been dug up and replaced with a thick bed of soil where dozens of people tended outlawed crops. Venthe. Bulbous knee-high white mushrooms riddled with blue veins. A peculiar creaking sound came from the fungus as it stretched and grew in the pale lantern light.

At the front of the warehouse a space had been cleared of soil where four alchemists worked at a large bench laden with glass tubes and brass instruments to turn the mushrooms into the addictive powder. Overseeing them were six armed jackals stationed by the front door. Standing not far away was a grizzled Morrin with curved horns and beside him a tall man dressed in grey. As Gorrax had said, the man's hair was chalk white and his skin pale and sickly.

At this distance Choss couldn't hear what was being said but the two men seemed to be arguing.

"I wish I could hear what they're saying," he muttered and Gorrax nudged him to one side. The Vorga's sail-like ears tilted away from the side of his face and he cocked his head to one side.

"The white one says the new batch will not kill. It will be more powerful and addictive. The Morrin is angry, saying the white one made promises that have not been kept."

There was no doubt now. Don Kal sought to control the supply of the drug in the city with a more powerful and addictive version.

Choss wondered what sort of deal Don Kal had made with the albino.

"The white one says he must be patient. That it is not an easy thing he does. Now he is showing his manhood," said Gorrax.

Choss squinted at the two distant figures in the gloomy warehouse and then glanced sideways at Gorrax. That wasn't what he could see.

"He's doing what?"

Gorrax sucked his teeth and tried again. "He is telling the Morrin he is bigger, stronger, more dangerous."

"Ah, I understand."

"The Morrin is not happy, but has no choice. The white one is dominant although the Morrin pretends otherwise."

Gorrax hissed through his teeth and ducked down, pulling Choss with him. "What is it?"

Gorrax looked surprised. "The white one. He knows we're here."

"How?"

Gorrax didn't have an answer, so, despite the Vorga's protests, he risked a glance through the window. Both Don Kal and the albino were staring at him, the jackals beside them mustering for a fight.

"There's no need to hide any more," said Choss, standing up and kicking in the window. He and Gorrax cleared a space large enough and then slipped inside the warehouse, glass crunching underfoot. The front door slid open and workers streamed out, running for their lives. The alchemists were not far behind. There was no sign of Don Kal or the albino, but for now they didn't matter. All of Choss's attention was focused on the six jackals, three of whom had crossbows.

Without being told, Gorrax moved to the right as Choss went left, sticking to the heavy shadows around the edge of the warehouse. When Gorrax stepped out of the shadows two jackals immediately fired, both completely missing. With an inhuman shriek the Vorga ran at them and they drew their swords. Choss roared and charged from the other side, startling the remaining archer. The last crossbow bolt went into the ceiling and before he had time to reload Choss was among them.

The first jackal, a tall Morrin woman with green eyes, hacked at him with a curved blade which he ducked and then retaliated by slicing her across the stomach. As she stumbled back clutching the loops of her innards, he stabbed her in the middle of her chest in the heart. She fell backwards off his blade and Choss deflected a blow from an axe on his left bracer. The force numbed his arm and made him stumble to his knees, but he ignored it and lashed out with his right. His blade bit into the man's groin.

The jackal squealed and fell back, desperately trying to staunch the bleeding.

As he looked for another opponent Choss saw Gorrax rip the throat out of a local Yerskani woman with his claws and bite off the hand of another. The man fell back in shock, clutching at his stump and staring at the Vorga, who spat fingers onto the floor. With a disappointed shake of his head Gorrax twisted the man's head around on his shoulders. The other two were already dead or choking out their last breaths.

"Nothing. Only that one offered any challenge," he said, pointing at the woman with the torn throat. Choss cut the throat of the last man and silence returned to the warehouse. "Do we go after the white one and the Morrin?"

Choss shook his head. "We can't. He's a Don for this territory. Many more will come to fight us. More than we can handle," he added quickly, before Gorrax suggested they stay and fight.

"Then we are finished here?"

"Almost."

Choss looked at one of the strange blue lanterns. A closer inspection revealed a metal frame holding a sealed glass dome in place, its interior filled with glowing water. He guessed it was some sort of alchemical liquid.

Taking a shirt from one of the dead he pulled up one of the large venthe growths, making sure he didn't touch any of it with his skin.

"Why do you want that?" asked Gorrax.

"To show Doña Jarrow."

"What about the rest?"

Choss grinned. "I have an idea."

They tipped over the laboratory, spilling chemicals all over the ground. Choss soaked several shirts and blankets in the chemical liquid then spread them out across the field of venthe. He gathered up the lamps and cracked each one before spreading the contents around as well.

Gorrax cocked his head to one side. "I hear many heavy men approaching."

"Time to go," said Choss, striking flint and tinder. The dead man's shirt ignited and the flame turned blue and then red. He tossed it onto the soil, which started to smoke and steam.

They went out the front door and as they ran Choss felt heat building up behind him. There was a loud inhalation and looking over his shoulder he saw flames burst out of the front door. The warehouse began to burn and the roof quickly caught fire, destroying all of the toxic venthe inside.

It was over. He'd destroyed the venthe and found proof of who was responsible. Doña Jarrow owed him now. She had promised she would speak to the right people. It might be only a matter of days before they could reopen the arena. Choss quickened his pace, eager to share the good news.

CHAPTER 23

Byrne borrowed a sack from a nearby tavern and took their grisly find with them back to Bav's house. Fray's hands shook as the adrenaline wore off and he began to feel lethargic. Byrne showed no ill effects and didn't say anything, but Fray could see by the set of his jaw that he was annoyed Bav had escaped.

Fray bought a hunk of bread and a couple of skewers of smoked fish from a street hawker, which he wolfed down. By the time they got back to the house he wasn't shaking, but was no less anxious.

Bav's mother was where they'd left her, sat at the kitchen table, staring at its surface for answers. She didn't stir as they came inside, or even when two more Guardians and a squad from the Watch showed up. One of the Watch was sent to fetch reinforcements and the rest to keep away onlookers, leaving Fray and Byrne to search inside.

"There's something behind there," said Fray, pointing at the wardrobe. "I saw it earlier." Byrne peered through the small gap into the gloom and his nose wrinkled at the smell. Even working together they couldn't move the wardrobe any further and had to get two members of the Watch to help them, all four trying to ignore the stench. Behind the wardrobe was a handmade opening and a narrow set of crude stairs leading down.

Byrne lit a couple of candles and after stripping off his weapon and jacket, he could squeeze through the hole. He'd barely been down there a minute when his voice drifted up.

"Fray. You should come down here."

Fray stripped off his jacket and sword, and bracing himself against the crude walls, slowly made his way down the stairs. Eight steps down Fray ducked under a low wooden support beam and found Byrne standing in the centre of a small room.

"Tell me what you see," said Byrne. The tone of his voice suggested this was another teaching moment.

The earth walls had been covered with wooden planks and then crudely plastered, creating a mottled and uneven surface. Several thick wooden support beams criss-crossed above their heads. It gave Fray some hope that the ceiling wouldn't collapse and bury them alive any time soon. It must have taken Bav months to dig out the stairs and tunnel.

The walls, ceiling and floor had been painted white and then every inch covered with letters in a strange swirling language he didn't recognise. Fray tried to make sense of the script and find letters or words, some kind of pattern, but it seemed nonsensical and random. At the centre of the room sat a stone plinth as high as his shoulder with several alcoves on the base. Each of these held an old yellowed scroll. Even without embracing his magic he didn't want to go near them as they made him uncomfortable. Being in this room made the hairs stand up on the back of his neck and it had nothing to do with his fear of the roof collapsing.

Resting on top of the plinth sat a fat book, its pages covered with more of the same language.

Sat in the furthest corner was the source of the unpleasant

smell. The desiccated corpse of a man with tight skin and hands turned into claws. Just like the other victims.

"What do you see?" asked Byrne.

"It's an altar and maybe this is a temple," said Fray, gesturing at the walls. "Someone was murdered upstairs and I think it was Bav. The real one. The killer took his place and has been posing as him for some time. Months, judging by all of this."

"Your father and I faced something like this before," said Byrne. "Twice in fact. The first was maybe ten or eleven years ago. A woman from Zecorria. The last one was five years ago."

Fray's head whipped around, seeking out Byrne's face for more detail, but he'd already turned away.

"What is he? What is all of this?" asked Fray, desperate for answers.

"Your father called them Flesh Mages," said Byrne. The name made sense given the grisly find they'd made after chasing Bav through the city.

"How does it work? What do they want?"

Byrne didn't answer. Instead he picked up one of the scrolls and slowly unrolled it. Fray noticed a strange symbol on the back of the yellowed paper. Byrne glanced at its contents before putting it back.

"It's the same as before," he said, gesturing at the scrolls. "They're written on human skin."

Fray hiccupped and tasted his smoked fish again, but thankfully didn't vomit. The symbol on the scroll was a tattoo that had come with the skin.

"We need to get all of this catalogued. Then have someone fill in the hole."

"Why won't you tell me about the killer?"

Byrne's face looked gaunt and slightly villainous in the flickering candlelight. "Let's speak to the mother first. Here's not the right place to talk about all of this," he answered, gesturing at the corpse by his feet and the human-skin-covered books. Fray wasn't satisfied but he took a deep breath and some of the tension eased from his shoulders. This wasn't the end of the discussion, but he put it to one side, for a little while at least.

Despite moving away from the altar Fray still felt unclean and in desperate need of a wash. His skin itched with a peculiar sensation as if encrusted with grime that moved. Byrne seemed unaffected and his expression gave nothing away. Even when they were settled at the kitchen table opposite Bav's mother, with sunlight coming in through the open door, Fray still felt uncomfortable. Slowly he realised it wasn't just the magic, it was the whole house. It was saturated with sorrow and fear.

"I knew it wasn't him, not really," said the old woman. "At first it was just the little things. Phrases my Bav never used. The way he said things, like he didn't care about them and that people were just things. Once, near the start, I asked him what was wrong and he told me I was senile."

"When did you first notice he was different?" asked Byrne.

"Maybe six months ago, but he'd been pretending for longer. Over time the changes became more obvious, like he'd forgotten who my Bav was. Like he'd worn him thin, like an old shirt full of holes."

"You saw something," said Byrne, studying the old woman's face. All Fray could see was her fear, regret and a terrible sense of loss.

"I came home early one day and found him in his room. He never used to spend any time in there. I heard him moving things around and digging, but I barely saw him. That day I pushed open the door and saw him lifting that old wardrobe." The old woman's haunted eyes found Fray. "He picked it up like it was light as a feather and covered that hole with it. Then he saw me watching from the door."

The old woman looked away, her eyes drifting into the past and shame crept into her face.

"I knew then, but I was scared. So scared," she whispered. Fray moved to take her hand but she flinched away. Byrne gave him a withering look and shook his head. "He said he'd skin me and use my old bones in his dark magic."

"Did he say what it was all for? Why he was doing any of it?" pressed Byrne.

"No. After that we barely spoke, except when we had to," she said, and then swallowed hard and revulsion crept into her expression. "He insisted on calling me mother."

Four more Guardians came in through the front door and Fray felt relieved at their presence. While Fray showed them what they'd found, Byrne asked the old woman a few more questions, but it was obvious she didn't know anything more.

They left her sat at the table, staring at nothing. Members of the Watch and Guardians moved around the house, never interacting with her. She'd been a prisoner and was now a ghost in her own home.

Byrne set a fast pace and Fray had to concentrate on where they were going to keep up and avoid walking into anyone.

"We need to speak to the Khevassar. Tell him what we've found," said Byrne. "He might know something about this. He and your father talked at length about cases. I'll also look through my old notebooks at Unity Hall. After that we should go through your father's journals."

"I've read them several times," said Fray. "There's nothing in them like this. I'd remember someone shedding their skin like a snake."

"What about his last case?"

"There's no reference to it. The last few pages were torn out," said Fray. Up to now he had assumed Byrne had done it to protect him. Being told that his father had died was traumatic.

Reading diary entries written by his father in his last few days about the case, his fears, suspicions and hopes, when Fray already knew the outcome, would be unbearable. However, buried in those pages might be clues about how to fight this Flesh Mage, whatever that was. Fray knew they would be looking to him to use his magic to fight, but without any training or being shown how, it would be nearly impossible.

Fray felt a terrible weight settle on his shoulders and his mood darkened until he and Byrne wore matching scowls.

The hallways of Unity Hall echoed with the sound of their heavy boots as Fray and Byrne marched to the Khevassar's office. Rummpoe, his ageing assistant, could see from their grim expressions that the matter was urgent. Even so he held up one hand, pointed at the chairs beside his desk and let himself into the Khevassar's office. Less than a minute later he re-emerged and gestured for them to go straight in.

As ever the Old Man was surrounded by a stack of documents spread out across his desk. A stack of unopened letters sat on a side table awaiting his attention.

"Close the door," he said without looking up, quickly scribbled a signature on one document and then put it to one side on the stack. "What have you found?"

They laid out the investigation so far, from the dockside workers to the arena, to finding the Flesh Mage and then Bav's body. Byrne didn't mention what had happened to Fray at the arena, but he knew now wasn't the right time to mention it. When Byrne had finished, the Khevassar sat back with a thoughtful expression.

"Flesh Mage. Yes, I remember that first case," he said with a sour twist to his mouth. "She was working her way up the social ladder. Killing people and becoming them for a short time, before they met with untimely accidents. By the end she'd accumulated quite a lot of wealth, but money wasn't her goal. I think she wanted to kill the Queen and assume her position."

"What can you tell me about Flesh Mages and their magic?" asked Fray. "How did my father beat them?"

"I can tell you about the cases, but little about magic. Your father never told me how it was done," said the Old Man. "Don't look so disappointed. I'll have his old journals and Byrne's brought up from the archives. They may give you some answers."

"And in the meantime?" asked Byrne. "What do you want us to do?"

"In the previous cases the murders were almost incidental. They were a way for the Flesh Mages to manoeuvre themselves into position and gather power."

"How?" asked Fray. "How does it work?"

"You're the one with the magic," said the Khevassar. "You tell me and I'll share what I know."

"From what I've seen a Flesh Mage is like a mosquito, or a sponge," said Fray, and Byrne grunted in agreement. "They soak up energy from other people."

"There's more to it than that. Do you remember what you felt at the arena?" asked Byrne. "They also feed on strong emotions, but they amplify them, twist them, and feed them back to people."

That made sense given the web of energy Fray had seen and felt at the arena.

"The organiser at the arena," said Fray. "He said there was something in the air and that people were hungry for blood."

"He's trying to accumulate power for something. It's just like the last time," said Byrne. "But something must have gone wrong at the arena."

Maybe the Flesh Mage had lost control or he'd tried to absorb too much energy and there'd been a backlash. Fray just didn't know enough about how the magic worked and could only guess.

"With the fights shut down he'll need a new source of power," the Old Man was saying. "You need to focus on that and you'll find him."

Now more than ever Fray wished his father was still alive so he could ask him about all of this. More than once he'd tried to contact his father using his magic, but nothing of him had lingered. It was a small comfort to know he was beyond this place, but right now Fray could really have used his help.

"We'll do what we can," said Byrne, moving towards the door, and Fray stood up to follow.

"Give us half an hour," said the Old Man, dismissing Byrne. A small frown creased the Guardian's brow but he left without further comment.

"Tell me about Byrne," said the Old Man without preamble.

Fray thought for a minute and chose his words with care. "He's more callous than I remember. He's completely focused on solving the case, but I overheard him talking to another Guardian about a missing person case. He just didn't seem to care about the people involved."

"Even you?" asked the Khevassar. Fray should have known better than to try and hide the truth. The Old Man had decades of experience with reading people. "Something happened, didn't it?"

Fray felt guilty and said nothing at first, but the Old Man waited patiently. Eventually Fray told him what had happened at the arena and how unpredictable Byrne had become.

"He's not the same man I remember," said Fray. "The old Byrne was always calm and he genuinely cared about people. Now he's angry and bitter most of the time. There's also urgency to him, like he's running out of time."

The Khevassar grunted, as if he'd been expecting Fray to say that. "I think Byrne needs some help and time away from the job. In fact I can't remember the last time he took a day off."

"He's determined to solve this case," said Fray, still feeling guilty.

"There are many capable and experienced Guardians, Fray. He's not the only one." The Old Man's tone was one of reproach.

"Yes, Sir."

"But I admire your loyalty to him, in spite of everything."

"When will you tell him?"

"Today. I'll assign you to another Guardian for the remainder of your apprenticeship."

The Khevassar waved him towards the door and turned back to the endless mountain of paperwork. Fray felt ashamed but he didn't think he could make the situation any worse, so he stayed in his seat.

"What is it, Fray?" asked the Old Man, tapping his pen in the ink pot.

"How did my father really die?"

The question floated around the room and then settled on them both with the weight of iron manacles. Fray would not be moved until he had some answers and the Old Man knew it. He suspected that both the old Guardian and Byrne knew more than they were saying, but now it might be important to solving this case. He needed to know.

The Khevassar heaved a long sigh, cleaned the nib of his pen and laid it to one side.

"Five years ago a man came to the city," said the Old Man. "We didn't know at first, but later we realised it was what your father called a Flesh Mage. Then there were a series of events, each one more violent and widespread than the last. The Flesh Mage was feeding and building up his power towards something catastrophic. Your father explained it to me at the time and I'm still struggling with how it works, but I accepted it."

Fray was shocked by the admittance and how rattled the Old Man looked, even all these years later.

"What was it?"

Instead of answering directly the Khevassar took a key from a chain around his neck and unlocked a drawer in his desk. He drew out a series of pages torn from a notebook, which he passed across the desk. Even before he saw the familiar handwriting Fray knew what they were.

"I took these from your father's private journal," he told Fray. "I told him not to write it down in his official report and he agreed. The information is just too dangerous. I was going to destroy it, but I thought you had a right to know."

"How much does Byrne know?"

"Not much. His memory of that time is patchy. I think what he saw at the end, as much as what happened to your father, is responsible for how he is now." The Khevassar pointed at the pages in Fray's hand. "It's all in there, but don't tell anyone, especially not Byrne. Read them, and then burn them."

Fray tucked the pages away safely inside his jacket but he didn't make the promise to destroy them. He might change his mind later, but right now it was another link to his father and finally the answer about how and why he'd died.

Byrne was pacing in the waiting room outside and immediately set off at a fast pace when Fray appeared.

"What did he want?"

"To see how I was getting on," said Fray. Byrne seemed uninterested and his eyes were distant as they marched along the corridors.

They left Unity Hall and walked through the city in silence for a time, each wrapped up in their own thoughts when the sound of raised voices caught their attention. He exchanged a look with Byrne who pointed off to the right and they both sprinted towards the disturbance.

As Fray came around a corner he saw an angry mob was trying to attack someone huddled on the ground. Crouched over the fallen victim was another Guardian who had her sword in hand, but it was still in its scabbard. The crowd were screaming and shouting, a few tried to shove the Guardian aside but she knocked down four men with sharp punches to the face that sent them reeling. But those four were quickly replaced by several more angry faces baying for blood.

Byrne didn't hesitate, he launched himself at the crowd, elbowing a man in the face and kicking a second in the stomach. He laid into the crowd using fists and knees to create a pool of space around the Guardian. Fray followed closely behind him, using his sheathed blade on anyone who tried to attack Byrne's exposed back. The crowd fell back at the viciousness of their combined assault, which gave the other Guardian a chance to get to her feet.

A tall shadow fell over Fray and he tilted his head up to stare at Tammy Baker, the tall Guardian.

"Get back!" Byrne bellowed at the crowd, drawing his sword with a flourish which made the steel ring. Fray heard another sword being drawn and followed suit. Some of the aggression seeped out of the crowd now that they were facing three armed Guardians. Byrne swung his sword in a few wide arcs, which made the mob move back a few more steps. "The next person who gets within arm's reach is going to bleed."

"They won't cut us," sneered one woman, boldly stepping forward with two men. When nothing happened the woman grinned at them. "Told you they wouldn't do nothing."

She screamed and fell back as Byrne's sword left a long trail down her left arm. Baker sliced one man above his eyebrows and the other on his outstretched hand. Fray could see the cuts were just scratches, but they all bled profusely, which convinced the crowd to keep their distance.

Baker and Byrne were both exceptional with a blade. Despite his moderate skill Fray wouldn't have attempted such a trick. He'd probably cut off someone's ear by accident.

"Who's next?" asked Byrne, but no one volunteered. "What's going on here, Baker?"

Fray risked a glance at the figure on the ground behind him. A local teenage boy with pale skin and red hair lay on his side. One half of his face was bruised and his clothes were soaking wet and smeared with dirt.

"They were trying to drown him in a trough," said Baker.

"He's not right. He's cursed," said one woman, stepping forward and then quickly retreating as Byrne's blade whistled through the air in front of her.

"Give us to him and go on about your business," said one doughy man with a bristly moustache. "There's nothing here for you. Just family business."

"Twenty adults trying to drown a boy isn't family business," said Baker.

"I'm his mother," said the woman with the cut on her arm. "You've no right to get involved."

"This gives me the right," hissed Byrne, gesturing at his uniform.

"It won't happen again," whimpered the boy, who seemed confused and dazed. "I'll be good. I promise!" he pleaded, reaching out a beseeching hand. His mother recoiled in horror as if he were a venomous snake.

"You're no son of mine," she said before spitting.

"You can't stop us all," said a chubby man, finding his voice. "And you can't stay here all day. Just walk away."

Despite their injuries the crowd had not dispersed. Even without using his magic Fray could sense the pressure was building. Their anger had not been sated and, worse, they still felt they were in the right. The other two Guardians sensed the shift in the mood as well, as they simultaneously fell back a step into a fighting stance.

"No one has to get hurt," said the boy's mother. "Just leave him to us."

Fray could hear the boy weeping; horrible wrenching sobs. Everyone knew what would happen if they walked away.

"This is your last warning," said Byrne. "Walk away now. I will kill the first person who crosses the line," he warned them, sketching a line in the air between them. A few in the crowd looked uneasy, but most seemed to take strength from their numbers. Fray wasn't sure Byrne's had been an idle threat and he believed he was capable and willing to carry it out if they pushed him.

As the hair began to stand up on the back of Fray's neck he heard a strange thumping in his ears. At first he thought it was just his frantic pulse, but he soon realised it came from the boy. There was a peculiar echo and he sensed a connection with the boy. He'd not felt anything like it since waking up to find a masked Seeker in his room.

"He's not cursed," said Fray. Byrne raised an eyebrow but there wasn't time to elaborate. The mob started to move towards them en masse, one step at a time. Part of Fray didn't believe the crowd would actually do this. Try to get past three armed Guardians to injure a defenceless boy. He expected members of the Watch to turn up any second but no one appeared.

Just as he'd been instructed, Fray took a deep breath to centre himself and then picked his first target.

"Stop," said a woman's voice. The sound was so loud it made his ears hum. "Do not move," said the commanding voice and everyone looked around in surprise. A figure dressed in black, with gloves and a deep hood, marched towards them up the street. The woman's face was covered with a gold mask which Fray recognised, but no one else showed any signs of recognition.

He didn't need to hear the uneven breathing to know it was Eloise.

Someone in the crowd decided to ignore the latest distraction but as they tried to shove the Guardians aside, Eloise intervened. She made a small twisting motion with one hand and the attacker's forearm snapped in the middle. Suddenly his clenched fist pointed at the sky. Fray could see broken white bone and stringy muscle poking through the skin.

Shrieking in pain the man stumbled back, clutching his ruined arm. The rest of the crowd took several steps back. Eloise stood in the middle of the two groups, completely unafraid at facing down a hostile crowd.

"Leave this place," said the Seeker, pointing one finger at a couple of people. Those targeted quickly ducked or moved to one side, trying to avoid being in front of that dangerous finger.

"What about the boy?" persisted the mother.

Eloise stared at the woman and, despite the mask, Fray could feel the hatred in her stare. "He doesn't belong to you."

The other Guardians exchanged confused glances, but they both knew not to upset an already delicate situation. Any orders they gave, even if they didn't conflict with the Seeker, might upset the balance and reignite the crowd's ire. Instead, they stayed silent and immobile, carefully watching for signs of violence.

"Good riddance," muttered the boy's mother. She tried for a sneer until Eloise pointed at her and started to twist her hand. The woman screamed and ran, quickly followed by the rest of the crowd. Within less than a minute the street was empty.

"Who are you?" asked Byrne but the Seeker didn't answer. She looked at Fray and seemed to be waiting.

Eloise had told him that when he discovered a child with potential, someone would find him. He hadn't thought it would happen so quickly.

"She's a Seeker from the Red Tower," he said. "The boy should go with her."

"We can't just give him to a masked stranger," said Baker, kneeling down beside the boy.

"What other choice is there?" asked Fray, directing his question at Byrne. "We can't take care of him. He's too old to go into an orphanage, and we can't just leave him here. They'll come back and finish the job, or he'll end up on the streets. If he's really unlucky he could get pulled into one of the Families."

"I will make sure that his natural magical talent is nurtured," promised Eloise. "He will never go hungry and we will teach him to control his power. What he does after that will be his choice."

Fray noticed the other Guardians still had their blades held ready. Neither of them trusted the masked Seeker, but Fray felt an innate sense of kinship with her. He could feel the echo of power that connected them in a way he'd never experienced before.

"Take the boy," said Byrne, sheathing his sword, but Baker didn't follow suit.

"This isn't right," she said.

"What other choice is there? At least this way he has a chance."

Baker and the Seeker stared at one another in silence. For a long time neither moved and they barely seemed to blink.

"We will look after him. I promise," said Eloise.

Eventually Baker relented, sheathing her sword and stepping aside. The Seeker crouched down beside the boy, quickly running a hand over his body, looking for injuries. The boy hissed when the Seeker touched his shoulder.

A strange prickling sensation ran across Fray's scalp and the boy twitched in surprise. "My shoulder. It feels better."

"I've healed your injuries," said Eloise, helping the boy to stand up. The bruises on his face had also disappeared.

"How did you do that?"

"If you come with me then you'll learn how to do that and a thousand more things with magic."

"You don't have to go with her," said Baker, trying one last time. "We can find somewhere for you to live. You can stay in Perizzi."

The boy considered it but eventually shook his head. "I want to go. There's nothing for me here any more."

As the boy walked away Fray could feel the other Guardians staring at him, waiting for some answers, but he said nothing. It seemed as if he would have to keep secrets for the rest of his life. What was one more secret on top of the others?

CHAPTER 24

Katja stared at the steam rising from her cup of tea, but her mind remained in the recent past. Her thoughts swirled in slow muddy circles and she felt as if she were teetering on the edge of an abyss. Every time she closed her eyes she could see him, smell his body pressed against her and hear his frantic heartbeat. She'd held him like a lover at the end. No one deserved to die alone.

"Who was he?" said Roza from the chair opposite. Katja was startled by her voice. She'd forgotten anyone was in the room. They were in the kitchen at the back of the shop. Glancing at the sky out the window Katja idly noticed the sun had finally risen above the horizon. She'd been watching it since dawn and had been awake for hours before that.

The kitchen smelled of freshly baked bread, honey and hazelnut from the ghastly coffee that Gankle insisted on drinking. Perhaps a cup of it would have been a better idea than tea. It would certainly have woken her up and helped shake off some of her lethargy. But not all of it was in her muscles. She felt a deep weariness in her bones and a weight on her soul, if such a thing were even possible.

"I've gone over and over it," Katja said finally. "As far as I can tell, he wasn't anyone important. But somehow, he was obstructing their plans."

"What can you tell me about him?"

Katja closed her eyes, trying to recall as many details as she could about the man she'd murdered.

"He had thick arms and shoulders, so his job was quite physical. He didn't have any calluses or burns, so he's wasn't a smith. He's not a sailor because he didn't smell like the sea. And at the end he said a prayer to the Maker, and I've yet to meet a seaman who didn't favour Nethun."

There was something she'd forgotten. A small detail she'd noticed as she let go of his body, which suddenly felt so heavy and still. It was right there, but her thoughts were just too slow and she couldn't grasp it. Digging her fingernails into her palms brought a short sharp pain which started to cut through the fog in her mind. She tightened her grip and as she focused on the pain the fog receded just enough for her to dig down and recall the elusive detail.

"He was a baker," said Katja, opening her eyes. "There was a smudge of flour behind his ear and a certain smell on his skin."

"I'll get some people to do some digging. See if we can find out if any local bakers have gone missing. Why would they want to kill him?"

Katja didn't have an answer and she knew Roza was just thinking aloud. It was a question she had asked herself a hundred times already. She could see some of the pieces on the board, but not all of them, or how they all fitted together. Rodann was loud and full of himself, but there was a sly cunning behind his friendly manner. And then there was Teigan. She wasn't just there to intimidate people. There had to be another reason she was involved.

"Something has been nagging at me," said Katja and Roza

raised an eyebrow. "Rodann and Teigan, I don't get the impression that either of them comes from money, which means someone else is providing it."

"I've got people looking into it and all of their history," said Roza, draining the last of her tea. "We'll find out who they really are."

"I think Rodann has some connection to Queen Morganse. Every time he speaks about her it almost sounds like it's from personal experience. As if she's personally aggrieved him somehow. There's also been no mention of Queen Talandra, not even any sly comments. Are we sure they're going to target her?"

"You heard what the Silent Order said. Queen Morganse was only half of the contract they turned down. You just have to be patient," counselled Roza. "You've shown them your commitment, but I doubt they really trust you yet. When are you seeing them next?"

"This afternoon. Rodann is sending me on my first mission."

"Keep me posted. I'll send word if we find anything," said Roza, getting ready to leave, until Katja put out a hand to stop her.

"About the other night. Those two men I killed."

"You're lucky, so far the Guardians haven't found any clues and eye-witnesses are scarce. No one saw you."

Katja shook her head. "I don't care about that. It was self-defence and I had no choice. But last night, murdering a defenceless man while they watched, that was something else. The weight of it is unbearable."

"What are you saying?" asked Roza.

"I think you might be right. I'm not sure this life is for me."

Roza was quiet for a long time, lost in thought. "If I could take your place I would, but they want you. When this is over, if you still want to go home, that's fine. Can you hold on for a few more days?"

Katja wanted to say no. To forget about Teigan and her dead eyes. Forget about Rodann and his stupid face. She just wanted to crawl into bed and wait for it all to be over. But she didn't. Her Queen was still in danger, and it was Katja's duty to protect her. Not just because of the damage her death would cause in the west, but also because of the impact it would have on the people of Seveldrom. They were still deeply wounded by the loss of Talandra's father and barely a year on they had not recovered. A sense of normality had returned, but like here in Perizzi, it felt like a paper mask covering the horrible truth. It wouldn't take much to hurt them again. She was sworn to protect the Queen and would give anything to keep her alive.

"I will see this through to the end," said Katja, calmly meeting Roza's stare.

Katja spent the next few hours trying to rest, but only managed to fall asleep for a few minutes at a time before coming awake from a nightmare. Every time she closed her eyes she saw him again. Sometimes he was whole and he begged her to spare his life. Other times he was already rotting and he reached for her with skeletal hands from an unmarked grave, trying to pull her down into the cold, damp earth beside him.

Feeling more tired than when she lay down Katja gave up on sleep. She washed and dressed in fresh clothing, then ate some fruit with a little bread and soft goat's cheese. Gankle came into the kitchen from the shop and his normally bland face was tense.

"There's a woman here to see you," he said.

The word sounded alien in his mouth, as if he'd never seen a woman before in his life. Katja raised an eyebrow and followed him to the front.

Standing in the middle of the shop with her back to Katja was a priestess of the Blessed Mother. Her white robe shone like fresh snow and it wasn't until she turned around that Katja saw why Gankle was so nervous.

The Faithful of the Blessed Mother preached purity of spirit, which they said could only be achieved through a balance of maintaining a pure body and mind. That meant never eating to excess, avoiding all intoxicants and cleansing the mind through prayer, chastity and being generous to others.

Her priests were supposed to lead by example, but the sacrifices that demanded proved too difficult for some and discipline varied in different countries. In Morrinow the priests flagellated themselves to maintain their purity and drive out wicked thoughts. Here in Yerskania they were more lenient, but not nearly as relaxed as the woman standing in front of Katja.

Her white silk robe was not transparent, but it was so tight it left little to the imagination and showed off her generous proportions. As soon as Katja saw her face she recognised the faux priestess. It was the wealthy escort from Rodann's group of conspirators.

"Good afternoon, sister. I believe we have an appointment."

Katja said nothing and played along, pulling her grey robe on top of her clothing. Gankle lurked at the back of the shop, gawping at the escort, his eyes lingering on her hips and breasts. The escort heaved a few deep breaths, making her bosom swell against the material, which made Gankle sweat. She laughed at his expression and Katja wanted to punch her perfect rosebud mouth. Even her laugh was generous and warm.

Katja flung open the front door and marched out, picking a direction at random. The escort caught up a short distance away and Katja slowed down to a more sedate pace.

"What should I call you?" asked Katja, knowing that she would have many different names.

"Faith."

"Is that supposed to be a joke?" asked Katja, gesturing at the robe.

"Faith is what my parents named me at birth. My working name is Violet, if you'd prefer."

Katja didn't know if it was Faith's idea at humour, or an attempt to get under her skin, but she tried to ignore it and not let it bother her.

"So where are we going?"

Faith offered her a wry smile. "To reward some true believers. But first we need to pick up a few more of the Faithful."

She led Katja into one of the seedier areas of the city, away from the main streets that were regularly patrolled by the Watch. Here people lurked in doorways offering any number of services, and several buildings had roses painted on their front door, indicating that companionship could be purchased within.

Faith led her to a building that looked in a better condition than either of its neighbours. The windows were clean, the paint was fresh and colourful flowers in pots brightened up an otherwise drab street.

Faith knocked loudly and the front door quickly opened to reveal a statuesque blonde woman. She wore a pair of long curved daggers on her belt and Katja noticed a small scar on the woman's chin and more on both hands. The blades were not decorative.

"Did you get everything on the list, Laure?" asked Faith and the enforcer nodded. Laure gestured for Katja to take a seat while they went into the back room. Katja's eyes briefly scanned the room, noting the rich and brightly coloured furniture, all of it covered with lots of soft cushions and no sharp corners. Wine and several other bottles containing spirits sat idle on a side table beside fluted glasses. A bowl of fruit with apples, grapes and even succulent spiny pears stared at her, tempting her to try something. Expensive items to leave gathering dust. All of which told her the clientele who came through the front door had very deep pockets.

Faith returned with Laure and four strangers, two men and two women, who she guessed were prostitutes. All of them were very beautiful, and given her expensive surroundings Katja would've been disappointed if they weren't.

"Has Laure explained what you need to do?" asked Faith and the four prostitutes all made sounds of agreement.

Laure handed out white silk robes like Faith's and they quickly stripped off without any signs of being self-conscious about their nudity in front of strangers. All of them were lithe with well-toned bodies that seemed without any flaws. Next they removed any indications of wealth as befitting Faithful of the Blessed Mother. All rings, piercings from ears and nipples, necklaces and bangles, were secured in a cloth bag for their return. The women washed off all make-up, leaving them slightly red faced and looking more vulnerable. Katja noticed Faith didn't wipe her face clean.

Faith handed Katja a white robe, which she swapped for her grey, but she kept her small clothes on underneath. Faith gathered up two bulging satchels, which she passed to the others to carry, then gestured for Katja to follow her. They went out the back door and along several alleys before rejoining the main streets. With their hoods pulled up the six had become a clutch of the Faithful, going about their work for the Blessed Mother with eyes demurely downcast and mouths closed.

"What are we doing?" whispered Katja. "And what, exactly, is my role in all of this?"

Faith glanced behind and a smile flitted across her face as she saw where Katja's thoughts were leading. "Don't worry. You're not here for that. We're on our way to the home of Lord and Lady Venarra. They're rich and easily bored, so they're always seeking new distractions. Their latest is embracing the religious fringe. For years there's been a rumour about an inner circle in the church of the Blessed Mother. A higher echelon which unlocks great spiritual mysteries for those daring enough to explore it."

As part of her job Katja was aware of the rumours, but after years of working in the shadows, she knew it to be false. There was no sacred text or ritual that could bring about enlightenment. Any who claimed such a thing existed were charlatans exploiting weak-minded or desperate individuals. She wondered which category the Venarras fell into.

"You still haven't explained my role," said Katja.

"They'll keep the Lord and Lady busy," said Faith, jerking a thumb over her shoulder. "While you and I have other work to attend to."

"Which is?"

"You know scripture. You could probably quote the whole book chapter and verse. We need you to set the scene for the Venarras. Build expectation in their minds of what they might discover if they have the courage. Then we'll put a little something in their drinks and they'll drift off. I've brought all sorts of religious paraphernalia to help create a tableau. When they wake up they'll believe whatever they want to."

Faith hadn't mentioned what she would be doing while she and the others conducted the elaborate charade. Despite Rodann's declaration that she was now part of the group, Katja was still being kept in the dark about the plan.

"I can do that," said Katja, staying positive, and she saw Faith smile. "But what are we actually doing?"

"Just focus on your job," said Faith with finality. Katja bit her tongue to stop herself slapping the other woman and shaking her for answers.

Long before they reached the Venarra estate Katja knew the

owners were not ordinary nobility, but one of the older families. As they started the climb into the wealthier district, the number of houses on either side of the street started to dwindle. The houses became bigger with more fanciful architecture, often designed simply for the sake of decoration rather than function.

By the time they stood at the front gates of the Venarra house Katja could only see half a dozen houses and most of those were hidden from view by high walls. Armed household guards in yellow and black livery greeted Faith with sincere reverence. They were escorted through the grounds and deposited in a large sitting room decorated with black metal furniture stuffed with white cushions and expensive silk tapestries on the walls depicting passages of scripture.

"Welcome, welcome," burbled a middle-aged balding man dressed in an expensive but ill-fitting outfit of yellow and black trousers with a matching shirt. He greeted them warmly, shaking hands and chatting as if they were old friends. Following behind at a more sedate pace was a tall woman, dressed in a high-necked dress in the family colours. Her demeanour was far less welcoming and she studied them all with a critical eye.

"Welcome to my home," said Lord Venarra. "And this is my Lady wife. I am a wealthy man, but all of the gold is dull in comparison to her beauty."

"Which of you is the High Priestess?" asked Lady Venarra, ignoring her husband's attempt at flattery.

"As I'm sure you know, Lady Venarra," said Katja, "there is only one High Priest and no other hierarchy below that, just the Faithful. However, I am the most knowledgeable."

"Ah, then I'm sure you recognise the miracle of rebirth," said Lady Venarra, turning Katja's attention to one of the tapestries hung over the marble fireplace. It depicted an old woman dying in a cave, apparently forgotten by the crowd who stood around a crib, cooing over a new-born child.

"Taken from the second book of the Harvest, verses seventy-eight to one hundred and eleven."

She tested Katja on half a dozen more passages, sometimes obscure and ambiguous parables, but nothing she mentioned came as a surprise. Katja could recite it all if necessary, as well as several more religious tomes.

Finally Lady Venarra sniffed and fell silent, apparently satisfied but somehow still unimpressed. Faith made a peculiar flipping gesture with her hands and Katja understood.

"Perhaps I should test the limits of your faith," said Katja, the tone of her voice making Lady Venarra raise an eyebrow. "You may be nobility, Lady Venarra, but I am one of the Faithful and I did not come here to be quizzed like a child."

"My wife meant no offence," apologised Lord Venarra, wringing his hands.

"I can speak for myself, Tommo," said Lady Venarra, smoothly gliding over to stand in front of Katja, who held her gaze evenly. "I apologise. I've heard stories about charlatans robbing gullible nobles."

"Money can be useful, but it is not the core of my belief or the stone on which my faith rests," said Katja, paraphrasing a verse from the Book of Sorrows, one of the old texts of the Twelve. At the hint of something that sounded vaguely religious Lady Venarra seemed to come awake.

"We're ready to be guided by you," she promised, suddenly as eager and accommodating as her husband.

"We'll see," said Katja as Faith approached and whispered something in her ear. "First, you need to cleanse your body and your mind."

Faith poured glasses of water for everyone from a large jug while Katja span out more mystical-sounding promises of enlightenment if they were willing to throw off the shackles of the mundane.

From her eye corner she noticed Faith added some white powder to two of the glasses, which briefly fizzed before settling. Moving to the table Katja added a single drop of red wine to every glass of water. The Venarras raised an eyebrow but said nothing and accepted the drink.

"Water brings life, but within you is the seed of corruption." Katja showed her glass of pink water to the room. The Venarras watched her with rapt attention. "You can pretend it's not there, but impurity stains us all. First we must identify and embrace it, before we can be cleansed."

Katja gestured at everyone's glass and then drained hers in three quick gulps. The others followed suit and looked at her again as if expecting to feel instantly different. Faith ushered the two male prostitutes to stand beside Lady Venarra and the two women stood beside her husband.

"Now you must cleanse the body," said Katja. "They will help you, while we prepare the room for the ritual of awakening."

The nobles were led away while Faith helped her move the furniture to the edges of the room. Inside the cloth bags she found an assortment of candles, incense, chalk, a few pots of henna paint and several coils of thin white rope. There was also a pot of red mud that came from the coast of Shael. There were several religious icons and books in the bags, but Katja ignored them. If they were to create a lost ritual it would work against her to stick too closely to scripture.

After twenty minutes of painting a complex geometric shape on the floor with black henna and using incense and candles to decorate the room, it started to look vaguely mystical. The outline of the design was complete, but she still needed to tie all of the different symbols together to create the impression of a web, connecting the seven deadly sins.

"It still needs some work," said Katja as Faith moved towards the door.

"You can finish it. I have other business elsewhere," she said, checking the corridor before slipping out. Katja followed her to the door, listened briefly and then stepped into the corridor.

From further along the corridor she heard women laughing and the sound of splashing water. Faith had completely disappeared. She considered her options and then stepped back into the room to finish arranging things quickly. A different idea occurred and Katja changed the centre of the design to save time, leaving two large empty spaces.

Walking with purpose she strode down the corridor, ready to be challenged but the Venarras must have dismissed their staff as she saw no servants or guards in the house. The sound of intimate moaning drew her towards an open door through which she saw the Lady Venarra in a huge tiled bath. It was large enough to fit twenty people, but now it held only three naked occupants. Lady Venarra was being pleasured by both of the prostitutes and was completely oblivious to anything else. Whatever Faith had slipped into their drinks had removed all of her inhibitions.

Her groans echoed off the bare walls and Katja hurried away, keen to find Faith and discover the real reason for their visit. In the next room she could hear Lord Venarra, who was equally busy, but she kept walking and came to a narrow set of spiral stairs. At the bottom the corridor split left and right but a faint scraping to her left drew her attention.

Moving as quietly as possible Katja crept to the end of the corridor where she peered through a door left ajar. Inside, Faith was sat on the floor inspecting documents taken from a vault, its huge metal door swung open on hinges as thick as her leg. Inside the vault she could see shelves stacked high with rare and special valuables from all over the world, but Faith only had eyes for the documents spread out on the floor. She carefully picked her way through several before finding those that she wanted, which she took out of the stack.

Katja made her way back to the sitting room where she poured herself a glass of wine. Faith appeared a few minutes later carrying two thick robes in the house colours.

"It shouldn't be long now," she said, cocking her head to one side as the sounds of pleasure reached fever pitch. She glanced at the design on the floor and raised an eyebrow.

"It's a mix of all sorts, symbols of rebirth, together with nonsense I've made up. Where did you go?"

At first Katja thought Faith wouldn't answer but it seemed as if her actions had bought her some goodwill. "To obtain some leverage, just in case."

"Do we need to come back here again?"

"Perhaps," said Faith. Katja rolled her eyes and was about to say something sarcastic when she noticed something in Faith's expression.

"You don't know what all of this is for either."

Faith grimaced. "No, but I can guess."

"So can I," said Katja. "Blackmail. But why them?"

Faith didn't have an answer.

Katja shook her head in dismay. "You're letting Rodann treat you like just another puppet."

Faith paused in the door, a wry smile on her face. "Don't try to turn me against him. I'm not easily manipulated."

"No, you're not. And yet despite not paying for the hour, he's still getting you to do what he wants." Her words made Faith flinch as she went out the door.

A few minutes later, dressed once more in their white robes, the prostitutes carried the naked Venarras into the room. Both were partially conscious and they seemed only vaguely aware of their surroundings.

The prostitutes wrapped each of them in a robe then lay them down in the centre of the pattern on the floor. Katja painted more of the geometric pattern on their hands with henna while the others daubed red mud between their toes. They dribbled a little more mud on the floor, lit the incense and carefully backed out of the room.

When they were a few streets away Katja turned to Faith.

"What happens now?"

"The fox-root will give them vivid dreams. When it wears off they'll wake up with a strong sense of euphoria. They may ask us to go back. You'll have to come up with something else at that point," said Faith, giving her fair warning.

Katja didn't ask why, as she knew Faith hadn't been told how the disparate pieces of the plan connected. The brooding silence and twitching muscles in Faith's jaw told Katja that this wasn't over. Her words had stung Faith more deeply than she had admitted. Now Katja wasn't the only one desperate to uncover the truth about what lay ahead.

For the first time since she'd agreed to infiltrate the group, Katja felt as if she was doing something proactive. It wasn't much but it was a start to finding some real answers.

CHAPTER 25

Early morning sunlight shone through the glass roof of the theatre, bathing one section of the seats in golden light. In the glow Choss could see the grain of the wood beneath the varnish, swirls and knots that should have felt rough but were smooth under his fingertips. Someone had spent countless hours crafting the chairs, honing the wood, sanding and polishing until it was perfectly smooth.

It brought back memories from his childhood of sitting in the back pew of the church of the Maker. He'd listen to the sermons, but not watch or engage with anyone else. Instead he'd focus on the wood beneath his fingers, tracing lines and patterns, imagining they were mighty rivers or secret maps that led to hidden treasure.

Closing his eyes Choss let the silence of the theatre wash over him as light played across his eyelids. The silence felt very different here compared to the church. The building was quiet, but there was no peace to be had, no comfort in the uniform empty seats or silent stage. The air hummed with expectation, like the moment before a fight.

Far below he stared at the two empty chairs on the half-stage. They'd soon be occupied by Don and Doña Jarrow. When one stood in front of them the chairs were imposing, but from up here they looked small and insignificant.

A set of heavy feet thumped on the stairs and a minute later Don Jarrow sat down, his wife beside him. Choss didn't look around but the two shadows that fell over him told him that Vargus and Daxx were in the row behind. Waves of anger and hostility poured off Daxx towards him but Choss ignored it.

"My wife tells me you've been busy," said Don Jarrow, gesturing at the cloth bundle on Choss's lap. He passed it over and the Don carefully unwrapped it, making sure his bare skin didn't touch any part of what lay inside. The venthe plant looked fairly innocuous, a grey white stalk with bulbous white and blue mushrooms, but all of them knew how lethal it could be.

"Tell us what you found," said Don Jarrow.

Choss glanced at Doña Jarrow for some guidance as to how much he should mention about her involvement, but as ever her expression remained unreadable.

Choss started with the Don's plea to his people to find out who was responsible for the new lethal dose of venthe. He skipped over how he knew it had come from Don Kal, as it would put some of the blame on Vinny and the arena for not dealing with Brokk sooner. Instead he focused on his ventures into the meat district and finding the warehouse where they'd been growing the venthe.

"The albino. Did you recognise him?" asked Don Jarrow.

Choss shook his head. "No, first one I've seen in the city."

"And you're sure it was Don Kal?" asked Doña Jarrow, her piercing eyes locking onto him. She probably thought he'd been hit in the head too many times and couldn't tell one Morrin from another.

"It was him. I'm certain."

Don Jarrow sat back and the chair creaked under his weight.

He closed his eyes and tilted his chin up until the sunlight fell across his face.

Seeing Don Jarrow up close Choss noticed the bags under his eyes looked more pronounced than usual, the notches between his eyebrows deeper. White hairs amid the black in his beard sparkled in the light, glinting like broken glass. Don Jarrow sat perfectly still, taking deep breaths, soaking up sunlight like a cat. Choss could see his eyes twitching beneath his closed lids and knew the Don rarely had moments of peace like this.

After a couple of minutes Don Jarrow cracked open one eye and tilted his head towards his wife. "Will the other Families agree to a meeting tomorrow night?"

"I think so," she mused and shook her head, faintly annoyed. "This can't wait. I'll make sure they understand the urgency."

Don Jarrow grunted and turned towards Choss. "You've done well, far better than any of my incompetent Silver and Gold. I would thank you, but my gut tells me this is going to get worse before it gets better."

"At least give the man something for his trouble," said Doña Jarrow but Choss felt a cold prickle up his spine at her words. For some reason it felt more like a threat than the promise of a reward. He turned his head slightly and from one eye corner saw a look pass between Daxx and Doña Jarrow. She shook her head slightly and Daxx frowned, clearly disappointed. The moment passed and Choss would've thought he'd imagined it, if not for the worrying prickle across the back of his scalp.

"Yes, of course," said Don Jarrow, clapping Choss on the shoulder and offering him the semblance of a friendly smile. "How about I arrange for you to spend a little time with one, no, make it two girls from the Blue Lotus?"

The Blue Lotus was one of the most elite and expensive brothels in the city. It only catered to the rich and hired the most beautiful and talented women from across the world. Choss had heard the stories, but knew of no one who had actually set foot inside the establishment.

"That's very generous, but I'm not interested," said Choss, which wasn't strictly true, but there were more important issues to think about than his gratification.

Don Jarrow raised an eyebrow and Choss heard the chairs creaking behind him as Vargus and Daxx shifted, but he didn't turn around to see their faces. Only Doña Jarrow seemed unsurprised and her expression didn't change, but he sensed tension in her body as if she were poised to fight.

"The arena," said Choss, before Don Jarrow could offer something else or speculate about the nature of his refusal. "That's all I care about. I want this thing with the venthe and Don Kal settled as much as you do, so I can get back to work. If there's anything else I can do to help, just ask."

"You're a strange man, Choss. There's not many who would turn down a night at the Blue Lotus." Don Jarrow chuckled and shook his shaggy head. "But I'll keep your offer in mind. You've certainly proved yourself."

Despite all the money he'd made over the years Choss had few possessions and most of those held more sentimental value than monetary worth. Perhaps it came from growing up with so little and having to fend for himself in one way or another from an early age. The only exception to the rule was the investment he'd made in buying his own home.

After every fight, right from the start when he'd begun making money, he'd put a little of his winnings aside. Years later it allowed him to buy a house overnight. He never had to risk getting caught in a cycle of borrowing from unscrupulous lenders to pay his debts, or making deals with dodgy landlords when times were lean. Whatever happened he would always have a roof over his head. He'd seen too much of it as a boy. Families turfed out of their homes for falling behind on the rent. Corrupt people wielding tiny amounts of power over others as if they were kings, taking away what little remained from those already at the bottom of the pile.

Choss shook his head as he ascended the steps of his home, trying to get rid of the melancholy that had settled over him. His meeting with the Jarrows had gone well and yet something nagged at him.

Gorrax was exactly where he'd left him, asleep in one of the bedrooms upstairs. At first the Vorga had found the idea of sleeping on such a soft surface quite distressing, but now he looked quite comfortable lying with both arms spread out. His ears flicked slightly as Choss came into the room but he kept his eyes closed.

"There are many things about your city and your people that I will never understand," said Gorrax. "Why you cover everything in stone. Why you eat cows and pigs and why many of you live away from the sea inland. But this," said the Vorga, opening his eyes and smoothing out the woollen blanket. "This is nice. It feels very soft."

"I'm glad you like it," said Choss, leaning against the doorframe. "Don't you have anything like it in your country?"

Gorrax sat up and clacked his tongue. "Yes, but only a little. Wool is not so good when wet. Mostly we trade for cotton." He thumbed the vest he always wore. "More useful. Lasts longer and less expensive."

It wasn't often the Vorga spoke about his homeland so freely, and despite being friends with Gorrax for years, Choss still knew very little about his family.

"Why did you come here? To this city?" asked Choss. It was a question many had wondered about, but no one had felt brave enough to ask.

Blue Vorga were the most common tribe seen in the human

cities. They understood trade far better than the rest of their people and they had the most even temper. Brown Vorga rarely ventured out of their swamps and the coastal green Vorga were notoriously ferocious and the most unsociable outside their own people. At one time Gorrax had told him they were also the biggest and best warriors in the world, respected and feared by all. Choss had a different opinion but he didn't argue the point. The blue Vorga also seemed the most intelligent, but Choss kept that to himself as well.

Gorrax said nothing for a while and sat with his head bowed and eyes closed. The bruising and injuries from his beatings in the tombs had completely healed, returning his skin to its usual green and white hue. Eventually Gorrax looked up and Choss saw something in the Vorga's eyes he'd never seen before. Uncertainty.

"Explain this to me. What is a prostitute?"

The question took Choss by surprise, but he chose his words carefully before answering. Gorrax had been living in Perizzi long enough to grasp all aspects of human society, including the sex trade, but as ever with the Vorga a simple question hinted at something else. "Someone who sells their body for money."

"Among my people no one buys or sells sex. Everything is within marriage."

"Did you visit a prostitute?"

Gorrax clacked his teeth in frustration. "How do you choose a husband? A wife?"

"You spend time together. You talk and learn about the person. Then you decide together to get married."

"There is no deciding made for the woman or the man?" asked Gorrax.

"Some faiths have arranged marriages, but it's uncommon these days. Mostly people choose for themselves."

"Among my people strength always decides. A female can

choose a male and challenge him to a fight. If she wins she is the main provider and they will marry. If she loses she was weak and unworthy. A male may also choose the female in this way. One always leads the other. Nethun wants only the strongest to survive and have children."

"Is that why you left your people? You didn't want to marry the female who defeated you?"

"No. No one bested me, not until you," hissed Gorrax, getting frustrated. Choss sat down beside him and laid a hand on his shoulder.

"It's all right. You don't have to tell me."

Gorrax let out a sigh that went on for a long time before he spoke again. "No, Choss, you should know this, but it is hard to explain. Years ago I found someone I liked, someone worthy. We fought and I was the strongest, but the one I chose was not the same. My people could not accept my choice."

"They were from another Vorga tribe?"

"Something like this," said Gorrax. "My family killed them for being different. I did not share in their shame so I left before they killed me as well."

Of all the possible reasons to explain why a green Vorga had fled his own people, forbidden love was not one Choss had considered. He'd expected it to revolve around revenge or a blood debt, which Gorrax had spoken about, or one of the long-running feuds between the tribes. Most people thought all Vorga were war-hungry savages who ate their own young and did nothing but fight. After years of hearing stories from Gorrax, Choss had a better understanding of their culture than most, but this latest revelation skewed everything he knew.

"I must go," said Gorrax, getting up and heading to the front door in a rush. If he'd been human Choss would have said he was embarrassed, but until today he'd not thought the Vorga capable of it.

"Wait," said Choss, taking the stairs two at a time and catching up to Gorrax at the front door.

"I have been behind stone walls for too long," said Gorrax. "I need to swim in the sea. I will come back in a few hours."

"Thank you for telling me. I'm honoured you shared this with me," said Choss, knowing that Gorrax had found it difficult. The Vorga tried to say something but changed his mind and went out the door without another word.

Choss tried to imagine all that Gorrax had been through but struggled to compare it to something from his own life.

He had very few memories of Seveldrom, as his father had moved the whole family to Yerskania before his third birthday. For many years the winding streets of Perizzi were all he knew. Eventually he'd made the pilgrimage back to the country of his birth, but by then it had become just another place. He had no family ties in the area and no friends or memories to anchor his emotions. He'd quickly grown bored of exploring and come back home to Yerskania. Being forced to flee his home and leave behind everything familiar or risk being murdered by his family was difficult to imagine.

A loud knocking at his front door pulled Choss from his reverie. Much to his surprise he found Doña Jarrow standing in the street. He glanced up and down the road but there was no sign of Daxx.

"I came alone. May I come in?" she asked. Choss wasn't aware that she even knew where he lived, but then again he shouldn't have been surprised. There was very little that Doña Jarrow didn't notice.

He moved back and she stepped inside. Doña Jarrow glanced around his front room before perching on the edge of a padded seat by the fire. Choss sat down opposite and tried to mirror her neutral expression and relax in her presence, but he found it almost impossible. Instead he went down into the calm place in his mind that he focused on before a fight. A place where he could lock away all of his emotions and shackle his rage. Eventually Doña Jarrow spoke, her husky voice shattering the quiet.

"We've already heard back from the other Families. They've agreed to meet tomorrow night on neutral ground at the arena." A nerve twitched in Choss's face at the mention of the arena.

"What can I do to help?"

An unsettling smile briefly touched Doña Jarrow's mouth, but it never reached her eyes. "Don Kal will try to talk his way out of what happened. He'll claim the venthe farm wasn't his. Or that his men were doing it without his knowledge. He's forgotten who we really are."

"Which is?"

"We're not diplomats who negotiate with words, or kings who barter with signed pieces of paper. I earned my position through blood and sacrifice, the same as every other head of a Family. Don Kal needs to be reminded of that."

"Why come to me?"

Doña Jarrow hesitated and a sour twist quirked her lips as if she'd bitten into a lemon. "Because I can't trust my own people. Someone has been passing information to the other Families. I will deal with them soon enough, but right now I need someone I can trust."

Choss considered her request, noting that she'd been very careful with her words. It was a stark contrast to their last meeting at the Emerald Dragon. So far she'd not mentioned their previous arrangement about him leaving the arena to work for her. Perhaps if he did this it would make them even, although he doubted it would be that simple.

"What do you want me to do?" he asked.

"Don Kal isn't stupid. The farm you destroyed won't be the only one. Venthe takes weeks to grow and he needs several to maintain a steady supply. I want you to find the other farms and destroy them tomorrow night while he's at the Family meeting."

"That's a lot to ask, especially now. They'll be extra careful after I burned down the other one."

"But it's not impossible for a man with your talents," said Doña Jarrow. It sounded like a compliment, but he knew she viewed him simply as a tool to be used. He couldn't help himself and had to ask the obvious.

"Why should I do it?"

"I would've thought that was obvious."

Choss leaned forward on his chair, struggling to control his temper. "I want to hear you say it."

"If the Families go to war over this, the city will tear itself apart. We need to destroy every single stalk of the new venthe. Then everything can go back to normal, including fights at the arena."

There it was. She'd set out the cheese and didn't think he could see the trap beneath, ready to snap his neck.

"You must think I'm an idiot," snarled Choss. Doña Jarrow fidgeted in her chair but didn't respond. "That's not why you want me to do this. I know what this is really about."

"And what's that?"

"You want to eliminate Don Kal from the venthe business. It will weaken his business and drive more addicts to your dealers. That's what you're really after."

A rare smile touched Doña Jarrow's face and she grudgingly nodded. "You're right. His recklessness has cost all of us a lot of money. I want to weaken his Family's position and drive him out of the city, but one thing at a time. For now I'll settle for taking his piece of the venthe business."

Choss sat back, letting the tension ease out of his shoulders. At least she'd not lied to his face. As he contemplated his choices Doña Jarrow spoke again.

"There's a price to be paid for everything that matters. I want to weaken him. You want the arena."

"What sort of price?" asked Choss, although really he already knew the answer. It was a price he'd paid many times in his life.

"For people like us, it's normally paid in blood. Nothing of worth comes without pain and sacrifice. Can you do it?"

He knew what it would cost him. The question wasn't if he could do it, but if he was willing to pay the price. Choss took a few minutes to think it through, but eventually he realised there was only one answer he could give. One more time, just one more.

"Yes, I can do it."

And with that Doña Jarrow smiled again and he felt a chill run down his back.

CHAPTER 26

After an incredibly long day Fray should have just collapsed into bed when he got home. The missing journal entries from his father weren't going anywhere. He could get some real sleep and read them in the morning when he was refreshed. He'd waited this long. One more night wouldn't make any difference.

Instead of going to bed Fray lit every candle stub in his dingy room. In the flickering glow he smoothed out the pages and began to sort them into order, starting with the oldest. After reading so many of his father's private journals he immediately recognised the crisp clean letters. Everything was neat and tidy. Everything had its proper place and Fray suspected his father's mind had been the same, organised into different sections.

The chaos and disorder of the real world must have agitated his father no end. He'd tried so hard to keep his work and home life separate but they'd bled together around the edges. Fray had come to know Byrne from the many times he'd visited their home and had overheard countless conversations about investigations. Equally, thoughts of Fray and his mother must have pushed his father to work harder to keep them safe from all of the horrors he saw on a daily basis.

Bringing his mind back to the present Fray stared down at the pages. There were more pages than he had been anticipating. Finally, after five years of wondering, the answers about how his father had died were in front of him. Fray took a few deep breaths and tried to stop his hands from shaking.

The first few pages detailed the initial encounter with what would later come to be known as a Flesh Mage. To begin with the journal entries detailed a case, from twelve years ago, about a series of seemingly unconnected disappearances. However, each disappearance was preceded by a period of out-of-character behaviour by the victim. After the first few the Guardians assumed people were being abducted or murdered. But there were never any witnesses, no ransoms were ever received and no obvious suspects were found.

Eventually they had found a pattern and from there tracked down a key witness. The hunt for the Flesh Mage began in earnest. Thankfully, due to his father's ability to see through her disguises with his magic, they found the Flesh Mage before she'd transformed into someone else.

From the moment the woman was caught and put into a cell she never spoke a single word. That changed when Fray's father used his magic to look at her again.

Her features changed dramatically, moving from a bland stare to one of wonder. Just as I'd never seen an ability like hers before, she admitted with delight that my magic was completely new to her. She agreed to answer my questions, but only if I answered one of hers each time in return. There seemed little harm since she had an appointment with the hangman in a few days. Anything she learned about my magic would go no further.

She named herself as a Flesh Mage and admitted that she had been taught this ability, although she would not name her teacher. When I suggested it had been someone at the Red Tower her contempt was palpable. The passion and joy with which she described her magic and the feeling it gave her was like that of a black crystal addict. To her, it was the greatest feeling in the world and she couldn't be without it. She would do anything to feel that way again.

Looking on her with my magic, I saw a complete absence of light. Every other person is filled with a rainbow of colours, but her whole body was nothing but a featureless landscape. She could not explain this to me as she'd not known until I had described it to her. Even now I am at a loss to explain it.

It reminded me of an old story from the book of the Maker about evil creatures stealing people's souls and consuming them as they didn't have one of their own.

I came away troubled after my first meeting with her. There was so much more to this woman than it appeared. She was full of life, not some creature that ate the souls of her victims, and yet she was a remorseless murderer.

At our next meeting the following day I asked her more specific questions about her magic and her purpose in coming to Perizzi. She explained that her physical transformations were only possible by draining all energy from a living person, right down to the last drop of moisture. She had burned what little remained which explained why we never found the first few bodies.

The murders themselves were only a means to an end. The violent events were connected to her real goal. Despite understanding all of the words she used, I still can't explain how her magic works.

My father made the choice for me, keeping me hidden when the Seekers came to our village, to prevent them from taking me away. They could not bear the idea of being parted from me for ten years or more, missing out on large parts of my childhood. I never regretted his decision until this moment when I am faced with something I can barely comprehend. Perhaps if I had studied at the Red Tower I might be better prepared, but most likely I would not have become a Guardian or even lived in Perizzi.

I have made the same choice for Fray, because in the wake of my wife's death, the thought of being without him for years is one I cannot face. I hope that my son never experiences such a moment of confusion in the face of strange magic, but if he should, I hope that he forgives me.

Fray put down the pages for a minute and stared out the window at the sky. He wiped his face and took a few minutes before turning back to the journal.

The Flesh Mage was the spark that began each violent event. She shoved someone, spilt a drink, uttered an insult or even threw the first punch. Once it had begun all she had to do was sit back and wait, as without her influence the violence would spread. Then she fed on the raw emotions from those around her, filling her up to the brim before releasing it back into the crowd. At this point the violence increased tenfold and she gorged herself again.

Somehow she was able to summon the most primal parts of a person, no matter how deeply buried, and bring them to the surface. She was very clear on that point and wanted me to understand she created nothing.

I have dealt with violent men and women for years, but in that time I have also met spiritual people who are incapable of harming another. The pessimistic voice in my head believes the Flesh Mage is right and that deep down we are all alike and capable of terrible violence in the right circumstances.

The optimist tells me she is wrong. On good days it is easy to ignore the inner cynic, but there are times when the optimist is drowned out by the cruelty I see people inflict upon each other without reason.

It's late, I'm tired and rambling.

The end goal of the Flesh Mage is to absorb large amounts of this primal power and channel it to create a rift in the world. It will open onto a place beyond the Veil. She speaks about it as if it were simply opening a doorway to another room, but she cannot explain to me where this other place is, or what it is.

She could not tell me how many lives it would cost to open such a doorway, only that she came very close on her last attempt before she was captured. Eighty-seven people died and hundreds more were exposed to some of the darkest corners of their soul. Some of them committed cruel acts upon strangers and friends that they must somehow find a way to live with and justify what happened.

Such a thing could not be ignored or swept under the rug. The Queen and the Old Man have agreed to distribute a more palatable lie, an outbreak of a virulent disease that caused hallucinations. Some will be able to swallow the story and go on with their lives as if nothing has changed. My fear is that, in time, others will begin to see through the lie and I cannot imagine what might happen then.

Many times I asked her why she was attempting to open a doorway and each time her answer worried me greatly. To my surprise she asked me about my faith and truthfully I told her that I followed the Maker. She held nothing but contempt for all of the Gods. She claims they are dead and we pray to nothing more than ghosts of old powers that abandoned humanity long ago. Sensing my disbelief she asked me to show her any proof of the Gods in the last thousand years. She wanted me to point at some miracle, some clear indication of divine intervention that proved their existence. I could not come up with any and my retort about faith not requiring proof was met with derisive laughter.

The Flesh Mage claimed that she regularly prayed to her God. While not unusual in itself the most disturbing part was her claim that her God answered. Despite asking her several times she would not name her God, but she did tell me that he had been banished long ago. By opening this doorway he would be able to return to our world for the first time in ten thousand years.

I have searched through the archives, consulted with a dozen historians and theologians, spoken to several priests and yet none of them can find a reference anywhere to such a celestial myth.

This leaves me with three possibilities. First, that she is mad and the voice that answers her prayers exists only in her head. While it is possible I think it unlikely. My instincts tell me not all of it is in her head.

The second option is that the religious experts are ignorant, but this seems the most unlikely. This leaves me with the third option, which is that something is talking to her, but I do not believe it to be a God. Stories of demons exist in every piece of scripture, from the Maker to the Blessed Mother to the old pagan faiths. They are always said to live elsewhere, sometimes beyond the Veil, and they demand blood sacrifice and violence being committed in their name.

I believe something monstrous, and not of this world, is speaking to the Flesh Mage and if she had continued unchecked, she may have succeeded in bringing it into our world.

Fray's stomach rumbled but he ignored it and focused on the last entry connected to this case.

The Flesh Mage is to be hanged at dawn for her crimes. When asked if she wanted anything she asked to see me one last time before the end. Spending time in her company is becoming more difficult, because after each visit I realise how little she cares for other people. However, I am still curious about who she really is, where she came from and who made her this way. I do not believe she was always so callous and indifferent about murder. The number of bodies we recovered has been counted and we estimate two hundred and twelve people died as a result of her actions.

As on all of my previous visits we traded answers. I have never spoken to anyone at such length about how my magic works, what it can do and the limits I am still exploring. Her impending death had not stunted her inquisitive nature and she pressed me for more details.

I will not be there in the morning to watch her hang. I cannot bear to look upon her sweet-natured face any more. Up to now I have avoided describing her appearance because it is too difficult to bring together the crimes she has committed with the innocent young woman I see looking back at me, chained to a wall by wrists and ankles. It is not until you look deep into her eyes that you can see the hollow space where her conscious, perhaps her soul, should be.

Tomorrow at dawn they will hang her until she is dead and then burn the body. There will be no marker of remembrance to denote her passing. She will be nameless but never forgotten.

The date on the next ripped-out entry was from five years ago, just three months before his father had died. Fray put the pages down for a minute and made a short trip to a nearby tavern, managing to grab some food before they closed for the night. The day had been hot and unpleasant but now much needed cool air was blowing in from the sea, giving everyone in the city a little relief. Fray took his time walking home, trying to clear his head and prepare himself.

By the time he reached home and sat down again with the torn journal pages, some of the candle stubs had burned out. He moulded the still warm wax together and created a multi-coloured monstrosity that would provide light for a little while longer.

The final journal entries began like the others, with precise handwriting and a structured approach. A fight in a dockside bar had turned from rowdy, which wasn't unusual, to one where eleven men were killed. Witnesses reported the men turning vicious like rabid dogs, tearing into each other with every weapon available including their nails and teeth. Blood was sprayed all over the walls and ceiling, and bits of bone and innards were scattered across the floor.

I went over the bar looking for something to explain their behaviour, but found nothing. The brutal nature of the murders was not something I had seen in a long time. Even before I asked everyone to leave the room and embraced my magic, I knew what I'd find. For a moment, when I saw the echo of magic clinging to the pieces of dead men scattered about the room, I thought that somehow she had returned. That somehow she had cheated death or escaped the hangman and we'd killed someone else in her place.

After a little while I realised that although the residue was similar there was a difference. This had been the work of a Flesh Mage, but it was someone else.

Once we knew that another Flesh Mage was involved the Khevassar made missing person cases a priority. I'm ashamed to say that because of the size of Perizzi, and the number of people coming and going each day, a lot of people go missing. We look into them when we can, but now they are as important as the violent event at the bar.

Once again a pattern began to emerge, where victims exhibited unusual behaviour before disappearing, but this time we started finding the bodies. They were dry husks, like ancient remains, rather than people who had died only a few days before. Despite knowing what was responsible and even a little about how it was done, it was difficult to find the Flesh Mage. If the pattern of escalation was to be identical then we anticipated a violent event on a grander scale, but we had no way of knowing where it would occur. Guardians and members of the Watch were stationed at the largest of gatherings around the city, including the music hall, the markets and the largest churches.

Despite our best efforts we didn't anticipate the next move. Seven Zecorran women were killed by a local Yerskani man. Witnesses reported hearing him screaming racial insults as he gutted them with a knife. It took five members of the Watch to restrain him. At first we didn't even realise the Flesh Mage was responsible. Two days later a group of merchants from Seveldrom were murdered by a Drassi mercenary for no reason. More incidents followed and with each unexplainable attack tension in the city began to mount.

The first Flesh Mage had used her power to turn people into brutal creatures. With each attack her strength increased and the scale of the events grew. This time the Flesh Mage is letting others do the work for him as racial divisions threaten to tear the city apart. When that happens the Flesh Mage will feed on the violence and magnify the effects. If the goal is the same, then the Flesh Mage will open a doorway to some other place, perhaps some other world, and whatever is on the other side will cross the threshold.

If the Flesh Mage succeeds I believe the death toll would be catastrophic.

Fray noticed the usually neat handwriting of his father had changed over the last few pages. Towards the end it was starting to become illegible, suggesting it had been written at speed or that his father's hands had been trembling. Either way it told Fray his father had been afraid. With hands that wouldn't stop shaking, Fray turned to the last journal entry, which was very short.

It's happening tonight. Every member of the Watch and every Guardian will be on duty patrolling the streets, doing their best to keep the city calm. The Queen has called in the army, but they will only be deployed if the situation gets out of hand.

I should be out there, but the Old Man has me sitting here, waiting for the first murder. The Flesh Mage will be close by and then it will be up to me to stop it, before everyone in the city is ripped apart by friends and family.

I have so many regrets, so many things I wish I had said, but I'm out of time.

I was always proud of you, Fray, and I love you.

Fray dropped the pages and began to weep.

CHAPTER 27

Just as she'd done a few nights ago, Katja followed Rodann's directions to the abandoned temple. She hadn't known it was a temple on her last visit, but had since looked into the worn-out building. Long ago it had been dedicated to an old God, one whose name no one remembered. Over the decades it had been rented by various people, merchants, a group of scribes, a silversmith, countless others, but they never settled for long and the building constantly changed hands.

A few months ago someone had bought it, but so far Roza's contacts couldn't tell her who owned the building. Katja suspected the mysterious benefactor behind Rodann and Teigan had arranged it.

Whether it was imagined or real Katja believed someone had been following her since leaving the shop. She'd taken extra precautions, doubling back several times and going in a long circuitous route, until she felt confident she'd lost them. Even so, something niggled at the back of her mind.

Shrugging off the feeling as nothing more than paranoia she knocked on the door, one hand on her dagger in case of trouble. As before, Teigan answered the door and carefully locked it before leading Katja to the comfortable room at the end of the corridor. This time as they passed by the storage rooms Katja

looked more closely at the worn statues, but despite her knowledge of religious texts nothing looked familiar.

As before, the room at the end of the hall was kept warm with
glowing embers in the fireplace but the heat didn't touch Katja.
A chill ran down her spine as she crossed the threshold and her
eyes came to rest on a spot in front of the fire where the baker
had died. Where she had murdered a man. It wasn't the first life
she'd taken, but his face wouldn't leave her thoughts.

Rodann sat at a table off to one side with Faith and he gestured for Katja to join them. He drained the last of some soup
and mopped up the dregs with a hunk of bread. To Katja's surprise Teigan sat down at the table as well. Faith regarded
everyone coolly over a glass of red wine. The smell of it, and the
soup, turned Katja's stomach and she tasted bile. To see them
eating and drinking as if nothing of consequence had happened
in the room made her feel sick. The ample cushions on the chair
did little to relieve her discomfort and she sat upright. All of it
served as a reminder that despite any words to the contrary she
was not among friends and their work did not serve the greater
good.

"Faith told me what you did with the nobles," said Rodann
as he washed down the bread with a gulp of ale. "Very impres-
sive. Lord and Lady Venarra were convinced. They still have no
idea why you were really there."

"That's good news," said Katja. "Do I need to go and see them
again?"

"No, I don't think so," said Rodann before looking at Faith
expectantly. "Shouldn't you be on your way?"

"No," said Faith, calmly sipping her wine. "Actually I'm not
moving from this chair until you explain what all of this is for."

"We've spoken about this. We're helping to—" said Rodann
but Faith cut him off.

"Save your platitudes and talk of the greater good. I'm not a dullard like the penny-pinching nobles, or that shrew Marcella and her lump of a husband."

Teigan glared and started to reach for her sword but Faith froze her with an icy stare. "And you can stop your pathetic posturing, Teigan. I'm not intimidated by your bulging muscles and pea-sized brain."

"I'll fucking gut you," snarled Teigan, starting to draw her sword. Rodann jumped to his feet and shoved Teigan back, while Faith watched them both with a bored expression. Teigan continued to twitch and snarl but Rodann slowly talked her down until eventually she sheathed her sword.

Faith sighed dramatically and rolled her eyes at Katja, who offered a brief grin which vanished when Rodann returned to the table. Teigan stayed on her feet, leaning against the door, but Faith just shook her head at the feeble attempt to intimidate her.

"I'm not a cat's-paw for you to play with. You haven't paid me, you couldn't afford me and I wouldn't let you touch me for all the gold in Yerskania."

"No need to be spiteful," said Rodann, who'd lost some of his familiar arrogance.

"So we're clear, I'm here because I want to be," stressed Faith. "But if you don't tell me what we're doing, I'll leave and not return. While you may not miss me, I know you'll miss having access to my contacts. So, make your choice."

Faith didn't glance at the door, or the rather large woman stood in front of it, and didn't seem concerned about getting out of the room. Katja suddenly wondered what the escort had concealed beneath her expensive dress. Probably something nasty in case Teigan tried to get in the way.

"You're right," said Rodann. "I have been treating you like the others and clearly you're a remarkable woman."

Faith's top lip curled into a sneer. "Save your flattery for someone who needs it. Just tell me the truth."

"All right," he said, holding up a hand towards Teigan, who had started to protest. "We need her and she can keep a secret."

"Fine, but Katja leaves," said Teigan.

"She stays," said Faith, which surprised everyone, including Katja.

"May I ask why?" asked Rodann with exaggerated politeness.

"Because you need her too, and she's almost at the same place as me. You may as well just tell us both."

Rodann made a pretence of seeing to the fire, but he obviously needed a few minutes to think things through. Once the fire had been built up he returned to his seat and poured himself another mug of ale. Katja declined his offer as her stomach was still churning.

"Queen Talandra of Seveldrom will shortly be arriving here for a state visit. On the first night of her visit there will be a formal banquet in her honour." A tremor passed through Rodann's body, but Katja didn't know if it was a thrill of delight or anger held in check. It was also the first time he'd mentioned Talandra in one of their meetings. Katja realised she was holding her breath and slowly breathed out. "To free our people from the shackles of foreign interference, Queen Talandra must die."

Faith's cool façade cracked and she sat back in her chair with a shocked expression. Katja tried to look equally surprised as if she were hearing the news for the first time.

"Why?" asked Katja. "Why kill Queen Talandra?"

Rodann stared at her as if she had asked why water was wet. "In many ways she's worse than Morganse. The west was united in peace, but she wouldn't join us and in doing so caused the war."

"Taikon was a mad man and a butcher," said Faith. "It was a mockery of peace." Rodann started to protest but Faith held up a hand, cutting him off. "We could argue all day about that, but right now it doesn't matter. The war happened and now he's dead. You cannot change the past. So why kill Talandra now?"

"Because we lost," snapped Rodann, grinding his teeth. "And we're still paying the price."

Faith looked as confused as Katja felt. "What price?" Katja asked, a second ahead of the escort.

"What normally happens when someone loses a war and sur-renders?" asked Rodann, his tone bordering on this being a lecture.

"Reparations are paid and treaties are signed."

"Exactly. And where are they? Money was paid to Seveldrom, but what about the treaties?" he asked, and neither Katja nor Faith had an answer. "Do you really think the Queen of Seveldrom would make the long journey to Perizzi on a whim? She's here to check up on her growing empire."

Faith arched an eyebrow. "Talandra rules Yerskania?"

"Morganse sits on her throne only at Seveldrom's behest. That was the price of surrender after the war. Morganse is nothing more than a puppet for Talandra. Yerskania has always been a nation that has dealt with others, but we've never been their sub-jects. Morganse is weak and not fit to rule. She was given her throne back only because Talandra allowed it. Seveldrom must be shown that we are our own people and we must have some-one worthy sitting on the throne."

There was a form of twisted logic to Rodann's words. Katja could see how some might believe the lies. After all, Morganse had stepped down from the throne when her son was threatened. But his idea that Yerskania was secretly being ruled by Talandra seemed ridiculous, and yet he had convinced at least a dozen people that it was true.

"So, you want to kill both Queens during Talandra's state visit?"

"Yes."

Katja looked at Teigan for confirmation that Rodann hadn't lost his mind. She met Katja's gaze for a second and in that look she saw the depth of the warrior's commitment. Teigan believed in this cause absolutely and would die trying to see it happen.

"A bold move," said Faith. "Incredibly stupid though. By killing Morganse all you're going to do is create chaos and probably trigger another war."

"Ahhh," said Rodann and some of the smugness returned to his demeanour. "But if the blame were to fall squarely on Seveldrom's shoulders, well ..." he said with a shrug and left the rest unspoken.

Most people primarily blamed the Zecorrans for the war as it was their Mad King who had united the west with the help of the Warlock. It wasn't that simple or easy, but people just needed someone to blame. It was why Zecorrans now travelled in groups and merchants always used Drassi mercenaries as guards. But there was still an undercurrent of hatred in Yerskania towards Seveldrom for killing so many of its soldiers during the war. The early massacre had been orchestrated by Taikon, but it was Seveldrom that had wielded the swords.

"There will be chaos for a while, and unfortunately some innocent lives will be lost," admitted Rodann. "But the west will unite against a common enemy. Seveldrom must be taught they cannot interfere in our sovereign affairs. As the heart of the west, Yerskania will need a worthy new leader to make urgent decisions. One who is worthy of wearing the crown."

Whoever Rodann was working for wanted to sit on the throne, but in a city littered with nobles where many of them had viable claims, it would take a long time to identify his benefactor. Even so, it gave Katja a starting point.

She also noticed he kept saying someone who was worthy, and Katja didn't think Rodann measured worth by their deeds. They would need considerable wealth, and Yerskania had only half a dozen families that could trace their lineage back to the founding of the capital. Their claim would have to be a strong one.

"Who are you working for?" asked Katja, but Rodann just grinned at her.

"Once Morganse is gone a number of supporters will speak out in favour of my benefactor taking their rightful position on the throne. Some of the nobility will also add their voices to the cause, like Lord and Lady Venarra."

"Will we ever get to meet her?" asked Katja, knowing she had a one in two chance of guessing the gender of his benefactor.

Rodann offered another of his annoying grins. "Maybe, one day." He hadn't corrected her, which could mean something, or was he just playing with her?

"Why kill Queen Talandra at the palace?" asked Faith. "Why not on the road?"

"It must be here, to ensure there are witnesses who will help point the finger at Seveldrom. It will happen in such a way that there will be no doubt as to who is responsible."

"You're still not telling us everything," said Faith. "Where are you getting your information?"

Rodann crossed his arms and leaned back in his chair. "I receive orders the same as you and there are some things I won't share. If that's a problem you're free to leave."

"Fine," said Faith. "I still think you're deluded, but I'm curious to see where this goes, so I'll stay."

"What about you?" asked Rodann, turning his attention to Katja. "Are you still with us?"

"You said some innocent lives will be lost. It will be a lot more than a few."

Rodann shrugged. "The price of freedom is steep. I'd rather die trying to free my country than live under the boot heel of someone else."

Katja drew her dagger, pulled Rodann across the table and put the blade against his throat. "If you're keen to die, I'm happy to oblige."

Rodann's eyes widened but he waved Teigan back and Katja heard her step away.

"I'm not ready to die, just yet."

"And yet you assume much by speaking for others. Who are you to decide their fate?" asked Katja, pushing the steel just a little harder until it drew blood.

"I'm just the catalyst," said Rodann, doing his best to stay absolutely still.

"You're not doing this for the greater good. You're doing it for yourself. So what do you get in return?"

Rodann shrugged, a tiny lift of his shoulders. "I've faithfully served the Crown for years. The only reward is what I'm rightfully due."

Katja shoved him away from her in disgust and sheathed her blade.

"What did you expect?" said Faith. "Everyone is selfish. Everyone wants something. Revenge, money, power. Why are *you* here?"

"I'm not sure any more," said Katja, shaking her head. The room was starting to feel too hot and small. Pain was blossoming behind her eyes.

"Your compassion is a strength but also a weakness," said Rodann, dabbing at the tiny cut on his throat with a cloth. "I ask you to put it aside until the worst is over. After that I'm sure we could find you a position and put it to good use to help the people."

"Once this is over, I never want to see you again."

"Fine, but I assume that means you're still with us. Time is short, and we don't have long to get everything in place."

"So what do you want me to do now?"

"It's time we utilised your network of contacts," said Rodann.

Katja's heart skipped a beat. Her hand crept back towards her dagger. "My what?"

"We didn't recruit you because of your knowledge about religion, although that has proven useful," said Rodann. "We chose you because of the people you've dealt with. All of them have come to you in their darkest hour, when they were at their most vulnerable. They lean on you, talk to you and ask you for all sorts of favours. They pay you for your silence. Now it's time to ask them for a favour in return."

"And if they won't help us?"

"I'm sure you can think of a way to motivate them," said Rodann with a villainous grin.

CHAPTER 28

Munroe felt out of her depth but she did her best not to show her unease. She'd tried to appear mean and intimidating, but quickly gave up on the idea when it made her look constipated. She sighed and wondered again why she'd agreed to do this. She also wondered why Don Jarrow had asked her instead of Vargus to accompany him.

Part of her knew she should be excited by the change, as this wasn't her usual job, but the tail-end of a hangover still niggled at the back of her brain. Every time they passed a rowdy tavern she wanted to stop off and have a couple of whiskies to ease her head, but Don Jarrow had forbidden it. He hadn't given her an order as such, but he had indicated how disappointed he'd be if she were drunk and not at her best for the meeting. It made sense, but she didn't have to like it.

A few paces ahead Don Jarrow walked with purpose, his shaggy head constantly moving as his eyes swept the streets for signs of trouble. Munroe remembered she was supposed to be doing the same, given that she was the Don's bodyguard for the night. The only thing she saw was people averting their eyes and sometimes changing direction to move away from Don Jarrow. The man had a fierce reputation and although they were no longer on his turf people knew better than to interfere in his business. He carried no visible weapons but she knew him to be a cautious man. She thought he had a short sword strapped to his leg. Either that or the rumours were true after all.

Munroe shook herself and tried to focus. She still had no idea why the Don had chosen her instead of Vargus or the grisly Daxx for protection. There were fifty people more qualified, but not even his wife had been able to change his mind.

"We're almost there," said Don Jarrow over his shoulder. "Keep your eyes open."

Munroe bit the inside of her mouth to stop herself from pointing out that she had to keep her eyes open to see where she was going. Another sarcastic retort bubbled up and she bit down harder until the pain made her wince.

They turned a corner and at the end of the street the roof of the arena came into view. Munroe's thoughts immediately turned to Choss. She'd not seen him since that night at the Emerald Dragon. She vaguely remembered their conversation and that he'd been quite sombre, which was unusual. Part of her recalled she'd made a pass at him, but the details kept slipping away. She would have to pay him a visit at home, if she made it out of this meeting alive.

Munroe liked spending time with Choss and missed his gentle heart and his self-assurance. Some people were so uncomfortable in their own skin, so afraid of what thoughts might occur, they couldn't sit quietly for five minutes. They had to fill the air with meaningless words, say anything to distract themselves from deeper thought. Choss knew exactly who he was and, more importantly, who she really was. She didn't have a connection like that with anyone else.

A massive bald man with tiny ears stood guard at the door to the arena. A dozen jokes sprang to mind and Munroe had to bite her mouth again. If this continued all night she'd bite a hole in her cheek.

"Jakka," said Don Jarrow. The big man studied them carefully, raising one eyebrow slightly when he spotted Munroe, but she gave him a look, daring him to say something. Instead he let them inside without saying a word and she blew him a kiss as she went past.

She followed Don Jarrow between the rows of seats towards the ring at the centre of the arena. The ropes had been taken down from around the edge and a table and five chairs set up in the middle of the raised platform. Two of the other heads of Families had already arrived and were making small talk while their bodyguards glared at one another.

Doña Parvie wore the same grubby leathers as always and her long greasy black hair looked as if it hadn't been washed this year. Parvie and her twin sister were ghastly creatures who relished violence in all its forms. They also had fewer morals than a cutthroat who'd steal the gold teeth from their dead grandmother's mouth before the body was cold. But there was a sly rat-like cunning about her that enabled her to stay one step ahead of other people.

Doña Parvie lounged idly on her chair, but her beady eyes never stopped moving. When she saw Don Jarrow she sat upright and her burly bodyguard flexed his muscles. Munroe had never met him before but she knew the type. Huge muscles, except where it counted, and a cabbage for a brain. He glared at everyone but completely dismissed Munroe, which made her hands twitch.

The other Don looked as if he'd wandered in by accident. Don Lowell looked and dressed like someone's grandfather, with wispy grey hair, round glasses and a kind face with so many wrinkles he resembled a piece of crumpled paper. He smiled often and with genuine warmth, but he was also known to smile as he watched people being butchered and fed to his dogs. Behind Don Lowell stood a scarred woman with a face only her mother could love. It looked as if someone had repeatedly hit it with a shovel until all of her features were flat. Worst of all was her eyes. There was nothing inside, just two black holes as if she were already dead.

"Ah, Don Jarrow," said Don Lowell, getting up slowly and warmly greeting his competitor as if they were friends, or perhaps father and son. No one knew how old Don Lowell actually was, but he played up the part of being the most senior. He'd probably outlive everyone, just to be spiteful. "Come, join us."

Don Jarrow glanced at Doña Parvie, who just grinned, showing a set of yellow teeth which she'd had sharpened to points.

"And who is this lovely young lady?" said Don Lowell. Munroe felt his gaze settle on her as if it had actual weight. His eyes moved over her in a way that made her skin crawl, and when he looked towards Don Jarrow she couldn't repress a shudder. "Not your usual. Is Vargus unwell?"

"He's fine," said Don Jarrow. "This is Munroe."

"Ah, the infamous Munroe," said Don Lowell. She didn't know which disturbed her more, the way he said her name or that he knew who she was. "Perhaps I could persuade you to come and work for me. I'll double whatever you're being paid."

Don Jarrow had told her this might happen and that she had to be nice.

"That's generous, but no thanks," she managed to say.

Doña Parvie laughed, a nasty snuffling sound like a rutting pig. "I wouldn't pay two copper pennies for her. She couldn't protect a warm cup of piss."

"Is that what he's for? Guarding your piss bucket?" said Munroe, jerking her chin towards the muscle-bound idiot behind Doña Parvie.

"Otto can do a lot more than that."

"I'm sure. He looks very ... dense," said Munroe, remembering that she wasn't supposed to provoke anyone. Otto glared at her and took a step forward, which was probably supposed to be threatening. Munroe just rolled her eyes and ignored him.

"Don't," said Don Lowell, giving Doña Parvie a warning shake of his head.

"Why are you all afraid of this little whore? Otto could snap her like a twig."

"What did you call me, you skanky cunt?" asked Munroe. Technically she was the daughter of a whore, but that wasn't the point.

"Otto, teach her some manners," said Doña Parvie. Otto took another step towards her and Munroe pointed a finger at his chest. He stopped suddenly, expecting a weapon, but when she didn't produce any steel he grinned inanely. Otto took one more step and then collapsed on his back, choking and grabbing his chest as his heart and lungs started to burn. Doña Parvie looked at the others for some help, but everyone was watching Otto turn purple.

"That's enough," said Don Jarrow and Munroe relented, withdrawing her curse. Otto fell unconscious but his face returned to its normal colour. Doña Parvie stooped down to check he was still breathing but left him on the ground. She glared at Munroe with murder in her eyes.

"It looks like I missed all the fun," said a rich, cultured voice, which broke the tension.

Tonight the Duchess wore an emerald silk dress edged with white lace and a swooping neckline that revealed a generous portion of her cleavage. Munroe wished hers were a little bigger, like the Duchess's, but then again she'd probably look weird with a small body and giant tits constantly pulling her off balance. At least the Duchess had the build to carry them. Her luscious red hair was gathered on top of her head revealing an elegant long neck and gold earrings with red stones at their heart. A simple

silver chain and a tiny locket was her only other piece of jewellery, but she didn't need gold to turn heads. Munroe had seen
a lot of women during her time at the Emerald Dragon and the
Duchess pissed all over the others in terms of natural beauty. Not
that the Duchess would actually piss on someone, unless that was
her kind of thing.

The two Dons politely rose from their seats as she climbed the
steps to the ring, while Doña Parvie just rolled her eyes and spat
onto the floor. Behind the Duchess was a tall Seve man with a
shaven head and keen blue eyes. His build was lean compared to
the others, but he walked with a certain grace Munroe had seen
in dancers.

The two Dons waited until the Duchess had sat down before
retaking their seats. The Duchess was first cousin to Queen
Morganse, putting her about fifth in line to the throne. She lived
among the nobility and yet none of them knew that all of her
wealth came from running one of the city's crime Families.

"Always lovely to see you gentlemen," said the Duchess, completely ignoring Parvie.

"Sorry to hear about your cousin getting his balls chopped
off," said Parvie, feigning concern about the Crown Prince. "Still,
it does mean you're one step closer to the throne."

"Where is our fifth?" asked the Duchess, not rising to the bait.

"Here," said the raspy voice of Don Kalbensham, who stalked
towards them with a strange grace. Morrin weren't like other
people. They had all of their bits in the same places, at least on
the outside, but they were a different breed. When Munroe
stared into a Morrin's eyes she had no idea of what they were
thinking. That wasn't to say they couldn't be nice, but Don Kal
wasn't the best specimen to represent his people. The Morrin was
at least twice as old as everyone, including Don Lowell, but he
moved like a man in his thirties. The only clues about his age
were the small patches of white hair among the brown. Long

before Don Jarrow had cheated, murdered and bludgeoned people to take control of a Family, Don Kal had been here in Perizzi, selling flesh and drugs.

Walking behind Don Kal was another over-muscled specimen like Otto, who stared at the others with open hostility. The Morrin took his seat and everyone looked at Don Jarrow expectantly.

"I think you all know why I requested this meeting," said Don Jarrow.

Just as he was about to continue something whistled through the air, making everyone look around. A meat cleaver landed in the middle of the table with a thunk as it bit into the wood. All of the bodyguards drew their weapons and put their backs to the table.

"I assume my invitation was mislaid," said a man as he calmly walked towards them. One look at him and Munroe knew exactly who he was. So did everyone else by their expressions. The Butcher was taller than she'd expected, a burly Seve dressed only in trousers and a white leather vest which showed off well-built arms and shoulders. An intricate black tattoo of swirls and knots ran up his left arm into his vest and came out down his right, ending at the wrist.

Don Lowell touched his bodyguard on the hip and she lowered her weapon. Slowly the others followed suit but kept them drawn. The Butcher picked up a chair from the front row and dragged it up to the table. He sat down and nodded amiably to the others as if they'd been expecting him.

The Butcher didn't seem worried by the armed bodyguards who were watching his every breath for the first hint of violence. The Dons just stared and not even Doña Parvie had anything to say. In fact, Munroe thought she looked afraid. After all it was her territory that the Butcher had cut into to create his own little empire. Also, the majority of people who'd been found hacked into neat packages of meat like cuts of beef had belonged to her.

"Welcome," said the Duchess, almost without stuttering. "Don Jarrow was just about to talk about the reason for this meeting."

"Ah, yes, the lethal venthe. Nasty stuff," said the Butcher, nodding his shaven head. Munroe tried to fix his features in her mind so that she would recognise him later but they were unremarkable. She'd probably seen him in the past and not realised because he was neither handsome nor ugly. If not for his dramatic entrance and the cleaver, she wouldn't have known who he was.

"The venthe killed over thirty people and several fighters in one night," said Don Jarrow. "And we all know where it came from."

All eyes fell on Don Kal but he didn't squirm under their scrutiny and his face gave nothing away.

"Where is your proof? Show me?"

Don Jarrow smiled in a way that made several people shift uneasily. Munroe pulled on her gloves and unwrapped the cloth bundle on her back. The gnarled venthe plant thumped onto the table beside the Butcher's cleaver.

"This was taken from one of your warehouses in the meat district," said Don Jarrow. "There would have been more, but unfortunately the building burned to the ground."

"That was an unfortunate accident," said Don Kal.

"And the venthe farm inside?" asked the Duchess. "Do you deny that was yours?"

"One of my people must have been growing it. I knew nothing about it."

"Come now," said Don Lowell, trying to be amicable. "We can all move on if we just put this in the past. Assure us that the rest of this batch has been destroyed and then business can go back to normal."

Munroe noticed sweat trickling down the sides of Don Kal's narrow face. "I knew nothing about it," insisted the Morrin.

"My people tell me otherwise," said the Duchess. "They saw you leaving the warehouse just before the fire."

"You were spying on me? On my turf?" said Don Kal. Munroe thought he sounded aghast, but it was hard to tell.

"Yes, yes. We've all done this for years," said Don Lowell. "You spy on me, I spy on the Duchess. Round and round it goes. Has all of the venthe been destroyed?"

"I will not sit here and be accused by you," said Don Kal getting to his feet. "Someone in my Family was responsible for this. I will find them and they will be dealt with. It is not a matter for you to interfere in."

With that he stormed out of the arena.

"Did anyone believe him?" asked the Butcher, crossing his arms. No one rushed to defend the Morrin.

"Something needs to be done about it," said Don Lowell. "He puts us all at risk."

"I vote we kill him and cut up his turf," said Doña Parvie, looking around the table for supporters. "More for all of us."

"Killing him would only anger his people and start a war," said the Duchess, dismissing the idea with a wave of her hand.

"Whatever Don Kal's original purpose for the new venthe, it failed. It's lethal and must be destroyed or it will continue to cause problems for us all," said Don Jarrow. No one wanted more squads of the Watch trooping through their territory, or worse the Guardians digging into every crime, turning every building inside out for clues. That kind of scrutiny would drive away customers and cost all of the Families a lot of money.

"We all have eyes and ears," said the Duchess. "It wouldn't take much to find out the location of his other venthe farms."

"A coordinated strike," mulled Don Lowell. "On the strict agreement that this is only to remove him from the venthe business, not claim territory." The old man stared at Doña Parvie and she showed her pointed teeth, but eventually grunted in agreement.

"If we all send people to take out one or two farms at the same time, he won't risk attacking us all in retaliation," said Don Jarrow and the others agreed.

"I know I'm new at this compared to some, but aren't you risking a war?" asked the Butcher.

"Don Kalbensham is many things, but he's not a rash man," said the Duchess. "He will pout and sulk for a while, but he won't attack us. He can't. He doesn't have the numbers."

"He's very patient," said Don Lowell. "I've seen him wait a decade before settling a score. Time moves at a different pace for the Morrin."

"But the rest of us have to live in a world where we don't live for two hundred years," said Doña Parvie. "If we're going to do this we need to hit him soon."

For once she was talking sense and no one disagreed.

"Tomorrow, or the night after at the latest," said Don Jarrow.

"Agreed," said the others.

"One thing," said Don Lowell. "I don't want to see any of your people getting involved," he said to the Butcher.

"Why not?"

"You might sit at this table, but you're not one of us. I don't trust the others, but if they give me their word I know they'll stick to it. I have no idea what you'll do." The old man suddenly didn't look so kindly and Munroe saw some of the steel beneath his deceptively soft exterior. She managed to repress a shudder this time.

"I agree with Don Lowell," said the Duchess. "While we're burning down venthe farms you could be expanding your territory. If you move against one of us, we will all retaliate in kind."

"So keep your fucking hands off," spat Doña Parvie, clearly

still stinging from having some of her turf taken over by the Butcher.

The Butcher smiled at Doña Parvie like a cat staring at a mouse but to her credit she didn't look away.

"We'll be watching," said Don Jarrow, drawing the Butcher's attention.

"As you wish," said the Butcher, getting to his feet. "I'll stay out of this, but next time there's a meeting, make sure I receive an invitation."

He yanked the cleaver out of the table with one hand and sauntered away. Munroe could admit it to herself, even if none of the others would say it aloud. The Butcher scared her and had rattled the others. Between him, creepy old Don Lowell and making a new enemy in Doña Parvie, Munroe hoped this was her first and last meeting.

Not for the first time Munroe wondered what she was doing with her life and how she could escape her prison.

CHAPTER 29

Fray spent the morning training with the other novice Guardians and for them nothing had changed. If anyone noticed that he was pushing himself harder than normal they made no comment.

At lunch in the mess hall he sat alone and although he was hungry he barely tasted the food. Fray's mind kept going over what he'd read in his father's journal. He had always thought his father had written the journals as a way of exorcising some of the darkness inside by committing it to the page. Throughout the many notebooks he'd read, the tone of voice had never changed. The Khevassar had known the truth from the beginning. They had been written for Fray, to guide him if he ever became a Guardian.

After lunch Fray would normally have gone out on patrol with Byrne, but when he approached the Old Man's office his assistant had a note for him. Fray would be assigned a new partner tomorrow and for the remainder of the day he was to go home and rest.

At first he was angry at being dismissed like a child, but then he was glad for the time to be alone with his thoughts.

As Fray headed for home he passed a few squads of the Watch and each time they made note of his presence. A smile, or a little wave to indicate his status. Once again he was part of the city and its people, and yet now he was a member of another group that sat apart from others.

Just over a year ago his magic had forced him to the fringes, to hide in the shadows and do his best to go unnoticed. Now, because of the uniform, the opposite happened and Fray couldn't walk down a street without drawing attention. It was rarely negative, but never overtly friendly as no one offered to buy him a drink or wanted to stop and chat. If you saw a Guardian, then it usually meant something bad had happened.

Part of Fray wanted to rip off his uniform and just blend into one of the crowds. To walk through a group of people without anyone staring. To drink and sing and feel part of a community. Suddenly he understood how much his father must have cherished coming home to his family every night. A safe and welcoming place where they were always happy to see him and didn't dread the uniform. Fray believed that the other Guardians would offer him friendship over time, but it wasn't the same. Coming home was a feeling that he struggled to describe, even to himself. It had been lacking from his life for a long time.

For once when the narrow stairs that led up to his tiny rooms came into view Fray wasn't dismayed by the sight. He locked and bolted the door, lit a few candles and found some comfort in the familiarity of his surroundings, if not the ringing silence that echoed in his ears. He considered just going to sleep for a few hours but his mind was whirling with so many questions. Instead he pulled out his father's journals and started to read them again from the beginning. This time, because he knew they had been written for him, he saw each entry in a different light.

After a few hours Fray knew that the journals would only get him so far. His father wasn't here to help him but he was not without contacts who could offer advice.

Moving to the window he painted a symbol for the Maker on

the glass with the red paint Eloise had provided. Many people had small shrines in corners of their home dedicated to their faith, but the poorest simply painted their windows in the hope of receiving some blessing and protection. Fray drew the stylised hand that represented the Maker and set a candle in the window beside it.

For the next few hours he read his father's journals as he waited, but as the night stretched on, he dozed and finally slept. A strange tingling sensation across his scalp woke him and he sat up to find Eloise sat in the window.

"You've found another child," she said without preamble. Once again her rasping breath sounded incredibly loud.

"What happened to the boy? Where is he?" asked Fray, shaking off the remnants of sleep.

Eloise's masked face turned towards him, the metal glinting in the candlelight. She watched him in silence for a minute before answering. "He is safe. We asked him what he wanted and again he chose the Red Tower. He's on his way there with a group of merchants delivering supplies."

"Is that safe?" asked Fray, thinking of the accidents he'd heard about.

"We've taken precautions," said Eloise, waving a hand to brush the topic aside. "Where is the other child?"

"There isn't one. I need your help with something else."

"You want to hire me?" asked Eloise, and Fray sensed a smile behind the mask.

"No, I need you to help me stop a killer."

"That's a job for the Watch and the Guardians."

"You don't understand," said Fray and this time he fell silent for a time as he mulled over his decision. "Can I trust you?" he finally asked.

"I have kept your secret and many others. Whatever you share with me will remain private."

Despite her promise Fray still hesitated. Eventually he realised there was little choice. Part of him knew that already, or else he would not have painted the symbol on his window.

"You mentioned my father. You know he died just over five years ago, but do you know how or why?"

"No, the details have never been revealed."

"He died fighting a man called a Flesh Mage. Do you know what that is?" To his surprise Eloise shook her head. "It's a parasite. Someone who feeds on the life and raw energy of other people. Five years ago a Flesh Mage tried to open a doorway. A rift to somewhere beyond the Veil. Don't ask me how because I don't know. But he was communing with something on the other side that he, and others, believe is a God."

"It is not." Eloise's words brooked no argument. "And even if it were, allowing a being that powerful to cross over would be worse than any plague."

"Last time the death toll was in the hundreds and now it is happening again. Another Flesh Mage is threatening the city."

Starting at the beginning, from when Byrne had come into his shop, Fray told Eloise about what had happened in their investigation into the Flesh Mage. She sat in rapt silence throughout, never questioning the validity of what he told her.

"I need you to teach me about magic," he said in conclusion. "I need to know how it works so I can fight him and stop this."

"What you're asking is not something that can be taught overnight. There are many aspects to magic. It is not a single straight road."

"But isn't what I can do a form of magic?" asked Fray.

"Yes, but yours is a Talent that is incredibly rare. To you it's just like flexing a muscle. It would take me months of study to unravel how it's done, before I could try to mimic it."

"Months?"

"Why do you think the Red Tower takes in children as young

as possible? Control can be taught in a few weeks or less to prevent accidents. It takes years to master some aspects of magic. Every year new Talents are discovered that have to be unravelled before they can be safely taught to others."

Something clicked into place in Fray's head. "You healed the boy. I've never seen that before, but there are old stories of such things."

"It was lost for a long time. I learned how to heal in a very dark place," said Eloise with a catch in her throat.

"I don't have months or even weeks. We came close once, but the Flesh Mage slipped away. I need to find him."

"There is one thing I can teach you that may help," said Eloise, "but it will not be easy."

"I'm willing to try."

"Even if you don't know how something is done with magic, it can be unravelled."

"Show me," said Fray.

They practised for hours until the sun came up, by which time Fray's eyes were sandy and painful. But when Eloise left he could unravel her constructs two or three times out of ten. It wasn't much but at least he had a way of fighting back.

CHAPTER 30

Sol, the Flesh Mage, kept one eye on the ranting Don Kalben-sham and the other on the door. So far no one had bothered to investigate the noise, which suggested they'd been expecting it. Don Kal had been shouting for some time and Sol had barely been listening since the start.

Plans were in motion that could not be stopped and the normally long-sighted Morrin didn't seem to have the vision to let events play out. For one who had lived for over a century his patience seemed to be incredibly short these days.

Finally he started to wear himself out and flopped down in a chair.

"All of them, just gone," he lamented about the destruction of his venthe farms in one night. It had been a daring and dangerous attack but very thorough, as every stalk had been turned to ash, every guard killed and left for the crows.

"There's no choice, I'll have to take a step back and wait. Plant an old crop of venthe and go back to how it was before."

"You mean bowing and scraping to the other Families?" asked Sol.

Don Kal didn't rise to the bait. "I should never have listened to you. You're bad luck. Ever since the start you've made promises and none of your plans have worked."

"The arena didn't go quite as planned," admitted Sol. He'd miscalculated and the first strain of venthe had proven too strong, driving the fighter into a blood rage. However, it had proven useful in that it had given him a boost in power. He'd then fed all of that fury back to the crowd and increased his strength again.

"I want you out of here, Sol. It will take time to recover from this, maybe a few years, but I will grow strong again, because I'm a patient man."

"I'm getting very tired of your constant complaints," said Sol.

"This is still my house," said Don Kal. "You will leave now before I take offence."

When the guard didn't move towards them Don Kal finally turned around and stared at the silent man. "Escort him out of here."

The man made no move but he looked towards Sol for instruction.

"Some of your people have lost their faith in you," admitted Sol. "They belong to me now."

"One or two turncoats will change nothing," said the Morrin.

"I think it's time you became more proactive," said Sol. "Watch the door," he said to the guard as he moved towards the Morrin. Don Kal started to scream but Sol clamped one hand over his mouth as the guard moved to stand watch outside. Don Kal surprised him by producing a dagger but his arm lost all of its strength as Sol started to draw out his life force. The dagger clattered to the floor so instead he tried to shove Sol away, but it was already too late, they were joined and the process had begun. Energy flowed out of the Morrin, a trickle and then a river, as the years of life ahead were pulled from his body and channelled into Sol.

Blue veiny lines sprouted all across the Morrin's face, until it became more blue than white. His hair turned grey then white all over, the skin sagged on his face and his horns lost their sheen. The Morrin's body shuddered and then started to contract as all fluids evaporated. The skin on his face became tighter and tighter, the eyes shrinking in their sockets to tiny raisins, the hands twisting into claws. A final gasp escaped the dead Morrin's lips and once again Sol thought he saw something flickering at the edge of his vision, but he brushed it aside. His senses could not be trusted during this part of the process.

Finally there was nothing more to take. Sol stumbled back and then fell into a chair. The dry husk of Don Kal stared back at him from across the room. A skeletal husk dressed in clothes that sagged off a stick-thin figure.

The first wave of pain ran through Sol's head and he braced himself for the onslaught. Of course, it started in the skull, a twisting snapping sound as the bones came apart and his jaw broke. He bit down and muffled the first scream but knew it wouldn't last. As the first nodule of horn split his scalp Sol shrieked in agony and would have fallen to the floor if he'd not gripped the arms of the chair. Out of the corner of his eye he could see the guard had come back into the room and was staring in horror, his eyes wide with terror.

Another lance of pain ran down his spine and he felt it stretch and realign itself. His jaws stretched wider and wider, snapped again, and then stretched as his whole skull became longer and leaner. The pain became too much and soon he didn't know if he was screaming or not. All he remembered was seeing the colours in the room shifting from dull browns and blacks to a sea of red and blue. A popping sound followed by a rushing noise close to his ears came next, and somewhere nearby he could hear two heartbeats, one frantic and scared, the other slow and regular.

The frantic pounding of feet approached before the transformation was complete and he waved towards the door. The guard understood enough to quickly slip outside and try to delay them before the transformation was complete. Searing pain in his jaw told him it wasn't finished and he felt fresh teeth rip their way through his gums. A twisting sensation made him look up and the horns started to curl backwards and turn from black to a deep brown.

As his feet and spine swelled he started to choke, gagging and coughing before hunching forward and spitting out a wad of something red and black. He kicked it towards the fire where it sizzled for a few seconds, turning the fire blue. Raised voices came from outside the door as a crowd had gathered, drawn to the room by his tormented screams.

Finally the pain started to subside, but echoes of it remained, running down his spine and across the new edges of his skull. Without drawing power it would take weeks before they settled, months for the skull to harden.

Standing proved more difficult than anticipated but he managed to shuffle across the room and yank open the door, sticking his head out. Ten of Don Kal's Silver and Gold filled the hallway, all of them armed and angry, facing off against the guard. They all relaxed when they saw him.

"What's this?" asked Sol, his voice alien to his ears.

"We heard screaming, Don Kal," said a tall muscular woman with red hair. It took him a couple of seconds to retrieve her name.

"It's fine, Tandir. The Flesh Mage and I are having a disagreement. He no longer works for me." Sol made sure he didn't smile as he dismissed them with a wave. They started to disperse as he leaned on the doorframe, trying to get used to his new body. When they'd all gone he grabbed the guard's arm to keep himself upright.

"Put me in the chair," he gasped. The guard bore his weight easily, lowering him slowly into the chair.

Sol spent the next hour getting used to his body and into some of Don Kal's clothes while the guard disposed of the corpse. No one questioned him as he carried the wrapped body away and more than a few seemed pleased by the old Morrin taking a more active role. He made a note of who they were for later, as they would likely be more in favour of what came next.

Next he sent runners out to gather all of his Gold and Silver, as well as the Brass for a meeting that night. By the time they'd all arrived, news about the destruction of the venthe farms had spread. Sol could see many angry faces in the crowd and he could feel several more who concealed it better than the rest. Their simmering rage felt like a warm breeze blowing against his skin, making it tingle and itch.

Sol held up one hand for silence, copying the mannerisms of the late Don Kal. His own memories and feelings were there, securely locked away in a corner, but the rest seemed taken up with Don Kal's. The edges were bleeding together, mixing up recent fresh memories from the last few weeks. Sol had to work harder than ever before to maintain his sense of self and not let the Morrin take over. It had happened only once before and he'd lost two weeks, living as his host before waking up in the night screaming at seeing a stranger's face in the mirror.

"By now you've all heard," said Sol as Don Kalbensham. "All of our venthe farms have been destroyed. Burned to the ground by agents from the other Families." A few people shuffled their feet and glared but no one spoke out. Their loyalty to Don Kal was absolute. "I put my trust in the wrong person and he let me down. The Flesh Mage is gone and now we must start from scratch. The other Families expect me to lick my wounds, say nothing and rebuild. I did consider it. It would be the wise thing to do, if only it ended there." Sol shook his head sadly as if disappointed by the recent turn of events. "A friend brought me some troubling news. The venthe farms were only the beginning. The other Families are restless. They want to drive me out of the city all together, cut up my turf and make it ruled by four Families instead of five."

People in the crowd grumbled and muttered among themselves. He let it continue for a few seconds before raising a hand and the noise quickly drained away.

"The other Families think I am old and weak. They think we will just walk away. I have been in this city longer than any of them and it is my home. Wisdom tells me to wait, but they've forced my hand. We will take the fight to them. We will cut into their territory. We will rule this city!"

The roar from the crowd made his ears ring. Somewhere in the back of his mind Sol felt Don Kal's disappointment and frustration at seeing his people so easily manipulated. A smile felt out of place but Sol couldn't help it. The tide of strong emotions coming from the crowd was already so dense it didn't take much to absorb a trickle of energy and feed it back to them.

Don Kal had forgotten most of his people were not Morrin. They didn't have his patience or his decades to plan and scheme a complex form of revenge. All of them were men and women of action, but lately there hadn't been enough to satiate them.

He gave individual orders to all of the Gold and Silver, who seemed pleased by his change in behaviour. A few made comments about having the old Don Kal back, which made him smile and a tiny voice howl in the back of his mind. Eventually the last jackal left and Sol collapsed in a chair, feeling tired and hungry. Normally he would have eaten a couple of chickens, some bread and cheese to fill the hole, but Don Kal favoured seafood. Instead he sent someone for a large portion of smoked fish and rice.

The Families would go to war and slaughter each other for nothing. The streets would run red with blood and he'd feed the city's misery and anger back to its people until it spread beyond the criminal underworld. Neighbours would turn on each other, family members would savage their own kin, and chaos would spread until every street was littered with the dying and the dead.

Then, when he had amassed enough energy, he would open a hole in the world and his God would cross over from beyond the Veil. He would be raised up on high and together they would reshape the world.

CHAPTER 31

Munroe had to knock on the door several times and shout that she wasn't going away, before she heard someone shuffling around inside. Finally the door opened to reveal a battered and bloody Choss. He leaned heavily on the wall with one arm and the other was wrapped in a makeshift sling. Half of his face was swollen, his right eye completely closed with a huge purple bruise, and the rest of him looked in much the same shape. He looked like a steak that had been pounded with a hammer.

"Maker's balls," whispered Munroe. She immediately shoved her way inside, doing her best to prop him up and close the door at the same time. Together they shuffled down the hallway into his front room where they slowly crab-walked across the tiled floor before falling back into a wide chair. Patches of blood and a heap of bandages indicated this was where Choss had been resting until she'd made him get up.

Despite him having had some medical assistance, as Choss's bandaging looked fairly competent, the dressings needed changing. Up close she could also see dozens of cuts on his face, blood seeping from a wound in his bandaged forearm and he favoured one leg over the other.

"I'm calling for a surgeon," said Munroe.

"No, don't," said Choss. "One came out to see me yesterday. She left me all the stuff I'll need," he said, pointing at several packets. One smelled rancid but the handwritten label clearly indicated it was a herbal tea to reduce swelling. The other had dozens of long narrow seeds that were slightly sticky, coating the inside of the paper bag in a fine white powder. Rinna seeds. She took out six and held them towards Choss.

"I'm all right. I don't need them."

Munroe gritted her teeth to stop herself from screaming. "Choss, you're a fucking mess. It took you forever just to walk to the front door. If you don't take these I'm going to twist your nutsack until you're sick and your balls turn purple. Then I'll do it again. At that point you'll beg me for these. Do you think I'm lying?"

Choss regarded her for a couple of seconds before taking the seeds and grinding them between his teeth. By the time she'd filled the kettle and brought it to the boil, some of the lines of pain on his face had eased. She poured two small spoons' worth of the stinky powder into a cup and made him drink every drop.

Next she stripped off the sling, moving his arm as gently as possible. He winced a couple of times but didn't cry out. When the old bandages came off she nearly wept at what was underneath. Part of her didn't understand how he could absorb so much physical pain and keep moving. But then he'd spent years in the ring, night after night of smashing his fists into another man's face and body. Perhaps you could become used to horrendous injuries after a while. You could become used to anything if it was all you knew. She understood a little of that.

Munroe cleaned the scrapes and gashes as best she could, dabbing unguent on the worst, sewing up the longest and then bandaging his arm again. She managed to persuade him to lift up his vest, which showed purple ribs on one side and green on the other.

"A couple are broken on the left. The right are just bruised," he said in a way that told her this wasn't the first time. Irritated at the tears that fell against her wishes Munroe angrily wiped them away.

"What about the leg?"

"It's fine. Just a scratch."

Munroe raised an eyebrow. "You wouldn't be lying to me, would you?"

Choss started to answer but then just closed his mouth. "It's pretty deep."

"Take off your trousers," she said. Choss fumbled at his belt with one hand and she moved to help.

"I can manage," said Choss. She thought he was blushing but couldn't tell for the bruises and blood on his face. She slapped his hand away and eventually he relented.

"I'd hoped that one day I'd get your trousers off, but this wasn't what I had in mind," said Munroe, trying to keep the mood light. Choss didn't even smile and her grin faded.

Working together they managed to get his trousers down to his knees. Halfway down his left thigh was a gash twice as long as her hand. A comment about his thighs rose in her throat, but Munroe swallowed it, instead fetching needle and thread. Thinking of it as nothing more than a stubborn bit of embroidery, she slowly pulled the gash closed. It wasn't neat or very tidy, evidence of another ladylike pastime she'd failed at, but at least it stopped the oozing. She smeared some more of the foul-smelling paste on top then wrapped his thigh in fresh bandages before helping him back into his trousers.

Finally she tended to his face, cleaning the cuts and then holding a cold wet cloth over his swollen eye. Munroe fetched herself a normal cup of tea and made Choss another cup of his foul brew. He sipped at it without complaint despite the putrid smell and bits floating on the surface. That told her something about the level of his pain.

"Tell me."

Choss sighed before speaking. A long deep sound that seemed to come from the bottom of his boots. "I was blind. I was so single-minded and naïve that I actually thought she wanted to help."

In all the time she'd known him, Munroe had never seen Choss look defeated. She knew his nickname from the ring, but it was his implacable spirit, not a talent with his fists, that she admired. Whenever obstacles came up he always found a way to get over or around them and keep moving forward. He was utterly relentless and had inspired her to try and find something at which she excelled, apart from drinking. Unfortunately none of her attempts had panned out yet, but it hadn't stopped her from trying new things.

"Doña Jarrow told me the city would tear itself apart and that I could stop it. I never thought I had much of an ego until now. Part of me knew she was doing it for her own reasons, but I hoped I could help the arena in the process."

Munroe swallowed a gulp of her tea and felt it settle in her stomach like a stone. She already knew some of it, but needed to hear it from him. "What did you do?"

Choss's eyes were haunted. "We destroyed all of Don Kalbensham's venthe farms. We burned them to the ground."

By the time she and Don Jarrow had returned to the theatre word had started to trickle in about fires in the meat district. It had taken the rest of the night for a clear report to come back from his contacts in the area. It shouldn't have mattered, since all of the Families had planned to destroy the venthe farms, but something had changed.

All of the venthe farms were gone but Don Kal was gathering his people for a fight. The war that they'd all hoped to avoid seemed intent on happening. When she'd left him, Don Jarrow had been busy arming his people.

No one could understand why Don Kal was doing it. She'd heard the other Dons say the Morrin was normally so calm. So why had he suddenly had a change of heart?

Given the odds it didn't seem like he could win. All Munroe knew was that Doña Jarrow was involved in some way. She had manipulated Choss and somehow persuaded Don Kal that going to war with the other Families was the right course of action.

"Who did you have with you?"

"Just Gorrax. Munroe, what have I done?" asked Choss. There was such terrible loss in his voice that she held him tight, trying to offer some comfort.

Part of her didn't want to know, but she needed to ask and could see Choss needed to tell someone. "What happened?"

Choss stared in the distance and the tension returned to his battered features. "I've seen people die. Seen men killed in horrible ways. Found bits of people washed up on the shore weeks after. By then you can't really tell what it is, just a hunk of meat and a bit of white bone. But last night, there was so much blood." The haunted look in his eyes was starting to scare her. "I've never seen anything like it. I've always known, part of me at least, but I lied to myself. I believed he was different, but he was just hibernating, like a bear in winter."

"Who was hibernating?"

"Have you ever seen a Vorga fight? I mean really fight without restraint?" Choss shivered and then groaned in pain, clenching his fists. Munroe started to reach for some more rinna seeds, but he grabbed her arm and pulled her close. He felt so warm and his body heat seeped into her. Her body started to respond to his touch and the terrible ache in her heart resurfaced.

"I saw it once before, when I beat Gorrax. But I was so arrogant. I was blind to what they really are."

A creeping sense of horror started to spread out from the dull weight in her stomach. The tea had turned bitter and her tongue felt fuzzy. "What did you do?"

Choss's eyes stayed locked in the past. "We found the first venthe farm and burned it to the ground. A few tried to fight but they died so quickly. Gorrax seemed to dance between them and they fell like toy soldiers. By the time we reached the second farm they'd seen the fire and were ready for us. It didn't matter. We hit them like a hammer striking an anvil. After a while, Gorrax started to show his true nature," whispered Choss. He gulped down the last of his tea, absently chewing the bits at the bottom of his cup. Munroe felt him start to shake and she held him tighter, but didn't know if he felt her.

"It's how I beat him, all those years ago," he said, suddenly coming back to the present and staring at her. "I became Vorga."

Munroe shook her head. "I don't understand. What does that mean?"

Choss struggled for a minute but eventually spoke, his words halting as if he were still trying to unravel it.

"In every previous fight I always fought to win, but never relished my opponent's weakness. I celebrated my victory, but never my dominance over them. People think the Vorga are savages who love to kill, but they don't. The strongest lead their people. Vorga want to be challenged and they relish a good fight, because it tests them, their heritage and lineage. They are born with knowledge of the sword, the spear, the axe, so many weapons. It's passed down in the blood. Even before they know how to speak, they can fight. To reject combat is to reject the heart of Vorga society. I tested myself against Don Kal's men as a Vorga would, using my heritage and history with my fists and sword. I fought without restraint and killed because I found them weak and I was disappointed."

Choss looked away, suddenly afraid of what she might see. He tried to pull away as well but she held on tightly, unwilling to leave him alone in such a dark place.

"We killed them all and then moved on to the next farm, and the next. As the night progressed I barely felt my wounds, only a rising sense of disappointment at my opponents. They came at me in twos and threes, but just got in each other's way, which only made it easier."

"Where is Gorrax?" asked Munroe, suddenly afraid the hulking Vorga was lurking nearby.

"He was badly wounded, worse than I've ever seen, but he'll live. I thought to bring him here, but he needed salt water to heal, so I dropped him in a river and he swam out to sea."

"Have you heard the news about Don Kal?" asked Munroe.

His grimace spoke volumes. "Everyone always said Don Kal was slow to anger. Why would he declare war on the other Families? He can't hope to win."

It was the one question being asked over and over and no one had come up with an answer. It would be suicide for him to try and fight all of the other Families at the same time. Perhaps Doña Jarrow had done it to manipulate the other Families into wiping out Don Kal. Or perhaps she was intending to separate from her husband and claim Don Kal's territory. Whatever her motivations they were not known to Don Jarrow, who was having to do a lot of fast talking to avoid sharing the blame for the upcoming war.

"What are you going to do now?"

"I don't know," said Choss, his voice thick with despair. "You were right."

"What do you mean?"

When he looked at her Munroe felt her resolve waver and something tightened in her stomach.

"A few years ago you warned me about getting involved with the Families. You told me what would happen, but I didn't listen. All I could think about was myself and the arena. We should have just walked away together."

Much to her surprise Choss kissed her, pulling her close and encircling her with his strong arms. She resisted for a second but then her hunger rose up and she kissed him back.

They had held back from each other for so long. Munroe straddled his hips and gently held his battered face between her hands before seeking out his mouth again. Her heart began to pound and she pressed herself again his body, making him wince in pain but his hands didn't stop exploring the curve of her hips and back. She ran her hands across the thick muscles of his shoulders and arms before gently touching his chest.

While his mouth explored the nape of her neck she arched her back and her mind started to go blank. The only things that mattered were the feelings surging through her body and her rising passion. Choss made a wet coughing sound but soon resumed kissing her neck and exploring her skin with deft fingers. But his brief sound of discomfort was enough to trigger something deep in her brain and Munroe quickly scrambled off his lap.

"Stop, just stop," she said, fresh tears welling up. "I don't want to hurt you."

"That night at the Emerald Dragon. I should have taken you upstairs and forgotten about the rest of the world. I want that now, more than anything."

"Please, please stop," said Munroe, her heart aching as she tried to control the surging emotions that raged through her. She desperately wanted to rip off his shirt and kiss him again, to live in that place where nothing else mattered but the feel of his body pressing against hers. Sobs wracked her and she tottered back-wards, knocked something off a table, slowly edging out of the room. The look in his eyes sent fresh waves of pain surging through her heart.

"I can't, I can't," she said, over and over, her vision blurring with tears.

"Please don't go," he begged.

"I'll come back soon. I promise."

Before he could say another word she ran out the door. If he'd asked her to stay just one more time she didn't know what she would've done. Her lips were still tingling with the feel of him and she could smell him on her clothes and skin.

Half blind with tears Munroe stumbled on, walking and run-ning until she was far enough away that she didn't consider going back.

As her ardour faded, hatred for Doña Jarrow began to burn inside like a hot coal. She'd preyed on Choss's trusting nature and had fooled him. She didn't care about him or the arena. She'd used him for his own ends and now, because of her, the Families were going to war. No one knew what she was really up to but now it didn't matter. Countless people Munroe had known for years would die because of Doña Jarrow and her scheming.

All other thoughts were pushed aside as Munroe stormed down the streets towards the theatre. Doña Jarrow needed to pay for what she'd done.

CHAPTER 32

Despite the news of a pending war between the crime Families flooding every bar and tavern across the city, the hallways of Unity Hall were surprisingly quiet. After another gruelling morning of training, Fray made his way to the Khevassar's office.

Rummpoe, the old man's assistant, looked up from his paperwork with no apparent sense of urgency. No one else sat waiting for an appointment so Fray was shown in almost immediately.

The paperwork on the Khevassar's desk seemed higher than the last time he'd been here, but the Old Man appeared no more daunted by it. Fray waited until Rummpoe had closed the door before speaking.

"Sir, can I speak freely?"

"This isn't the army, Fray. Speak your mind."

"If I'd never joined the Guardians, would you have given me those pages from my father's journals?"

The Old Man took his time before answering. "The short answer is no. I thought about it, many times, but knowing what you do now is not a burden I would wish on anyone."

"My father wrote that over two hundred people died because of the first Flesh Mage. How many died because of the second?"

"Four hundred and seventeen." The Khevassar didn't even

have to think about it. "Most of those died on the same night as your father."

"How did you cover it up?"

"We didn't, not really," admitted the Old Man. "Just like the first time we told a range of convenient lies. Tainted meat coming from overseas. Poison in the water. Ergot blight in the bread. An infestation of rats in a food warehouse."

"How? How could anyone believe those stories?"

"Fray, you're forgetting that most people just want to live a quiet life. They don't knowingly put themselves in harm's way. When violence or crime comes into their lives it's a rarity, and it can take them a long time to recover. Over the years I've become immune and now there's little that upsets me. Most people don't know how to cope. At first some didn't believe the lies, but after a while when things settled down they began to forget the small details. People told themselves they'd imagined seeing their neighbours biting each other or perhaps it had been ergot poisoning. Perhaps what they'd seen had been hallucinations."

"That's it?"

The Old Man shrugged. "What do you want me to say? People want to feel safe. If we tell them something, they'll inevitably believe it. They need to believe we can protect them. We try our best, but sometimes we will fail. Most people can't live with that knowledge every day."

Fray could see that revealing the truth about what had happened at this stage would only do more harm than good. Over six hundred people had died because of the previous two Flesh Mages. Their friends and families had been given an answer and hopefully they had now moved on with their lives. They may not have found peace with what had happened, but at least they had some form of closure. To take that away from so many people wasn't something he even considered. At least they'd had the opportunity. He had been unable to rest or move on, as he'd never known why his father had died.

"If I ask, will you tell me everything about the night my father died?" asked Fray.

"I will," said the Old Man, who suddenly looked his age as he sagged in his chair. "But how much do you really want to hear? Do you want to know about some of the horrors that people witnessed from that night? Do you want a description of the bodies and their wounds?" The old Guardian took a long deep breath and stared intently at Fray. "I know that when the city began to tear itself apart your father tracked down the Flesh Mage. He and Byrne were able to disrupt the spell and stop the Flesh Mage from opening the rift. But there was a terrible backlash and it killed your father. Byrne's memory of that time is patchy and he doesn't remember the lies we told the people."

"But then he started to remember," said Fray.

"Perhaps, or maybe he was more seriously injured than I realised," admitted the Khevassar. "Regardless he was irreparably changed. How much more do you need to know?"

It was a good question, but not one Fray was sure he could answer at the moment. Hearing more of the grisly details would not change the facts. His father had fought and beaten the Flesh Mage. He had died saving the city from worse bloodshed. And now it was his turn to try.

"What are you willing to do to solve this case?" asked Fray and the Old Man raised an eyebrow. "Would you consider an unusual approach?"

"Now you sound like your father," muttered the Khevassar, before gesturing for Fray to continue.

"I've heard stories about a brewing conflict between the crime Families. People are saying it's out-of-character behaviour and no one saw it coming. What if the Flesh Mage orchestrated this feud?"

"I don't believe in coincidences," said the Old Man. "Even if the Flesh Mage isn't involved, he would benefit from such widespread violence. So, assuming he was involved, I tried reaching out to the Families through channels. As you might expect, they've not been very receptive. If he orchestrated this, if he has that kind of reach, then he's deeply embedded in their world. We can't just walk in there. They practically know every Guardian by name. If we went in with larger numbers they'd see us coming and scatter. Any Guardian who went in solo would disappear and wash up in the river."

"No one knows my name, or my face," said Fray.

The Khevassar sat and steepled his fingers, his eyes distant and thoughtful. Fray remained silent, letting him ponder the risks and potential rewards.

At the beginning he'd been following Byrne's lead on this case, but now he had a chance to do something by himself. No one else apart from Fray could identify the Flesh Mage, regardless of whose face he was wearing. Even though Fray knew he was in over his head, his unique Talent meant it had to be him.

"You understand the risks?" asked the Old Man.

"Yes."

"No one will come for you. One wrong word and it will be your body we're fishing out of the river."

"I know."

"I'm an old man," said the Khevassar suddenly. "I've lived longer than most, but I'm lucky to have few regrets. One of those is you."

Fray was confused. "Sir?"

The Old Man shook his head. "I know you and your father weren't close for many years. You wanted to be your own man, find your own way. Even so, I wish you'd joined us sooner, and not because of your magic."

"Why?"

"Because you remind me of him. If you'd started your training even five years ago things would be different. Your father was one of the best Guardians I've ever met. I'd hoped that one day he'd take over my office."

Fray was speechless. He knew other Guardians respected his father but he'd had no idea the Old Man had been making long-term plans.

"No matter. One day someone else will have to shoulder the burden. Are you sure you want to do this?" asked the Khevassar.

"Not really, but I need to."

"Then I hope the Great Maker keeps you safe," said the Old Man, offering his hand. "Do you know where to start?"

"I have a couple of ideas."

"If you'll indulge me, I have one piece of advice. If you feel threatened, don't hesitate to do whatever is necessary. Mercy will get you killed."

Fray shook his hand and walked back along the silent corridors towards the front door.

He'd lived on the fringes of the underworld, even helped a few criminals find closure when they'd lost friends and relatives, but never something like this. Despite not being known as a Guardian, walking in by himself would be suicide. He needed a guide. Before he did that Fray had one last visit to make while there was still time.

Fray had to knock on the door for a long time before Byrne answered. He looked genuinely surprised and while he recovered his composure Fray tried to get used to seeing him out of uniform. Part of Fray expected Byrne to react angrily to his surprise visit but he seemed genuinely pleased. They moved to his front room and stared at one another for a minute in silence.

"Where's your uniform?" asked Byrne. "Did you decide to leave the Guardians?"

Fray's suspicions were confirmed by how hopeful Byrne sounded at the idea. "It took me a while, but I eventually worked out what you were doing."

"I don't understand."

"The Old Man said you'd changed after my father died. I didn't believe it at first but then I saw it. You seemed more callous and yet you were determined to solve this case. It didn't make any sense. Then there was how you kept treating me."

"I didn't mean to hurt you, Fray."

"But you did," said Fray with a gentle smile. "You made a promise to my father to protect me. Once you realised I couldn't help you with the case you kept pushing me away in the hope that I'd leave the Guardians. You were trying to keep me safe."

Byrne sat back in his chair and his expression became unreadable. Eventually a smile formed on his lips. "You're right. I didn't expect the Khevassar to force me to take some days off. I've been trying to get a meeting with him to explain my behaviour, but he's ignored my letters. I was about to go down to Unity Hall."

"I don't think he'd listen, because we both know not all of it was an act." Fray felt a lot of sympathy for Byrne as he'd lost not only a mentor but also a friend who was practically family. But ever since that night he'd not taken the time to mourn and deal with what had happened and now the cracks were beginning to show. "I have to go, but I'll try to come and visit again."

"Where are you going?" asked Byrne, following him to the front door.

"I've found a lead on the Flesh Mage."

Byrne grabbed him by the shoulders and span him around. "You can't do this by yourself. It's too dangerous."

"There's no one else who can do this. I have my father's gift and I can help stop this."

"Let me come with you."

"You can't," said Fray, gently easing Byrne's hands away. "I'm going to speak with the Families and they know you're a Guardian. They'd kill you before we had a chance to explain, and I couldn't live with that."

Byrne looked terrified. He tried to say more, to come up with another argument, but Fray didn't give him a chance. Instead he hugged Byrne tightly to his chest for a moment and went out the door in a hurry.

Despite not being in his Guardian uniform the bald man at the arena door recognised Fray.

"Are you working undercover?" he asked.

"Something like that. Can I speak to Vinny?" asked Fray. The big man crossed his arms and didn't move. "It's Jakka, isn't it?"

"You're not going to have another seizure, are you?"

"No, not today. I'm better," promised Fray, although he couldn't be sure the residual energy from what the Flesh Mage had done wouldn't affect him again. He hoped that it had been long enough since his last visit that it would have faded. Even so he was bracing himself for another onslaught.

"Follow me," said Jakka, finally letting him inside before locking the door again. Fray felt something on the edge of his awareness. An echo of what the Flesh Mage had done and other strong emotions which suffused the building. He kept a tight rein on his magic, as opening himself to it could cripple him again.

Fray followed Jakka down a corridor that was so narrow the big man's shoulders brushed the walls on either side. He knocked on a door at the end and then gestured for Fray to step inside.

As before, Vinny sat behind a desk in an office where everything had been neatly filed. Vinny briefly glanced up as they came in but continued making a few more notes in a ledger. He waved Fray towards one of the chairs and finished what he was doing before carefully cleaning his pen and setting it to one side. He looked no less pale and skeletal than last time, but despite his appearance, Vinny had probably not seen fifty winters.

"Thank you, Jakka, I'm sure my young friend isn't going to harm me," said Vinny, dismissing the big man. "Something to drink?" he said, gesturing at a steaming pot of pungent tea.

"No, thank you."

"You were here the other day," said Vinny, pouring himself a cup.

"Yes, with my partner."

Vinny sipped at his tea, grimaced at the taste and gulped more of it down. "Did you find that dock worker?"

"Yes, that's why I'm here. I need your help again."

Vinny raised an eyebrow. "Where's your uniform?"

Fray wondered how much he should tell Vinny and whether or not he should try lying. Looking around the room and at the man behind the desk, he was suddenly struck by the similarity between Vinny and the Khevassar. Both were physically unassuming men who ran empires with their intellect. Fray realised it would be pointless trying to outwit him so he went with the truth.

"I'll tell you what I can, but I assume you can be discreet," said Fray, waiting for Vinny to nod before continuing. "I'm hunting a killer. He's responsible for several deaths, and for what happened the other night at the arena."

"Magic," said Vinny.

"Yes. And now I believe he's involved with one of the Families."

Vinny's face quirked into a lop-sided smile. "What do you know about the Families?"

"A little. I've dealt with a few Brass, even one or two Silver."

Vinny grunted in surprise. "Then you know more than most. Enough to stay out of their business."

"I wish it were that simple," said Fray.

"They'll deal with the outsider, one way or another."

"That's the problem. He can make himself look like other people. They won't know it's him."

"Magic again?" asked Vinny. "Is it even worth me asking how he does it?"

"Not really, but I think he's involved with the feud. The more bloodshed and violence there is, the stronger he becomes. You saw first-hand what happened at the arena. Imagine what will happen when the Families go to war. He'll gorge himself and then ... " Fray trailed off, leaving the rest to Vinny's imagination. It was a lot easier than trying to explain opening a tear in the world and things Fray didn't really understand himself.

Vinny sipped at his tea for a minute, his eyes troubled and distant.

"You remind me of someone," he said absently. "Another Guardian that used to come here from time to time."

"Was it my father?"

"That could explain the resemblance," muttered Vinny. "I knew him a little, passed information his way from time to time. Sometimes he came just to watch a fight." Vinny shrugged, leaving the rest unsaid. "This killer, can you find him?"

"Yes. I just need someone to show me around, someone who can vouch for me with the Families."

"I have someone in mind," said Vinny, scribbling down an address. He also wrote out a separate note, which he signed and passed across the desk. "Give him this note. Whether he agrees to take you or not is his decision. Be honest with him. He's not someone to trifle with."

"Thank you."

"Don't thank me. All I've done is point you in the direction of the bear pit. Tread carefully, because if they think you're lying they'll kill you."

It took Fray thirty minutes to cross the city and find the address Vinny had given him. The house was a modest but well-tended building on a quiet street, a far cry from what he'd been expecting. He thought Vinny would have sent him to one of the dark corners where Guardians never walked alone.

He knocked and waited but there was no answer inside. He knocked again and was just about to leave when he heard a scuffing noise inside and the sound of heavy footsteps approaching. A minute later the door opened to reveal a massive man with a swollen face and a black eye.

"Vinny sent me," said Fray, holding out the note. "I'm Fray."

"Choss," murmured the big man, taking the note and quickly scanning the contents. He stared at Fray, who tried not to squirm under his gaze or reach for his sword. Choss unsettled him and seemed to exude a feeling of pent-up aggression.

"You'd better come inside," he said and Fray felt the threat of violence begin to fade. "I believe you have a story to tell me."

CHAPTER 33

Katja scrubbed at her face with a wet cloth, then dried it vigorously. Her reflection still looked pale in the mirror. Sleep had evaded her yet again and she felt dizzy and weak. The dark smears under her eyes had become bags and all of the skin on her face seemed to be slipping towards the floor. Even as she watched it started to ooze and trickle down her face like wet mud, exposing the muscles and grey bone underneath. One of her eyeballs started to wiggle about as if it might pop out of its socket.

Katja scrunched up her eyes and took long deep breaths. After a few minutes she managed to slow the frantic beating of her heart. Looking in the mirror again she saw nothing unusual and turned away before the hallucinations started again. She needed to stay busy, focus on something and wait for it to pass.

She dressed quickly, tied her hair in a braid and went downstairs to the kitchen where she found Roza having tea with Gankle.

Both of them looked up at her with matching worried expressions. Gankle quickly moved to the stove where he'd been warming some eggs and sausages. He filled a plate, added a thick chunk of bread and put it down in front of her with a crock of butter. Katja's stomach growled at the smell and she started gobbling down her food.

Roza poured her a cup of tea and for a while no one said anything while she ate. Gankle sipped his tea, looking at her over the rim of his cup with concern while Roza watched her from an eye corner.

"What happened with Lord and Lady Trevino?" asked Roza when Katja had almost finished.

Rodann's first task for her after revealing the full extent of his plan had been for her to revisit the Trevinos. Previously she'd only known them as Sim and Belle, rich nobles who'd asked for discreet funeral arrangements to be made for their son, an Eater. She'd sent his body to a farm to be eaten by pigs. She'd thought that concluded their business but Rodann had other ideas. It made her wonder if Rodann had known about the couple's beliefs and arranged their son's murder in the first place.

Rodann had informed her that the Trevinos were shipping magnates and one of the oldest and richest families in the city. They could trace their lineage back to some of the first settlers who'd built Perizzi. Over the centuries they'd turned a single fishing boat into a fleet of ships that now transported goods around the world. They were very rich and advised the Queen on matters concerning trade and shipping.

With a heavy investment in a new fleet of ships the Trevinos were at a critical business juncture. Katja's second visit, at the dry dock amid the skeletons of a dozen new vessels, had been less than cordial. If information about their son and their beliefs were to emerge it would cause a scandal. Investors might want to distance themselves from the Trevinos and withdraw their money from the project, leaving them with huge debts to pay. It might be enough to threaten their business and all that their family had built over the centuries.

The hatred emanating from Lord Trevino had been palpable, but he'd stiffly agreed to her request. People knew he smoked a pipe and the small pouch would not look untoward on his belt when he entered the palace. Even a cursory glance at its contents would not reveal anything unusual.

"What was in the pouch?" asked Roza.

"I think it was poison," said Katja. Rodann hadn't been specific, but it seemed the most plausible answer. "It was hard to tell as they'd mixed it with tobacco, but it's the only thing that makes sense."

"You think Rodann intends to blackmail them into poisoning one of the Queens?" asked Roza.

Katja shrugged. "Maybe, but what if he's blackmailing them for another reason as well."

"Such as?"

"Rodann wants to replace Queen Morganse with his benefactor, whoever she is." Katja had settled on it being a woman in her mind for now. "The Trevinos are one of the oldest families in Perizzi and their opinion carries a lot of weight. Perhaps he intends to get them to support his patron's claim to the throne."

"It's possible. I'll look into the other founding families."

"I've had my people following all of those from the meeting," said Roza. "The shrew-faced woman, Marcella, works at a bakery with her husband, Borren. The banquet tonight is so big the palace has some food brought in from outside. The man who died," said Roza, careful not to say that Katja had murdered him, "has been replaced by Borren and he's due to make a delivery to the palace."

"Do you think they're going to poison the guests?" asked Katja, but Roza was already shaking her head.

"It's too imprecise. Why have such an elaborate conspiracy if all you're going to do is poison everyone? Rodann told you everyone would know Seveldrom was responsible, and poison doesn't fit."

"Then why are they there?" asked Katja.

"Access to the palace? Maybe they're smuggling in weapons

through the kitchens. Whatever it is, I've got someone in place to keep an eye on them."

"What do you know about the others?"

Roza ticked them off on her fingers. "The servant, Lizbeth, she works at the palace and is working tonight. She'll be able to move about freely and go almost anywhere. Servants are invisible to most people, so she won't be noticed. Keeping an eye on her will be more difficult, but we'll do what we can."

"That just leaves Faith and the nobles."

"Lord and Lady Kallan. They're not very well regarded, and fairly poor in comparison to most of the nobility."

"Then how did they get an invite to the palace?" asked Katja.

"Someone with authority secured them an invitation," said Roza. "Rodann's patron again."

"But why would Rodann want them there?"

Roza didn't have an answer for that and shook her head. "Keeping them in sight will actually be very easy. Once they sit down for dinner they can't go anywhere for hours. And if they leave the table midway, it will be easy to follow them."

Katja was starting to feel like she was drowning. They had the names of some of the people involved, and knew a little more about them, but were still no closer to their purpose.

"Faith?"

"As far as I know she has no reason to be there," said Roza with a frown. "My contacts actually found out very little about her."

"Then what about the first group?" said Katja, trying not to let her frustration show. "I saw Rodann talking to other people before he approached me."

"We have people throughout the palace," said Roza, dodging the question. "Queen Talandra will be surrounded by her royal guards and has been briefed about everything. It was up to her and she decided to go ahead as normal."

"We're out of time. We should just take Rodann off the street," said Katja. "It's too risky to let this continue. We can make him talk."

"He's been very cautious since the start," said Roza. "There will be contingencies if he disappears. Then there's Teigan to deal with as well."

"Then we could make both of them disappear," said Katja, feeling the onset of hysteria.

"What do you think would happen?" asked Roza.

"The others would continue with their individual tasks. They're zealots and they believe what they're doing is for the greater good."

A knock at the front door ended their conversation. Katja finished the last of her breakfast while Gankle went to answer the door.

"Don't hesitate if you see an opportunity to turn any part of this to our advantage," said Roza. "Use whatever means are necessary."

"Meaning what?"

"I can surround the Queen with a ring of swords, but all it takes for them to succeed is one person who's willing to die for their beliefs. If you see anything that will give us an advantage, take it."

Gankle returned from the front room. "A carriage is waiting outside."

Katja checked her weapons, pulled on her bulky grey robe and went out the front door. A rat-faced man with short red hair and a crooked nose waited for her inside the carriage.

"Rodann sent me. Get in," he said in a nasal whine. She sat down opposite and kept one hand resting on the dagger at her waist. As soon as the carriage pulled away he reached under his seat and started to pull on a loose white robe with a deep hood.

"I'm Mallanc," he said, rearranging the robe until it covered his plain and rather worn clothing. There were brown stains around the wrists and something brown had trickled onto one of his boots. If Katja had to guess she would have said Mallanc was a cutpurse or a thief, not someone Rodann would normally deal with.

"So what's the job?" she asked.

Mallanc gave her a lop-sided grin. "You hear about those two rich kids that went missing?"

"No, what happened?"

"A few nights ago the sons of some nobles went for a few drinks down on the docks. To show the little people that we're all the same. Two of them never made it home." Katja remembered hearing something about the Guardians searching the river for a missing boy.

"Rodann grabbed them," said Katja, taking a guess.

"Just one, the son of Lord Mullbrook. The other washed up in the river a couple of days back. Fell in drunk and drowned. Terrible accident," said Mallanc with a nasty grin.

"So who are we going to see?"

"Lord Mullbrook. We need something from him for tonight. If he doesn't agree, his son will end up like the other one."

At least the other family had some sort of closure. Not knowing would be worse. With no body a sliver of hope would always remain, tormenting grieving relatives with the possibility of good news. Getting to see Lord Mullbrook would normally be difficult, but Mallanc's white robe for one of the Faithful, and Katja's reputation in the city for dealing with the bereaved, would get them in the front door.

"What's the favour?" asked Katja.

"He's got an invite for the big party but said he isn't going. We need him to get you inside."

"He'll want proof we have his son," said Katja.

Mallanc gave her a feral grin. "Don't worry. I've got that covered."

Twenty minutes later the carriage stopped outside a fairly large estate. A servant in sky blue livery trimmed with silver met them at the front door and at the promise of news about Lord Mullbrook's son he let them inside. They only had to wait a few minutes in a plush front room before Lord Mullbrook marched in. Somewhere in his fifties, with wavy brown hair going white over the ears, he was a lean man with craggy features and pale blue eyes. A drooping grey moustache gave him a permanent scowl and his stiff posture told Katja he'd served in the army at some point.

"I was told you have news," he said, his manner abrupt and his lack of protocol suggesting a no-nonsense attitude.

"If we might speak in private, my Lord," said Mallanc, glancing at the lingering servant by the open door. Lord Mullbrook flicked his hand and the servant stepped outside and closed the door.

"Should your wife be here to hear the news?" asked Katja, ignoring Mallanc's frown at her interruption.

"I'm a widower. What's the news?" demanded Lord Mullbrook.

"You son is alive," said Mallanc.

"Praise the Blessed Mother," said Lord Mullbrook, letting out a long slow breath. He turned his back for a minute and crossed the room to look out the window. When he returned his eyes were a little red but there were no tears.

"Is he well? Is he on his way here?"

"He's well for now, but he will only stay that way if you cooperate." Mallanc threw off his hood and sat down without being asked. He gestured at the chair opposite but Lord Mullbrook didn't sit down.

"You're not one of the Faithful," he sneered. "Who are you? What have you done with my son?"

"Sit down, old man," snapped Mallanc, pointing at the chair.

Katja saw Lord Mullbrook's hands ball up into fists but he took a deep breath and slowly relaxed before sitting down as instructed.

"What do you want? Money?"

"That's more like it," said Mallanc, grinning at Katja. "Now we can have a nice conversation."

"Just get on with it," she said, taking a seat beside Mallanc.

"It's very simple. Tonight is the big banquet at the palace. You're going to attend."

Lord Mullbrook raised an eyebrow. "And? What else?"

"You got two invites. You're going to take my friend here with you," said Mallanc, gesturing at Katja.

Lord Mullbrook thought about it for a moment while Mallanc eyed an expensive jade statue with envy. She saw his fingers twitch and knew he desperately wanted to stuff it into a pocket.

"I want proof that you have my son, and that he's alive," said Lord Mullbrook. "Only then will I agree to your terms."

"No problem," said Mallanc, reaching inside his robes for something. "Your son wears a big ring on his finger. Gold with a symbol on it."

"That's the family crest, and that's not proof. You could have stolen the ring."

Mallanc dramatically slapped his forehead. "You're right. If only there was another way to prove it." He pulled out a bundle of cloth from inside his clothes and dropped it on the table between them.

Lord Mullbrook looked at the bundle and carefully unwrapped the material. When his eyes fell on the contents he sat back with a grimace.

"I will kill you for this," he promised.

Katja leaned forward to take a look. Nestled in the middle of the cloth was a severed finger with a ring still attached bearing the Mullbrook crest.

Mallanc ignored the threat. "Tonight you'll get all dressed up and go to the banquet. You'll smile and pretend that everything is good because your son is home. If anyone asks about your new friend, you tell them a convincing story. If nothing goes wrong then tomorrow we'll release your son."

Lord Mullbrook didn't ask what would happen if he failed to cooperate. Katja could also see him struggling with the idea of trusting Mallanc to be true to his word. His son could still end up being cut into chunks no matter how well he performed.

"Did you cut off the finger?" Katja asked Mallanc.

"What?" The question caught him off guard.

"Did you do it, or someone else?" she asked, while putting her hand in her pocket.

"I did it. So what?"

"So if he doesn't play nice, you'll cut off the rest."

Mallanc relaxed and grinned again. "That's right."

Katja drew the long blade strapped to her thigh and stabbed Mallanc in the leg, pinning him to the chair. He screamed as she drew a dagger from her boot and straddled his hips, pressing the steel to his neck. Forcing his throat back over the back of the chair she pressed a little more until blood began to run down his neck.

"What are you doing?"

"Where is he?" she asked.

"Who?" Mallanc managed to gasp, his eyes wide with terror and pain.

Katja shuffled her legs backwards, nudging the blade buried in Mallanc's leg and he howled. His eyes started to roll up in his head but she slapped him and shook him until he refocused. A second later he started to drift off again.

"If you want to see your son, get me some water," she said to

Lord Mullbrook. He only hesitated for a second before hurrying to the side table, coming back a moment later with a pitcher of water. Katja stood up and dumped the whole jug over Mallanc's head.

He came awake sputtering and immediately looked down at the handle of the blade buried in his leg. It had gone straight through the meat of his thigh into the wood underneath. She rested one hand against the hilt and started to waggle the knife from side to side.

"Don't," pleaded Mallanc, suddenly less smug.

"Last time. Where is he being held?"

"At the Kallan estate," gasped Mallanc. "In the back room of their house."

"Do you know where they live?" Katja asked Lord Mullbrook, who stared at Mallanc's injured leg with grim satisfaction.

"Yes. They're black penny nobles. They were given their title by the Queen a few years ago."

Black penny nobles had little money and usually nothing more than a title to their status. Katja doubted they were interested in helping Rodann's cause. They only wanted to further their own status and wealth.

"Who are you?" asked Lord Mullbrook.

"I'm an agent for the Crown," said Katja, which technically was true, just not the Queen of Yerskania.

"You lying sow," snarled Mallanc.

Katja lunged at his chest with her dagger.

"Wait!" said Lord Mullbrook, but it was already too late. She'd aimed for his heart and hit it right in the centre, burying the dagger to the hilt. Mallanc's eyes widened in surprise and then drooped. She yanked both blades out of Mallanc's corpse and cleaned them on his clothes before sheathing them.

"We could have questioned him," lamented Lord Mullbrook.

"There's no time. I will send someone to the Kallan estate to retrieve your son, but I still need you to take me to the palace as your guest."

"Why?"

"Because there are others players involved in this conspiracy."

"If you can prove to me that he's alive, I'll do as you ask," said Lord Mullbrook. "But I'm not letting you out of my sight until then. I don't trust you."

Katja asked for paper and wrote a coded note to Roza, which a servant raced off to deliver. She spent the next two hours helping Lord Mullbrook dispose of Mallanc's body and then trying to find one of his late wife's dresses that would fit her comfortably. Most were too baggy and they gaped at the chest, but eventually she found a few old-fashioned dresses from when Lady Mullbrook had been younger and slimmer.

Two armed guards kept an eye on Katja at all times and she could see several more stood outside in the gardens beneath the window. Lord Mullbrook wasn't leaving anything to chance. He changed into more formal clothing as well, but seemed less confident that he'd be leaving the house. Katja busied herself trying different hairstyles and eventually managed to pin it up with the assistance of a servant, who cooed over her slender figure. She even went so far as to allow the woman to put some make-up on her face, covering up the purple smudges and adding a touch of colour to her skin and lips.

Finally the front doors flew open downstairs and a dishevelled young man came in alongside Roza. One of his hands had been wrapped in bandages, but apart from a few bruises and a scrape over one eye, he seemed in good health. While father and son were reunited, Katja had a little time to talk with Roza.

"Four men were guarding him," whispered Roza. "I've left a couple of our people inside, just in case anyone returns, but I don't think they will. The banquet is only a couple of hours away and the house looked abandoned."

Roza fell silent as Lord Mullbrook approached. "I'm a man of my word. I'll get you into the palace," he promised. "But I'd like you to do one thing for me."

"Which is?"

"You can't take any weapons into the palace, but I think you should wear this," he said, producing a gold necklace with a long rectangular pendant decorated with a symbol for the Blessed Mother. He held up the pendant between his fingers and then twisted the bottom half. Something clicked and he pulled it in half, revealing a hidden blade. "I thought you might need it," said Lord Mullbrook with a vicious grin.

CHAPTER 34

Walking through the streets of Perizzi without his Guardian uniform was a surreal experience for Fray. He'd just started getting used to people looking in his direction or acknowledging him to the point where he could ignore it.

Even without using his magic, part of him could feel their benign attention, like a faint prickling on his skin. Now it felt as if he had stepped back in time, as no one looked at him. In fact more people stared at his hulking, battered, companion and rarely noticed he was even there.

From what little the big man had said, and from what Fray knew from living in Perizzi for so long, Choss was quite the local hero. Born in Seveldrom, he'd come to the city as a young boy and dragged himself up from the streets using his skill in the ring to earn a fearsome reputation. Unlike others who had gone on to become enforcers for one of the Families, Choss had gone into business running the arena with Vinny.

Most remarkable was a story he'd heard about Choss fighting and beating a Vorga. Apparently it was the same Vorga who'd torn apart the other fighter when the Flesh Mage had struck at the arena. Something niggled at the back of Fray's mind about what had happened at the arena but he still couldn't bring it into focus.

As they made their way towards the meat district and Don Kal's territory, some of the looks Choss received were not related to his status. His injuries worried people and their eyes were drawn to him because he moved with a stiff gait. Despite the bruises Fray was glad to have Choss as a guide as they went deeper into Don Kal's territory.

Fray had dabbled a little in the underworld, but it had never been through choice. Living in a run-down area meant catering to a variety of clients that often included those connected to violence in some way. Inevitably people connected to a Family, or sometimes an unfortunate victim, would come into his shop seeking closure. It had taught him a little about how their world worked, but this was completely different and without Choss he would've been lost.

Fray felt something brush against the skin on his arms but the air around him was still. He touched Choss on the arm and the big man stopped, one hand reaching for the sword at his waist.

"What is it?"

"Can you feel that?" asked Fray, holding up a hand and moving it one way and then the other in front of him. Further up the street he felt a thickening in the air and a wispy presence like a cloud of fog, but there was nothing to see. Something nipped Fray on the arm and he jumped. He pulled up his sleeve, expecting to see a red welt from a biting fly. The skin on his arm was unmarked.

"Keep an eye out. I need to look at the street using my magic," said Fray. He'd explained to Choss what he could do and had even given a warning about how his eyes changed colour so that the big man didn't react badly.

They ducked into a side road while Choss watched for anyone coming their way. It wasn't that late and yet the further they'd gone towards the meat district, the quieter the streets had become. A lot of shops had closed up early and their shutters were down. Even without being told, people in the area knew something was in the air and they were doing their best to avoid being caught in the middle.

Reaching out towards the waves at the edge of his hearing, Fray focused his magic and the world changed around him. Keeping his breathing slow and regular he glanced up the street towards the meat district. A gasp of surprise lodged in his throat and he spluttered and almost choked.

"What is it?" asked Choss.

At the end of the street a thick swarm of sparrow-sized motes of energy danced in the air. And beyond them Fray could see hundreds maybe thousands more, spread out across the city like a living net that ebbed and flowed, constantly moving with the tide. One of the energy motes drifted towards Fray, brushed against him and burst. A tiny spark of energy ran across his skin and it felt as if someone had pinched him.

It had to be the work of the Flesh Mage but Fray could only speculate about its purpose. Whatever the cause, the build-up of energy in the air wasn't a good sign. The Flesh Mage's plans were escalating and it looked as if they would happen soon, maybe tonight. Perhaps the energy motes represented a build-up of the emotions in the area.

Fray withdrew his magic and they set off again with Choss leading the way. Someone connected to one of the Families was working with the Flesh Mage. It made sense when Choss had explained they start with the person acting the most out of character. Don Kal, an old Morrin and perhaps the oldest head of a Family in Perizzi. He should have been calm, bided his time and waited for his moment to get revenge. Instead someone had manipulated or pressured him into starting a war. It seemed likely that the Flesh Mage was involved since he would benefit the most from such widespread violence.

"What's happening?" asked Choss.

"I can feel something in the air. It's like that calm moment just before a lightning strike."

"The air does smell strange," said Choss. Fray took a deep breath, noting that the usual smell of the sea and the city had become muted. A dry, crisp tang tickled his nose and the hairs on the back of his hands itched.

Fray felt the first trickle of nervous sweat run down his back. He wanted to say something witty to show Choss he wasn't scared, but nothing came to mind. Instead he just kept a firm grip on his sword to stop it tripping him up, and wiped the sweat from his brow.

With a slightly uneven gait because of his injured leg, Choss jogged down the street, his eyes constantly scanning for signs of trouble. Fray did his best to keep up and ignore the prickling against his skin as they crossed over into the meat district. He'd thought it would be a net of energy that would be hollow inside, but every street was the same, full of jostling sparks that pinched him.

After a few minutes at a slow jog Choss stopped abruptly and held up a hand. A couple of seconds later Fray heard the faint scuff of approaching footsteps. Choss pointed at a side street and they sprinted into it a few seconds ahead of a patrol. Three local men came into view, dressed in an assortment of armour, and all were armed with axes or swords. Fray and Choss crouched down in the shadows of a shop doorway, hands on weapons as they waited to see what the patrol would do. Fray expected some sort of idle banter, but the three men spoke tersely in harsh whispers. They were nervous and unsettled. Perhaps they could feel what was coming as well.

As they neared, Choss drew a punching dagger from his belt, slowing and quietly. There wasn't enough space for Fray as well, but he readied himself as best he could, bunching up the muscles in his legs and tightly gripping his sword. As he'd been instructed, he studied the men and their movements and picked out a target. His heart started to thump as they came closer and closer.

They were only half a dozen steps away. All one of them had to do was turn his head slightly and he'd see them hunched down in the meagre shadows. Fray's breathing sounded impossibly loud in his ears so he held his breath, sure that it would give them away. A tight band of pain started to form across his chest, but he ignored it as he willed the men to turn away. When black spots started to dance in front of his eyes he saw the men turn. Only after they'd disappeared around a corner did he dare breathe again.

Choss sheathed his dagger and led the way. Five more times they had to quickly duck into alleyways and once they were forced to hide on the bed of a cart between barrels of fish. Whether it was the stink or something else Fray didn't know, but the patrol went past them without stopping.

"Not much further," said Choss. "I've never seen so many patrols." His grimace held more than annoyance, but it took Fray a while to realise it was guilt. The stories of the destruction of several buildings in one night had reached the Guardians, but it had sounded ridiculous. Tales of a giant masked man dressed in black, carving a bloody path through the meat district, burning buildings with a flaming sword. A God made flesh, daring men to fight him and then mocking their weakness when they failed. The fiery sword might have been an exaggeration but looking at Choss he suspected the rest contained an element of truth.

As they slid off the cart something caught at the back of Fray's throat, a metallic tang that filled him with a sense of dread. It was blood. A lot of old blood. Run-off from the bulky slaughterhouses that loomed all around him. A giant congealed river of what had once been the essence of life ran in a sludgy mess beneath his feet. Someone had dipped into that river and summoned the pain from those final moments, twisting them into something for their own purpose. The Flesh Mage had fashioned it into a weapon, one that no one could see or touch, but Fray could feel it vibrating in the stones beneath his feet. It was the catalyst and a spike of terror. The Flesh Mage would then use the pain and suffering from the street war as a hammer to tear open a tiny fracture. He didn't want to think about what would happen after that.

Fray stumbled and would have fallen if Choss hadn't caught him by the elbow.

"What is it? Are you all right?"

Fray tried to find the words but knew that it would sound like gibberish. Instead he went with a version of the truth.

"He's summoning his power. I can feel it starting to build."

Choss's eyes widened in alarm. "Quickly."

They raced down narrow alleys, splashing through puddles of blood, their boots crunching bones and bits of gristle into dust. Past rotting skins and carcasses of long dead animals stacked like firewood, forgotten and now nothing more than feasts for flies. Fray didn't stop or look down, afraid that none of what he saw was real. At first he thought that only he was being affected but then he heard Choss muttering to himself.

Finally they reached the heart of Don Kal's territory, but all of the streets were closely guarded. Choss gestured at a nearby building set close to its neighbour. The alley between the two stank and the ground was littered with rotting filth and red sludge. The back door of the building had been forced open by someone in the past and poorly repaired. It flew open with a well-timed kick and then sagged on its hinges, the wood rotten and warped. Inside, the carcass of the building looked no better, black mould climbing the walls and more rotting filth clinging to the floor, making their feet stick. Everything of value had been stripped away, leaving nothing but a grimy green and black shell of a building that smelled like an open sewer. Fray gritted his teeth against the assault and followed Choss up the stairs, which creaked alarmingly under their combined weight.

In one or two places the wood had completely rotted through and they had to jump up a few steps or cling to the metal railing and pull themselves across a wide gap. It slowed their progress, which made Fray sweat even more, but not from exertion. Being this close to the centre of the Flesh Mage's power made his skin feel as if it were covered with a host of writhing maggots.

Eventually they reached the top floor and crouched down beside a window. Peering through the grimy pane into the street below Fray could see the front of one building which seemed to be the centre of activity. The faces weren't clear at this distance but he could still see a tall Morrin giving orders. A large group of people started to gather in front of the building.

"That's Don Kal," said Choss, gesturing at the Morrin. "And those at the front are his Gold and Silver jackals."

As they watched even more people came out of nearby buildings, lining up in front of Don Kal. The Morrin climbed up onto the back of a cart and began to speak to the crowd. After a few minutes two figures appeared from one of the buildings and made their way to the front of the crowd to stand beside Don Kal. The appearance of the newcomers sent a ripple through the assembly. From the way everyone reacted it was clear they recognised the two identical-looking women.

"Who are they?" asked Fray.

"Doña Parvie and her sister," hissed Choss. More armed people started filtering into the square at the back. "We all assumed Don Kal had lost his mind. It would be suicidal to take on the other Families alone, but he was working with Parvie all along."

Fray heard what Choss said but he was focused on scanning

the crowd. Choss had described the unusual albino he'd seen with Don Kal and he'd hoped it would turn out to be the Flesh Mage. After a few minutes of frantic searching Fray realised that if the Flesh Mage was in the crowd he would be in disguise.

The cold prickle along his scalp and the churning energy in the air meant he was close. Don Kal's speech started to excite the crowd and even though he couldn't hear every word, Fray picked up on the general theme of riches and ruling the city.

"Is he down there?" asked Choss.

"I think so, but I need to be sure," said Fray, tapping the side of his head. He reached out for his magic and it flowed into him with ease. Fray braced himself mentally for the onslaught and then peered out the window. His heightened eyesight sharpened until he could clearly see every face in the crowd and hear every word. The air crackled with the build-up of energy, and sparks of what looked like lightning flashed out from the centre of the crowd towards the sky. Most surprising of all was the Morrin himself. Whereas everyone else in the crowd had become suffused with a mix of orange and yellows, colours that spoke of their passion, Don Kal stood apart. His body was nothing more than a shadowy outline of a man filled with an endless black void.

"By the Maker," whispered Fray. "Don Kal is the Flesh Mage."

"Then where's the real Don Kal?"

"Dead. The Flesh Mage has become him. He doesn't care who wins or dies in this war, he just needs there to be as much violence as possible."

"We need to tell Don Jarrow. He has no idea what he's getting into."

"Wait, something is happening," said Fray. Disguised as Don Kal, the Flesh Mage started to pass out packets of something from the back of the wagon. Each person in the crowd ate something before passing it on to the jackal beside them. Almost immediately Fray saw a change among the crowd. The Flesh Mage started talking again, whipping the crowd into a greater frenzy with provocative words and promises he couldn't keep. But they were too drunk, too stupid or too arrogant to realise, and whatever he'd fed them started to affect their mood.

Cheers and shouts became something wild, a chorus of animalistic rage and wordless cries that hungered for blood.

"He's feeding something to the crowd. It's making them feral, almost like they're berserk."

"I've seen something like that before," said Choss, the blood draining from his face. "It happened at the arena."

It had to be to create more chaos and bloodshed. The Flesh Mage would need a vast amount of energy to open a rift. He didn't want any of his people losing their nerve and running from a fight. This way they would feel no pain and keep killing until they dropped dead from their injuries. The other Families would have no idea what was about to hit them.

Fray let go of his magic with some relief, suddenly glad he couldn't see or feel the Flesh Mage in such detail any more.

If they didn't warn the others and somehow convince them to work together, there would be slaughter among the Families unlike anything they'd seen before. The Flesh Mage would get exactly what he wanted. The rift would open and the nightmare that his father had died to prevent would be unleashed upon the world.

"Even with Parvie and her people, I don't see how they can win," said Choss, staring at the crowd.

Just then a beautiful woman with dark skin stepped out of a nearby building and moved to stand beside the Flesh Mage and Doña Parvie. Fray heard Choss gasp in surprise and a ripple of displeasure ran through the crowd at her presence. From the stance and gestures of the Flesh Mage he was doing his best to tell them she was a friend but the jackals seemed unconvinced and were visibly angry. A tall man with golden skin from Shael stepped up beside the newcomer and, if anything, that seemed to make the crowd even more upset.

"Who's that?" asked Fray.

Choss clenched his teeth and shook his head. He seemed unable to answer and was shaking with rage. Fray could see the muscles tensing across his shoulders and arms. With considerable effort the big man regained control of his emotions, although when he spoke his voice was ragged.

"That's Doña Jarrow. She must have been working with Don Kal all the time as well. She manipulated me, used me to start this war."

"I don't understand."

"By himself Don Kal couldn't win, but with Parvie's people behind him, and if Doña Jarrow has convinced people to follow her, I don't know what will happen."

"Then we need to go," said Fray, but the big man didn't move. He tried pulling Choss's arm but it was like trying to move a mountain. "We need to tell the others. What about Don Jarrow? Do you think he knows about his wife?"

The question caught Choss by surprise and he sat back on his haunches, staring into the distance.

"I bet he has no idea about what his wife has done," said Choss.

"Or any of this," said Fray, waving at the square below them. Finally Choss started to move, but not before glaring at Doña Jarrow. The war was almost upon the Families and they were totally unprepared. It would be a massacre and the Flesh Mage would get exactly what he wanted. Time had run out.

CHAPTER 35

Talandra really tried to listen carefully as Hyram detailed her security arrangements at the palace but her mind kept wandering. He was still sulking with her for having gone on ahead of the main caravan, making him escort Sasha her body-double in her place during the long and slow journey, but he would get over it. He was on more familiar ground now, protecting her in an environment he could control, with doors and walls.

The few days she'd been able to operate in Perizzi without being observed had been wonderful. She had squeezed in so many meetings every day and yet still managed to get seven hours of sleep at night. Normally she managed six but since finding out about the baby, and with the trip here sapping her stamina, she needed that extra hour. Even now she had to fight back a yawn.

"She doesn't need to know every tiny detail," said Alexis, cutting off Hyram mid-sentence.

"I trust you, Hyram. You've been very thorough," said Talandra, offering her brother a smile to soften the blow. Hyram grunted and turned towards the door. No doubt he'd have a good sulk about this later. Alexis mimed weaving a noose and hanging herself behind his back and Talandra fought back a snigger.

Alexis had proven to be the perfect foil for her brother. Her sense of humour balanced out her brother's moods and she understood subtlety and how to read body language far better than Hyram.

Alexis had known about the baby without being told and had promised to keep it a secret. No one else knew yet, not even her husband, as she'd left for Yerskania before he'd returned home. When she got back to Charas she intended to tell him first. When it became impossible to hide her growing waistline others would be told.

Alexis followed Hyram to the door. "Get some rest," she called back over her shoulder.

"I can't. I don't have time," said Talandra.

Alexis raised an eyebrow. "Nothing is happening for a couple of hours, then the harpies will descend to dress you up like a solstice duck, so what else are you going to do until then?"

Talandra didn't have an answer. Alexis glanced pointedly at the bed and then closed the door behind her. It did look tempting and had proven to be very comfortable last night. Queen Morganse had been incredibly generous with the accommodation she'd provided, giving Talandra an entire wing of the palace for her staff. In addition to her royal guards, who were stationed in the rooms closest to hers, there were also rooms for her maids, house staff and all of the others who were required for such an important visit.

For now there was very little to do except rest, and most of her people were taking advantage of the lull before the storm. After the banquet, the formal greetings with local dignitaries, and necessary ceremonies had been completed, Talandra would be able to have some important meetings. From the tone of the letters she'd received from Queen Morganse she too sounded keen to get past the formalities and move onto the business they had been discussing.

A loud knock repeated three times on the door disturbed her

thoughts. Three knocks meant someone important had arrived. Talandra heaved a long sigh, stared with longing at the bed and then composed herself.

"Come in," she said.

Alexis pushed open both doors and then stepped inside, Hyram moving to stand with his back against the opposite door. A small balding man dressed in crimson and white tottered in before clearing his throat.

"May I present Her Royal Majesty, jewel of the Argent Sea, noblest daughter of—"

"That's enough Poe," said Queen Morganse, sweeping into the room and dismissing the little man with a wave. He shuffled off and she watched him depart with a fond smile. "If I don't stop him early he will go on and on."

Many people had described the Queen of Yerskania to Talandra, but this was the first time that they'd met in person. For a woman who had four grown children, and grandchildren too, she looked surprisingly young. A closer look revealed fine lines at the corners of her eyes and mouth, and deep ridges between her eyebrows. Given everything that she'd been through, even just the events known to the public, Talandra thought she still looked amazing for her age.

With a generously curvy figure that Talandra somewhat envied, and flawless pale Yerskani skin, the tall Queen was a striking woman, even wearing a plain green dress, bereft of any jewellery or trappings of state.

Her dark brown eyes studied Talandra carefully as one hand casually played with the loose plait of her hair. Even if Talandra had not been watching she would have felt it when Morganse entered the room as her presence filled the space. She could see it affecting the others as they twitched at their posts.

"Your Majesty," said Morganse, curtseying formally and inclining her head.

"Majesty," said Talandra, imitating her and sinking slightly lower as this was Morganse's palace and she was the more senior. She was also a woman who had successfully ruled her nation for many years by herself after the death of her beloved husband. Talandra admired the woman and all that she had achieved, so was happy to bow just a little lower.

Morganse approached and warmly clasped her hands before kissing her on both cheeks.

"It's so good to finally meet you."

"You also."

"The stuffy formalities will come later, but I thought we should meet first and talk," she said before pointedly glancing at Talandra's guards.

"Thank you, both."

They took the hint and stepped outside, firmly closing the doors.

"How was your journey?" asked Morganse, taking a seat and gesturing for Talandra to sit down opposite. Talandra waited until Morganse was settled before sitting down.

"Long and tiring, your Majesty," said Talandra, which technically was true. It had meant a few nights sleeping outdoors in a tent.

"Formalities and rituals weigh on me after a while. Please, call me Morganse in private."

"I'd like that, Morganse," said Talandra with a smile.

"I remember that journey from Seveldrom to Yerskania. I did it when I was a girl. My father took me with him all the way to Charas as part of a trade delegation. This was almost forty years ago, before you were born. I think your mother was pregnant at the time."

"Did you meet her?" asked Talandra, trying to dislodge the catch in her throat.

"Briefly," said Morganse, staring off into the distance. "She left quite an impression. She was beautiful and very kind. You look a lot like her. So how many weeks along are you?"

Talandra thought about denying it but changed her mind.

"Is it that obvious?"

Morganse's laugh was a rich sound that filled the room with warmth. "Not at all, but after four children and a few grandchildren, I know all the signs. I'll leave you to your rest in a minute, but I wanted to talk to you briefly about a few things."

"Like men and women in gold masks?" suggested Talandra.

"Yes. In the last two weeks, eight children from Perizzi alone have left for Shael."

"I assume your agents saw the children arrive safely at the Red Tower?"

"They did. Everything the new Seekers have promised seems to have happened, but that doesn't mean I trust them."

"Nor me," admitted Talandra. "Half a dozen children from Charas recently made the journey. So far my agents have seen only two Seekers in my city. There might be a couple more, but not many."

"They're stretched," said Morganse, mirroring Talandra's thoughts. Whoever had taken over the Red Tower was doing their best, but they were still few in number. It explained why she'd not heard any reports of masked people in the countryside, visiting towns and remote villages. Morganse had shared similar information with her about Seekers only appearing in Perizzi.

"If we take them at face value then what they're doing will save lives," said Talandra.

"True. So, the question becomes, do we publicly support them in their efforts?"

They both understood that eventually the public would become aware of the masked Seekers and would expect a formal response from their respective Queens. The real problem was they had no way of knowing what the children were being trained for. The optimist in Talandra said that in a few years the Red Tower would be strong again and if someone like the Warlock should appear, she and other rulers could call on them for support.

The pessimist in her worried that those in charge could be teaching whole classrooms full of children to hate their own people, creating a hundred new Warlocks. She could suddenly see the wisdom in what she'd always thought of as barbaric branding of magic users in the desert kingdoms.

"I can see from your expression you share my concerns," said Morganse.

"If only there were some way we could send in an agent. Someone to report back what was happening inside the Red Tower."

Unfortunately few people with sensitivity to magic made it past their teenage years without some training to control their power. Accidents were common, with some children dying in their sleep and others simply exploding with power, often killing their family in the process. Those who did become adults without training often had such a tenuous link to magic they could ignore it and live normally. Despite the time she'd spent with the Battlemages during the war, Talandra still knew so little about how magic worked.

Not for the first time she regretted how things had ended with Balfruss. More than that, she hated how his name had become a curse, a word people would not say out loud for fear of attracting his attention. No one seemed to remember that it was Balfruss who had defeated the Warlock and if not for him the war would not have ended when it did.

"I think this requires more thought and a longer discussion," said Morganse. "Perhaps we can talk about it later."

"I agree."

"I also wanted to ask you about the other personal matter we discussed," said Morganse, staring off into the distance. For the first time since entering the room she looked uncertain and a little afraid.

Talandra's wasn't the only family that had been affected during the war. Although Morganse's son had not been murdered like Talandra's father, she'd still lost him. The country had also lost a future King, as he should have taken the throne after his mother.

In the final days of the war the Crown Prince had boarded a ship and sailed away. Since then, using their combined network of contacts, they'd been tracking his movements as best they could.

"After spending almost six months in Drassia, my contacts tracked him sailing north. I believe he made port in Zecorria," said Talandra.

"I have two contacts that report seeing him around the capital, Herakion. Then he seemed to disappear for three months before resurfacing. Do you know where he went after that?"

"He came to Seveldrom, to Charas," said Talandra, passing Morganse a note she'd received from a local agent. "He stayed in the capital for two nights and then travelled east towards the desert."

Morganse sat back to ponder this latest bit of information, her frown growing deeper. Talandra didn't think the Prince's movements were random. He wasn't aimlessly wandering from place to place, but so far her agents couldn't uncover the reason. From Morganse's expression she also hadn't determined why her son was travelling across the continent.

"I'll leave you to your rest," said Morganse, coming out of her reverie. Her smile was genuine but her eyes were still distracted. "I hope we can talk again soon."

"I'd like that," said Talandra.

She'd just settled down and was starting to doze off in the chair when there was another knock on her door.

Roza came into the room before Talandra had a chance to speak. She looked flustered and agitated, and sat down without asking permission.

"I was discreet, no one saw me come in," said Roza, tucking a loose strand of red hair behind an ear.

"Has something happened?"

"Katja has secured her invitation to the banquet. I've also managed to get a couple of extra agents inside the palace."

Talandra raised an eyebrow. "But?"

"There are still players we haven't been able to identify. We still don't have the full picture."

"You think we should tell Queen Morganse."

"At such an important event she will have her own people in the palace. We could combine our efforts."

Talandra took a few minutes to consider it, weighing up the alternatives before coming to a decision.

"For now, I think we should keep this to ourselves. While I trust Morganse up to a point, there's no way to know if any of her people have been compromised. Their first priority will be to protect their Queen. I don't want to be left behind and forgotten if things start to unravel. At least this way I know my people will be looking out for me."

"I have a number of agents inside the palace, plus all of your royal guards have been briefed," said Roza. "There's also the other idea we discussed. I think it would be prudent, just in case."

"I agree. See that it's done," she said and Roza sighed with relief.

Talandra knew it was a risky plan, but despite their best efforts to identify all of those involved in the plot to assassinate her, some remained hidden. At least she knew she was walking into a trap. She put her trust in her people, their ability to protect her, and the contingencies they'd made. It didn't sound like much, but Talandra also had a few tricks up her sleeves and would not be caught unawares. If anything, what would normally be a tedious and lengthy banquet might prove to be the most memorable she'd ever attended. She just hoped it wouldn't be her last.

CHAPTER 36

It felt to Choss as if his lungs were burning, but he did his best to ignore the pain and keep moving at a steady jog. The cracked and broken ribs were healing, his arm ached less than before and his leg constantly throbbed with pain, but worst of all was his head.

The physical pains of his body were familiar, comforting in their own way, as they followed a certain path. He knew what came next in the cycle of bruise, broken bone, sprain and torn muscle. By simply looking at the colour of a bruise, experience told him when it would recede and fade from angry purple to yellow and green. He knew the familiar itching meant the bone had started to knit back together and soon it would be ready to bear more weight.

The path of recovery for the imbalance in his head could not be so easily charted. Choss had no illusions. He knew there were many people more intelligent than him. He'd worked for some and had not tried to keep up or pretend they were evenly matched. But equally he'd also thought he knew himself well enough that it made him difficult to manipulate.

Everyone had a weakness, a flaw in their character, or a passion that made them blind and easy to control. At some point the

arena had become his life and then his obsession. He had forsaken and ignored opportunities thrust under his nose in order
that it succeed and become legitimate. Some had been there for
years and he'd not done anything about them, his biggest regret
being Munroe. Thoughts of her touch as she'd nursed him lingered in his mind. The feel of her lips, the warmth of her breath,
the taste of her skin.

Choss stumbled but quickly righted himself, focusing his
mind on the present. He'd done it to himself. By keeping people
at a distance, by isolating himself from his friends, he'd created
a void which he'd filled with the arena. Eventually friends had
stopped asking him to join them for a drink or a meal and he
hadn't even noticed. The only people he saw every day were those
connected to the arena like Vinny and Jakka, but each of those
had families, friends and lives. He had nothing else.

"Are you all right?" asked Fray, jogging a few steps back.

"Just thinking," said Choss.

"Do you think Don Jarrow will believe us?"

"We're about to find out," said Choss, pointing at the tall theatre in the heart of Don Jarrow's territory. Men and women
armed with crossbows saw him coming and Choss slowed to a
walk as they came into range.

"I need to see Don Jarrow," he said to a tall woman with red
hair. He recognised her as a second to one of the Gold, not normally someone who'd guard the theatre. A quick look at all of
those nearby showed him faces he knew well. The most loyal and
trusted that Don Jarrow could rely on, not people who might
have been tainted by his traitorous wife. Perhaps he already
knew.

"It's not a good time," said the guard.

"This is important. It's about Don Kal," he insisted. The
guard glanced at Fray, her hand twitching on her crossbow.
"Give her your sword, Fray."

To his credit Fray didn't argue. He unbuckled his sword belt and passed it across to the guard, together with two daggers. She still patted Fray down thoroughly while two other guards watched, nervously clutching their swords. Choss spotted two archers looking down at them from nearby rooftops and a few spotters as well. A direct assault on Don Jarrow at the theatre seemed unlikely, but he wasn't taking any chances. Choss passed across his punching daggers and for a moment thought they would search him as well for other weapons. The others looked to the redhead for guidance but she shook her head.

Inside, the theatre was more crowded than Choss had ever seen it before. Weapon racks leaned against the walls and most of them were already empty. A huge pile of arrows sat off to one side and several people were stuffing their quivers full before going out the back door. Several Gold were giving orders, grouping men and women together before directing them to points in the city. A huge map had been set up on a table in the centre of the room where Don Jarrow and several men and women stood around it. Vargus had positioned himself a few steps back from the huddle, but they'd left a space so that he could see the map. His experience would be invaluable in such a situation.

Behind Don Jarrow on the platform sat the two throne-like chairs. His wife's absence highlighted the betrayal to Choss but no one else seemed to have noticed.

More men and women filled the first tier of seating above Choss's head. All of them were armed and restless, awaiting orders that were gradually being given out. The air was so thick with tension it felt as if he were wading through a river to reach the table.

Don Jarrow and one or two glanced up as he approached, but they quickly turned back to the map.

"I want at least two people on every roof in this area," said

Don Jarrow, stabbing the map with a thick finger. "And get me another dozen runners. Pull in the Paper jackals if you need to. As long as they're fast."

Don Jarrow looked up again at Choss and made a dismissive gesture to those nearest, who stepped away to give him some privacy. Vargus didn't move from his post, but he did turn slightly so that he could keep Choss and Fray in plain sight. His right hand remained resting on the hilt of a dagger on his belt, and the expression on his face wasn't one Choss had seen directed at him before. It took him a moment to realise it was suspicion. Vargus no longer held him in high regard.

"I was angry with you for a while," said Don Jarrow, which drew Choss's attention back to him. "But then I realised she'd fooled and manipulated us all."

"We went into the meat district and—"

"Was she there?" asked Don Jarrow, cutting him off.

Somehow he already knew. Perhaps his wife's prolonged absence had confirmed Don Jarrow's suspicions or maybe she'd left him a note. Either way it seemed pointless for Choss to dance around the subject since the Don had brought it up.

"Yes. And Daxx was with her."

Don Jarrow grimaced. "It doesn't matter. She only took about two dozen people with her. Even with them, Don Kal can't attack all of the Families. Not at once. They'll come here first on her orders and we'll make them suffer."

"There's more bad news," said Choss. "Doña Parvie and her sister have signed up with Don Kal."

Don Jarrow's eyes widened and his mouth hung open before he regained control. He lowered his head to the map, hiding his surprise from the many faces watching. Now wasn't the time to show weakness. It could prove deadly. If Don Jarrow couldn't protect his people then someone else would remove him and try to do a better job.

"Parvie's people were filtering into the square while Don Kal gave a speech."

"She and her sister always were sneaky rats," muttered Don Jarrow. "They must think he's going to win, otherwise they'd just sit back and pick through the bones."

"If I were them, I'd send some people here and some against another Family," said Choss.

Don Jarrow shook his head. "No, they'll send everyone here first, try to recruit those who might be loyal to my wife," he said with a sneer. "They'll kill everyone else and then move on to the other Families."

"Could you go to the other Dons? Ask them for help?"

Don Jarrow considered it. "Don Lowell won't help. He's not lived this long by sticking his neck out. He'll barricade himself into his district and emerge when the fires have burned out. And the Duchess, she's not one for direct assaults. She'll keep her distance, work behind the scenes and make deals to keep herself safe. No, we're on our own."

Don Jarrow frowned and stared at the map, trying to find something that he could use to his advantage. There was another obvious suggestion but Choss doubted many would dare put it forward. He had little to lose and was already held in low regard so it seemed worth the risk.

"What about asking the Butcher for help?"

At first Choss didn't think Don Jarrow had heard, as he kept staring at the map, but eventually he looked up. His eyes were furious and Choss was suddenly reminded of how Jarrow had earned his position. All too quickly the rage drained away as reality set in. If he wanted to survive and protect his territory then he would have to compromise.

"We all told the Butcher to keep his distance with this business and he agreed," muttered Don Jarrow, in a low voice so that it didn't carry to the many ears nearby. "If he does help us there will be a cost. What puzzles me is that all of this isn't like Don Kal."

"Don Kalbensham isn't giving the orders any more," said Fray, stepping forward.

"Who's this?" asked Don Jarrow.

"Fray. He's a friend. He also has some magic."

As soon as the word left his mouth Choss thought it might have been a fatal mistake. Before he had a chance to say anything more, Vargus had drawn his sword and pressed it against Fray's neck. Without turning, Choss heard the creak of a few bows and felt several arrows pointing at his back.

"We came here to help you," said Fray.

Don Jarrow glared at Fray. "I don't know you. And right now," he continued, pointing at Choss, "his judgement can't be trusted. So speak quickly before I lose my temper."

"Don Kal is dead. Someone has taken his place and they're giving the orders."

Don Jarrow shook his head. "His people wouldn't switch allegiance that quickly."

"They can't tell the difference. The new leader looks exactly like Don Kal."

"Is this a game? Some kind of a joke?" said Don Jarrow, quickly losing patience.

"It's true," said Choss. "Fray can see things with his magic."

Don Jarrow shook his head. "I thought better of you, Choss. Not a man that could be fooled twice so easily."

Choss gritted his teeth to keep himself calm. "Fray, can you show them? Prove what I've said is true."

"Yes, as long as no one cuts my throat," he said, nervously glancing at the sword resting on his throat.

"Step back, Vargus," said Don Jarrow. "But at the first sign of someone acting peculiar, chop off his head."

Vargus lowered his sword and took two steps back, but his

steely gaze never wavered from Fray. If he chose to, Vargus could kill Fray before Choss had a chance to intervene. He might be a veteran but there wasn't a man or woman in the room that was his equal with a blade.

"Well?" said Don Jarrow.

Moving slowly, Fray reached into his pocket and drew out a narrow strip of cloth. He tied it across his eyes and bowed his head. Choss could hear his heart thumping in his ears. As the minutes ticked past and nothing happened he started to sweat. Everyone in the building had fallen silent and all eyes were locked onto Fray.

Don Jarrow shook his head and started to speak when Fray cried out and fell to his knees. "You killed a boy," whispered Fray, pointing at Don Jarrow.

"Is that it? Because I've probably killed dozens."

"This was when you were a child. He drowned."

Don Jarrow staggered back a couple of steps. Vargus started to move towards Fray, his sword a silver blur.

"Wait," cried Don Jarrow, holding up a hand. Vargus's sword paused a finger's breadth from Fray's throat. Don Jarrow righted himself and then sat down on his chair. Choss could see his hands were shaking. "Let him speak."

Vargus stepped back but kept his sword ready. Fray still had his eyes covered so he probably had no idea how close he'd come to dying.

"You were nine years old. This boy bullied you. Sometimes threw rocks, because you didn't have a father. This went on for years." Despite the press of bodies Fray's voice echoed around the theatre. "One day you saw him playing down by the river with some friends. He fell in but none of them could swim. They tried to help but couldn't, so they panicked and ran, leaving him to die."

Don Jarrow had turned pale and his left hand trembled until

he grabbed it with the right. "How?" he whispered, but Fray wasn't finished.

"He tried to swim but couldn't. Then he saw you and begged you for help. He'd seen you swimming down at the docks. You just stood there and watched him sink. They found his body three days later."

"How could you know that?" asked Don Jarrow.

Fray slowly unfastened the cloth from around his face. Despite their orders Choss heard the slow creak of several bows being drawn tight. A gasp ran through the crowd and there was a loud rasp of metal as swords were drawn. Fray's blue eyes had turned amber in colour and they glowed with an unnatural inner light, giving him an inhuman quality. When he spoke his voice sounded rough and it echoed around the theatre.

"Because the boy's ghost speaks to me and I can see him clearly," said Fray, pointing over Don Jarrow's left shoulder. "It lingers around you, caught between here and whatever comes next. There are more, many more, but his is the oldest spirit connected to you."

Fray turned to address the theatre and his words caused ripples throughout the crowds with people shifting in discomfort.

"I can see into the hearts of men and speak with the lingering dead. This theatre is full of spirits. They cry out for justice and revenge for the brutality you have visited upon them in life."

Fray's words may not have dented the thick skins of those assembled, whose crimes were many, but none would meet his bright gaze as he looked around the building. Each person turned their face away in fear, scared of seeing their own sins reflected. For some reason an amused grin touched Vargus's face at Fray's display.

"Don Kal is dead," said Fray. "A changeling has taken his place. A man who wears his face and skin. He's also fed Doña Parvie and Don Kal's people a twisted form of venthe, laced with magic. It drives them berserk and they won't retreat or stop fighting until they're dead. If you don't believe me then think of what happened at the arena and imagine that across the whole city."

"Can they still be killed?" asked Don Jarrow. Fray's revelation had unsettled the Don in a way Choss had never seen before. Even so, he recovered quickly and his hands had stopped shaking.

"Yes, but they won't feel pain in the same way."

"What does the changeling want?" asked Don Jarrow.

Fray shook his head. "He doesn't care about your people or anyone else. He needs a slaughter to fuel his magic. If he succeeds, what he will summon will tear this city apart and thousands will die."

"We need to tell the other Families," said Choss to Don Jarrow. "Even if they won't work with you, they should know what they're up against."

Don Jarrow considered it, absently waving at his people to stand down. The tension eased and Vargus sheathed his sword. Fray closed his eyes and when he opened them next they'd returned to their normal colour. It seemed to help but even so people who had previously ignored him now watched him warily. An echo of fear lingered throughout the crowd as each man and woman wondered about the spirits that trailed after them.

"I'll send word to the other Families," said Don Jarrow, moving to the table and frantically scribbling a few notes. "It may not help, but at least I can warn them. I need to prepare my people for the worst. Someone find me some runners," he yelled and the room became a hive of activity again.

"Head or heart," said Choss to the nearby Silver and Gold. "If they're as berserk as Morrin, nothing else will stop them. Tell everyone."

They began to spread the word around the crowd and a few men and women disappeared out the door to alert the sentries. A few minutes later a dozen lanky youths turned up and several were sent out with a note for the other Families. The rest left at a sprint to inform all of Don Jarrow's people about what to expect. Two left with messages to contact the Butcher. Don Jarrow grimaced the entire time he wrote those last two notes but it had to be done if he wanted to survive the night.

As people went about their business the central table stopped being the focus of attention. For a few seconds Don Jarrow closed his eyes and Choss saw a shadow of sorrow pass across his features. It was there for only a moment. The sum of all the guilt and anguish he felt about his actions over the years. Or perhaps he mourned the loss of his wife who had been his partner and oldest friend for many years. A second later the pain was gone and the old Don Jarrow stared at him again, an implacable and dangerous man.

"I would be happy if you fought for me," he said, which Choss knew was the closest thing he'd ever get to an apology.

"I'm needed elsewhere," said Choss.

"Then I hope the Blessed Mother protects you," said Don Jarrow, offering him a brief smile before turning back to his map.

By the time he and Fray had passed through the crowd and stepped outside, the mood of the guards had changed dramatically. Any lingering doubts about his loyalty were gone and their weapons were immediately returned to them without hesitation. Fray received a few lingering stares but mostly it was behind his back.

"Well, that was quite a performance," said a smoky voice that made Choss smile.

*

As Fray watched, a petite woman with a mischievous grin sauntered up to them. Dressed in tight black trousers, leather knee
boots and a white shirt over a black vest, she didn't look like any
of Don Jarrow's people. She carried four identical daggers in a
baldric around her narrow waist and a pair of black leather gloves
tucked behind her belt. At the sound of her voice he noticed a
shift in Choss's stance. A relaxing of his shoulders and a smile
tugging at the corners of his mouth. As she approached, Fray felt
a familiar prickling at the edges of his perception. Just as Eloise
had taught him he slowly opened his senses without embracing
his magic.

"By the Maker," he whispered, staggering back a step.

Choss raised an eyebrow. "Munroe, what did you do?"

"I'm not doing anything," she said.

"Fray, what's wrong?" asked Choss. Instead of answering, Fray
embraced his magic. A loud pulse, one much stronger than any
he'd ever felt before, echoed through his head, making him
wince. As he stared at Munroe his mouth fell open in surprise.

Where the Flesh Mage had been filled with nothing but a
bottomless void, Munroe shone with golden light so bright it
hurt his eyes. It suffused her entire body, transforming her into
a being of majesty that made his heart ache. Wave upon wave of
energy flowed outwards from her in time with her pulse, filling
the air around her with power. The connection he felt between
her and the Source was stronger than any he'd ever felt before.

"You're beautiful," said Fray, struggling to translate what he
was seeing, but his senses were overwhelmed.

"You're not bad yourself," said Munroe.

Slowly, bit by bit, he withdrew his magic. The wrench against
his senses was so intense it felt as if he'd carved out a piece of his
own soul and locked it in a box. It took him some time to settle
and regain control of his emotions. Tears ran unchecked down his
cheeks.

"What just happened?" asked Choss.

"Has anything strange ever happened to you? Something you couldn't control?" he said to Munroe.

"Once or twice," she said with more than a little sarcasm. "Why?"

"I can sense when someone is sensitive to magic. Your connection is so strong, it's amazing," he said to Munroe.

"What are you saying?"

"You have an ability, a magical Talent. Whatever it is, you can be taught to control it."

For a few seconds Munroe just stared at him and then she began to laugh, a rich sound that made the hairs prickle across his scalp. She laughed so hard she bent over double and started to cough until Choss gently patted her on the back. After a couple of minutes she recovered, but a smile still lingered.

To Fray's surprise Munroe grabbed him by the ears and kissed him hard on the mouth. She soon pulled away and sighed.

"Typical."

Munroe told him about her curse and the many horrible things that had happened to her over the years since it had manifested.

"If I don't do something with the feeling, it builds up and just gets worse. So I share my bad luck with others. Don Jarrow appreciates it."

"But it doesn't have to be bad luck. You could control it, and do so much more," said Fray. "When we get back, there's someone I'd like you to meet."

"Get back? Where are you going?" she said, addressing the question to Choss.

"To kill Don Kal," said Choss, as if it would be that simple. Fray hadn't explained all of what might happen and Choss hadn't asked. He knew everything he needed to.

"Then I'm coming with you," she said.

"That's not a good idea," said Choss. Munroe glared up at him but it had no effect on the big man. "It's too dangerous."

"I didn't nurse you back to health just to stand around and do nothing. Especially now, when we might have a future together."

After hearing just a little of what Munroe had done with her power, Fray thought she would be incredibly useful, but he kept his mouth shut. There was a lot more going on between them than either one of them had said.

Eventually Choss relented. "Please, be careful."

"I promise," said Munroe, smiling up at him.

"I think the three of us should be able to sneak in amid the chaos," said Fray.

"Four," said Choss. "There's one other who's coming with us."

Choss led the way through the city, taking them out of Don Jarrow's territory and then surprisingly down to the docks. He picked up half a dozen fist-sized stones and walked out to the end of an empty dock. In the flickering light of scattered torches and lanterns, Choss cast a long shadow across the water. The tide was out and the sea very still, its surface a murky blue grey that looked more like glass than water.

This late at night the docks were quiet. All ships were tied up and the only noise came from the waterfront bars behind them. But the sound of merriment seemed removed and part of another world to Fray. One full of light, music and joy. The revellers knew nothing about the Flesh Mage and the destruction he threatened to unleash. The city would fall in hours and after that it would only get worse.

One at a time Choss threw the stones as far as he could out into the sea. They splashed down close to each other, creating ripples across the water, spreading out in an ever-widening circle that eventually faded out of sight. Choss joined them back at the start of the dock but his eyes stayed on the waves.

Fray heard a faint whisper and a quiet rush as if something huge had passed through the water. As he turned towards the others the dock creaked and something bumped against the wood beneath his feet. A huge green hand and then another appeared on the edge of the dock, followed by the broad lumpy head of a Vorga. It hauled itself out of the sea, rising higher and higher as if the ocean had just given birth to it. It stood eye to eye with Choss, making it at least six and a half feet tall. The Vorga grinned at Choss, showing off razor sharp teeth, and the big man clapped it on the shoulder as if they were old friends.

"Is it time?" it grated, in a voice softer than Fray had expected. Water ran down its green and white skin and its whole body shivered.

"Yes, old friend. We're going to war," said Choss. This time it was Fray who shivered with fear and a terrible sense of dread.

CHAPTER 37

It had been a long time since Katja had worn a beautiful dress and been waited on hand and foot. Now that his son was safe and in good health Lord Mullbrook was happy to be an accomplice and guide her through what would happen when they arrived at the palace. When he'd offered her his arm at the front door it had taken her a couple of seconds to remember why. Katja thought Lord Mullbrook looked handsome in his elegant suit and must have been very dashing in his youth.

"You'll be fine," he said, helping her into the carriage.

On the ride to the palace Lord Mullbrook outlined the normal order of the evening at such events.

"Once all the guests have arrived we'll have about an hour to mingle over drinks."

Katja slipped her shoes off and then back on quickly. They looked great but she couldn't run in them. "Then what happens?"

"We'll all be called to dinner and the formal banquet will begin. With so many people to feed at once it will take hours," explained Lord Mullbrook.

At first Katja thought Rodann had wanted her in the palace to assist with the plan. Now she had a growing suspicion it was the opposite. He didn't trust her at all. He wanted her in plain sight where his people could keep an eye on her and she wouldn't be able to act against him until it was too late. Or perhaps he simply wanted a scapegoat to take the blame for any sudden and unusual deaths.

"No one is allowed to take any weapons inside the palace apart from the royal guards. So don't use that unless absolutely necessary," he said, gesturing at her necklace. "You don't have any other weapons do you?" he asked, suddenly suspicious.

"No. Of course not." She'd been forced to give up her usual array of daggers, but had kept the long blade strapped to her thigh. The late Lady Mullbrook's elegant dress hugged her figure, leaving few places to conceal a weapon, but she didn't think any guard would search her that thoroughly.

The gentle rocking of the carriage and the rhythmic clopping of the horses' hooves on stone started to lull Katja to sleep. A few minutes later she suddenly awoke when the carriage stopped outside the palace gates. Through a gap in the curtains she could see tall black iron gates and through them the five square towers of the palace. A brief conversation took place between the driver and the guards before they were let through the gates into the courtyard.

"A few people might stare or gossip," said Lord Mullbrook, apologetically. "I suggest you just ignore them."

Katja raised an eyebrow. "Why would they?"

Lord Mullbrook coughed and cleared his throat. "I've been a widower for a few years. This is the first time I've come to court with someone."

"And?" said Katja, still not seeing the problem.

"Well, you're quite a bit younger than me and I'm reasonably wealthy. They might make the wrong assumption."

"Then maybe we should give them something to gossip about," said Katja, touching him on the knee.

"My dear, if I were thirty years younger, I would show you a night you'd never forget," he said, patting her hand affectionately.

"You're not that old. I'm sure there are a few things you could show me," she said with a wink.

Lord Mullbrook was spared any further embarrassment as the carriage stopped again and the door opened to reveal a palace servant. Lord Mullbrook jumped out and then offered his hand, while forcing a smile. Katja took her time and carefully stepped out of the carriage, doing her best to avoid getting tangled in the dress and falling over.

A few other carriages were arriving at the same time and several richly dressed couples disembarked. They all glanced around, waving or nodding at Lord Mullbrook, before giving her a searching and quite often scathing look.

Katja was tempted to say something but bit her tongue instead. Lord Mullbrook had been very cooperative and she didn't want to add to his woes. She only had to pretend to be one of these people for a night. He had to deal with them for the rest of his life.

She took his arm and followed the other couples up the wide path and through the gardens to the main doors. They formed a leisurely queue under the careful scrutiny of palace guards who were stationed at intervals around the outside of the palace, and there were more at every door.

Although no guests were searched Katja felt several pairs of eyes on her as she walked towards the building. From experience she knew people held themselves in a different way when they carried a weapon, often casually resting one hand on their belt to stop a scabbard tangling between their legs.

Several men in front didn't seem to know what to do with their free hand and in the end they tucked it behind their belts. Katja pretended not to have noticed, tried to act relaxed and pointed out some of the more interesting flowers in the garden as they waited.

At the door a balding middle-aged servant only casually glanced at the invitation before smiling at Lord Mullbrook and gesturing for them to go inside.

"Big smile," said Lord Mullbrook from the corner of his mouth as they crossed the threshold.

"Lord Mullbrook and Lady Katja Smallwood," shouted the Marshall, two steps behind Katja and nearly deafening her in one ear. The majority of the richly dressed crowd didn't bother to turn around, but a dozen or so heads glanced across. Katja saw a few raised eyebrows in her direction but in such surroundings it would go no further than that. They would sidle up to her or Lord Mullbrook later to find out more if they were interested. Lord Mullbrook had carefully chosen the name Smallwood. It belonged to a modest family with minor holdings who never came to the capital, so her identity was secure for one night.

Even though she didn't really keep up with minor court politics and which of the nobles were gaining power, Katja recognised many of the faces in the crowd. There were several distinct groups. People of the same social standing huddled together, glaring, ignoring or trying to put a brave face when looking at others depending on their status.

It was a complex game in itself and she had no patience or time to worry about it. A quick scan of the crowd revealed no sign of Rodann or Teigan among the guests or the many palace servants moving through the room with drinks.

"You have some time," said Lord Mullbrook from the side of his mouth as he smiled and waved. "Just get back here when they ring the bell for the banquet."

"Thank you," she murmured.

Lord Mullbrook stepped back and kissed the back of her hand.

"Good luck," he whispered before they separated. He headed one way deeper into the crowd and she went the other, towards the edge of the grand ballroom.

A constant stream of servants emerged from one door, which she bypassed, but beside it was an archway to an adjoining corridor. Katja ducked into it to get away from the crowd, found she was alone and followed it for a few minutes. She'd memorised the map of the palace layout Roza had given her, but it took her a few minutes to orientate herself. If she were either Rodann or Teigan, they wouldn't want to be too far away from the banquet, but also needed to be close enough to observe events.

Circling the corridors and open spaces around the busiest areas revealed nothing unusual except numerous narrow stairwells partially hidden behind screens or worn tapestries. They were the backstairs designed for servants to quickly criss-cross the palace without running into guests. Eventually she chose one at random and descended slowly, listening carefully for approaching footsteps. Halfway down the narrow winding staircase she heard a woman crying up ahead, her voice echoing off the plain stone walls.

With only a few alcoves to duck into, Katja had the choice of either going back up or pressing on. She conjured up a few excuses just in case a servant proved bold enough to ask her why she was downstairs, then continued. Sat on the bottom step was a young woman barely out of her teens dressed in a white and grey palace uniform. The girl's hands shook and tears ran down her face as her breath hitched in her throat. She hiccupped a few times before continuing to whimper and cry.

Katja scuffed her foot on the final few steps to announce herself and the girl shot to her feet.

"What's happened?" asked Katja, before the girl could ask a question of her own. She tried to speak a few times but the words just wouldn't come out. Eventually she just pointed down the corridor. Katja offered her a reassuring smile and followed the girl's directions.

At the far end of a long narrow corridor she could see the back of a crowd of servants. There was an accompanying murmur of whispers and muttering, shaking of heads and other signs of distress. Katja moved up behind the crowd and tried to peer past everyone but could see little except a huge room from which a vast array of tempting smells emerged. She could hear the crackle of several fires and smell roasting meat, which meant it had to be the main kitchen.

"Is someone hurt?" she whispered.

A broad matronly woman with thick arms spoke without turning around.

"Worse than that. She's dead."

"When did it happen?" asked Katja.

"A few minutes ago. She clawed at her throat and started wheezing, then turned purple and collapsed."

"Chef said it was poison," muttered someone.

"Or maybe she got something stuck in her throat," said another in the crowd. "My cousin got a fishbone stuck and choked to death."

"I bet your cousin didn't have blue foam coming out their mouth," said someone at the front.

"It was poison," said Katja. The confidence in her voice made a few heads turn in her direction. When they realised she wasn't another servant a pool of space quickly opened up around her.

"I'm a doctor, let me through," she said and was immediately given access.

A huge table down the centre of the massive room was covered with food in various stages of preparation. Whole hog roasts sizzled over fire pits, dozens of pots bubbled away while being casually attended by an army of servants. Most were more interested in what was happening than in preparing the food but they could stir with one hand and watch.

Two wide archways led to the next section of the kitchen. More than fifty more people were loitering, all of them staring at the woman's body on the floor lying in one of the archways. Someone had covered the top half of the body with an apron but Katja knelt down and pulled it aside before anyone could stop her.

A familiar face stared back at her. It was Marcella, the shrew-faced woman from Rodann's meeting. The last expression on her face was one of pain and terror. One hand was curled up into a tight claw held against her chest and the other reached out beseechingly for assistance. A pale blue smear, which had dried on her chin, ran from both corners of the woman's mouth. Her clothes were different to those around her and although people were upset, no one seemed to be grieving.

"Who is she?" asked Katja, feigning ignorance.

"Outside help," said a gaunt man wielding a ladle. "For a banquet of this size, chef brings in people to assist. She and her husband were from Seveldrom. They were supposed to be feeding all of the royal guard and Queen Talandra's warriors."

A cold prickle ran up Katja's spine. "Where's the food she brought with her? Has anyone eaten it?" said Katja, rounding on the man.

"No," he said, taking a step back. "We think the meat was spoiled. The butcher is taking it away."

The prickle of fear turned into something else and Katja stood up sharply. Even before she asked the question the man was pointing through the archway and she followed his arm. The next section of the kitchen was the bakery, where people were slowly getting back to work, and beyond that was an area devoted to desserts. Katja marched as fast as her dress and high shoes would allow, passing through several more sections before eventually reaching an open door.

A cart had been backed up to the building where a bald and tattooed Seve man was loading chunks of meat onto a wagon. The back of the cart was covered with a grey cloth, but as he threw another side of beef onto the back the blanket slipped and an arm flopped out. He saw her approaching but made no move to stop her from pulling back the cloth. Katja had last seen Borren at Rodann's meeting with Marcella, his shrew-faced wife. Now his face was also constricted in terror and there was a blue smear around his mouth. She also noticed several fingers on one of his hands had been broken.

"You're the Butcher, aren't you?" said Katja, staring at the thick muscles across the man's chest and arms. Intricate tattoos ran the length of both arms. "Did Roza send you?"

"Talandra upset a lot of people during the war," he said, ignoring the question. "Seveldrom won and the people here in the west lost. It doesn't matter that their rulers were blackmailed or coerced. All they remember is that a lot of Yerskani died at the hands of Seves during the war. Talandra gave the orders, so they blame her."

"That's what Rodann kept saying," said Katja.

"People here lost a lot of friends and relatives. They're scared of Talandra, because of what she did in the past and what she might do in the future. They're worried about her influence over Queen Morganse, and after being held captive once, they don't want to be prisoners again."

"It's insane. Can't they see all the good she's been doing? She's been working so hard to maintain the peace. It's one of the reasons I'm here."

At the end of the war there had been a purge in Perizzi, where every Chosen was killed, but also a number of foreign agents disappeared overnight. For a very short period of time the city was open, allowing Talandra to send in more agents like Katja and several others. By the time other nations had sent in replacements she was firmly entrenched and part of the landscape. The more eyes and ears they had, the easier it would be to identify rifts between nations and hopefully stop them before they developed.

"That's true," said the Butcher, "but while all of that was happening, and the war was raging, very little changed for the Families. They're suspicious and very careful, which meant getting inside their network, and having access to their information, wasn't something that could happen overnight."

"You're still working for the Queen," said Katja.

"My loyalty remained unchanged," said the Butcher. "King Matthias died while I worked for Talandra. I can do more working here in the shadows to ensure that it never, ever, happens again."

Katja was speechless as she tried to grasp what he had sacrificed and what he was willing to do to protect the Queen. The Butcher had a fearsome reputation and like her he had become part of the landscape.

"None of the royal guards or Seves protecting Talandra ate any of the food," said the Butcher. "I've delivered something safe instead. It was supposed to make the Seves go berserk, so they'd kill Queen Morganse. Now that this part of the plan has failed, what will Rodann's next move be?" Katja shook her head and glanced at Borren's body.

"He didn't know anything," said the Butcher.

"It's how Rodann operates. He doesn't trust anyone, so only he knows the whole plan."

"Then you need to get back upstairs and find out what he's planning. I'll take care of this," said the Butcher.

By the time Katja made it back upstairs the last of the guests were just arriving as the front doors closed behind them. She slipped into the crowd and slowly moved through it, looking carefully at all of the guests for a familiar face. Across the room she spotted Lord Mullbrook talking to a woman with long black hair and an hourglass figure. As she turned to pick up a glass of wine from a passing servant Katja saw her face in profile. It was Faith. As ever, her stylish pale blue dress with a daring bare back and silver trim was equal to that of any noble in the room. Her ears, fingers and neck were adorned with gold and jewels but even then she looked underdressed compared to some in the crowd. Katja doubted any of them knew who Faith really was but she also noticed that no one was staring, which suggested her presence at such events wasn't unusual.

As Faith slipped away to speak to another noble, Lord Mullbrook spotted Katja across the room and raised a questioning eyebrow. She shook her head and frowned before scanning the crowd again. A part of Rodann's plan had failed but it would only be one part of the whole. If she were in his position she would have contingencies to ensure the outcome remained the same.

Katja was starting to feel despondent until she saw another familiar face in the crowd. Lizbeth. She was dressed in palace livery and wouldn't have stood out if not for her gloves. Every other servant had bare hands. Hers, Katja recalled, were red and chapped from physical work, probably scrubbing floors. They might upset the delicate sensibilities of the guests so had been covered.

Katja moved across the room, keeping Lizbeth at an angle so she could see her face, but remained at the periphery of the servant's eyesight. There was no mistaking her. Katja assumed she worked for a noble house and somehow Rodann had arranged for her to serve drinks to the guests in the palace.

A raucous laugh from an old man beside Katja made a few people glance around. Lizbeth was nervous and her hands shook as she collected up the empty glasses. She jumped slightly at the old man's laugh and then looked around for the source of the disturbance.

She and Katja stared at one another across the room for the space of three heartbeats. A second later Lizbeth passed her tray to another servant and hurried out of the room with Katja racing after her.

CHAPTER 38

Choss tried to ignore his injuries and push the pain to the back of his mind, but despite his best efforts they were starting to intrude. He led the way into the heart of Don Kal's territory with Munroe and Fray a few steps behind and Gorrax bringing up the rear.

So far the streets had been unusually quiet but he wasn't surprised. Word would have got around and even those who weren't involved with Family business knew when to stay inside and lock their door.

What they were attempting felt like a fool's errand and yet he wouldn't turn aside. Too stubborn, or perhaps too stupid, he didn't know, but either way it didn't matter. Choss had played his part in starting the war between the Families, working for Doña Jarrow and unknowingly furthering her goals, and now there was a price. She'd told him once that there was a price to pay for the things that mattered. There was also a cost for making a mistake.

"Are you all right?" asked Munroe behind him. Choss turned around, thinking she'd noticed his limp despite his best efforts, but found she was staring at Fray. He'd gone incredibly pale and was shaking as if freezing cold, his teeth clattering together.

"Don't you feel it?" Fray asked Munroe, who shook her head. "The air is full of energy. The Flesh Mage has already begun summoning his magic. We don't have long."

Choss couldn't feel any magic but he could smell a change in the air. Normally the city smelled of a hundred flavours that were so familiar he barely noticed any more. Woven into them all was a faint tang of the sea, but now the air felt dry in his lungs and it prickled against his skin like the moments before a storm.

"We're getting close," said Choss, gritting his teeth against the pain before setting off again. The swelling around his right eye had reduced a little but his vision on that side was less than perfect. To compensate he swung his head left and right as they crept along deserted streets, the air tingling with expectation. He felt a growing sense of dread and his scalp prickled as if ghostly fingers were being drawn through his hair.

Somewhere in the city Choss heard an angry roar from a hundred voices mixed together. More joined in, adding their own rage to the din, and shortly after came the echoes of steel against steel. Men and women began to scream in pain and soon it all meshed together into one horrendous din that spoke of violence and bloodshed.

Perhaps one of the other Families had decided not to wait and had attacked first. Perhaps Don Jarrow had managed to convince the other Families to join with him against the imposter who posed as Don Kal. It really didn't matter, as long as the fighting stayed away from his group. They needed the distraction to try and slip through unnoticed. Even so Choss didn't think they would be able to avoid a fight all together. If the Flesh Mage was half as devious as Fray suggested he wouldn't leave himself open to attack. He would hold back some of his best muscle to avoid interruptions.

Choss just hoped he was up to the task. For the first time in his life he wasn't sure how long his stamina would hold out. It galled him to be injured and possibly not up to what lay ahead. He'd fought with injuries before but never this severe.

They reached a wide crossroads and he gestured for the others to move against the side of the building. They were now inside Don Kal's territory and normally the streets in the area would be busy with customers enjoying one of the many available vices. Instead an eerie silence gripped the area. Choss moved to the corner and quickly stuck his head around, scanning the streets. They looked empty but Choss thought he heard a faint scuffing not far away.

"Are you all right?" he heard Munroe whisper. He thought she was talking to Fray again until he felt a tug on his arm.

Choss didn't trust himself to speak so instead he just nodded. Her smile warmed him inside but he turned away before he grinned back. He didn't want to think about her and tried to force away all thoughts about tomorrow that were now possible.

He was brought back to the present by a patrol of six thugs, probably Wooden jackals, foot soldiers who worked in teams. They were coming this way, scanning doorways and alleys, and would reach Choss and the others in a few minutes. They could run, or try to hide until the patrol passed by, but their options were limited. Gorrax's ears perked up at the sound of the approaching squad and he tapped one side of his head. Choss held up six fingers and the Vorga just grinned. The odds meant nothing to him.

"There's a patrol coming," Choss whispered to the others. "We could double back, try and get deeper into Don Kal's territory from somewhere else."

"Won't there be patrols elsewhere?" asked Fray.

"He's right," said Munroe. "And we don't have much time. I can feel something in the air. Something sour," she said with a grimace as if she'd just bitten into a lemon.

"We fight here," said Gorrax, weighing in.

Choss took a deep breath, rolled his shoulders to loosen them and led the way into the street. He drew both punching daggers and heard the ring of steel as Fray drew his sword. Munroe had a dagger in each hand and Gorrax carried no weapons. Choss wasn't worried as the Vorga didn't need any. He was a weapon.

They spread out across the street and waited for the patrol. Choss wasn't sure what he expected, taunts or threats would've been usual, but the empty stares were worse than anything he'd anticipated. Instead of speaking, the patrol just drew their weapons and charged, screaming and snarling like animals.

The first man died with a dagger buried in his throat courtesy of Munroe, but it took him a few steps to realise. Eventually he slowed from a run to a walk and fell forward, a look of surprise on his face. It didn't slow the others or perhaps they didn't care.

Choss ducked a crude swing and retaliated, jabbing at his opponent's ribs with his left hand and lashing out with a riposte from his right. The jackal fought with reckless abandon, barely turning aside blows before pressing forward. Twice Choss felt his blades slice into the man's flesh but the two injuries had no effect. The jackal didn't slow down or show any signs of feeling his wounds.

All around him Choss could hear the others fighting for their lives as they were pressed by opponents who seemed to have no sense of self-preservation. Their inhibitions had been removed and their stamina appeared to be unlimited. After only a couple of minutes of fighting a series of sharp jabbing pains ran through Choss's chest from his damaged ribs. His breathing became increasingly loud in his ears and on all sides he could hear the others struggling with their opponents. The sound of steel on steel echoed in the night, broken only by that of shuffling feet on the stones and the occasional hiss of pain.

Although his opponent seemed unstoppable he was ultimately limited by his skill with a blade, which was moderate at best. He took more risks in an attempt to compensate and bully his way through Choss's defence, but it wasn't working. Choss was able to match his recklessness with caution while he bided his time and waited for an opening.

It took another minute but eventually he saw it, blocking an overhand hammer blow with his left while grabbing the jackal's wrist. As the thug moved to wrestle for control of his sword Choss buried his other punching dagger in the jackal's chest. No matter how frenzied or immune to pain, a man couldn't fight with six inches of steel through his sternum. The man stared in shock at Choss and then crumpled to the ground.

As Choss turned to look for another opponent it was nearly over.

Munroe danced around her opponent, a tall woman with red hair. Already the woman bore over half a dozen wounds, long red gashes on her chest and arms, but it hadn't slowed her down. Finally Munroe managed to get the woman to make a sound when she cut the tendons on the back of both legs. With a scream the woman dropped to her knees but even then she reached for a dagger. Before she had a chance to use it Munroe stabbed her in the side of the neck. The woman gagged and tried to say something around the blade, spraying blood across the ground. With feeble hands she reached for the weapon but Munroe pulled her blade free and stepped back, careful to avoid the growing pool of blood.

Several figures lay on the ground already and Fray ran another through before quickly yanking his sword free with a grunt of effort. Gorrax picked his opponent up off the floor, batted away the sword and casually snapped the Morrin's neck with a sharp twist. As ever the Vorga looked disappointed at the ease with which he'd dispatched his opponent.

Fray had a couple of minor cuts and Munroe a shallow nick on one arm, but generally they were unharmed. Choss took a minute to catch his breath while the others cleaned or retrieved their weapons. The burning pain in his side was only growing worse and each breath still hurt.

"Should we hide the bodies?" asked Munroe.

Choss shook his head. "There's no time."

Even if the bodies were discovered by another patrol it wouldn't matter. The Families were already fighting each other and the Flesh Mage wouldn't send someone to investigate a few missing bodies. From what Fray had said the number of dead didn't matter to the Flesh Mage, as long as he had enough time to complete his ritual. Choss was also growing increasingly worried about Fray, who looked pale and sickly, as if he'd been struck down by a sudden illness. Choss knew it wasn't the fight that was affecting him. Fray had mentioned that something like this might happen because of the foul magic in the air and had told Choss to ignore it. Even so, Choss wasn't sure how much longer Fray, or he for that matter, would be able to continue fighting. It was better to press on now and give the others a chance at finishing this.

"There's someone following us," said Gorrax, pointing back the way they'd come.

"If they catch up we'll deal with them, otherwise we don't have time," said Choss.

After getting his bearings and catching his breath a little, Choss pressed on towards the square where he'd last seen the Flesh Mage. Several times they heard the nearby clash of fighting but they didn't encounter another patrol. Whether it was his imagination or dark magic Choss thought the air started to smell foul, like bad eggs and rotting fruit. Sweat ran freely down Fray's face but he gritted his teeth and seemed determined to carry on.

Finally they reached the end of a familiar alley, one of several that led to the square where the Flesh Mage had made his proclamation. At the mouth of the alley stood two jackals but Gorrax crept up behind them and ripped out their throats before they had a chance to turn around.

Wheezing like an old man with the damp lung Choss steadied himself on one wall and followed the Vorga's broad back down the alley. Behind him Choss could hear Munroe asking if he was all right, but he didn't have any breath to speak so just nodded and pretended that all was well.

They emerged into the square and quickly spread out into a line. Choss was expecting the most desperate fight of his life, but remarkably the square was abandoned except for a group of five people. Doña Parvie and her twin sister were giving orders to a couple of runners, who quickly raced off when they saw Choss and the others. Stood beside the sisters was Pietr Daxx as well as two big jackals.

The twins didn't wait to see what happened. They ran in the opposite direction to Choss, disappearing down an alley, shadowed by their two bodyguards. Daxx didn't run. He stared at Choss and barely seemed to notice the others were even there.

"The Flesh Mage is that way," said Fray, gesturing off to the right.

"Then you should go. He won't stop you," said Choss, never taking his eyes off Daxx. "Munroe, you should go as well."

"What?"

"He'll need your help to stop the Flesh Mage."

"Choss."

"We need to go after Doña Parvie and her sister. Doña Jarrow is probably with them. I have to try and stop this war. It's my fault."

"Choss, look at me," insisted Munroe.

Even though Choss didn't want to look away Munroe's tone of voice was not one that he could ignore. He broke off the staring match and turned to face her.

"I'm not leaving you here," she said.

"I'm not alone," said Choss, looking over Munroe's shoulder at Gorrax. The Vorga offered her what Choss thought was meant to be a reassuring grin.

"I promise no harm will come to him. He will be safe," swore the Vorga.

"I could kill Daxx in two seconds," she said.

"I know," said Choss, "but the Flesh Mage is more important. You need to save your strength for him. Let me and Gorrax take care of Daxx and the others."

Munroe still hesitated, biting her lip before muttering under her breath. "I fucking hate this." She pulled his face towards her and kissed him fiercely. "Don't you dare get yourself killed."

Choss thought about saying something witty but the look in her eyes made him change his mind.

"Yes, Ma'am."

"Please look after him," she said to Gorrax, who bobbed his head.

Muttering to herself Munroe supported Fray on one side with an arm around his waist and together they shuffled away in pursuit of the Flesh Mage. Choss watched Munroe until she disappeared around a corner, at which point the smile dropped off his face. All good humour drained from his body and he stuffed all thoughts of the future away in a dark corner of his mind. He couldn't risk the distraction. He needed to be wholly in the moment to have any chance of winning. Daxx was the most hideous person he'd ever met in the Families.

Across the square Daxx hadn't moved a muscle. In fact he barely seemed to breathe and the only indication of life was the slow blinking of his eyes. Choss expected threats, perhaps an insane speech about the inevitability of this moment, but there was nothing, just a tense silence that started to build.

Choss took a deep breath and tried not to groan out loud as his sides burned and his breath caught in his throat. With slow jerky movements he settled his punching daggers and tried to loosen his arms. His whole body ached and his vision was still impaired on one side. Across the square Daxx drew his sword in one fluid motion and in that moment Choss knew with total certainty there was no way he could win this fight.

CHAPTER 39

Lizbeth wasted no time with any attempt to make her flight look casual. She ran for her life and Katja chased after her, barging other guests aside as they raced for the far side of the ballroom. Lizbeth made it first without raising too many eyebrows, but Katja left a trail of angry faces and mutters in her wake. One or two people called out after her but she ignored them and didn't look back.

As Katja had expected, her shoes made running difficult and Lizbeth already had a decent lead. Just as she'd practised in the carriage ride to the palace, she flicked off her shoes then resumed her sprint. Her bare feet flew over the cold stone tiles and Lizbeth's eyes widened in alarm as she saw Katja narrowing the gap between them.

The servant let out a squawk of pain as she skidded around a corner and collided with a stone column. Katja gained a little more ground but fear gave Lizbeth a boost of energy and she pulled ahead again. She ducked around a corner and disappeared from view. When Katja reached the spot where Lizbeth had vanished she was at a T-junction. Doors were open on both sides and there was no sign of her prey.

Cocking her head to one side Katja closed her eyes and focused on the sounds of the palace. Behind her she could hear a rising tide of raised voices and the heavy clank of armed guards. Someone was coming after her but they weren't here yet. There was still time. Lizbeth knew something and Katja was determined to find out her role in Rodann's plan.

Somewhere to her right Katja heard a faint muffled wheezing. Reaching under her dress she drew out the long blade strapped to her leg and tip-toed down the hallway towards it. The first room on the corridor, a sitting room with couches and a cold fireplace, stood empty and silent and there were no places to hide except behind the luxurious curtains. But there were no suspicious lumps or feet poking out from the bottom so Katja moved on.

The second room held several small writing tables and a chalk board on a wooden stand at the front. The classroom furniture looked old and the wooden seats had been worn smooth from use. At first glance the room also looked empty but the door to a large cupboard was slightly ajar. The servant's quiet wheezing echoed around the room, which lacked any soft furnishings.

Katja dashed into the classroom, yanked open the cupboard and pulled Lizbeth out by her collar. The woman blanched at the sight of the blade, which Katja pressed against the base of her throat.

"You have one chance. Tell me why you're here," said Katja.

Lizbeth looked past Katja's shoulder, her eyes desperately searching for something that could help. She squealed in pain as Katja pressed the point of her blade hard enough to draw blood.

"Focus on me," said Katja. Lizbeth's eyes snapped back to her face. "Why are you here? What is your job?"

Lizbeth looked ready to answer and her mouth even opened when a sound caught her attention. Katja heard it too. The heavy footsteps were getting closer. Lizbeth's terrified expression drained away and was replaced by one of malicious glee.

"Help!" she screamed until Katja shoved her against the wall, driving the rest of the breath from her lungs.

"Down there," someone shouted.

Despite being winded Lizbeth grinned at Katja. "You're out of time."

Grabbing Lizbeth by her neck Katja pinned her to the wall and pressed the blade against her stomach. "I still have enough time to gut you. Tell me something useful or I'll cut you open."

Lizbeth bit her lip and shook her head, deciding to take her chances and test Katja's resolve. With a casual shrug Katja thrust the blade forward. Lizbeth shrieked and then looked down at the point of the blade, which had sliced through her clothes and nicked the skin across her stomach.

"Talk," said Katja, pressing the point slightly harder until a trickle of blood began to run down Lizbeth's stomach. She gasped in pain and pretended to faint until Katja slapped her across the face.

"Last chance," she warned Lizbeth.

"Rodann is here," she said in a hurry. "In the palace."

"Where?" asked Katja. She heard footsteps in the corridor outside the door. "Where?" she screamed.

"Behind you," whispered Lizbeth as strong hands grabbed Katja, pulling her off the servant. Lizbeth began to wail at her injuries then collapsed to the floor.

"She tried to kill me!" cried Lizbeth as a royal guard checked her wounds, which Katja knew were only minor. Lizbeth had missed her true calling and should have been on the stage. Despite the small patch of blood on the front of her clothes and the shallow cut beneath, she appeared to be dying.

Palace guards wrestled the long blade out of Katja's hand as she was held face down on the floor. She was roughly searched for other weapons and then dragged back to her feet. They failed to find the small blade Lord Mullbrook had given her in the necklace. Katja berated herself for having chased Lizbeth through the halls of the palace. She could have followed at a more sedate pace. Even though Lizbeth had recognised her Rodann knew Katja was in the palace and had in fact arranged it. That made her wonder why Lizbeth had run in the first place.

As the palace guards pulled Katja to her feet she saw a sneer creep across Lizbeth's face for a second before she resumed her mask of feigned agony. Katja had been manipulated and done exactly what Lizbeth wanted.

"Have you ever seen this woman before?" asked one of the royal guards, a burly man with a bushy moustache.

"No, never," said Lizbeth, managing to look the guard in the eye. "She started chasing me for no reason."

"That's a lie," said Katja. The moustached guard pointed a finger at her face. Part of Katja was tempted to snap it but the two armed guards standing behind her would make her pay so she resisted the impulse.

"Not one more word or I'll have you gagged," promised the guard.

"She kept asking me questions about the Queen," said Lizbeth, which made all of the guards come to attention.

"What sort of questions?"

"How to get into her quarters. She asked if I had keys, that sort of thing."

Katja had to admit the woman's story was convincing and she had played into Lizbeth's hands by chasing her through the palace. Rodann must have heard what had happened to his people in the kitchens. He'd probably orchestrated this little charade to stop Katja interrupting other parts of his plan.

One of the guards was sent to fetch a surgeon rather than move the patient, who heroically managed to bear her grave wounds in silence. A few minutes later Lizbeth was attended to by a portly woman with grey hair.

"Is everything all right in here, Captain?" asked a familiar voice from the doorway.

Despite being held by both arms Katja was able to turn slightly so that she could stare at the newcomer. At first she didn't recognise the smartly dressed man in blue trousers and grey shirt. His bald head gleamed from being recently shaved and part of his scalp still looked pale from lack of sunlight. Even more distracting was the broad jaw that should have been covered with a big red beard. But the eyes didn't change and, despite his attempt to conceal his identity, she knew it was Rodann.

Rather than looking alarmed at someone creeping up on them the guards relaxed when they saw who it was. Their change in posture indicated familiarity and some sort of deference to Rodann, but she didn't think he'd served as one of the palace guards. He wasn't the right sort of person and definitely wasn't a fighter. He liked the sound of his own voice too much.

One of the two men holding Katja smiled warmly at Rodann and even the Captain moved to greet him at the door.

"Everything's fine here," said the Captain, blocking Rodann's view of Katja and the injured servant. Rodann briefly glanced around the room over the Captain's shoulder then allowed himself to be turned around. The Captain and Rodann talked in hushed voices but Katja could just make out what they were saying.

"How is your youngest doing these days?" Rodann asked the Captain.

"Very well, thank you. She turns twelve next month."

The rest of their conversation was muffled but the pieces slowly started to slot into place. The look in Rodann's eyes when he'd peered into the classroom had not just been one of curiosity but also of nostalgia. He'd been a teacher at the palace, tutoring the Queen's children and those of her guards. That explained his familiarity with the guards and the lack of alarm at his presence in this part of the palace.

"Bring her," said the Captain, gesturing at the guards holding Katja, who marched her out of the room. Rodann lingered in the corridor a few steps away, feigning concern for Lizbeth, while actually making sure Katja was secure.

She considered rushing Rodann and cutting his throat with her hidden blade but resisted the urge. As she was led away Katja looked over her shoulder and saw him grinning at her back.

With her in custody Rodann believed his plan would be able to continue without further interruption. Even knowing part of his background she still didn't see how he fitted into the picture, or Teigan for that matter. There'd been no sign of the sour-faced swordswoman, but Katja suspected her role would be critical and not one that required subtlety. Part of her mind suspected the pieces were all there, she just needed to understand how they fitted together. However, as they locked her in a bare room with no windows, she realised any prospect of unravelling the puzzle by herself was looking bleak. Both Queens were almost out of time.

CHAPTER 40

Choss stared at Daxx across the square with a growing sense of dread. It had begun as a seed of fear in the pit of his stomach like a frozen stone, but now tendrils of trepidation were creeping out across his body.

Although he still trained every day it had been two years since he'd fought in the ring. Two years since he'd been under the same pressure. Two years since he'd fought and beaten his toughest competitor, who now stood beside him as a friend. At the peak of his fitness and in good health, he would've stood a fair chance of beating Daxx. But that was not today.

Daxx didn't fight for honour or money, but for something else. The fuel at his core was dark and unknown, but Choss had seen delight flicker across lifeless eyes when Daxx hurt people. He didn't relish the challenge or even victory over an opponent, but he took great pleasure in inflicting agony on others.

There would be no reasoning with him. No peaceful solution. Daxx didn't want anything except to hurt other people. The seed of fear swelled again but Choss did his best to shake it off and ignore its icy fingers. He had too much to live for and a chance at something new with Munroe.

"This man, he seems different," muttered Gorrax, watching

Daxx move towards them. A group of four jackals entered the square from the opposite side, their faces twisted into feral masks, driven berserk by the tainted venthe. Another present from Doña Parvie and her delightful sister.

"No, he's mine!" snarled Daxx, turning to attack the four men. He cut down two of them in seconds with vicious slashes, while one charged at Choss and Gorrax, ignoring the fate of his friends. His attack was clumsy and wild, which made it easy for Choss to dodge him and Gorrax to get behind him and then rip out his throat with his claws. There was a final squeal of pain as Daxx killed the last jackal, driving his sword into the man's chest where it burst between his ribs. With a sharp twist and yank Daxx retrieved his sword, letting the man drop to the ground.

Choss noticed Gorrax watching Daxx with a peculiar expression, one he'd not seen before.

"Gorrax? What's wrong?"

"This man, he is interesting," said Gorrax with a smile. "I will fight him."

"He wants me," said Choss.

As Daxx cleaned his blade on the dead men's clothes, Gorrax turned towards Choss with an eager smile.

"Choss, you are very important to me. You've taught me many things about your people and how they live, but I am not one of you. I will never be like you. I am Vorga. This man brings me something I have not seen since we fought."

"What's that?"

Gorrax smiled. "A challenge. I can see his hate. It burns inside and nothing will douse it. He will never stop. This pleases me."

"I can't ask you to fight for me," said Choss.

Gorrax put a hand on his shoulder, looking him in the eye. "I know this will not shame you, so I will speak plainly. You are injured. You cannot beat him like this. Do I speak the truth?"

he asked and eventually Choss reluctantly had to agree. "I will fight, not because you ask, but because I choose this and want this."

Much to Choss's surprise Gorrax touched him lightly on one cheek then kissed him gently on the mouth.

"What was that for?"

Gorrax took a deep breath, his chest swelling beneath the plain grey vest. "Once, you asked me why I left my people. I did this because the one I chose was Vorga in his heart like you, but he was not born Vorga. He was a human man and my people could not accept this."

Choss didn't know what to say. He didn't even know where to start. No one knew much about Vorga culture, but he'd been learning from Gorrax over the years. Even so he was struggling to fit what Gorrax had told him and how he should respond. He started to offer some words of sympathy but then noticed the swelling beneath Gorrax's vest had not receded. In fact it had grown further and resembled breasts.

Suddenly things started to come together in his mind. The way Gorrax deferred to him, the strange ritualistic greeting and the frequent but gentle physical contact.

"My name is Gorraxi," said the Vorga, smiling at his confusion. "No man ever bested me until you. You are worthy of Nethun."

Choss was still struggling for words, but he managed to gesture at the Vorga's breasts, which were starting to recede.

"Vorga females can control them. We swim better with them flat," she explained. All Vorga wore little clothing except kilts and vests, but Choss had never wondered why he'd never seen Gorraxi's naked torso from the front. At the arena the Vorga always showered alone, as she intimidated the other fighters. Choss recalled a few times he'd walked in when the Vorga had been getting dressed and had only seen her from behind.

Dozens of other little clues started to drift to the surface. He'd also wondered about the strange gestures and unusual greeting she made towards him and no one else.

Part of him wanted to tell her not to fight in his place, but the small part of him that understood her knew that this would hurt her worse than any blade. Strength and skill defined a person's position in Vorga society, nothing else. Squashing the voice of his ego Choss smiled and clapped Gorraxi on her shoulder just as he'd always done.

"I would be honoured to watch you fight," said Choss, careful not to mention the outcome or his desire to see her live.

Gorraxi stepped forward and casually bent down to retrieve the sword from one of the dead thugs. Choss couldn't recall ever seeing the Vorga holding a weapon, let alone fight with one. Even when they'd attacked the venthe farms she'd killed men with her bare hands. As she swung the blade a few times to get used to the weight he recalled the stories she'd told him about being born knowing how to fight with weapons.

If Daxx was concerned he didn't show it, his hateful gaze resettling on the Vorga.

"I have been waiting a long time for this," said Gorraxi, stepping forward and gesturing for Daxx to attack her. "Let us see what is in your heart."

Daxx sneered before launching into a blistering series of attacks, each slice carefully controlled and aimed at a different part of the body. Choss had seen this before when fighters tested each other's ability to see if they had a weakness in their defence. Gorraxi met Daxx's attacks with apparent ease, a puzzled and disappointed expression on her face. Such probing tactics were alien to her but she played along, perhaps only out of curiosity.

Daxx took a couple of steps back, reassessing his opponent, carefully studying the Vorga for the first time. This was unlike any fight he'd ever been in before and he was slowly beginning to realise that. Instead of waiting for Daxx to regroup Gorraxi attacked, launching a series of moves so fast Choss couldn't track the blade. Somehow Daxx managed to keep the Vorga at bay, but he took one and then a few more steps back as Gorraxi drove him across the square.

The sheer ferocity of her assault caught Daxx by surprise as he stumbled, his left heel slipping on the ground. He managed to keep his blade up but Gorraxi didn't press her advantage. Instead she waited just out of reach for Daxx to get back to his feet.

To beat him because he had slipped on wet stones would not satisfy her. He could be a worthy opponent, which meant she had to beat him with both of them on their feet, eye to eye. It wasn't honour as Choss thought of it, as he'd seen Gorraxi kill men from behind on the venthe raids. It was something he was still struggling to grasp despite her attempts to explain it.

Daxx mistook her gesture for kindness or some form of noble intent. With a snarl of rage he attacked again, doing his best to dismember or maim the Vorga. He hacked and stabbed at her in a way Choss had never seen before. Once, many years ago, Daxx may have been taught how to wield a sword by an instructor. Across the years, a river of blood and countless cruel murders, his technique had evolved into something as black and horrific as his soul. There was no grace, no fluidity to his style, only the intent to inflict as much pain as possible before killing his opponent.

Gorraxi stood her ground, parrying Daxx's blows with her own unorthodox style. She seemed able to anticipate his attacks. It was the only way Choss could understand how she maintained perfect balance and never once gave him an opening. They battled back and forth across the square, pressing each other hard, both doing their utmost to find an opening in their opponent's defence.

Sweat freely ran down Daxx's face and he showed considerable strain, from the grinding of his teeth to the taut muscles in his jaw. His breath hissed out from between his teeth and he barely seemed to blink, his eyes never leaving Gorraxi's face. Choss didn't know if Gorraxi could sweat but as far as he could tell the Vorga wasn't displaying any signs of discomfort at the relentless pace. Whether they were evenly matched or not, Choss didn't know, but a fight at this speed couldn't continue for long. Eventually one of them would make a mistake and even one small slip-up could prove lethal.

When it happened Choss didn't see it and he only realised when he heard the familiar clicking of Gorraxi's tongue. Something had caused the Vorga to lose her balance, perhaps an uneven stone or wet patch of ground, but one leg had slipped, creating a small opening in her defence. Daxx had no issue using it to his advantage and the point of his sword sliced Gorraxi across the ribs on her right. Pale green blood seeped from the wound, soaking into her vest.

At the clicking of the Vorga's tongue Daxx's expression twisted into one of malicious glee. He didn't understand what it meant. He thought Gorraxi was in pain, but Choss remembered the terror that had gripped him in the ring seconds after hearing that noise. Now the fight would truly begin.

Gorraxi shifted her grip on the sword to two hands and a peculiar calm settled on her. Her expression became serene and she stood poised with the sword held ready, silent and stiff as a statue. Daxx didn't care about the sudden change, he simply attacked, trying to disembowel the Vorga. Gorraxi parried his slice but barely seemed to move, swaying to one side and tapping his blade with hers, knocking it to one side of her body.

Her riposte flicked towards his face and, despite stepping back, Daxx cried out in pain, a red line appearing down his left cheek. When he saw the blood on his fingers Daxx flew into a rage but now Gorraxi was ready to fight in earnest.

Both swords moved so quickly they became silver blurs of light. The rhythmic sound of steel striking steel echoed off buildings around the empty square. Despite his obvious skill with a sword Daxx moved like a clumsy oaf in comparison to Gorraxi, who seemed to flow from one position to the next.

In all the years Choss had known the Vorga, he'd always respected Gorraxi and knew that she was as strong, if not stronger, and tougher than him. Not once had he thought her capable of being graceful, but now the creature before him moved in a way that was so instinctive and elegant he began to understand a small piece of her heritage. When a Vorga held a weapon they didn't have to learn how to use it, they knew and had always known since the moment of their birth. Down through the generations, since the first of them had swum up from the ocean and stepped onto dry land. Each generation gifted their experience and knowledge to the next, creating a legacy without comparison.

Daxx tried to overpower Gorraxi but his frustration and rage were insufficient. When they had run their course and faded, he had nothing to fall back on except his skill and experience from years of murder. His movements became less wild, more precise and focused, but still they carried a vicious edge. There were attempts to slice her fingers, take out an eye, kick her and do anything and everything to gain an advantage. Gorraxi met him with a calm expression and the combined knowledge of her ancestors.

Blocking a high swing, Gorraxi feinted a riposte towards Daxx's legs then did something with her arm so quickly that Choss couldn't follow. He saw her twisting her blade in a furious arc, then Daxx stumbled back with one hand clutching his stomach while red seeped out from between his fingers. For the first time since the fight had begun Choss saw a glimmer of fear in Daxx's eyes. The burning hatred had not diminished and perhaps it was this, despite his injury, which drove him to attack Gorraxi. Casually batting his sword aside she sidestepped his follow-up, then swung her blade in a wide arc that made the steel whistle through the air.

The blade bit into the side of Daxx's neck and carried on, cleanly severing his head from his shoulders. Daxx's head bounced across the square as his body collapsed to the ground, blood pouring from the severed neck. Gorraxi looked down at Daxx's body and shook her head in disappointment.

"You are not worthy of Nethun," she said.

Across the square someone began a slow clap, mocking Gorraxi's victory.

"Brilliant," said Doña Parvie, still clapping. "Brilliant, but fucking stupid."

Behind Doña Parvie came her twin sister and behind her a dozen jackals, all of them armed and several foaming at the mouth, driven to madness by the Flesh Mage's new venthe.

"Any last words?" asked Doña Parvie with a grin.

CHAPTER 41

Katja was out of time. Rodann had been careful to conceal parts of the plan from her and the others, but now it didn't matter. She needed to understand what he was planning and fill in the blanks. She had to work out who posed the greatest threat and find a way to stop them.

Rodann's two people in the kitchens had failed in their attempt to poison the guards with the tainted venthe and were now dead. If they had been given any other tasks to fulfil, those would now fall to someone else or the plan would have to change.

Despite her sneer at Katja, Lizbeth had also been neutralised from causing further problems. Her injuries were modest but she had overplayed her hand by claiming to be in agonising pain. She would be relieved of her duties for the next few hours and either sent home or dispatched to a hospital. Either way she wouldn't be able to assist Rodann and his people.

But just as someone can secure victory in a game of Stones, even with some pieces taken off the board, Katja thought Rodann could still win. He would have made alternative plans in case parts of the main plot failed, and now, with three people dead or injured, he would be putting those into action.

Something intruded on Katja's thoughts and it took a few seconds before she remembered where she was. Opening her eyes brought her back to the present and her current predicament.

Both of her arms had been tied to the chair and more ropes held her ankles in place.

Across the table Captain Cole of Queen Morganse's royal guards stared at her without sympathy. He was taking the threat against his Queen very seriously. The only thing she knew about him was his name and rank.

So far all he'd done was ask her the same questions over and over. What had she been planning? Was she working alone? Why did she want to get into the Queen's quarters?

"Who are you working with?" asked Cole for the umpteenth time. "Is Lord Mullbrook working with you?"

"No, he's a mark," said Katja, trying not to show any emotion. "I needed to get into the palace so I blackmailed him."

She wasn't sure if Cole believed her but Lord Mullbrook had done more than enough to help her. It was the least she could do to keep him away from this.

"Why did you attack the servant?"

"I'll take over from here, Captain," said a voice, startling them both. A woman in a black cloak with a deep hood watched them from the doorway. Despite the hood Cole recognised her, and he immediately stood up and stepped back. There was something familiar about the woman's voice, but she never took her hands from inside her cloak and her voice was muffled. Whoever she was, Cole deferred to her and, seemingly afraid, quickly hurried from the room.

The woman sat down opposite then took off her hood, setting it and the cloak to one side.

Faith smiled at Katja from across the table.

A hundred questions surged to the front of her mind but

Faith spoke before she could ask. "Did you think you were the only agent in the palace tonight?" asked Faith.

"You work for Queen Morganse," said Katja and Faith inclined her head.

"And you work for Queen Talandra," replied Faith. Her tone of voice carried a trace of reproach.

"How long have you known?"

"Quite a while. Why do you think I insisted Rodann bring you into his little circle?" said Faith with a slight shake of her head. "You're new at this, aren't you?"

It wasn't really a question and Katja didn't answer. "Why didn't you say something?" asked Katja.

"For the same reasons you didn't."

Orders. Katja knew Roza had wanted to share what they knew with Queen Morganse's people about the plot, but Talandra had overruled her.

"Now that we both know, are you willing to share?" asked Katja.

"You first," said Faith with a smile.

At this point Katja saw little point in lying. If Faith thought she was being dishonest, Katja would spend the rest of the night locked in a cell. Katja outlined what she knew about the others in the group and then came to the fate of Marcella and her husband in the kitchens.

"Tainted with what?" asked Faith.

"Given the blue stains around their mouth, some sort of venthe. It would have driven the guards into a berserk rage. It doesn't matter, they're dead and hopefully Lizbeth is not in the palace any more?"

"No, she's in a cell," said Faith.

"There was another group of people," said Katja. "When I first saw Rodann and Teigan they were talking to a group I've not seen since. We've been unable to trace them."

"They're an acting troupe, if you can believe it," said Faith. "Disillusioned by their lack of success they found it easy to blame those in charge."

"But how did Rodann get them into the palace?" asked Katja.

"Lord and Lady Venarra."

The pieces started to join up in Katja's head. "Rodann blackmailed them with whatever you took from their house."

"During the war, they supported the Mad King, Taikon, and funded some of the Chosen in the city. The documents I stole were rather incriminating letters. In return for their cooperation the Venarras persuaded their brother, the Chief Steward at the palace, to recommend the acting troupe. They were supposed to be this evening's entertainment."

Katja raised an eyebrow. "Supposed to be?"

"They all suffered terrible accidents and didn't show up," said Faith with a shrug of her shoulders. "More reliable entertainers have taken their place."

"That can't be all of the conspirators," said Katja. "Where are Lord and Lady Kallan?"

"Mingling with guests, but soon they'll be stuck at the banquet."

"What about Rodann and Teigan?"

Faith frowned. "I don't know. I've not seen her all night and he slipped away."

"I saw him briefly, but not her. It's not over. He won't stop, you know that," said Katja. "If someone threatened Queen Morganse in the palace, what would happen?"

"They would be detained or eliminated on the spot," said Faith with absolute confidence.

"What if you couldn't detain them? What if there were more than one, or the palace guards were absent or busy elsewhere?"

"We'd lock the Queen inside her chambers with trusted

guards until the threat had passed. And before you ask, yes, the loyalty of her guards is absolute," said Faith.

Something stirred at the back of Katja's mind. An idea, like a dangling piece of frayed cotton, was teasing her, drifting in and out of her mind's eye.

"Would anyone else be secured with the Queen in her chambers? Family? Friends?"

Faith pursed her lips in thought before answering. "Normally her cousin, the Duchess, but she's not here tonight. Her children are also elsewhere."

"No one else?"

"Half a dozen people from the oldest families."

Something clicked into place in Katja's mind and she pulled on the thread. An idea began to unfold and her mouth fell open.

Faith looked alarmed at Katja's expression. "What is it?"

"Rodann's patron is from one of the oldest families. If Queen Morganse dies, they will take her place on the throne."

"But no threat has been made against her tonight. Not yet anyway."

"And what about Queen Talandra? What happens to her in an emergency at the palace?"

Faith leaned forward across the table, a frown creasing her brow. "There would be a similar drill, except she'd be guarded by her own warriors. She'd be locked inside the east wing behind fifty of her own people."

"Maker's balls," whispered Katja.

"What is it? What?" asked Faith.

Just then, someone burst into the room, throwing the door open wide. Before the guard spoke, Katja heard sounds of alarm from elsewhere in the palace. People were screaming, there was the sound of breaking glass and the scrambling of many feet.

"What's happening?" asked Faith.

"All of the guests are panicking, running through the halls, trying to escape," said the guard.

Faith turned away from Katja towards the door.

"Take me with you!" screamed Katja. "I can help."

"Ma'am, what are your orders?" asked the guard.

Faith hesitated, caught between two worlds, but Katja could see her eyes were flickering as she ran scenarios through her mind. With a snarl she dashed back into the room, produced a dagger from inside a fold in her dress and slashed Katja's restraints.

"Stay close," said Faith over her shoulder before beckoning the guard to go ahead of them down the corridor. Katja stumbled to her feet and ran after Faith down the corridor towards the source of the chaos.

CHAPTER 42

F ray felt as if he were walking into the face of a storm. No
wind stirred the rubbish on the streets and the hanging
signs were still above his head. An invisible tornado raged
along the street, flattening his clothes against his body. A
vicious wind screeched past his ears, making them burn with
the cold. The combined wail of tortured voices mixed with
screeching metal made him wince and grit his teeth. Tiny daggers of ice pierced the exposed skin on his hands and face, but
there was no blood.

Munroe was feeling it too, but she didn't slow down. Fray
forced himself to keep up as they marched forward. She was
angry at leaving Choss behind, but he offered her no reassur-
ances, nor made any attempt to calm her down. Fray had never
seen anyone with such a strong connection to the Source and he
needed that power to fight the Flesh Mage. Working together
they at least stood a chance.

The air rumbled above his head but, staring at the night sky,
he saw no clouds, only a field of stars. He could feel a river of
energy up there, something malevolent and cruel, flowing
towards the Flesh Mage, but there was nothing to see. No lightning followed the thunder and then the rumbling changed pitch,
becoming something he'd never heard before.

Fray and Munroe both stumbled at the same time. He fell to his knees while she toppled sideways and slumped against a building. Before she could ask, he felt it again, a powerful jab just beneath his navel, a pulling sensation as if someone were yanking on an invisible umbilical cord. He had felt something like this twice before. Once when Balfruss had defeated the Warlock all those miles away, and on the day his father died. Fray gagged and swallowed bile while he heard Munroe spattering the ground with the remnants of her last meal.

They were too late. The Flesh Mage had opened a portal, tearing a hole in the fabric of the world. Their bodies were instinctively reacting to something alien and didn't know how to cope.

The assault on the senses continued and Fray sat back for a minute, trying to master his body and suppress the strange feelings.

As he looked up past the battered buildings, something seemed out of place.

"Maker protect us," hissed Munroe. "Where are the stars?"

The stars were disappearing. Fray could still see the sky but something was spreading out across the night like a wave. Where it touched a star the light began to fade and then it was extinguished. A growing void of absolute darkness swelled above them in the night sky. The centre wasn't far from where they huddled in the street, which meant they were close.

"We have to keep going," said Fray, trying to get to his feet.

Munroe wiped her mouth with the back of one hand and stood, using the wall for support. She pulled him up and, leaning on each other, they stumbled along the narrow road like a pair of drunks.

The pain was still there, a dull throb somewhere behind his

stomach, but Fray tried to ignore it. They rounded a corner and came to a square surrounded by houses on all sides. He felt Munroe stiffen beside him and Fray's mouth fell open in horror.

The glass in every window around the square had been shattered. The stone paving slabs in the square had been gouged up and shoved to the edges as if by an enormous hand, revealing the earth beneath. Three concentric rings had been cut into the ground and a thick black liquid sloshed in the narrow channel of each. Fray didn't need to see the cloud of flies or the pile of bodies in one corner to know what it was. He could smell the rot and blood.

Half a dozen metal spears had been embedded into the ground and arranged around the circles. An assortment of bones, talismans and seemingly random items had been tied to one. From another dangled the skin of a man, flapping gently like a flag, empty hands waving in supplication. On a third hung the skulls of animals and men, some recently killed, as they still had bits of hair and skin attached. There were other items scattered here and there, but Fray's eyes were drawn to the thing at the centre of the circle.

The portal. It hung in the air, flickering and pulsing in time with the pain he felt in his bones. A purple tear in the fabric of the world. Currently it was the length of his forearm, but Fray knew it would grow over time as the Flesh Mage fed it. Thin as a single hair and yet infinitely deep its mere existence screamed at him. One moment the portal was there and the next it seemed to vanish, but turning his head slightly he could still see it. The link to that other place, whatever lay through the portal, was tenuous. It required a huge amount of energy to stay open and nature kept doing its best to heal itself and close the wound.

"What do we do?" asked Munroe, holding a hand to her face to try and block out the stench of the decaying bodies. Fray could barely hear her voice above the phantom wind that moaned like spirits of the dead as it whistled through the broken windows.

"I'm going to try and disrupt it," he shouted, knowing how that sounded. He'd never attempted anything like this before, unpicking magic so complex that he couldn't even fathom where to begin. Even so he knew that the energy sustaining the portal had to go somewhere. There was a good chance the backlash would kill him and everyone else for a mile in every direction, but the alternative was far worse. The look in Munroe's eyes told him she knew that as well.

"Do it," said Munroe.

Fray had started to draw in his magic when Munroe shouted a warning. As he turned towards her something flew past his face, narrowly missing him. Across the square a woman in a green dress was flanked by two thugs, one of whom was desperately trying to reload his crossbow. The other pointed his crossbow at Munroe.

Fray recognised the woman as Doña Jarrow. The jackal with the loaded crossbow pulled the trigger, but Munroe made a sweeping gesture with her left arm and he jerked to one side, the bolt missing them both. Before either jackal could reload, Munroe screamed at the woman, flinging out her hands. The thugs screamed in unison. One clutched his chest and toppled over while blood fountained from the other's throat. They dropped dead and Doña Jarrow turned and fled.

"I'll keep them busy," said Munroe, running after Doña Jarrow.

"Wait!" shouted Fray but she didn't seem to hear him.

Suddenly alone in the square with the portal, Fray felt the weight of responsibility bear down on his shoulders. The pressure threatened to drive him to his knees but he forced himself to take a step closer to the portal, then another.

Stretching out with his mind to the sound at the edge of his perception, Fray embraced his magic. The world convulsed around him and a flood of new colours and sensations rushed in. Even though he braced himself for the onslaught the intensity was overwhelming and he staggered back a few steps and fell to one knee. The portal remained unchanged, a purple scar on the world that flickered in and out of existence. Everything else around it was dramatically different. Before, the river of power in the sky had been invisible, but now Fray could see black pulsing veins running through the clouds. A huge net had been spread out across the city and all threads flowed down to converge on the portal. More energy, red and sickly, also trickled into the portal from the three circles and talismans. Despite everything, it still wasn't enough. The portal was barely staying open, which gave Fray a glimmer of hope.

He reached out towards it with his magic and immediately drew back as the edge of his senses touched the portal. The unnatural feelings inside his body grew more intense and the squirming swelled, twisting and turning like ripe maggots burrowing through his flesh. Mewling like an animal in pain, Fray stretched out again, touched the portal and this time he felt something. A shape. Like a giant knot of corded rope that was constantly untangling itself. Every second the rope sheared and peeled back, threads stretched past their bursting point. And with every pulse of energy a fresh knot appeared, holding the rift open for another second. Fray tried to imagine the knots coming apart more quickly and desperately tried to apply his magic.

A scream drew his attention, snapping his focus away from the portal, as a man was dragged into the square. The person who held him was horribly familiar by his absence of light and colour. Everything else in the square was brightly coloured and suffused with energy, but the Flesh Mage's body held only darkness. An endless abyss filled him that would never be satisfied.

Before Fray could stop him the Flesh Mage slit the man's throat, holding him above the third circle so that his blood joined with the rest. The outer circle flared more brightly at the fresh sacrifice and the portal pulsed in response. The Flesh Mage dropped the corpse then turned towards the portal, raising his hands. Finally he noticed Fray and shouted something but his words were lost in the gale. Purple light leapt from his fingertips into the portal, which began to writhe and twist. The churning in Fray's guts became shards of glass. It felt as if he were being ripped apart from the inside as the Flesh Mage fed even more power into the rift. Fray felt as much as saw the tear in the world stretch longer and he screamed in response. Half as tall as a person, the rift still hung in the air, making every part of him ache.

Reaching out with his senses Fray seized hold of the squirming knot that tethered the portal to the world and frantically tried to tear it apart. The Flesh Mage saw what he was doing but couldn't move to intervene. Power still flowed out of him as a conduit so each of them remained tethered to the portal, one trying to force it open wider while the other tried to pull it apart.

For every small knot that Fray severed, two more seemed to grow over, fixing the portal more tightly to this place. The Flesh Mage was too strong. Without Munroe to help him there was no way for Fray to stop it.

Movement at Fray's eye corner caught his attention and a flicker of hope turned to fear as a dozen thugs came into the square, each dragging a squirming victim. Their life-blood was added to the rest before the thugs finally noticed Fray and turned towards him with their bloody weapons.

Despite the odds stacked against him and Gorraxi, Choss drew his punching daggers and prepared to fight for his life. As regret welled up for all the things he should have said, mostly to Munroe, he struggled to find the calm he needed.

The old anger that he'd learned to master so many years ago started to well up inside. It had been born of a young man's rage at the world when he found out it didn't work as he expected. Layers of frustration and disappointment at those closest to him had kept the fire hot for years. He'd used that anger as he was growing up and then, later, against his own father. Choss felt no regret about what he'd done, but it was the last time he'd let it take control.

"Remember how far you've come," said Gorraxi, sensing his distress. "Remember the long road that brought you to this moment. Remember the hours you trained that cannot be counted. Remember the sacrifice, the blood, the pain. Remember."

Her words brought up many memories of practising in the ring, training and sweating and forcing his body to the limit. Choss sank down in the cool place inside and all of his emotions drained away.

The jackals approached with caution, fully aware of who he was and what Gorraxi had done to Daxx. Despite the berserker effects of the drugs and the odds in their favour, Choss could see they were afraid. None of them wanted to be the first to attack as there was a good chance they would die or, at least, be horribly maimed. Finally one of the jackals found the nerve to attack as he charged forward with an inhuman howl.

An arrow burst the man's right eye, embedding itself in his brain. He managed two steps before dropping dead. Everyone turned to stare at eight newcomers, more jackals, but none of them looked familiar.

"Who the bloody—"

"The Butcher sends his regards," said a scarred Morrin woman with a pair of hand-axes. She tipped her head towards Choss and the others lined up alongside him. Two of the eight were archers, who spread out to the far corners of the square.

To everyone's surprise, even her own sister's by the look she was giving her, Doña Parvie laughed. "It doesn't matter. Either way this city will be ours after tonight. Kill them. Kill them all!" she screamed at her people. Whether it was her voice or the venthe burning in their blood, they charged towards Choss and the newcomers.

While the others around him shouted in defiance at Doña Parvie and her people, Choss remained silent. To his right Gorraxi was also silent and perfectly still, a reassuring presence whose loyalty was never in doubt.

Choss studied his opponent as she approached, a gangly local woman with a short sword and dagger. When she attacked he parried two quick slashes then retaliated, scoring a line across her forehead. As blood ran into her eyes, Choss stabbed her twice in the chest and quickly stepped back. The wounds were fatal, but she didn't notice and he had to slice open her stomach, spilling entrails onto the ground before she slowed down. Even as she tried to stuff the pink coils back inside her body she snarled at him. Choss stabbed her in the heart and stepped over the corpse.

Something whistled towards his head. By the time he started to react some part of Choss knew it would already be too late. But the fatal blow didn't land. He felt a rush of air by his ear and saw a bright spark as steel collided, then he was shoved to one side. Spinning around he saw Gorraxi had saved him again, blocking the sword and retaliating with an intensity her opponent could not match. For all of the man's obvious strength and bloodlust the Vorga seemed to dance around him before ending it quickly with a slice across the thigh. The jackal stumbled back then fell onto his arse, staring in bewilderment at the pool of blood beneath him.

The archers picked off two more and the scarred Morrin and her allies made short work of the rest. Soon only the sisters and their two bodyguards were left. When they realised the odds had suddenly become stacked against them Doña Parvie turned on her sister.

"This is all your fault. If you hadn't been so fucking greedy!"

"Me? You're the one who agreed to the deal without me."

Doña Parvie looked as if she would argue but then pulled a dagger and threw it at one of the Butcher's people. The jackal went down with a blade in the eye and both sisters attacked with vicious ferocity. Choss and Gorraxi held back, letting the others deal with the wretched sisters. Cornered and with nothing to lose they fought hard but were eventually overcome by sheer numbers.

The Butcher's people stepped away to reveal Doña Parvie stumbling backwards, one hand pressed to her stomach, the other holding a knife. Her sister and the two bodyguards lay dead at her feet. Blood trickled from the corners of Doña Parvie's mouth and from between her fingers.

"You big fucking—" she slurred at Choss and then toppled over.

The scarred Morrin approached Choss, but kept one eye on Gorraxi.

"You work for Don Jarrow, yes?" she asked.

"Yes."

The Morrin grunted. "This is just for tonight. After that things will change."

"Then follow me," said Choss. "Because it isn't over yet."

Gritting his teeth against the pain Choss led the way out of the square.

CHAPTER 43

Katja raced after Faith through the halls of the palace. Scared guests streamed past them in the opposite direction, screaming, crying and running for their lives. All were wide-eyed with terror and one or two were spattered with blood, but no one had any visible wounds.

Faith tried to stop one man to ask him what had happened but he pulled his arm free and wouldn't slow down. Something cold touched Katja's spine. Deep inside a primal instinct welled up that told her to turn around and flee with the others. To move away from whatever danger had caused the stampede and to let others deal with it. There were plenty of armed palace guards who were far better equipped than she was. She didn't need to do this and get involved. Katja's instincts had always served her well, helping her to avoid injury and walk away from situations before they grew worse, but now she ignored them. There was more at stake than her own life. Clenching her jaw, she pressed on as the stream of terrified people scrambled away from the banquet hall.

The closer they came to the source of the disturbance the worse the noise became. At first it sounded to Katja like an animal keening in pain. The sound was so high pitched and strained it made her wince. As she rounded another corner the sound became a little clearer and she heard words amid the screeching.

Katja reached a set of doors to the banquet hall a few seconds behind Faith and had just enough time to duck as something came flying through the air towards her. The dripping object landed a few steps away with a sodden thump. It was a severed human hand. A second glance revealed teeth marks in the torn flesh. It had been ripped off and chewed.

"Blessed Mother save us," whispered the guard as Katja came up beside him.

The royal banquet hall was a beautifully decorated room set out with three long tables in the shape of a horseshoe. At the far end of the room a raised platform held another long table where the two Queens and their close allies would have dined. Tall stained-glass windows ran down the right side of the room and on the left sat an array of pedestals with rare gifts given to Queen Morganse by guests from around the world. A balcony over-looked the hall with several doors leading off from it to rooms on the floor above. Rather than feeling awed, however, Katja felt queasy at the sight that met her eyes.

Several of the windows had been smashed. A storm had sprung up outside, wreathing the city in grey clouds, while fat drops of rain tapped against the remaining glass. The banquet had been ruined, with food thrown all over the walls, floor and even the ceiling. Blood had been liberally sprayed across the tables, up the walls and it dripped from the broken windows. Katja could see at least six dead bodies and she guessed there were others. All of the victims looked as if they had been savaged by a wild animal. Faces were chewed, limbs had been torn off and coils of intestines had been strewn about the floor. Two of those Katja could see were royal guards, probably the first who had tried to intervene. One guard had been decapitated and the other disembowelled.

Striding up and down on top of the banquet tables were two blood-soaked figures. It took Katja a moment to recognise them as Lord and Lady Kallan. Both had been transformed, seemingly possessed by some malicious spirit that had turned them completely feral. There was a wildness in their eyes that spoke of wanton bloodlust and a savagery she'd never seen before.

Their faces were daubed with gore but Katja noticed a blue stain at the corners of their mouths. The tainted venthe had driven them over the edge, beyond madness into something inhuman and unnatural. Rodann must have been desperate to turn to this strategy, one so unpredictable in its results.

Lord and Lady Kallan were smeared with blood all over their clothes and both had been wounded, but neither seemed to notice. When Lord Kallan spotted Katja and the others at the door he opened his mouth and let out an unholy shriek. Seeing the lack of humanity and recognition in his eyes made it infinitely worse. However petty and cruel he'd been, nothing remained of the man.

Lady Kallan howled in response to her husband, pacing up and down the tables, sending plates and bowls of food crashing to the floor. When one of the victims on the ground moaned she leaned down onto the woman's back and started hacking away with a sword. The woman's screams lasted only a few seconds. Lady Kallan ripped something away, an arm or possibly a leg, before taking a bite, hunching down over her food.

A dishevelled and bleeding royal guard came running up the corridor, followed by half a dozen more. They all looked worried but were heavily armed with swords, shields and helmets. Each wore a chainmail shirt, bracers and gauntlets, offering very little bare flesh to gnaw upon.

"Where is Queen Morganse? Queen Talandra?" asked Faith.

"Safe," gasped the officer. "They've both been sent to secure wings of the palace under heavy guard."

"They're not safe," hissed Katja, earning a few peculiar looks, which she ignored.

"Do you have this under control?" Faith asked the officer, who gestured to the balcony above their heads. Six royal guards armed with crossbows edged into sight, targeting Lord and Lady Kallan. He hissed at the newcomers, clearly recognising them as a threat, while Lady Kallan began to whoop and sway from side to side.

"I'll leave this in your hands, Captain," said Faith, pulling Katja away down a corridor. When they were out of earshot of the others, Katja turned to her.

"It's happening just like I said. Neither Queen is safe."

Faith shook her head. "Queen Morganse's people can be trusted."

"Do you know Lord and Lady Trevino?" asked Katja.

"Of course. They're old friends of Queen Morganse."

"Old enough to be secured with the Queen inside her quarters?"

"How do you know them?" asked Faith.

"Their son was recently murdered. I took care of his funeral arrangements."

All colour drained from Faith's face. "I heard it was an accident."

Katja shook her head. "I think Rodann murdered their son. The whole family are Eaters. Rodann had me blackmail Lord Trevino into smuggling something into the palace. I think it's more of whatever turned them savage," said Katja, pointing behind her towards the banquet room. She heard the thrum of several crossbows, followed by a scream of pain. "The Trevinos could be a last resort. Rodann is desperate and we've just forced his hand."

"They wouldn't," said Faith, but despite her words she started jogging down the corridor and Katja kept pace. "Why? Why now? They've been loyal supporters, almost since the beginning."

"Do they have any more children?"

"A daughter," said Faith, her eyes going wide. "She's supposed to be at their country estate."

"Rodann has her. If they don't go through with it she'll die too. If you can get to Queen Morganse quickly there's still a chance. My Queen isn't safe either. Is there another way into Talandra's rooms?" asked Katja.

"Yes, there's a secret tunnel, but it's locked," said Faith, skidding around a corner. She started fishing around inside her dress for something before finally pulling out a small ring of keys. With one eye on the corridor ahead she sorted through the keys until she found the one she wanted and slipped it off the ring. Passing it to Katja, she led her down several corridors before stopping in front of a wall that looked exactly the same as all of the others.

Faith pressed part of the wall at waist height, which seemed to trigger a mechanism, as something hidden clicked.

"Help me with this," said Faith. Together they pushed against the wall and a section moved backwards to reveal a narrow tunnel. Katja stuck her head in and saw that it extended both left and right. It was barely wide enough for one person, so she would have to shuffle sideways.

"Which way?" asked Katja.

"Follow the right path until you reach a junction," said Faith, taking a small globe from an alcove inside the wall. It contained a pale green liquid which glowed very faintly. She shook the globe and the fluid fizzed and frothed, glowing more brightly. "Then turn left, go up the stairs, take the third opening on your right and follow the tunnel to the end. You'll come to a locked door. Use the key and it will bring you out inside Queen Talandra's bedroom."

"Thank you," said Katja, accepting the globe and stepping into the tunnel. The globe illuminated the tunnel for only a few steps in each direction but it was better than fumbling along in the dark. "What about you? Can you get to Queen Morganse?"

Faith bit her lip. "I think there's a way. Good luck."

With Katja pushing from one side and Faith pulling on the other the wall quickly slid back into place with a dull boom, sealing her inside the tunnel. The darkness pressed in on all sides, making the pool of green light seem very small. Katja took a deep calming breath then started shuffling sideways down the tunnel as fast as she could manage in the cramped space. Muttering a prayer to the Maker, she hoped she wasn't too late.

CHAPTER 44

Doña Jarrow glanced once over her shoulder and the fear in her eyes made Munroe run even faster.

There were so many reasons to hate her. The way she viewed people in the Family as nothing more than tools, to be used and then cast aside without a second thought. The way she pretended to care that the word family meant something. Her general indifference to killing everyone else was also a good one. Recent crimes aside, of which there were many, the real reason Munroe hated Doña Jarrow was because of how she'd treated her when they first met. There were better reasons, and on some levels Munroe knew it was petty, but that first meeting spoke volumes about the type of woman she was. Upon meeting Munroe, and hearing about what she could do, Doña Jarrow's only comment had been "We can use her."

Over the four years she'd been working for the Jarrows, Munroe had seen many unpleasant things. She'd known about the Families and what they did before getting involved, but there were lines that the Jarrows set and their people were unwilling to cross. Munroe had respected Doña Jarrow's because of this and now her betrayal burned.

The rage welled up and with a scream of fury Munroe threw one of her daggers. She wished it would smack Doña Jarrow in the back of the head and willed it to happen. Whether it was luck or her magic Munroe didn't know and didn't care. The hilt caught Doña Jarrow behind one ear and she tumbled face first to the ground. She skidded through the gutter, smearing mud and something black and sticky on her expensive silk dress. Doña Jarrow stared in horror at the filth, which made Munroe's grin widen.

Rather than being cowed, Doña Jarrow's normally calm expression twisted into something vicious and cruel.

"You've had this coming for a long time, Sabina," said Munroe, unwilling to use her title. She didn't deserve it or the respect it commanded.

"Fuck you, Munroe," snarled Doña Jarrow, getting to her feet. She flicked the worst of the grime off her hands then wiped them down her dress, leaving grey smears. "You have no idea what's going on."

Munroe cocked her head to one side. "Let me see. Betraying your husband. Probably fucking the Flesh Mage. Magic portal. Gang warfare, mass murder. Did I miss anything?"

Doña Jarrow shook her head. "You're short-sighted. This was never about what happens next year. There are too many Families. After tonight there will be only one. The city and its people need stability."

"Don't even pretend you care about anyone except yourself. We're all just ants to you."

"You're wrong," said Doña Jarrow with a sneer. "You're nothing but maggots."

Munroe laughed in her face. "I'm glad we can be honest because I've never liked you, Sabina. You've always been a cold-hearted cunt. Showing emotion isn't a weakness."

Doña Jarrow's laughter was mocking. "I'm supposed to take lessons from you? You're a coward. You'll never achieve anything because you're too scared of the risks."

Munroe's witty retort died in her throat. "Well, now you've just pissed me off." She flexed her fingers and Doña Jarrow shook her head in dismay.

"Taking the easy route again I see."

"Oh no, I'm not going to use my curse," said Munroe, drawing a dagger from her belt. She rotated her shoulders and stretched her arms left and right. "That would be too easy. Too quick."

Doña Jarrow showed her teeth in the approximation of a grin. She produced a dagger of her own and, taking hold of her dress, she cut the silk until it ended just above her knees. She threw the material to one side and kicked off her shoes. "I clawed my way up the ranks to rule a Family. You're nothing but a street rat. It's time you learned your place."

But Munroe wasn't listening any more. She knew whatever was being said was designed to make her angry. The countless hours of training and the painful stretching exercises Ben had made her endure day after day suddenly seemed useful. Twisting her arms one way and then the other Munroe felt the different muscles pull and flex, perfectly in balance. She tensed and relaxed her legs next, gradually moving from one muscle group to the next.

Somewhere in the distance she could feel the hum of the Flesh Mage's magic, but it wasn't part of her. Not now, not at this moment. Her curse, her magic, whatever it was, didn't belong in this fight.

When Doña Jarrow realised her words weren't having the desired effect she rushed forward, slashing wildly with her dagger. Munroe carefully gave ground before blocking a crude jab and retaliating, backhanding Doña Jarrow hard across the face. She stumbled back and spat blood from her split lip before attacking again.

Whether it was anger or something else that fuelled her, Doña

Jarrow's technique was crude but dangerous. Munroe had heard the stories and knew how she'd earned her position, mostly by outsmarting other people, but not everything could be settled that way. Sometimes it came down to a bloody knife in a dark alley and you had to be the one holding the weapon.

Apparently she'd not lost her touch. Munroe was too slow to move out of the way and Doña Jarrow sliced her across the left forearm. Munroe hissed in pain and glanced at the wound, but couldn't see if it was deep. All she knew was that it hurt like a bastard.

Much to her surprise Doña Jarrow didn't gloat or threaten her. She stayed utterly silent. Her face remained an expressionless mask that barely twitched in an imitation of life. Munroe was used to bravado, overconfidence and aggression, but Doña Jarrow's silence was unnerving.

This time when she attacked Munroe moved to meet her and they started to dance. One stabbing while the other twisted away, slicing and jabbing, swaying to one side and then the other. Their daggers clacked together and sparks flew. They kicked and gouged, punched and elbowed, constantly trying to unbalance the other. Back and forth they moved, Munroe pushing herself off one wall and painfully bounced off another with her hip.

When she slipped on some filth Doña Jarrow managed to get behind her. While they battled to keep each other's blades at bay she put Munroe in a headlock and tried to choke her. Rather than try to wrestle, Munroe grabbed Doña Jarrow's hand and bit down until she tasted blood. With a desperate scream Doña Jarrow tried to pull away and shake her off. Eventually Munroe relented and let go, spitting out a lump of skin. She wiped the blood from her mouth and spat, trying to clear the taste.

Munroe stepped back, flipped her dagger in her grip and attacked with an overhand stab. As Doña Jarrow moved to block her knife arm Munroe kicked out with her left leg and followed up with a right hook. Doña Jarrow dodged the kick and saw the punch coming. She twisted her face aside, but it still clipped her on the jaw. Munroe kept up the offensive, hammering blows which Doña Jarrow had to either block or move backwards to avoid. Her back collided with a wall and Munroe twisted her dagger, holding it flat against her forearm. She spun and dragged her right arm in a diagonal arc, then quickly stepped back out of reach.

Doña Jarrow stared at her in shock and then down at herself. Two long red lines had appeared on her dress. One ran horizontally across her hips and the other down one leg. The wounds weren't deep but they were bleeding profusely and would ebb away at her strength. A little deeper and they would have spilled her innards all over the street. She wobbled on her feet but quickly righted herself, one hand pressed against the wound at her stomach.

Perhaps it was the sight of Munroe's bloody grin, or the bits of skin stuck between her teeth, but whatever the cause Doña Jarrow lost control.

As Munroe had expected she came out fighting. Her dagger became a silver whirlwind that whistled through the air. But for all of her skill and history with a blade, Doña Jarrow hadn't fought in a long time. She was rusty and her aggression made her sloppy. Her balance was off and Munroe punished her for it, ducking beneath Doña Jarrow's arm and punching a nerve cluster low on her back. She squawked and stumbled away, holding herself awkwardly. She managed to parry two of Munroe's attacks but missed the third, which sliced through the top of her left thigh. Hissing in pain she hopped back, her dagger held high, one hand pressed against the wound.

"What's wrong?" asked Munroe. "I thought you were going to put me in my place."

Undeterred by her injuries Doña Jarrow came forward again

with a snarl. Munroe swayed to one side and sliced her opponent across one cheek, then ducked under her arm and darted behind her back. As expected, the shallow cut on her face made Doña Jarrow even angrier. Pride in her appearance was her greatest weakness and until now her face had remained free of blemishes and scars.

She muttered something, a final insult perhaps, then came forward, silent and relentless. Munroe grabbed her right wrist, stopping the attack cold while Doña Jarrow found her left. They started to wrestle for control, trying to stab one another while keeping their adversary's blade at bay. Kicking and twisting, they slammed into a wall then skidded across the street and fell against the other. Doña Jarrow's head cracked off the stone, stunning her for a second, and that was all it took.

Munroe dropped her blade, seized Doña Jarrow's wrist again with both hands and, twisting her hips, threw her. Doña Jarrow had a second to cry out before the world tilted and she flew over Munroe's back, then struck the ground. The impact drove the air from her lungs and she dropped her dagger. As she struggled for breath Munroe swept up her dagger and buried it in Doña Jarrow's stomach, pinning her to the ground.

Doña Jarrow's face paled and she started to gag, struggling to breathe as dark rich blood welled up from around the hilt. Munroe twisted the blade then wrenched it free. A streamer of gore followed her hand up into the air. Doña Jarrow screeched, throwing her head back and bashing it off the ground before passing out.

Munroe lay beside her for a minute, gathering her breath, then struggled back to her feet. Her clothes were torn, bloody and covered in filth, but she was alive. Part of her had thought to extend the fight, to take Doña Jarrow apart piece by piece, but the less savage voice inside had won. Doña Jarrow was still alive, but she wouldn't be for much longer.

Munroe stared down at Doña Jarrow and expected to feel something. Triumph. Satisfaction perhaps. But all she felt was empty, tired and cold. It wasn't over, though. Something far worse remained and she'd left Fray to fight it alone. Stumbling away down the alley Munroe raced towards the source of the pain inside her chest.

Fray was outnumbered thirteen to one. Every instinct in his body told him to run but he didn't. Something stopped him. Perhaps he'd just given up and knew that running would be futile. Perhaps he was just too stubborn. Or maybe some insane part of his mind thought he could still win despite the overwhelming odds.

Faced with certain death Fray's biggest regrets came to the surface. If only he'd joined the Guardians earlier. If only he hadn't been so determined to prove his father wrong they could have spent years together. By now he would've learned how to wield his magic properly. If they'd worked together five years ago his father might still be alive today. If only, if only.

The cold hard truth settled into Fray's bones. Everyone dies alone.

With nothing else to do, he drew his sword, tried to stop his arm from shaking and remember his training. The armed thugs stalked towards him, taking the long way around the circles of blood. The Flesh Mage ignored them all and resumed his ritual. The assault on Fray's senses continued and he felt something wet trickle out of his ears. He touched a finger to the side of his head and it came away red. Doing his best to ignore the mounting pain, he focused on not dropping his sword.

A husky voice behind Fray drew everyone's attention. "Catch you fuckers at a bad time?"

Munroe stalked into the square, a grim expression on her face. As she came alongside him Fray noticed her clothes were torn and blood-spattered. She had a few nasty-looking cuts, but none of them appeared life-threatening.

"Sorry I'm late," she whispered. "I had to take care of something."

Munroe raised an eyebrow at the dozen jackals, who had stopped in their approach. Their surprised expressions began to change into one of abject terror. "I guess my reputation is worse than I thought."

Someone cleared their throat behind Fray and turning again he saw Choss walk into the square. Behind him came the big Vorga and at least half a dozen armed jackals, led by a grizzled Morrin.

Munroe's grin stretched from ear to ear but it quickly faded when she saw the portal stretch even wider. Fray felt a stab of pain in his stomach. The Flesh Mage's voice rose in pitch and the blood in the three circles began to bubble and churn.

The time for threats and bravado was over. Screaming at the top of their lungs, Choss and the others charged at the thugs. The world changed colours as Fray stretched out with his magic towards the portal, desperate to unravel it.

At his side Fray heard something huge unfurl, like a sail flapping in the wind. Wave after wave of pure white energy flowed out of Munroe's outstretched hands towards the portal. A sea of blue sparks erupted where the two forces met, so bright it made his eyes hurt, like staring at the sun. Fray wanted to turn away but needed to see the knot in order to peel it apart, one strand at a time.

Munroe's magic made the impossible a reality. Whether it was good fortune for him or bad for the Flesh Mage he didn't know, but every time Fray seized a thread it immediately came apart. He turned the knot over and over, invisible hands feeling for the slightest lump to grab onto. Again and again he ripped it apart, peeling back layer by layer like an onion. Their combined magic seemed to be working, as the knot seemed smaller now and the portal flickered in the air, winking in and out of existence.

Above the noise of ringing steel and the howling phantom wind, Fray heard the Flesh Mage scream. He could feel the sound as well, deep down in his bones, a pain so intense that it threatened to knock him down. He could see that Munroe's mouth was moving but he couldn't hear the words. The defiance on her face told him enough. She would never surrender.

Bodies whirled around the square, blood sprayed into the air and the chaos only fed the ritual. Across the city rabid gangs of drug-fuelled jackals tore into each other, filling the streets with rivers of blood. A torrent of power flowed out of the sky, channelled through the Flesh Mage then poured into the rift. It came back into focus and then widened again.

Something stirred in the heart of the rift. Like ripples on a pond the black space in between moved and flexed. The surface began to stretch outwards, as if something from the other side was pushing hard, trying to claw its way into the world. He saw the outline of something massive, a huge hand with many fingers.

The rift was still not fully dilated and something from the other side was trying to cross over into their world. If they didn't stop it before it was too late, thousands would die.

Reaching out with his magic Fray cast about for anything that would help. Something flickering at his right eye corner and, turning his head, Fray saw a faint red wire hanging in the air. It sparkled as if it were made of a chain of tiny rubies, running at waist height into one of the surrounding buildings.

Just to the left of that he saw another, and now that he was focusing his eyes on the threads he saw dozens, maybe hundreds. The whole area was saturated with a network of threads that no one else could see. Across the square a blue vein rose from the ground and then it crystallised, turned red and hung motionless in the air. At the other end of the wire Fray could see the spirit of one of the Flesh Mage's most recent sacrifices.

Reaching out with both hands Fray pulled all of the threads towards him, channelling his magic into a request. Almost instantly the shades started to respond. A phantasmal river of blood burst up from the earth. An echo of the many beasts that had been slaughtered in the meat district. Riding out of the ground on the torrent came a hundred restless spirits, howling and screaming for justice. More started to flow upwards, covering the sky above the square, whirling around his head like a tornado that only he could see and hear.

Now that he had started it the spirits rose faster than Fray could summon them. Whether it was the magic of the portal or something else, but soon hundreds of angry spirits were crowding for space in the sky.

"It was him," whispered Fray into the storm of the dead. "The Flesh Mage." As one, the spirits turned to stare at him, and under the scrutiny of so many Fray felt his heart miss a beat. A second later they refocused on the Flesh Mage and then surged towards him.

Instead of passing through him the first shade collided with the Flesh Mage and there was a spark of energy, like the glow of a firefly. By itself the spirit did little but as hundreds started to attack the Flesh Mage together he staggered under the tide. The spirits were expending their essence and were starting to come apart but they persisted, ripping into the Flesh Mage, tearing at his magic defences.

While the Flesh Mage was attacked by the spirits of the dead Fray redoubled his efforts, ripping the knot apart as fast as he could. It was easier than before. He could feel the tiniest imperfection, seize hold and rip it away from the whole with little effort. Yet as fast as he pulled it apart the Flesh Mage was able to rebuild it, maintaining the rift's integrity. Or so it seemed at first, but Fray quickly noticed the Flesh Mage was starting to lag behind. The flow of power from the sky was not enough to combat him, the army of the dead and the efforts of Munroe. Fray could hear her breathing hard beside him, tired breath hissing from between her clenched teeth. None of them could go on for much longer.

Reaching out with both hands towards the rift Fray pushed himself as hard as he could, throwing everything he had at it. Fresh pain blossomed deep inside and a fire hotter than anything he had imagined started to well up.

The portal flexed outwards again, stretching further and further like the skin of some vast creature trying to give birth. Now he could see the arm of something inside the glossy sheath.

The shining black substance of the portal ripped apart. A massive blue-black hand, bigger than Fray's torso, touched the ground and the screaming began. It rang in his ears. It filled his head and his heart skipped a beat. He was aware of people falling down all over the square, thrashing around on the ground and howling like beasts. The hand began to blur as if his eyes were watering, then it began to change shape and colour. It twisted and writhed, his perception of it constantly in flux as it sought purchase in a world where it was utterly alien. The hand stretched forth and then it became an arm and the start of something's shoulder.

Fray didn't remember falling to his knees but as mud and blood began to soak into his trousers he raised both hands and pushed himself again. The flow of power beside him from Munroe resumed, hammering into the portal, and the thing's hand jerked as if in pain.

The Flesh Mage had stumbled to one knee but now he pushed himself upright. Reaching towards the sky he pulled down the energy and fed it into the portal. But the flow had started to recede and the flow of power was fading, now a trickle, now only a few drops. The phantom wind had started to fade as well and Fray's hearing was returning to normal. The shades were continuing to harry the Flesh Mage but their energy was almost spent. Nevertheless they'd done their job, as his power was depleted.

Screaming in frustration Fray saw the Flesh Mage draw on his own energy reserves from the stolen lives he'd taken.

Something flickered at the edge of Fray's vision on his left but he ignored it. The burning fire had spread from his stomach out to his legs and now he couldn't feel his toes. The stretching ache inside became worse and he felt something tear, like muscle being ripped away from bone. His mouth stretched wide in a silent scream and he fell onto his side, but didn't let go. His eyes never wavered from the knot and he continued his assault, shredding it as fast as he could.

Someone was running towards the portal, a blur of red and black. It was Byrne.

He threw himself at the creature, burying his sword into the flesh of its arm. It twitched and the fingers closed in response, forming a massive fist which pounded the earth. Roof tiles fell from the surrounding buildings into the square, adding to the chaos and noise. Byrne pulled his sword free and continued his assault, hacking at the arm as if it were a tree trunk.

The Flesh Mage raised one hand towards Byrne but then two arrows sprouted from his chest. Two more joined them shortly after but he didn't fall down, only took a step backwards. The skin on his face twisted and flexed like dough before resettling. The arrows started to move, inch by inch, being pushed forward until they fell out of his body.

Fray heard a faint whooshing and an axe slammed into the Flesh Mage's face, the blade buried alongside his nose. The flow of power from him into the portal wavered and then stopped. He took another step backwards and wobbled on his feet. Two more arrows hammered into his chest and then two more. Finally blood began to trickle from the wound in his face. More arrows and weapons found their mark on the Flesh Mage, distracting him from the portal, forcing him to try and regenerate his own body.

Byrne continued to cut into the thing's arm but it seemed to be having little effect except making the creature irate. It swatted him aside but he quickly scrambled to his feet and resumed his attack.

Despite the loss of power, the rift continued to thrive. Fray didn't know if the being on the other side was feeding it but even without the Flesh Mage it had not disappeared.

A scream of defiance echoed around the square. It took Fray a few seconds to realise it came from Munroe. Forcing herself forward, one step at a time, she grimly stalked towards the portal and the creature trying to force its way into their world. With one hand pointing at the rift she reached towards the sky with the other. A fat fork of lightning split the heavens, giving Fray a brief glimpse of the hidden stars, and a second later pure white fire slammed down from above into the rift. The sound was so loud it made his ears pop and his head ring, pain lancing behind his eyes.

Finally the knot holding the rift open began to come apart, faster and faster. It flickered once and then again, winking in and out of existence. The monstrous arm spasmed and out of the corner of his vision Fray saw the Flesh Mage fall backwards, his body a pin-cushion of arrows and weapons.

"Byrne!" he screamed, but Byrne couldn't hear him. He hacked at the creature's arm again and again, chunks of nightmare flesh flying into the air all around. As the portal flickered once more, the arm started to withdraw, slowly at first and then moving faster and faster. Byrne pursued it relentlessly, slicing at the retreating form.

At the last second before the monstrous hand disappeared it lashed out, seizing Byrne around the waist and lifting him off the ground as if he were a child. Fray thought it was going to smash Byrne into the ground but instead the arm vanished through the portal, taking Byrne with it.

Only a few strands held the portal open but Fray hesitated. The rift continued to hang there in the air and he waited for Byrne to emerge from the other side. He would come back. He had to come back. Fray had lost his father to a Flesh Mage. He couldn't lose Byrne the same way.

"Close the portal," screamed Munroe. "Close it!"

Fray was on his feet stumbling towards the rift, tripping over the totems and rings of blood, never once taking his eyes off it. He needed to give Byrne enough time to come through.

When he was finally in front of the portal Fray stared through the opening into the space in between. With magic heightening his senses Fray felt his mind start to unravel. He tried to make sense of what he was seeing but clarity of thought abandoned him. A scream welled up inside and he started to claw at his own face, trying to gouge out his own eyes to hide what he was seeing. Strong hands grabbed his before he could blind himself. Amid the screams inside and out he heard a voice whispering in his ear to close the portal.

Fray severed the last threads holding the portal open. It snapped shut like a slamming door and the aftershock sent him hurtling through the air. He hammered into something hard, cracking his head against stone, and tumbled to the ground in a boneless heap. All colour seemed to bleed from the world as the magic left him, until he was left with a drab and dreary version of reality. More colours began to drift away as an enveloping darkness crept in on all sides until it swallowed him whole and then he felt nothing.

CHAPTER 45

Katja shuffled along the passage as fast as she could manage in the cramped and narrow space. She'd tried running, but as slender as she was, both shoulders noisily brushed along the walls. Alerting Teigan to her arrival before she had a chance to intervene would not help the Queen.

Forgoing speed for stealth she sidestepped and skipped along the path, holding the fizzing globe aloft in one hand. She followed the right passage until she reached the first junction, turned left and pressed on. Katja had expected cobwebs, dust, even rats, but the secret corridors of the palace were empty of all three, which suggested they saw a lot of use. Through the walls she heard muffled screams and the muted sound of running feet. Whatever panic the Kallans had started was still causing guests to flee in terror.

The corridor ended at a very narrow set of spiral stairs. Katja had to almost hug the central shaft and started to feel a little dizzy as she went up and up. Another long black and silent corridor stretched out ahead, but now she was struck by the silence. Surely if something had happened to Queen Talandra there would have been some noise? The clash of steel. A scream. She hoped that meant she still had time. A more terrifying thought pushed its way to the surface. What if she was already too late?

What if the Queen and her guards were already dead and Teigan had fled?

Fear gripped her heart and she increased her speed. Holding up the pale green light she saw several openings on both sides. She turned down the third opening on the right and nearly walked headfirst into a huge black iron door. A complex lattice of thick scrollwork blocked her way with bars as thick as her leg. The hinges were set with heavy bolts and there wasn't even space to put her arm through the gaps in the heavy metal. It looked like an impenetrable barrier until she spotted a small keyhole tucked away at knee height. Katja knelt down, whispered a brief prayer to the Maker, and tried the key Faith had given her in the lock. There was a faint click and the door moved slightly.

Katja gritted her teeth and gently pushed the door, expecting a hideous squeak of rusty hinges. The door swung back silently and she had to dash forward and catch it before it collided with the wall. Holding the light aloft Katja could see the corridor extended another thirty paces and then ended in a solid stone wall. Towards the end on the right side she could see a catch or doorway of some kind.

Katja wrapped the light with the sleeve of her dress until a very small amount seeped out. As her eyes adjusted to the gloom she crept forward, head tilted to one side, listening for sounds of alarm.

When she stood opposite the secret opening into the Queen's chambers Katja took a minute to study the door. It looked fairly simple, a wooden panel with a counter-weight to pull it closed once opened. There was a spyhole at eye level and a catch that could be opened from either side. She didn't dare open the spyhole just yet, so instead she put her ear to the panel and listened.

At first the only thing she could hear was the pounding of her own heart. Gradually she began to pick out other noises coming through the wall. There was a low murmur of voices and the shuffle of feet on stone. Everything seemed normal. Katja covered the globe completely, so that no light from the secret passageway would show, before opening the spyhole. Pressing her eye to the hole she could see a large bedroom and beyond that a thick set of double doors. Immediately in front of her and to the left was a bed, beyond that a set of tables and chairs, wardrobes and a set of drawers. Queen Talandra sat reading at the table, a stack of papers spread out before her. Katja heaved a sigh of relief to see her alive and unharmed. The fear that had been gripping her chest eased.

She was about to push open the panel and sneak into the room when she heard the muffled sounds of a disturbance. From beyond the double doors Katja heard someone shouting, the clash of steel and a scream of pain. Talandra looked up in alarm and a second later the doors flew open. Her brother, Hyram, marched into the room looking flustered and annoyed.

"What's happening?" asked Talandra.

"The disturbance has spread. People are running in panic throughout the palace," said Hyram. "We've posted guards at the entrance to this wing. Alexis will make sure no one gets in. I've also posted two guards outside these doors. Once Queen Morganse's people have it contained we'll let you know."

"Thank you, Hyram."

He gave the Queen a peculiar look then turned towards the doors. They were opened from the other side and someone stepped into the room. For a couple of seconds Hyram and Talandra stared at the newcomer in surprise, but Katja was already trying to open the secret door.

She looked like one of Talandra's royal guards, right down to the uniform, but unusually she wore her helmet, which partially covered her face. Even so, Katja would never forget those eyes.

"Who—" asked Hyram, but before he'd finished asking the

question Teigan had lashed out. Her mailed fist cracked into his jaw and he stumbled back. She followed up quickly, clubbing him over the head with a wooden baton. The force of the blow was so hard the baton splintered as it collided with Hyram's head. He dropped to the floor in a heap, blood seeping from the gash in his scalp.

As Katja twisted the handle and started to pull open the secret door, Teigan closed and locked the bedroom doors, sealing her inside with Talandra. She wedged a chair under the handle for good measure before returning her attention to the Queen.

Instead of screaming or panicking Talandra now stood facing Teigan with a narrow sword held ready. She cast a worried glance at her brother but the point of her sword never wavered.

As the secret door slid closed behind Katja with an audible click both women glanced in her direction. Their initial reaction was much the same, shock and surprise, but then Teigan's face twisted into a vicious snarl. She drew her borrowed sword and cast the helmet aside.

"Majesty," said Katja, inclining her head towards the Queen.

Talandra silently regarded her for a moment then nodded. Katja turned her attention towards Teigan. She was suddenly aware that everyone but her had a sword.

"You deserve to die," Teigan said to the Queen, but she made no move to carry out her threat.

Talandra regarded her with a cool expression. "What have I done to deserve your wrath?"

"I've been trying to work out that for weeks," said Katja, slowly edging towards the Queen. "At first I thought it was something grand. Rodann spoke about a revolution, but you never showed any interest. You never cared about any of that. Everything you've done was to get you into this room."

Teigan watched her with seemingly lifeless eyes which gave

away nothing. By itself that told Katja she was on the right road.

"Once I realised it wasn't political, I knew your reasons were personal and petty."

"Petty?" shouted Teigan.

Katja smiled, knowing she was on the right path. "I think you lost a brother in the war. Either that or your father. Surely not a husband." She couldn't think of Teigan tolerating the attentions of any man and there were few that would want to grapple with her.

"I lost everything because of you," said Teigan, staring at the Queen with intense hatred. She'd been suppressing her emotions for months and now all of them were rushing to the surface in a flood. "My father, my brothers, my husband. All dead. Murdered in a field of mud for nothing."

"We all suffered losses during the war," said Talandra. "My father—"

"No. No! Do not pretend you understand. Do not tell me of your suffering," said Teigan. "How many thousands died because of your pride? Your arrogance?"

As she ranted Katja kept edging across the room, bringing her closer to the Queen.

"You claim that you won the war, but how many widows and orphans did you create? How many families did you destroy?"

Katja could see there was no reasoning with Teigan but the Queen wasn't ready to give up yet. "What would you have done in my place?" she asked.

"Surrendered. The west was united. It was at peace. If Seveldrom had joined the Alliance there wouldn't have been a war. We could have lived in peace. My family, and thousands of others, would still be whole."

Talandra heaved a long sigh. "You're wrong. The Warlock and the Mad King had summoned an army for war. They wouldn't have simply walked away. They would have slaughtered us and then continued their march across the continent. Many more people would have died if we'd done nothing."

Teigan laughed, a dry bitter sound. "We? Who is we? Did you take to the battlefield? Did you stand on the front line in the mud? Did you shed even one drop of blood during the war?"

There was no answer to her questions. Katja knew it and so did the Queen. Nothing Talandra said would satisfy Teigan. Nothing would bring back her family or heal the wound that still festered deep inside her soul. She was broken and driven only by revenge. Teigan had not thought beyond the moment of her revenge and had no intention of escape.

Someone began to pound on the doors from outside but Teigan didn't seem to notice or care. They would get through eventually but the doors were solid and had been designed to withstand a lot of damage.

"A reckoning must be paid, in blood, for your sins. For the lives you wasted," said Teigan, readying herself for a fight. Katja looked around for a weapon but saw none, just papers and a table and chairs. Just before Teigan charged she remembered the hidden blade Lord Mullbrook had given her but it was already too late.

As Teigan raced forward Katja picked up a chair and threw it at her. It hit her square in the chest making her stumble and cry out in pain. At the same time Talandra stepped forward and lashed out with her sword. Teigan saw it coming and twisted to one side, taking the blow on her mail shirt. Katja threw herself at Teigan and they went down in a tangle of limbs, biting and clawing at one another.

Katja got one of her thumbs in Teigan's right eye and was desperately trying to shove it into her skull. At the same time as trying to keep Teigan's sword at bay the swordswoman strangled her with one hand. With a surge of strength Teigan shoved Katja's hand away, bunched her legs together and kicked out. Katja had a moment of disorientation as she flew through the air before she collided with the table. The legs broke as she hit it and she tumbled to the ground amid the splinters.

Teigan rolled to one side, dodging an attack from the Queen, then retaliated and kicked out. Her foot caught Talandra on the hip, spinning her around, and she fell back onto the bed, banging her head on a wooden post. Her sword flew from her grip and it skittered out of sight under the bed. As Katja tried to shake off the black creeping in around the edges of her vision, Teigan retrieved her sword and then stalked towards the dazed Queen. The pounding at the door was much louder and Katja heard the crack of wood but they would be too late.

Lying prone on the bed the Queen desperately scanned the room for something. As Katja stumbled to her feet Teigan raised her sword on high. With a scream Katja yanked the short blade free from her necklace and launched herself at Teigan's back. She clung onto Teigan's shoulders and sword arm, desperately stabbing at the other woman, trying to find flesh. The dagger kept hitting mail and steel, doing nothing except annoy Teigan. The additional weight of Katja on her back made her stumble and they collided with a wall. Black spots danced in front of Katja's eyes but she held on more tightly, wrapping an arm around Teigan's neck, stabbing with the other.

Snarling like an angry dog Teigan tried to shake Katja free as they moved about the room. When that didn't work she twisted around. Katja slipped to one side but refused to let go. A sharp stabbing pain in her side made her look down to see Teigan's sword buried between her ribs. A scream lodged somewhere in her throat but now she was struggling for breath and it wouldn't come out. Her grip started to ease around Teigan's neck and her other arm flopped about, seemingly useless despite the dagger.

The darkness started to grow around the edges of the world

again and sounds began to recede. Even the pounding and shouting at the door was started to fade. Katja's fingers tried to hold onto Teigan's mail but they were sliding and scratching at the metal. Her head fell back and her legs began to slip down towards the floor. With numb fingers she tried one last time to stab Teigan but it only sliced her across one ear, annoying but hardly fatal. Katja slumped to the ground and fell back against the wall, Teigan's sword still buried in her right side. She thought it had pierced her lung as she couldn't catch her breath and she could hear a terrible wheezing sound. When Teigan ripped her blade free Katja heard a scream but didn't know if it was hers or someone else's.

As Teigan raised her sword for a killing blow, Katja stared up in defiance as her tired fingers sought to retrieve her fallen dagger.

With a loud crack the doors to the Queen's room burst open and two royal guards marched into the room led by a woman. Both guards carried loaded crossbows but her eyes were drawn to the woman's face. For a second Katja thought she was seeing things but Teigan was also disorientated. It was the Queen.

"Lower your weapon," said Talandra. "There's been enough bloodshed already."

Teigan was bleeding in a few places but all of her wounds were minor. Even so she wobbled on her feet as if dizzy, or perhaps she was simply exhausted. "Who?" she asked, glancing at the woman on the bed.

"My body-double," said the Queen. "Surrender your weapon. It can all end here."

"You're right," said Teigan, lowering her sword, holding it down by her side. "It must end today."

The tone of Teigan's voice sent a cold prickle of alarm down Katja's spine. The others heard it too, as the royal guards raised their crossbows and aimed at the Seve woman's chest.

"Don't," warned the Queen but Teigan wasn't listening.

"You must die for what you've done," she said. With a scream of rage she raised her sword and started to charge at the Queen. Even before she'd advanced a single step, two quarrels punched through the armour on her chest, burying themselves up to the fletching. At this distance they knocked Teigan off her feet, sending her flying backwards to collide with the far wall.

Despite her injuries she refused to stay down. Her arms and legs began thrashing about like a dying spider, but her body didn't have the strength to lift her up any more, and as blood trickled and then gushed from her mouth a look of surprise crossed her face. Her confusion drained away and was replaced by a look of agony. The Queen started to approach Teigan but one of her royal guards kept her back, just in case. The danger had passed, though. Teigan couldn't move but even so she continued to glare at Talandra. With her dying breath she cursed the Queen, spraying blood on the floor before she died.

Before the darkness closed in, Katja saw the Queen kneel down beside her. She felt gentle hands on her face and something pressing against the wound in her side. There was a loud rushing sound and then nothing, just an endless sea of black.

CHAPTER 46

When Choss woke up the next morning he was alone but the other side of the bed was still warm. He saw a note on the side table and reading its contents made him smile.

The Flesh Mage was dead and the rift had been sealed. He'd seen Munroe at the end, infused with magic and glowing like the sun, utterly terrifying and beautiful. It was her power that had tipped the scales and saved them all.

When they'd finally made it back to his house, bruised, battered and wearing blood-stained clothing, they'd felt bone weary beyond anything they'd ever experienced. Sleep had seemed like the best and only thing possible. But sleep had evaded them as another more urgent need rose up from within. They'd celebrated their victory but more than that, they'd celebrated life. When their passion had finally been quenched they'd talked until the sun had come up. Eventually they'd fallen asleep in a tangle of limbs and Choss had been content and at peace. It was a moment he'd not experienced for many years.

Yesterday there had been only one road for them both, stretching all the way to the horizon. Now the future wasn't set and anything was possible.

As Choss sat up, the aches and injuries came back into focus, making him hiss in pain. Last night he'd made promises about looking after himself that he intended to keep. With that in mind he went down to the kitchen and fished out the powder the surgeon had previously left. While he waited for the water to boil Choss crunched rinna seeds between his teeth, which took the edge off the pain. Just walking down the stairs had made his leg throb and other injuries were jostling for attention. Fresh bruises were starting to blossom across his torso but he did his best to ignore them. The foul-tasting tea made him gag but he gulped it down quickly. After a second cup Choss felt much better and able to move around the house without feeling like a man twice his age.

He washed and dressed in fresh clothes, laced up his boots and automatically reached for his punching daggers. At the last second Choss pulled his hand back and went out the front door without them. He didn't want to carry them any more. The streets would be safe enough but that wasn't why he'd left them at home. If he wanted to make a fresh start, to become someone new, then it would mean leaving many things behind. His experience with Doña Jarrow had shown him how naïve he could be. Choss had no illusions about the world, but today he could afford to walk the streets without them.

Appetising smells from a bakery made his stomach growl, reminding him how long it had been since his last meal. Choss stopped at the first shop to gorge himself on fresh warm bread, soft cheese and slices of juicy watermelon.

Walking through the streets he expected to see obvious signs of the widespread bloodshed from last night. At first he saw nothing amiss, except more patrols of the Watch than ever before. They marched along with hands on weapons, reassuring people with their presence and numbers.

There were no bodies, no discarded weapons and very little signs of damage to the surrounding buildings. He saw one shop with broken windows that had been boarded up, but little else.

Choss did spot a few stains that were being vigorously scrubbed but the rest of the blood had been washed away. It seemed as if most of the violence between the Families had been conducted against each other, to the point of ignoring everything else.

Someone had been very busy in the hours after the fighting had stopped. Choss suspected that the Queen was doing her utmost to shield the people of Perizzi from the worst. Most would know that something had happened but they would pretend otherwise. The war was still fresh in the minds of many and because the city thrived on trade, faking normality was good for business. Eventually the illusion would become reality, but that was still a long way off. Today, in the nervous glances of strangers, Choss saw the illusion was wearing very thin. If no more violence erupted in the next few weeks their fear would begin to fade.

By the time Choss made it down to the docks it was almost midday and several shipments had already been unloaded from waiting vessels. Some dockhands and merchants were having a drink or grabbing something to eat, but the docks were still busy with activity. Much to his surprise Gorraxi sat out in the open at the end of the longest wharf. She received a few curious glances from those nearby, but because the Vorga was just watching the sea and not ripping anyone into pieces, no one complained.

Choss was still getting used to the idea that Gorraxi was female. As he sat down beside her on the dock he found himself going over previous events for clues. If he thought about it long enough he'd probably find the signs were there, but that wouldn't stop his feelings towards the Vorga being in a jumble. He was struggling to understand how he felt about her, as they'd been friends for many years. In itself friendship with a Vorga was rare and unusual, which made him realise how lucky he'd been.

During the fighting Gorraxi had sustained a few minor injuries but they were already healing. While Choss had slept in a bed she'd returned to the healing bosom of the deep water to recuperate.

"You want to ask me something?" said Gorraxi without looking around. Her face was in profile, her eyes studying the waves. She seemed more pensive than Choss was used to, but she seemed happy to have company.

"Tell me about him. The man from before."

"He was strong and worthy. That is all that matters to me." Gorraxi sounded melancholy and bereft. In those rare situations in the past when he'd found the Vorga upset, Choss would make a joke or suggest they go out for a drink. Now he wasn't sure how to respond, or even if he should be worrying about it. Male and female relationships in Vorga society were very different from how men and women treated each other.

"Your silence," said Gorraxi, as Choss struggled to decide how he should respond. "This is another reason I never told you."

"I'm sorry."

"So am I," said Gorraxi, getting to her feet. She stared out at the water for a moment longer and then offered Choss a hand, which he accepted. Mindful of his injuries, the Vorga gently pulled him to his feet until they were stood face to face. He'd always found the Vorga's stare impenetrable and had seen how it made people nervous, but this was the first time it had the same effect on him.

Strangers were scared of sudden outbursts of violence, their minds full of old folk stories about the Vorga. Choss knew his friend would never hurt him. She'd already saved his life many times in the last few weeks.

"It's a shame you're still injured," said Gorraxi, breaking eye contact. "I would like to fight you again."

"Perhaps when I've rested," he suggested and Gorraxi smiled.

"Perhaps."

They walked down the dock and settled at a table outside one of the slightly nicer waterfront taverns. Choss brought drinks back to the table and they sipped their ale in companionable silence. A few minutes later Gorraxi turned towards him.

"Munroe, she is your wife now?"

"No, not my wife. Maybe one day, but we're just at the beginning."

"I can smell her on you," said Gorraxi.

"What will you do now?" asked Choss, keen to change the subject.

"I would ask you the same thing."

"I'm not sure, but last night we agreed to leave Perizzi. We both want to try something new, not live in fear of trying in case we fail. Wherever we go, it will be together."

"If she is the one, then it should be so," said Gorraxi, a note of approval in her voice. "What of Vinny?"

Choss sighed. "I'll speak to him today and tell him my plans. I feel guilty, for abandoning him, but I hope he'll understand."

"Is he a friend?" asked Gorraxi.

"Yes, a good friend."

"Then he will want you to be happy. He will understand."

Choss put down his drink and turned to face Gorraxi. "You've been a loyal and true friend to me. You saved my life last night. There was no way I could have beaten Daxx."

Gorraxi shook her head. "It was not done for you. I told you this."

"I know, but even so, I wanted to thank you. Earlier, when we raided Don Kal's venthe farms, you risked your life just because I asked and you protected me."

"Is this not what friends do for each other?"

Choss smiled and gripped one of Gorraxi's hands in both of his. "The best of them. I owe you everything."

Gorraxi regarded him in silence for a minute and all of Choss's anxiety faded. "You are offering me something?" she finally asked.

Choss nodded and placed his right hand over his heart. "A blood debt. If you ever need me, for anything, you only need to ask. Lead and I will follow, to the last breath. This I swear."

Over the years he'd learned many things about Vorga culture from Gorraxi. Blood debts existed in other societies, but to her kind they meant much more. Other people regarded them as favours to be called in when times were hard. To the Vorga a blood debt meant something else, something almost spiritual and binding. Some were passed from one generation to another before they were called in and ancestors would be expected to pay the debt in full without hesitation. They were not given as a matter of course.

"You honour me," said Gorraxi, giving his hands a squeeze before sitting back. In that moment Choss saw an array of emotions in her eyes and he maintained eye contact until she looked away first.

"Where will you go?" he asked.

"I'm not sure," said Gorraxi. "Like you I have become small in here," she said, touching her head and then her heart. "There are many places I have yet to see. Many lands where Vorga are not seen as monsters."

"You're not a monster."

They watched the waves and the busy docks until their glasses were empty. "What are your plans for today?" asked Gorraxi.

"After the last few weeks I thought I might just sit here and drink. For today, that seems like enough."

"I like this plan. It's a good plan," said Gorraxi with a grin. "I will buy the next round."

*

This time when Munroe walked into the arena she and Don Jarrow were the last to arrive. The others were sat waiting for them around a large round table in what felt like a tense silence.

Elegant and gorgeous as ever, the Duchess wore a dark blue dress that was unusually demure for her with a high neck. Even so it still hugged her body in all of the right places, showing off her figure. Munroe noticed there were bags under the Duchess's eyes and a couple of strands of red hair had escaped the artful tangle on top of her head.

Beside the Duchess sat the rumpled figure of Don Lowell, but there again Munroe noticed a few changes. He didn't slouch and Don Lowell's gaze was focused and sharper than she'd ever seen it. The charade of the kindly old grandfather was gone. His bodyguard scanned the room for signs of trouble, but most of her attention, and that of the other Naibs, was focused on the other person at the table.

The shaven head of the Butcher seemed to shine in the torch-light as if it had been oiled. Dressed in black trousers and a vest which showed off his thick arms, she saw they were criss-crossed with cuts and bruises. There was a bandage around his right wrist and another above one eye. Munroe thought about making a joke, but smothered it. The atmosphere became more tense as she and Don Jarrow mounted the stairs to the ring.

What followed proved to be routine and tedious for Munroe. In the wake of the deaths of Don Kal, Doña Parvie and her sister, the city had to be reportioned among the surviving Families. The Butcher's help against Don Kal's people would not be overlooked, but equally the other Families were not willing to just hand over Doña Parvie's territory to him.

At the end of two hours a compromise was reached. The Butcher would take over a portion of what had previously been Doña Parvie's territory and merge it into his current operation. Any of Doña Parvie's people who had survived would be given sanctuary for a week. By the end of that time they would be presented with a choice. Leave the city and never return or swear loyalty to one of the other Families.

Almost to a man, Don Kal's people were dead. Partly because they had been fighting wherever it was thickest, but also because of the tainted venthe. It had allowed them to fight longer and harder than normal, but once it wore off many had dropped dead from the severity of their wounds. His territory would be divided up among the remaining Families and that would be the end of it.

With that the meeting was adjourned, and as each person left Munroe noticed each gave her a funny look.

It had been two nights since they'd beaten the Flesh Mage. By now word had got around about what she'd done. Some of the details were wrong, as any eye-witnesses didn't know the full story. But as neither she, nor any of the others had volunteered information, the half-truths persisted. She let that continue, as it was easier to understand and far less scary. Munroe knew her dreams would be haunted for years by what she'd seen. There was no need for everyone else to have nightmares about it.

It took her a while to work out what the look meant. It was only when she saw it in Don Lowell's eyes that she understood. Her trick of manipulating the odds had previously earned her a certain amount of respect, but this was the first time people were genuinely afraid of her. Her grin made Don Lowell twitch and hurry out of the arena.

"Do you have time for a short walk?" asked Don Jarrow. It sounded like a genuine request and it was the first he'd ever made.

"Of course."

He'd been very quiet and more reflective than usual, which wasn't surprising given everything that had happened. Doña Jarrow's betrayal had hurt him far worse than anything else.

Munroe wasn't sure how much to tell him about what had happened to his wife. He knew she was dead but Munroe didn't know if he would be pleased to know how she'd died and who was responsible.

They walked in silence for a few streets before he finally spoke.

"When will you be leaving?"

"In two days," said Munroe. The morning after the death of the Flesh Mage, she'd told him that she'd wanted out. Whether it had been because he had a lot on his mind, or because he hadn't really been listening, he'd said yes. Now that he had been given some time to think about it, she was expecting an argument. Instead Don Jarrow just grunted.

"You sound very certain. You have somewhere in mind?"

"I'm going back to school," said Munroe, which had surprised her too when she'd agreed.

Don Jarrow raised an eyebrow. "School?"

"Choss and I are going to travel to Shael, to the Red Tower. I'm going to study my magic. Learn how to control it."

"I wasn't expecting you to say that," admitted Don Jarrow.

"I'm going to be a fucking Battlemage!" shouted Munroe.

A few people in the street stared at her outburst. Don Jarrow managed a brief grin but it soon faded.

"Whatever you need for the journey, horses, provisions, just let me know. I'll take care of it."

"That's very kind," she said, waiting to see the hook.

Don Jarrow glanced at her from his eye corner and shook his head. "I don't expect anything in return. You've saved me several fortunes over the years. It's the least I can do."

"Oh well, since you're feeling generous, any chance of a little travel money? I don't fancy sleeping in hedges on the way there."

Don Jarrow laughed. "Why not. You've earned it." The Horse and Cart, one of many taverns run by Don Jarrow, came into view at the end of the street. "I'm meeting someone," he announced.

"Will you be all right?" asked Munroe. It was disconcerting for Don Jarrow to be so quiet. It made her feel awkward and she almost felt sorry for him.

"I'll be fine," he said, but she didn't believe him. He gave her a wave and walked away, a lonely figure on a busy street.

When Munroe pushed open Choss's front door with the key he'd given her she had a big grin on her face. It drained away when she went into the front room and saw a familiar face waiting for her.

"Hello, Munroe," said Ben.

"What do you want?" she asked. "Because you made it very clear what the Silent fucking Order thought of me. So why are you here?"

Ben raised an eyebrow. "Are you done?"

Munroe shook her head. "No. Whatever it is, I don't care. I'm not interested. Get out, before I make you."

"That's why I'm here," said Ben, holding out a sealed letter towards her. "My employer requests your presence."

"Your employer?" said Munroe, taking the letter before she glanced at the wax seal. Even before she opened it she knew who the letter was from. Everyone in the country knew that person's seal. It hung above the throne. "You work for the Queen?"

"I serve the Crown," said Ben, as if there was a difference. "The Queen's grandfather created the Silent Order. She inherited it from her mother."

Munroe's mouth opened and closed a few times. "But, I thought it was hundreds of years old?"

Ben shrugged. "Just read the note," he said, gesturing at the letter in her hand.

As she read the brief message Munroe's eyes widened and her jaw fell open.

"I have a carriage waiting," said Ben. They went out the front door in silence, and Munroe had managed to regain her composure by the time they'd reached the palace. She noted a large number of heavily armed royal guards everywhere, but they merely glanced at Ben before waving them through the gate.

When the carriage stopped, the door was opened by a servant. Munroe stepped down but Ben didn't follow. "I'll wait for you here," he said.

Another servant led her through the huge corridors of the palace and Munroe did her best not to gawp at the finery. She'd never seen so many paintings of battles and people she vaguely recognised, which meant they were probably the Queen's ancestors. Eventually she was led into a rather plain sitting room where two women were sat waiting for her in front of the fireplace.

Munroe immediately recognised the older woman on the left as Queen Morganse and she guessed the younger tall woman on the right was the Queen of Seveldrom. The servant closed the door behind her without saying a word, leaving Munroe alone with the two Queens. She didn't know if she should bow or curtsey to one or both of them and if etiquette meant she should wait for them to speak first before saying something. She settled for silence and inclined her head towards them both.

"Thank you for coming," said Queen Morganse. "Please sit," she said, gesturing at the chair.

"You're probably wondering why you're here," said the Seve Queen.

"To put it mildly," said Munroe, doing her best not to swear. Would she end up in a cell for swearing at the Queen? Was that a crime?

"We need your help with the Red Tower," said Queen Morganse. "One of my agents tells me you're going there soon and I'm worried."

"About me?" said Munroe.

"No," said Talandra. "About the children. Have you seen the masked Seekers?"

"No, but my friend told me about them," said Munroe, being careful not to name Fray. She didn't want to get him into any kind of trouble. "They help children. Stop them hurting people or themselves when their magic develops."

"Do they really help the children?" asked Queen Morganse. "Because we only have their word. No one has seen what happens to the children once they reach the Red Tower. How do we know what they're really doing?"

Munroe could see where this was going. "You want me to spy on the Red Tower for you. For both of you."

Talandra sat forward. "Do you remember the Warlock?" she asked, barely waiting for Munroe to nod. "What if they're teaching children to be like him? Can you imagine what an army of them could do?"

The mere thought of it made Munroe shiver. "It sounds like a fucking nightmare." The words were out of her mouth before she realised. She clapped a hand to her mouth and started to babble an apology, but Talandra laughed and even Queen Morganse smiled.

"You're right," said Talandra. "It is a fucking nightmare. So we need to make sure it doesn't happen. All we want you to do is keep your eyes and ears open."

"And if you see anything that worries you, just send a letter home to your uncle Ben," said Queen Morganse. "Would you be willing to do that for the children?"

Munroe's head was spinning a little from turning towards one Queen and then the other over and over. She thought about their request for a minute and even though she knew there was more to it than they'd told her, she could see their reasoning. No one actually knew what happened inside the Red Tower, as outsiders were not allowed. For all they knew the new people in charge could be intent on training children to be like the Flesh Mage.

"I'll do it," said Munroe and the two Queens smiled with obvious relief.

Two days later Munroe and Choss rode south for an hour before stopping and turning their horses. They looked back at the distant city and she could see his feelings were mixed about leaving it behind.

"Are you sure about this?" she asked, not for the first time. They wanted to be together, but when she'd mentioned leaving Perizzi for the Red Tower he'd said yes without hesitation. It was a lot to ask. More than she'd anticipated. She worried about things not working out between them. That he might hate her for taking him away from everything familiar.

"I'm worried as well," said Choss, as if he could read her mind. "I don't know what will happen tomorrow, but whatever comes, we'll face it together. But I'm sure that I want to be with you, more than anything. Good enough?"

"Pretty good," said Munroe with a grin. "I'm convinced."

Turning their backs to Perizzi they rode east towards the sun and their future together.

CHAPTER 47

Katja awoke to the sound of rain rattling on the window. Gradually she became aware of her surroundings. The comfy bed, the clean sheets, the plain white walls. Next she heard the faint wheezing in time with her own breath and there was a tight band across her chest.

She tried moving and her body was slow to respond at first, as if it had forgotten how to, which meant she'd been unconscious for a while. Her right hand twitched and then slowly moved up to her side where Teigan's sword had pierced her.

"You're very lucky to be alive," said a familiar voice. "You lost a lot of blood."

Katja turned her head towards the sound and saw Roza sat in a chair beside her bed. A book and a pot of tea sat beside her.

"How long?" asked Katja, her voice dry and croaky. Roza helped her sip some water before she answered. Katja felt incredibly weak and the pain in her chest was not receding, but at least she was alive.

"You've been asleep for four days. They nearly lost you a couple of times."

"What have I missed?"

"Quite a lot," said Roza, sipping at her tea. "While you were in the palace, parts of the city turned into a war zone. The rumoured war between the crime Families became a reality. We're not sure how many died but when the sun rose there were a lot of bodies in the street. As a result it's created a lot of opportunities. I'm placing new agents as we speak."

It was the perfect time. Normally getting into one of the Families was incredibly difficult. People were referred or they started off at the bottom and worked their way up the ranks, which took years. It also meant a long time playing the role before any agent would have access to any useful information. A widespread cull meant there would be openings at many levels. Katja was sure Faith would also be putting some of her people forward to get inside one or more of the Families.

"Queen Talandra?" said Katja. She still couldn't catch her breath and speaking more than a few words was proving a challenge.

"She's well and sends her thanks. It was the royal surgeon who saved you."

Katja closed her eyes for a moment and felt the remaining tension ease from her shoulders. Sleep called to her, trying to pull her under, but she forced her eyes open.

"Queen Morganse?"

"Also alive and well. As you said, Lord and Lady Trevino were supposed to ingest the same substance as the Kallans and go into a frenzy. They were meant to kill Queen Morganse and all of the others in the room, but it didn't work. He summoned the courage to take it, but something went wrong and he died. Weak heart, I think."

"Lady Trevino?"

"She couldn't do it, even with the threat against her daughter," said Roza with a shrug. "By the time Faith got into the Queen's wing they had her tied up and Lord Trevino was dead. Their daughter was rescued the following day."

"That's good news."

"The two Queens had a meeting. It seems they're the best of friends," said Roza. She forced a smile but Katja sensed her unease. "As such they're encouraging us to share information more freely. Recent events highlighted the flaws of working in isolation. So I've agreed to meet with Faith from time to time. We'll have tea and talk."

There was wisdom in that, although it would prove a tricky and subtle relationship to manage. Roza didn't freely share information with others and she suspected Faith was the same.

The room was quiet for a time before Roza spoke. "A few days ago you were ready to quit and I asked you to hold on for a while, which you did. Do you still want to keep doing this?" she asked.

It had been on Katja's mind for some time. She knew that at times her actions had been reckless and could have got her killed. She also hadn't been able to stop thinking about the baker she had killed. Even now the scene played out in her mind's eye again.

"I don't know," she admitted.

"What else would you do instead?" asked Roza. "Run a shop? Become a merchant? Organise last rites full time?"

"I don't know what I want."

"Then perhaps you should take some time to think about your choices. Maybe take a break and travel."

Time away from Perizzi would do her good. A change of scenery and a new city would be refreshing for a time, but it wouldn't change what she had done.

Despite all of the nonsense Rodann had preached, he had been right about one thing. Katja had been looking for something; a purpose.

She needed to know that what she was doing mattered and the sacrifices made meant something. She couldn't pretend what she'd done hadn't happened, and there was no way to bring the dead back to life, but she could do her best to protect the city from people like Rodann. Roza had been right about that too. It wasn't just about her.

Katja knew that the pain of what she'd done would stay with her for a long time, but perhaps in time she would develop a way of coping.

"I need to be here. I need to do this," said Katja. She thought Roza would ask her to explain but instead she just smiled.

"What about Rodann?" said Katja. "What happened to him?"

Roza's smile was wintry. "Oh, he ran when it all went wrong, but we picked him up."

"Did he say why he hated Queen Morganse so badly?"

"Rodann taught all of the Queen's children and he was the Crown Prince's personal tutor for many years. Rodann helped shape the future King of Yerskania."

"He kept saying he'd served the Crown for years," said Katja. "That he wanted a reward that was long overdue."

"Queen Morganse granted Rodann a boon for his service and he asked to be made a minor Lord. She publicly refused and he disappeared shortly after."

That kind of insult must have stung Rodann's pride, especially after what had happened to the Prince during the war. It seemed that Rodann blamed Queen Morganse for what had happened to her son. If the Queen had died at the palace then his benefactor would have taken her place and given him the title he coveted so desperately, and, knowing his ego, probably a seat on her council.

"Did you find out who was funding him? Was it someone from one of the founding families?"

"Yes, it was. In fact we didn't have to look very far from the palace to find her," said Roza, showing her teeth.

CHAPTER 48

Queen Morganse looked up from her desk at the slow and somehow plodding knock at her door. Even before she opened her mouth she knew who was on the other side and a fond smile creased the corners of her mouth.

"Enter," she said in a loud voice.

Her ageing herald, Poe, shuffled into the room. He'd been a loyal servant to her household since she'd been a girl, long before she'd sat on the throne. She'd tried to get him to retire on several occasions but he'd refused each time.

His children had grown up and moved out of the country. His wife had died years ago, and most of his friends were feeble and doddering, barely able to remember their own names. Poe claimed that continuing to work kept him young and helped his mind to stay sharp. Morganse partially agreed with him and, besides, he was practically family, and there was nothing more important to her than family.

"The Duchess of Marrowood and Penk," said Poe.

"Cousin," said the Duchess sweeping into the room, dressed in a gorgeous grey silk dress, her red hair piled up on top of her head. Despite a liberal application of make-up, Morganse could still see the purple bags under her eyes.

"How are you, Bella?" asked Morganse, taking her cousin's

hands in hers before gesturing towards the chairs by the fireplace.

"It's a bit chilly in here, Poe," said the Queen.

"I can build a fire, your Majesty," replied Poe.

Morganse exchanged a look with her cousin.

"I'm sure you have more important matters to attend to," said Bella, offering the old man one of her most generous smiles.

"Perhaps you could send for a nice young guard to sort out the fire?" suggested Morganse, slyly glancing at her cousin. "Perhaps Captain Cole. Apparently he has very nice arms."

"Very good, your Majesty," said Poe, shuffling away.

"You're never going to let that go," said Bella when the door had closed. "I said it once, and that was years ago."

Morganse grinned. "Did you know he's been a widower for five years now?"

"Let it go, cousin," said Bella. "He's probably gone grey by now."

"Haven't we all," said Morganse, running her fingers through her hair and glancing knowingly at Bella's remarkably uniform red hair.

"How are things out there?" said the Duchess, changing the subject as she gestured at the city outside.

"Settling down," said Morganse, her expression turning serious. "We're still counting the dead and there's no way to hide what happened. Despite the war between the Families, a lot of people saw bright lights and heard strange noises. They know magic was involved."

"Magic," said Bella, curling her lip. "It's dangerous and unpredictable."

"It can be, in the wrong hands," admitted Morganse. "How are you, cousin? You look tired?"

"It was a long night," admitted Bella.

"So I hear," said Morganse. "How many jackals did you lose in the fighting?"

The Duchess frowned. "Cousin?"

"I've been suspicious for a long time," said Morganse. "I kept hearing stories about 'the Duchess', but I only had confirmation a few days ago that you run one of the Families." The Duchess started to protest but Morganse held up a hand. "Don't lie to me. There's no point any more. I know everything."

Bella took a long deep breath, studying Morganse's face intently. After a minute she looked away at the cold fireplace. "When my idiot of a husband died, he left me with a huge amount of debt. He'd lost all our money at cards. Everyone was very sympathetic, but they didn't offer any help. It started out small with a gambling den, then when that went well I bought a few more. After that it grew until I had an opportunity to take over one of the Families."

"If you'd come to me, things would have been different."

The Duchess's laugh was harsh and bitter. "Why would I want to change anything?" she asked.

"Isn't that why you started the war between the Families?" said Morganse. "You couldn't bear the thought of me sitting on the throne after the war." The Duchess's head whipped around, her eyes widening in surprise. "I told you, I know everything."

Bella's top lip curled into a sneer. "You gave in to that mad man, Taikon. You let him send thousands of our people to be slaughtered."

"I didn't let him," insisted Morganse. "He demanded I give him the throne."

"Which you did anyway," snapped the Duchess, her voice echoing around the room. "Thousands died and you did nothing. Your city was overrun by zealots and you did nothing. It was the people of this city that rose up and liberated it. You don't deserve to sit on the throne."

"You claim to care about our people, but do you even know how many have died in Perizzi because of your crime war?" asked

Morganse shaking her head. "No, you did this for yourself. You wanted me dead so that you could assume the throne."

"Why not someone more worthy? People have lost faith in their Queen. You can't maintain control in your own capital city. How can they trust you to run the entire country?"

After many years of running one of the Families, her cousin had built up an enormous amount of wealth, which gave her significant power in Perizzi. With it she could buy, manipulate and encourage much of the aristocracy to throw their weight behind her in a succession.

Even more useful were the many secrets she had accumulated when important figures had sought distraction and entertainment on an evening. With the throne empty, and all fingers pointing at Seveldrom as the culprit, the aristocracy would have looked for a powerful new leader.

Bella would have sat on the throne and run the country while her business partner, Doña Jarrow, ran the Families.

"Doña Jarrow is dead, by the way," said Morganse.

"I thought so," admitted Bella. "Either that or she'd run, but Sabina was never one to run from a fight."

"How did you meet her?" asked Morganse, out of curiosity.

"She was running a local brothel when I took over the gambling den," said Bella. "We came to an early arrangement and stayed in touch."

"And the Flesh Mage?"

"Is that what he's called," said the Duchess. "That was all Sabina. She hired him to scour the Families away so that she could start afresh. She was confident it would work, but I had my doubts."

The door opened and Captain Cole came into the room unannounced and without invitation. "Ah, Captain, do you remember my cousin, the Duchess of Marrowood and Penk?" asked the Queen.

"Majesty, your Grace," said Captain Cole, bowing slightly at the waist.

Bella stared at him. "You've gone a little grey since the last time I saw you, Adem. It looks good."

"You're very kind, your Grace."

"And still so polite," said Bella before turning back to the Queen. "What happens now?"

"I think you know," said Morganse, her expression turning grave. "Treason comes with a high price."

"This way, Duchess," said Captain Cole, gesturing at the open doorway where the Queen saw several royal guards waiting. All were armed but none had drawn their weapons.

The Duchess glanced down at her dress, smoothing the grey silk beneath her fingers. The next dress she wore would also be grey, but it wouldn't be made of silk. It had been a long time since someone had been hung. That was a rare form of punishment used only for treason, but they'd built the gallows quickly enough. It would be done in private though. It was a small mercy for such a vulgar and protracted form of execution. The war between the Families and the Flesh Mage had cost the city enough. Morganse didn't want to add to the woes of her people.

Bella cast one last glance around the room at the palace, perhaps picturing it all belonging to her, before she walked from the room with her head held high.

Captain Cole escorted her from the room, followed by a squad of his finest. As the sound of their footsteps receded down the hall Poe came back into the room.

"Do you want me to light the fire for you?" he asked, glancing at the hearth. Morganse felt a chill down her spine, but it had nothing to do with being cold.

"No, it's fine. Thank you, Poe," she said.

"She was always greedy," said the old man, jerking his head

over his shoulder. "Even when you were little girls. Any time you had a new toy, she wanted two, just as shiny and expensive."

He shambled out of the room, leaving her staring at the empty chair. Her thoughts whirled as she contemplated what could have been done differently to avoid it coming to this. She wondered if Bella was right. Had the people lost faith in her? Only time would tell.

Some plans were already in motion to prevent similar conspiracies in the future, but there were other areas that needed addressing. Putting her personal worries aside Queen Morganse turned her attention to the next matter at hand.

CHAPTER 49

After a week of rest and being treated like a child, Fray was overjoyed by the Khevassar's visit. He declared Fray ready to go back to work, ignoring the protests of the overzealous nurses. All of his wounds had been treated and he was healing, but it wasn't his physical wounds that were worrying everyone. Without knowing, they could sense something was out of place.

Walking the streets beside the Old Man in uniform brought them both a lot of attention. Fray was starting to get used to people staring, but now there was something new. At first he thought it was because of the Khevassar's reputation and position. But when the first squad of the Watch stopped to shake his hand Fray knew the stares had been directed at him, not the Old Man. Fellow Guardians greeted him warmly and despite his being a novice they treated him as an equal.

As they walked, Fray let the familiar sights and sounds of the city wash over him like a balm. Most of the people remained unaware of what had really happened.

The war between the crime Families had alarmed them, but such things could be understood. Criminals, like rats, were a part of the city and there were forces in place to keep them in check. Blood magic and tears in the fabric of the world could not be easily explained.

Fray and the others had agreed that it was better if most people remained ignorant. It would help to heal the cracks in the fabric of the city more quickly. The truth would only frighten people and make them even more scared of magic. Some were already terrified, willing to do horrible things to their own children, as he'd witnessed first-hand. Many people had also seen the white fire in the sky and watched as the stars were blotted out. Like most unusual events these days, such things would be blamed on magic and with no one to tell them otherwise the fear would continue to grow.

"Despite recent events, you'll still have to complete your training," said the Khevassar without looking at Fray. "That's assuming you want to continue."

Having had little else to do over the last week but think, it was one of the many things Fray had gone over in his mind. The moment that wouldn't fade from his memory was the image of Byrne being pulled through the rift by the creature. He should have pushed himself harder to seal it more quickly. He should have done something to save him.

"You can't blame yourself," said the Khevassar, easily reading Fray's thoughts from his expression.

"I think part of him wanted to die," said Fray.

"Survivor's guilt," said the Khevassar. "He's carried it with him for five years. I hope the Maker has finally granted him some measure of peace."

"I hope so too."

"He swore to my father to protect me," said Fray. "And he died to keep his promise. However much he might have changed, Byrne was still a man of his word."

They walked in silence for a while.

"I still want to be a Guardian," Fray said eventually.

"I'm glad," said the Old Man with a smile. "I'm going to partner you with Faulk. He's been a Guardian for a long time.

He's good at his job and asks a lot of questions. You can ask him anything and he'll always try to answer. Just don't ask him about his eye and you'll be fine."

"When do I start?"

"There's no rush," said the Khevassar, gesturing they take a road on the left. He had a specific destination in mind but Fray didn't care. He was just glad to be outside where he could walk and eat without someone constantly watching him.

"I heard the nurses talking," said Fray. "There's a rumour about the Queen and Seekers from the Red Tower."

The Khevassar grunted. "Everyone's talking about it. She should've done it sooner if you ask me, but better late than never. Once a month, starting next week, people can bring their children for testing by a Seeker in Regent Square. There will be a few squads of the Watch on hand to keep things civil, but hopefully they won't be needed."

"I just hope it stops people trying to murder their own children," said Fray, thinking back to the terrified boy and the angry mob.

"I heard about that," said the Old Man, his face thoughtful. "There have been a dozen more incidents like it in the last few months. Unfortunately we arrived at most of those too late. This is a step in the right direction, but it won't stop people being afraid."

"What do you mean?"

"It doesn't matter," said the Khevassar, waving it away. "Once a month is a good start, but there will be times in between when children will need testing. I'm hoping there's a way to contact a Seeker during that time."

Fray wondered if anything slipped past the Old Man. "Yes, there is."

"Good. That's all I need to know."

They continued walking for a while, each caught up in their

own thoughts, until they stopped outside a nice-looking building. It was in a much better part of the city than Fray was used to. The Khevassar handed him a key and gestured at the door.

"Third floor, last door on the left."

"What is it?" asked Fray.

"Your new home. We had your belongings moved here."

Fray stared around at the nearby streets, noting the shops and faces that would soon become familiar and part of his everyday routine.

"Your father would be proud of you."

"What makes you say that?" asked Fray.

This time the Khevassar's smile reached his eyes. "Because I know what kind of man he was. Because you were willing to sacrifice your life for this city and the people. And because you achieved something that no one else could. I'm proud of you, son."

Fray didn't know what to say. He tried to reply a couple of times but couldn't find the words.

The Old Man gripped his shoulder and walked away before Fray could thank him.

Fray never slept well the first night in any new bed so he was barely asleep when he heard someone else breathing in the dark. He lit a candle and sat up in bed. Even before he saw the golden mask he'd known who it was. Just at the edge of his perception was a faint pulse, a second heartbeat that would become much louder if he focused on it.

"Much nicer," murmured Eloise, gesturing at his new room. "I came to say goodbye."

"Where are you going?"

"Home. To the Red Tower. There's much I need to do."

"Have you heard about the Queen's announcement?" asked Fray.

"I did. My people are in place to test every child put forward. The more we find and have a chance to teach, the safer things will become in the future."

Fray's thoughts turned to the war and how few Battlemages had come forward to fight. He thought about his father and then himself, a very thin line against the darkness.

"Do you have a library at the Red Tower? Journals or histories of previous Battlemages?" asked Fray.

"We do. Why do you ask?"

"Five years ago my father fought a Flesh Mage. Three years before that, there was a woman, another Flesh Mage. She was intent on infiltrating the aristocracy in the city. Three Flesh Mages in less than a dozen years. Before that there's no record of any in Perizzi, according to the journals in Unity Hall. Perhaps there's something in your library?"

"Their Talent," said Eloise with a sour twist of her mouth. "It's not something that's ever been taught at the Red Tower. It's dangerous, uncommon and complex. Mastering it would take years of study."

"Then there's someone else out there."

The oppressive silence that followed weighed heavily on them both.

"I will look into it," promised Eloise.

"I did have one question you might be able to answer. Why here? Why did all of them come to this city?"

Eloise was silent and so still that for a minute Fray thought she'd died. It was difficult to make out the rise and fall of her chest under her bulky clothing and long robe. He moved the candle a little closer and saw her eyes. They were studying him and Fray had a sense that he was being weighed. Finally she reached a decision and gave him a sharp nod towards the candle, which he pulled back.

"You have a right to know. It's the reason I came to this city to establish Seekers ahead of any other place in the west." Her voice echoed around the room and the chill creeping up Fray's spine had nothing to do with the temperature outside. "The barrier, the skin between here and there, is thin around Perizzi. That's why the darkness is drawn to this place."

"What can we do?"

Eloise shrugged. "Stand watch and pray that we're ready the next time it happens. There may be more we can do, but if so I've not found anything yet. I won't stop looking though."

Eloise stood up and moved towards the bedroom door.

"I wanted to ask you something else," he said. Eloise paused with her back towards him. Suddenly he wasn't sure how to ask. He wanted to know but was also afraid of the answer. "Since waking up I've not been able to use my magic. Every time I try I have a searing pain in my head."

Eloise pulled up a chair and sat down beside the bed. "When I came into the room, did you feel anything?"

"A pulse. An echo of your magic."

"Then there's hope. Give it time. I'm confident you'll heal, but if something changes send word through one of the Seekers."

"Who are they?" asked Fray, relief washing through him. To be without his magic after only just beginning to embrace his inheritance would have been a heavy blow. It wouldn't have been the end of his career as a Guardian, and in some ways it would have made things easier, but it would have felt like a betrayal.

"They're people like you, young and old," said Eloise. "Those who've managed to hide or control their ability so they can live normally without alarming others. Some of them have so little strength they can barely light a candle, but they're all sensitive to magic."

"Are they all volunteers?"

"Of course. In the past a Seeker would roam from city to city, stopping off at most places perhaps once a year to test the children. The old method was flawed. Accidents still happened and children died." The bitterness in her voice was apparent. "People became afraid of magic because all they'd seen was the destruction it brought. I made the offer and each person chose to become a Seeker. None of them want to see any more accidents. They shouldn't have to hide who they are. It may be too late for them, but it's not too late for others."

"And what about those who make it to the Red Tower? What happens to them?" asked Fray, still suspicious of her motives.

"We train them long enough until they have control of their power. After that they're given a choice. They can continue with their studies or they can return home. All we ask is that if they do leave early, they do a small favour for the Red Tower."

"You ask them to become Seekers," said Fray.

Fray saw the mask shift and sensed Eloise's smile. "I've recruited eleven people in this city. Butchers, nobles, weavers, sailors, barmaids and priests. And now I'm asking you."

Eloise set a heavy cloth bundle down on the bed beside him. Fray unfolded the cloth to find a black robe, gloves and a gold mask.

"Will you help others? Will you become a Seeker for the Red Tower?"

Fray stared at the mask for a long time. He thought about what the Khevassar had said about children being murdered because people were afraid. He thought about his childhood and his father teaching him to hide his ability. Fray had hoped that if he earned people's trust they might accept him. Although Eloise had said he was naïve and foolish, he still hoped such a day would come. But until then children in his city were dying and he could stop it.

Fray picked up the mask.

CHAPTER 50

In Perizzi an old sailor and a grizzled warrior watched as the woman in the gold mask mounted up and rode away. No one on the street saw anything unusual but the two veterans could see the truth. They smiled at each other and carried on down the road to the dockside tavern. The warrior bought them some drinks and they sat at a table outside, watching the water. There was nothing remarkable about them and no one paid them any attention.

"Skinwalking is a very rare Talent," said Vargus. "It's not something that can be easily taught."

"Three Flesh Mages in so few years is very unusual," agreed Nethun, slurping his ale. "I thought it was the Lantern boy at first, interfering like he did when he dragged half the world into a damned war."

Vargus raised an eyebrow. "You knew that was him?"

Nethun chuckled. "You don't get to be my age without knowing what's going on. I take it you've dealt with him?"

"He's in the Void for now. It's up to his followers if he comes back or not."

Nethun grunted. "I recently heard a story from a sailor. A few years ago he remembers seeing the Warlock on board his ship. He travelled all over, up north to Zecorria and elsewhere."

"Really?" said Vargus.

"Apparently the Warlock learned many things on his travels, like dreamwalking. Isn't that how he killed King Matthias?"

"Yes, it was."

"The Warlock also sailed south, to the furthest corners of Shael. He spent years down there in fact."

"Is that so," said Vargus, taking a long drink.

"In fact I'd be willing to bet my gold against your copper that all of the Flesh Mages passed through the same place in Shael at one time."

Vargus leaned across the table and lowered his voice. "Do you know who's down there?"

"No. I've sent a few people to investigate but none have returned."

Vargus sat back and they drank in silence for a while, watching the hustle and bustle of the docks. Nethun turned his eyes towards the sea and smiled, like a parent watching his children at play.

"That information could prove very useful if it found its way into the right hands," said Vargus.

"Like a woman in a gold mask," said Nethun.

"I'll see to it."

The old sailor sniffed the air and drained his mug. "I have to go, the tide is changing. Let me know if you hear anything about Shael."

"I think when it happens, we'll all know about it," said Vargus.

Nethun gripped Vargus's hand and then hurried away towards a ship. Nethun was right, the tide was changing, and a storm was coming.

ACKNOWLEDGEMENTS

As ever, many people helped to make this book a reality. First and foremost, Juliet Mushens, for seeing the potential in my writing and pulling me off the slushpile in the first place. Sarah Manning, for her hard work on my behalf and enthusiasm for this story. The whole team at Orbit, who helped me wrestle with the text and beat it into shape. Also all of Team Mushens for being excellent and supportive people.

Lastly I'd like to thank you, the reader. If you've come this far then you've made it to the end of the book. Reading a novel by a new author is always risky, so I hope you enjoyed the story and will come back for more adventures in the future.

Look out for Book Three
in the Age of Darkness series

Chaosmage

Coming in late 2016!

extras

orbit

meet the author

Photo Credit: Hannah Webster

STEPHEN ARYAN was born in 1977 and was raised by the sea in northeast England. After graduating from Loughborough University, he started working in marketing, and for some reason he hasn't stopped. A keen podcaster, lapsed gamer and budding archer, when not extolling the virtues of *Babylon 5*, he can be found drinking real ale and reading comics.

He lives in a village in Yorkshire with his partner and two cats. You can find him on Twitter at @SteveAryan or visit his website at www.stephenaryan.com.

introducing

A CROWN FOR COLD SILVER

by Alex Marshall

"It was all going so nicely, right up until the massacre."

Twenty years ago, feared general Cobalt Zosia led her five villainous captains and mercenary army into battle, wrestling monsters and toppling an empire. When there were no more titles to win and no more worlds to conquer, she retired and gave up her legend to history.

Now the peace she carved for herself has been shattered by the unprovoked slaughter of her village. Seeking bloody vengeance, Zosia heads for battle once more, but to find justice she must confront grudge-bearing enemies, once-loyal allies, and an unknown army that marches under a familiar banner.

FIVE VILLAINS. ONE LEGENDARY GENERAL. A FINAL QUEST FOR VENGEANCE.

CHAPTER 1

I t was all going so nicely, right up until the massacre.
Sir Hjortt's cavalry of two hundred spears fanned out through
the small village, taking up positions between half-timbered
houses in the uneven lanes that only the most charitable of sur-
veyors would refer to as "roads." The warhorses slowed and then
stopped in a decent approximation of unison, their riders sitting as
stiff and straight in their saddles as the lances they braced against
their stirrups. It was an unseasonably warm afternoon in the
autumn, and after their long approach up the steep valley, soldier
and steed alike dripped sweat, yet not a one of them removed their
brass skullcap. Weapons, armor, and tack glowing in the fierce
alpine sunlight, the faded crimson of their cloaks covering up the
inevitable stains, the cavalry appeared to have ridden straight out
of a tale, or galloped down off one of the tapestries in the mayor's
house.

So they must have seemed to the villagers who peeked through
their shutters, anyway. To their colonel, Sir Hjortt, they looked
like hired killers on horseback barely possessed of sense to do as
they were told most of the time. Had the knight been able to train
wardogs to ride he should have preferred them to the Fifteenth
Cavalry, given the amount of faith he placed in this lot. Not much,
in other words, not very much at all.

He didn't care for dogs, either, but a dog you could trust, even if
it was only to lick his balls.

The hamlet sprawled across the last stretch of grassy meadow
before the collision of two steep, bald-peaked mountains. Murky
forest edged in on all sides, like a snare the wilderness had set for
the unwary traveler. A typical mountain town here in the Kutum-
ban range, then, with only a low reinforced stone wall to keep out

the wolves and what piddling avalanches the encircling slopes must bowl down at the settlement when the snows melted.

Sir Hjortt had led his troops straight through the open gate in the wall and up the main track to the largest house in the village... which wasn't saying a whole lot for the building. Fenced in by shedding rosebushes and standing a scant two and a half stories tall, its windowless redbrick face was broken into a grid by the black timbers that supported it. The mossy thatched roof rose up into a witch's hat, and set squarely in the center like a mouth were a great pair of doors tall and wide enough for two riders to pass through abreast without removing their helmets. As he reached the break in the hedge at the front of the house, Sir Hjortt saw that one of these oaken doors was ajar, but just as he noticed this detail the door eased shut.

Sir Hjortt smiled to himself, and, reining his horse in front of the rosebushes, called out in his deepest baritone, "I am Sir Efrain Hjortt of Azgaroth, Fifteenth Colonel of the Crimson Empire, come to counsel with the mayor's wife. I have met your lord mayor upon the road, and while he reposes at my camp—"

Someone behind him snickered at that, but when Sir Hjortt turned in his saddle he could not locate which of his troops was the culprit. It might have even come from one of his two personal Chainite guards, who had stopped their horses at the border of the thorny hedge. He gave both his guards and the riders nearest them the sort of withering scowl his father was overly fond of doling out. This was no laughing matter, as should have been perfectly obvious from the way Sir Hjortt had dealt with the hillbilly mayor of this shitburg.

"Ahem." Sir Hjortt turned back to the building and tried again. "Whilst your lord mayor reposes at my camp, I bring tidings of great import. I must speak with the mayor's wife at once."

Anything? Nothing. The whole town was silently, fearfully watching him from hiding, he could feel it in his aching thighs, but not a one braved the daylight either to confront or assist him. Peasants—what a sorry lot they were.

"I say again!" Sir Hjortt called, goading his stallion into the mayor's yard and advancing on the double doors. "As a colonel of the Crimson Empire and a knight of Azgaroth, I shall be welcomed by the family of your mayor, or—"

Both sets of doors burst open, and a wave of hulking, shaggy beasts flooded out into the sunlight—they were on top of the Azgarothian before he could wheel away or draw his sword. He heard muted bells, obviously to signal that the ambush was under way, and the hungry grunting of the pack, and—

The cattle milled about him, snuffling his horse with their broad, slimy noses, but now that they had escaped the confines of the building they betrayed no intention toward further excitement.

"Very sorry, sir," came a hillfolk-accented voice from somewhere nearby, and then a small, pale hand appeared amid the cattle, rising from between the bovine waves like the last, desperate attempt of a drowning man to catch a piece of driftwood. Then the hand seized a black coat and a blond boy of perhaps ten or twelve vaulted himself nimbly into sight, landing on the wide back of a mountain cow and twisting the creature around to face Sir Hjortt as effortlessly as the Azgarothian controlled his warhorse. Despite this manifest skill and agility at play before him, the knight remained unimpressed.

"The mayor's wife," said Sir Hjortt. "I am to meet with her. Now. Is she in?"

"I expect so," said the boy, glancing over his shoulder—checking the position of the sun against the lee of the mountains towering over the village, no doubt. "Sorry again 'bout my cows. They're feisty, sir; had to bring 'em down early on account of a horned wolf being seen a few vales over. And I, uh, didn't have the barn door locked as I should have."

"Spying on us, eh?" said Sir Hjortt. The boy grinned. "Perhaps I'll let it slide this once, if you go and fetch your mistress from inside."

"Mayoress is probably up in her house, sir, but I'm not allowed 'round there anymore, on account of my wretched behavior," said the boy with obvious pride.

"This isn't her home?" Hjortt eyed the building warily.

"No, sir. This is the barn."

Another chuckle from one of his faithless troops, but Sir Hjortt didn't give whoever it was the satisfaction of turning in his saddle a second time. He'd find the culprit after the day's business was done, and then they'd see what came of having a laugh at their commander's expense. Like the rest of the Fifteenth Regiment, the cavalry apparently thought their new colonel was green because he wasn't yet twenty, but he would soon show them that being young and being green weren't the same thing at all.

Now that their cowherd champion had engaged the invaders, gaily painted doors began to open and the braver citizenry slunk out onto their stoops, clearly awestruck at the Imperial soldiers in their midst. Sir Hjortt grunted in satisfaction—it had been so quiet in the hamlet that he had begun to wonder if the villagers had somehow been tipped off to his approach and scampered away into the mountains.

"Where's the mayor's house, then?" he said, reins squeaking in his gauntlets as he glared at the boy.

"See the trail there?" said the boy, pointing to the east. Following the lad's finger down a lane beside a longhouse, Sir Hjortt saw a small gate set in the village wall, and beyond that a faint trail leading up the grassy foot of the steepest peak in the valley.

"My glass, Portolés," said Sir Hjortt, and his bodyguard walked her horse over beside his. Sir Hjortt knew that if he carried the priceless item in his own saddlebag one of his thuggish soldiers would likely find a way of stealing it, but not a one of them would dare try that shit with the burly war nun. She handed it over and Sir Hjortt withdrew the heavy brass hawkglass from its sheath; it was the only gift his father had ever given him that wasn't a weapon of some sort, and he relished any excuse to use it. Finding the magnified trail through the instrument, he tracked it up the meadow to where the path entered the surrounding forest. A copse of yellowing aspen interrupted the pines and fir, and, scanning the hawkglass upward, he saw that this vein of gold continued up the otherwise evergreen-covered mountain.

"See it?" the cowherd said. "They live back up in there. Not far."

Sir Hjortt gained a false summit and leaned against one of the trees. The thin trunk bowed under his weight, its copper leaves hissing at his touch, its white bark leaving dust on his cape. The series of switchbacks carved into the increasingly sheer mountainside had become too treacherous for the horses, and so Sir Hjortt and his two guards, Brother Iqbal and Sister Portolés, had proceeded up the scarps of exposed granite on foot. The possibility of a trap had not left the knight, but nothing more hostile than a hummingbird had showed itself on the hike, and now that his eyes had adjusted to the strangely diffuse light of this latest grove, he saw a modest, freshly whitewashed house perched on the lip of the next rock shelf.

Several hundred feet above them. Brother Iqbal laughed and Sister Portolés cursed, yet her outburst carried more humor in it than his. Through the trees they went, and then made the final ascent.

"Why..." puffed Iqbal, the repurposed grain satchel slung over one meaty shoulder retarding his already sluggish pace, "in all the... devils of Emeritus...would a mayor...live...so far...from his town?"

"I can think of a reason or three," said Portolés, setting the head of her weighty maul in the path and resting against its long shaft. "Take a look behind us."

Sir Hjortt paused, amenable to a break himself—even with only his comparatively light riding armor on, it was a real asshole of a hike. Turning, he let out an appreciative whistle. They had climbed quickly, and spread out below them was the painting-perfect hamlet nestled at the base of the mountains. Beyond the thin line of its walls, the lush valley fell away into the distance, a meandering brook dividing east ridge from west. Sir Hjortt was hardly a single-minded, bloodthirsty brute, and he could certainly appreciate the allure of living high above one's vassals, surrounded by the breath-taking beauty of creation. Perhaps when this unfortunate errand was over he would convert the mayor's house into a hunting lodge, wiling away his summers with sport and relaxation in the clean highland air.

"Best vantage in the valley," said Portolés. "Gives the headperson plenty of time to decide how to greet any guests."

"Do you think she's put on a kettle for us?" said Iqbal hopefully. "I could do with a spot of hunter's tea."

"About this mission, Colonel…" Portolés was looking at Sir Hjortt but not meeting his eyes. She'd been poorly covering up her discomfort with phony bravado ever since he'd informed her what needed to be done here, and the knight could well imagine what would come next. "I wonder if the order—"

"And I wonder if your church superiors gave me the use of you two anathemas so that you might hem and haw and question me at every pass, instead of respecting my command as an Imperial colonel," said Sir Hjortt, which brought bruise-hued blushes to the big woman's cheeks. "Azgaroth has been a proud and faithful servant of the Kings and Queens of Samoth for near on a century, whereas your popes seem to revolt every other feast day, so remind me again, what use have I for your counsel?"

Portolés muttered an apology, and Iqbal fidgeted with the damp sack he carried.

"Do you think I relish what we have to do? Do you think I would put my soldiers through it, if I had a choice? Why would I give such a command, if it was at all avoidable? Why—" Sir Hjortt was just warming to his lecture when a fissure of pain opened up his skull. Intense and unpleasant as the sensation was, it fled in moments, leaving him to nervously consider the witchborn pair. Had one of them somehow brought on the headache with their devilish ways? Probably not; he'd had a touch of a headache for much of the ride up, come to think of it, and he hadn't even mentioned the plan to them then.

"Come on," he said, deciding it would be best to drop the matter without further pontification. Even if his bodyguards did have reservations, this mission would prove an object lesson that it is always better to rush through any necessary unpleasantness, rather than drag your feet and overanalyze every ugly detail. "Let's be done with this. I want to be down the valley by dark, bad as that road is."

They edged around a hairpin bend in the steep trail, and then the track's crudely hewn stair delivered them to another plateau, and the mayor's house. It was similar in design to those in the hamlet, but with a porch overhanging the edge of the mild cliff and a low white fence. Pleasant enough, thought Sir Hjortt, except that the fence was made of bone, with each outwardly bowed moose-rib picket topped with the skull of a different animal. Owlbat skulls sat between those of marmot and hill fox, and above the door of the cabin rested an enormous one that had to be a horned wolf; when the cowherd had mentioned such a beast being spied in the area, Sir Hjortt had assumed the boy full of what his cows deposited, but maybe a few still prowled these lonely mountains. What a thrill it would be, to mount a hunting party for such rare game! Then the door beneath the skull creaked, and a figure stood framed in the doorway.

"Well met, friends, you've come a long way," the woman greeted them. She was brawny, though not so big as Portolés, with features as hard as the trek up to her house. She might have been fit enough once, in a country sort of way, when her long, silvery hair was blond or black or red and tied back in pigtails the way Hjortt liked... but now she was just an old woman, same as any other, fifty winters young at a minimum. Judging from the tangled bone fetishes hanging from the limbs of the sole tree that grew inside the fence's perimeter—a tall, black-barked aspen with leaves as hoary as her locks—she might be a sorceress, to boot.

Iqbal returned her welcome, calling, "Well met, Mum, well met indeed. I present to you Sir Hjortt of Azgaroth, Fifteenth Colonel of the Crimson Empire." The anathema glanced to his superior, but when Sir Hjortt didn't fall all over himself to charge ahead and meet a potential witch, Iqbal murmured, "She's just an old bird, sir, nothing to fret about."

"Old bird or fledgling, I wouldn't blindly stick my hand in an owlbat's nest," Portolés said, stepping past Sir Hjortt and Iqbal to address the old woman in the Crimson tongue. "In the names of the Pontiff of the West and the Queen of the Rest, I order you out here into the light, woman."

"Queen of the Rest?" The woman obliged Portolés, stepping down the creaking steps of her porch and approaching the fence. For a mayor's wife, her checked dirndl was as plain as any village girl's. "And Pontiff of the West, is it? Last peddler we had through here brought tidings that Pope Shanatu's war wasn't going so well, but I gather much has changed. Is this sovereign of the Rest, blessed whoever she be, still Queen Indsorith? And does this mean peace has once again been brokered?"

"This bird hears a lot from her tree," muttered Sir Hjortt, then asked the woman, "Are you indeed the mayor's wife?"

"I am Mayoress Vivi, wife of Leib," said she. "And I ask again, respectfully, to whom shall I direct my prayers when next I—"

"The righteous reign of Queen Indsorith continues, blessed be her name," said Sir Hjortt. "Pope Shanatu, blessed be *his* name, received word from on high that his time as Shepherd of Samoth has come to an end, and so the war is over. His niece Jirella, blessed be *her* name, has ascended to her rightful place behind the Onyx Pulpit, and taken on the title of Pope Y'Homa III, Mother of Midnight, Shepherdess of the Lost."

"I see," said the mayoress. "And in addition to accepting a rebel pope's resignation and the promotion of his kin to the same lofty post, our beloved Indsorith, long may her glory persist, has also swapped out her noble title? 'Queen of Samoth, Heart of the Star, Jewel of Diadem, Keeper of the Crimson Empire' for, ah, 'Queen of the Rest'?" The woman's faintly lined face wrinkled further as she smiled, and Portolés slyly returned it.

"Do not mistake my subordinate's peculiar sense of humor for a shift in policy—the queen's honorifics remain unchanged," said Sir Hjortt, thinking of how best to discipline Portolés. If she thought that sort of thing flew with her commanding colonel just because there were no higher-ranked clerical witnesses to her dishonorable talk, the witchborn freak had another thing coming. He almost wished she would refuse to carry out his command, so he'd have an excuse to get rid of her altogether. In High Azgarothian, he said, "Portolés, return to the village and give the order. In the time it will take you to make it down I'll have made myself clear enough."

Portolés stiffened and gave Sir Hjortt a pathetic frown that told him she'd been holding out hope that he would change his mind. Not bloody likely. Also in Azgarothian, the war nun said, "I'm... I'm just going to have a look inside before I do. Make sure it's safe, Colonel Hjortt."

"By all means, Sister Portolés, welcome, welcome," said the older woman, also in that ancient and honorable tongue of Sir Hjortt's ancestors. Unexpected, that, but then the Star had been a different place when this biddy was in her prime, and perhaps she had seen more of it than just her remote mountain. Now that she was closer he saw that her cheeks were more scarred than wrinkled, a rather gnarly one on her chin, and for the first time since their arrival, a shadow of worry played across the weathered landscape of her face. Good. "I have an old hound sleeping in the kitchen whom I should prefer you left to his dreams, but am otherwise alone. But, good Colonel, Leib was to have been at the crossroads this morning..."

Sir Hjortt ignored the mayor's wife, following Portolés through the gate onto the walkway of flat, colorful stones that crossed the yard. They were artlessly arranged; the first order of business would be to hire the mason who had done the bathrooms at his family estate in Cockspar, or maybe the woman's apprentice, if the hoity-toity artisan wasn't willing to journey a hundred leagues into the wilds to retile a walk. A mosaic of miniature animals would be nice, or maybe indigo shingles could be used to make it resemble a creek. But then they had forded a rill on their way up from the village, so why not have somebody trace it to its source and divert it this way, have an actual stream flow through the yard? It couldn't be that hard to have it come down through the trees there and then run over the cliff beside the deck, creating a miniature waterfall that—

"Empty," said Portolés, coming back outside. Sir Hjortt had lost track of himself—it had been a steep march up, and a long ride before that. Portolés silently moved behind the older woman, who stood on the walk between Sir Hjortt and her house. The matron looked nervous now, all right.

"My husband Leib, Colonel Hjortt. Did you meet him at the crossroads?" Her voice was weaker now, barely louder than the quaking aspens. That must be something to hear as one lay in bed after a hard day's hunt, the rustling of those golden leaves just outside your window.

"New plan," said Sir Hjortt, not bothering with the more formal Azgarothian, since she spoke it anyway. "Well, it's the same as the original, mostly, but instead of riding down before dark we'll bivouac here for the night." Smiling at the old woman, he said, "Do not fret, Missus Mayor, do not fret, I won't be garrisoning my soldiers in your town, I assure you. Camp them outside the wall, when they're done. We'll ride out at first"—the thought of sleeping in on a proper bed occurred to him—"noon. We ride at noon tomorrow. Report back to me when it's done."

"Whatever you're planning, sir, let us parley before you commit yourself," said the old woman, seeming to awaken from the anxious spell their presence had cast upon her. She had a stern bearing he wasn't at all sure he liked. "Your officer can surely tarry a few minutes before delivering your orders, especially if we are to have you as our guests for the night. Let us speak, you and I, and no matter what orders you may have, no matter how pressing your need, I shall make it worth your while to have listened."

Portolés's puppy-dog eyes from over the woman's shoulder turned Sir Hjortt's stomach. At least Iqbal had the decency to keep his smug gaze on the old woman.

"Whether or not she is capable of doing so, Sister Portolés will *not* wait," said Sir Hjortt shortly. "You and I are talking, and directly, make no mistake, but I see no reason to delay my subordinate."

The old woman looked back past Portolés, frowning at the open door of her cabin, and then shrugged. As if she had any say at all in how this would transpire. Flashing a patently false smile at Sir Hjortt, she said, "As you will, fine sir. I merely thought you might have use for the sister as we spoke, for we may be talking for some time."

Fallen Mother have mercy, did every single person have a better idea of how Sir Hjortt should conduct himself than he did? This would not stand.

"My good woman," he said, "it seems that we have even more to parley than I previously suspected. Sister Portolés's business is pressing, however, and so she must away before we embark on this long conversation you so desire. Fear not, however, for the terms of supplication your husband laid out to us at the crossroads shall be honored, reasonable as they undeniably are. Off with you, Portolés."

Portolés offered him one of her sardonic salutes from over the older woman's shoulder, and then stalked out of the yard, looking as petulant as he'd ever seen her. Iqbal whispered something to her as he moved out of her way by the gate, and wasn't fast enough in his retreat when she lashed out at him. The war nun flicked the malformed ear that emerged from Iqbal's pale tonsure like the outermost leaf of an overripe cabbage, rage rendering her face even less appealing, if such a thing was possible. Iqbal swung his heavy satchel at her in response, and although Portolés dodged the blow, the dark bottom of the sackcloth misted her with red droplets as it whizzed past her face. If the sister noticed the blood on her face, she didn't seem to care, dragging her feet down the precarious trail, her maul slung over one hunched shoulder.

"My husband," the matron whispered, and, turning back to her, Sir Hjortt saw that her wide eyes were fixed on Iqbal's dripping sack.

"Best if we talk inside," said Sir Hjortt, winking at Iqbal and ushering the woman toward her door. "Come, come, I have an absolutely brilliant idea about how you and your people might help with the war effort, and I'd rather discuss it over tea."

"You said the war was over," the woman said numbly, still staring at the satchel.

"So it is, so it is," said Sir Hjortt. "But the *effort* needs to be made to ensure it doesn't start up again, what? Now, what do you have to slake the thirst of servants of the Empire, home from the front?"

She balked, but there was nowhere to go, and so she led Sir Hjortt and Brother Iqbal inside. It was quiet in the yard, save for the trees and the clacking of the bone fetishes when the wind ran its palm down the mountain's stubbly cheek. The screaming didn't start until after Sister Portolés had returned to the village, and down there they were doing enough of their own to miss the echoes resonating from the mayor's house.

introducing

If you enjoyed
BLOODMAGE,
look out for

THE LASCAR'S DAGGER

The Forsaken Lands: Book 1

by Glenda Larke

Faith will not save him.

*Saker appears to be a simple priest, but in truth he's a spy for
the head of his faith. Wounded in the line of duty by
a Lascar sailor's blade, the weapon seems to follow him home.
Unable to discard it, nor the sense of responsibility it brings,
Saker can only follow its lead.*

*The dagger puts Saker on a journey to distant shores, on
a path that will reveal terrible secrets about the empire,
about the people he serves, and destroy the life he knows.
The Lascar's dagger demands a price, and that price
will be paid in blood.*

1

The Touch of Spice

S aker paused, nose twitching. Good Va above, the *smell*.
No, not smell: aroma. The intense, rich aroma of spices saturating his nasal passages and tickling the back of his throat. Gor-
geously pervasive fragrances, conjuring up images of faraway lands.
Perfumes powerful enough to scent his clothes and seep into the
pores of his skin.

He recognised some of them. The sharp tang of cloves, the
woody snippiness of cinnamon, the delicious intensity of nutmeg.
Saker Rampion, witan priest of the Faith, was privileged enough to
have inhaled such fragrances wafting up from manor kitchens, but
never had he smelled spices as pungent as these. Never had he been
so tantalised by scents redolent of a world he'd never visited.

Crouching on the beam under the slate shingles of the warehouse roof, he inhaled, enjoying the richness of an olfactory dec-
adence. Any one of the bales beneath him could make him a rich
man, for life.

Enough of the daydreaming, Saker. Witans are never wealthy...

His early-morning breaking and entering into merchant Uthen
Kesleer's main warehouse did have a purpose, but it wasn't theft.
He'd come not as a thief, but as a spy for his employer, the Pon-
tifect of Va-Faith.

Several hours remained before the city of Ustgrind would waken
to another summer's day, but slanting sunbeams already filtered
through the ill-fitting ventilation shutters to illuminate the interior.
In one corner, ledgers were neatly aligned on shelving behind the
counting clerks' desks. The rest of the warehouse was stacked high
with sacks and casks from the holds of the thousand-ton carrack

Spice Dragon, recently docked with a cargo purchased halfway around the world. Narrow aisles separated the rows of goods. Seen from his perch on the beam, it was as confusing as a hedge maze.

He had already seen—or rather, smelled—enough to glean some of the information he'd been sent to obtain, but he wasn't about to leave without proof.

Tying one end of his rope to the beam, he lowered the other end on to the burlap of the bales. He rappelled down the wall until his feet hit the top bale. Leaving the rope where it was, he crouched to examine the sacking beneath his feet.

He peeled off his leather gloves and tucked them into his belt, then used the tip of his dagger to tease apart the strands of burlap. The hole he made was just large enough to insert the tips of two fingers and pull out a sample. In the dim light he wasn't sure what he had. It felt like wood and was shaped like a star, no larger than his thumbnail. He lifted it to his nose and inhaled. A tantalising smell similar to aniseed, but stronger and subtly mixed with a hint of...what? Fennel? A spice obviously, but not one he knew. He slipped several of the wooden stars into his pouch, smoothed over the hole in the sacking and moved on to another bale.

After quarter of an hour he'd extracted samples of eight different spices and done a rough count of sacks, bales and casks. In the interests of secrecy, he'd resisted the temptation to break the seal around the bungs on the casks to see what they contained. His instructions had been explicit.

"Just for once, no one is to know what you are doing, Saker," the Pontifect had said with weary sternness after giving him his instructions. "No adventuring, no brawling, no sword fights, no hair's-breadth escapes. You're supposed to gather intelligence, not be a one-man army."

"Not so much as a bloody nose," he'd replied cheerfully. "I swear it, your reverence. I find out if Lowmeer's merchant traders have found the Spicerie and, if they have, what their intentions are, then I return with the information. No one will know the Pontifect's witan spy was even in Ustgrind. Simple."

"Somehow nothing is ever simple if you're involved." As this was said with a sigh that spoke of a long-suffering patience not far from being shattered, he'd had the wit to stay silent.

Now, however, he smiled wryly at the thought of Saker Rampion keeping out of trouble. He seemed to *attract* trouble, swinging towards it like a compass needle pointing north.

A moment later, right on cue, he knew he wasn't alone in the warehouse.

He wasn't sure what had alerted him. A faint inhalation of a breath? The almost inaudible scrape of a shoe against the rim of a cask? Something. While counting the cargo, he'd circled the whole warehouse, walked down every narrow alley between the stacks. *I didn't see or hear anybody.* The hair on the back of his neck prickled.

He eased himself down into a crouch, holding his breath. No one shouted an alarm. The silence remained as intact as the aromas saturating the air, yet every instinct told him he was being stalked. It wasn't a mouse or a warehouse cat. It wasn't the creak of timber warming up as the sun rose. Someone was there, in the building, following him.

Va rot him, he's good, whoever he is.

The warehouse doors were barred on the outside, and the street was patrolled by arquebus-toting guards of the Kesleer Trading Company. His only escape route was the way he'd come in, over the roofs.

Edging down a narrow canyon between stacked casks on one side and layers of bulging sacks on the other, he headed back to the rope. Each step he took was measured, silent, slow. As he moved, he ran through possibilities. A thief? A spy for another trading company? A warehouse guard? The thought of someone skilled enough to stay hidden and quiet all this time sent a shiver tingling up his spine. His hand dropped to the hilt of the dagger at his belt. Confound his decision to leave his sword back in his rented room! He'd feared it would hamper his climb to the roof; now he feared its lack.

He'd almost reached the rope when a soft slithering sound gave him a sliver of warning. Too late, he threw himself sideways. A man dropped on him from the top of a stack of sacks, his momentum sufficient to send them both sprawling. His heart skidded sickly as he tried to roll away, but there was no escaping the grip on his shoulder. Face down, his nose ground into the floor hard enough to start it bleeding, his dagger inaccessible under his hip, he was in trouble.

So much for his promises...

He relaxed momentarily, allowing his muscles to go soft. The hand jamming him down to the floor was powerful, yet the body on top of his felt surprisingly slight.

A *woman*? Surely not. His assailant had the muscles of an ox. A strong smell of salt, though. A sailor, perhaps. Yes, there was the confirmation—a whiff of tar from his clothes.

He arched his body up and over, reaching backwards with his free arm. Clutching a handful of hair, he wrenched hard. The fellow grunted and punched him on the side of his face. He let go of the hair and they separated, rolling away from each other and springing to their feet.

The young man facing him was at least a head shorter than he was, but the real surprise lay in his colouring. Black eyes stared at him out of a brown face, framed by black hair long enough to be tied at the neck. Not Lowmian, then. Pashali? A Pashali trader from the Va-forsaken Hemisphere? He was dark enough, but his clothes were all wrong. He was dressed in the typical garb of a tar straight off a Lowmian ship. In the dim light it was hard to guess his age, but Saker thought him a few years younger than himself. Nineteen? Twenty?

Not much more than a youth, crouching, arms held wide, body swaying slightly. The stance of someone used to hand-to-hand combat. Bare feet. *A brown-skinned sailor and no shoes.* He'd heard about them: skilled sailors from the Va-forsaken half of the globe, but not from Pashalin. They were recruited from the scattered islands of the Summer Seas and their reluctance to wear shoes in all but the coldest weather was legendary.

What did the Pashali call them? Lascars, that was it.

But what in all the foaming oceans was he doing in Lowmeer? Lascars crewed Pashali trading vessels half a world away. They didn't turn up in warehouses in chilly, wet Ustgrind, capital of Lowmeer, though he'd heard they occasionally reached the eastern coasts of his own nation, neighbouring Ardrone. He'd never glimpsed one, though.

He dropped his hand to pull out his dagger, but barely had it free of his belt before the young man sprang at him, turning sideways as he came, his front leg rising in a kick. Confused by the move, Saker hesitated. The man's heel—as hard as iron—slammed into his wrist. The dagger went flying and he was left gasping in pain. Consign the whelp to hell, a wallop like that could kill. And with bare feet too – his heels must be as thick as horn!

He ducked away and, to give himself time to recover, said with all the calm he could muster, "Can't we talk about this? I imagine you don't want to get caught in here any more than I do."

That was as far as he got. The youth came barrelling at him again, his speed astonishing. Saker reacted without thinking. He slid one foot between his opponent's legs, laid a hand flat to the floor to give himself leverage, and pushed sideways. His legs scissored around the youth's right knee, pitching him over. The lascar fell awkwardly, grunting in pain. Saker threw himself on top, and for a moment they wrestled wildly on the floor.

The sailor might have been small in stature, but he was all sinew and muscle. Worse, he was a scrapper. He head-butted Saker's face, sending fierce pain lancing through his cheekbones. His nose gushed fresh gouts of blood. Only a lucky blow using his knee to jab the fellow's stomach saved him from further ignominy. They broke apart, panting. Saker cursed. His shirt was torn all down the front, so he used it to wipe the blood from his face.

His opponent had scooped the fallen dagger up from the floor and drawn another from his belt. His blade was oddly sinuous. Saker's mouth went dry. Sailors said there was sorcery in blades like that.

Fobbing damn, Fritillary will be furious. Sorry, your reverence, I think trouble has come calling again . . .

Sometimes life just wasn't fair.

He back-pedalled away, fast, relying on his memory of the configuration of the cargo heaped behind. The lascar leapt after him.

Saker grabbed a barrel balanced on top of another and pulled it to the floor between them. The metal rim rolled over his attacker's bare foot. He didn't flinch. Saker tumbled another after it, and then a third, a smaller one, bound around the bulge with cane. The cane broke when it hit the floor, splitting the staves apart to release a cloud of bright yellow powder which billowed up around him. Disorientated, he tripped over one of the staves and fell face down into brightly coloured ground spice. He pushed himself up, blinded, utterly vulnerable, dripping blood and sneezing, blowing out clouds of gold-coloured powder.

He blinked away the spice and found himself looking into twinkling black eyes. His assailant's amusement didn't prevent him from pricking his ribs with the point of his wavy dagger, or twisting his other hand into his torn shirt to haul him to his feet.

Pox on the cockerel!

Saker could have said any number of things. Instead, he wiped bloodstained powder from his face and selected the most harmless question he could summon. "What *is* this stuff?"

"*Kunyit.* Here, men say turmeric."

"A spice, I hope, and not a poison."

The grin broadened. "Maybe you no live long enough to be poisoned, yes?" The fellow jabbed the point of his dagger a little more firmly into his side.

Saker sneezed again, a series of explosive paroxysms. Each time, the point of the dagger jabbed unpleasantly through the cloth of what was left of his shirt. Va help him, he was as helpless as a featherless squab!

The side door of the warehouse swung open with a loud creak. Light and the sound of voices flooded in. Both of them froze, then—as one—ducked down below the level of the stacked cargo. The lascar eyed him warily, keeping his wavy blade at the ready, even as he slipped Saker's knife into his belt in a deliberate gesture of ownership.

Their danger was now a shared one. If the newcomers wanted to inspect the cargo, there was no way they'd miss the broken cask with its contents spilled. Any man caught in an Ustgrind warehouse could expect no mercy. Lowmian law protected trade and traders, and punishment of transgressors tended to be lethal.

Va-blast, we could soon be as dead as soused herrings in a firkin.

Silently he shrugged at his unwelcome companion. The lascar leaned forward, until his mouth was almost at his ear. "Betray me, my blade stick your heart. You understand, no?"

Saker rolled his eyes to signal his lack of interest in continuing the fight. He glanced at his rope where it hung against the wall. It suddenly looked all too obvious. Carefully he reached for his gloves. The lascar watched, alert, as he pulled them on.

Footsteps rattled floorboards at the entrance. He counted the number of shadows cast across the light as men entered the door one by one: five. Five people. Only one spoke, directing the rest to the desks. Relieved, Saker breathed out. Clerks, then?

No, too early for clerks. This was a clandestine meeting.

Chairs scraped, more murmured conversation. Then one voice, authoritative, irritated, spoke above the rest. "Well, Mynster Kesleer, what's all this about, then? Dragging us out of our warm beds at this Va-forsaken hour! I trust you have good cause."

Kesleer? Kesleer himself? The Ustgrind merchant who not only owned the warehouse, but who possessed the largest fleet in all the Regality of Lowmeer.

The idea that such a powerful man had called a meeting at five in the morning in a dockside warehouse was startling. Saker's astonishment paled, though, under his growing fear. If he was caught and identified as an Ardronese witan working for Fritillary Reedling, the Pontifect of the Faith, he would not only be hanged as a thief and a spy, but his involvement would drag the Pontificate into an international incident. He winced. The repercussions would be horrendous.

He strained to hear the conversation, but the men had dropped their voices to a murmur. Beside him, the lascar peered around the edge of the bales to see what was happening. His frown told Saker he wasn't having much luck either.

The next audible words were uttered by a different man, his tone incredulous. "That's a preposterous proposal! Your skull's worm-holed, Kesleer, if you think we'll agree to that!"

Once again, the reply was muffled. Saker gritted his teeth. What proposal? To do what? Between whom? Without a second thought, he hoisted himself up the side of the bale until he lay flat on top. He was nowhere near the front row of the stacked cargo, and stuffed sacks on top of the bales still hid him from the Lowmians, but there was a gap between them, several inches wide.

A slit he could look through.

He had a narrow view of the counting table near the desks, now scattered with papers and charts, and the face of a man seated there. A lantern on the table provided more illumination, and there could be no mistaking him: Uthen Kesleer. Although they'd never met, the merchant had been pointed out to him on the street, and a bulbous growth on the side of his nose made for a distinctive visage.

A soft scrabbling behind told Saker the lascar had followed him. The young man, baring his perfect white teeth in a grin that might have been infectious in another situation, burrowed his way between Saker and the sacks, until he was sharing the same view.

One of the men raised his voice to growl, "Profit? Not from this recent venture of yours, I think, Mynster Kesleer. I notice neither of your other carracks followed the *Spice Dragon* up the Ust estuary home to the berth outside."

"Scuttled in the islands. Shipworm. Three in every four men in the fleet died, so there weren't enough to man all three vessels anyway. Those still alive sailed the *Spice Dragon* home. The dead were no loss. More profit for the rest, in fact."

The lascar drew breath sharply and his muscles tautened against Saker's torso. His hand groped for his wavy-bladed dagger, now thrust through the cloth belt at his waist.

He was on board, Saker thought with sudden insight. *He sailed on the* Spice Dragon *to Ustgrind*. Those poor bastards who'd died had been his shipmates. Scurvy-ridden fish bait, probably, or dying of bloody flux and fever in strange ports.

"Come now," Kesleer was saying, "you know how it is, Mynster Mulden. Since when have any of you rattled your brains about such things? It's the way Va has ordered life. There are always plenty more tars willing to take the risk and seek their cut of the trade. I'm sure Mynster Geer and Mynster Bargveth agree with me."

The shoulder muscles of the youth rippled like a cat about to spring. Saker gripped him, shaking his head. The fellow turned to glare, dark eyes flashing, daring him to say something.

He kept silent.

The conversation mellowed, the softer words unintelligible, but he had gleaned the identity of three of the other four men. Geer, Mulden and Bargveth, all merchant families with shipping interests, families not just wealthy, but influential at the Regal's court. The Geers hailed from Umdorp, the second largest port of Lowmeer. The Muldens controlled the docks and fleets of Fluge in the north, while the Bargveths had a monopoly of trade out of Grote in the far south.

That they were talking to one another astonished him. Competition between ports was a normal part of the country's commerce. Lowmian shipping merchants didn't cooperate; they prattled the whereabouts of rival merchantmen to Ardronese privateers instead.

Cankers 'n' galls, what's going on? The Pontifect won't like this, whatever the truth. When rich men played their games of wealth, they endangered the independence of Va-Faith and the neutrality of the Pontificate.

He strained to hear more, but caught only fragmented snatches. And he still didn't know the name of the fifth man.

"...new design of cargo ship. They're called fluyts..." That was Kesleer speaking.

"...the Regal will want a privateer's ransom!"

"Well, we can't succeed without him, that's for sure."

"…I have just such a tasty bait…" Kesleer again. The words were followed by a short silence, then a rattling sound.

"A piece of wood as a bribe for the Regal?" someone asked, tone scathing.

"This is bambu," Kesleer replied, "from the Summer Sea islands. It grows like that, with a hole down the middle."

The lascar jerked, the expression on his face an odd mixture of both pleasure and fierce rage as the conversation murmured on.

Oh, Va save us, what now?

"This hollow stuff is valuable?" someone else asked, incredulous.

"No, no. The value is in the contents." That was definitely Kesleer again. The next few words were indecipherable. Then, also from Kesleer, "Here, take a look…"

Saker couldn't see what Kesleer was showing them. He pulled a face, frustrated.

More muttered words, then, "I agree, they're certainly magnificent, yes, but what value can they have?"

What the rattling pox were they looking at? With a sudden movement the lascar pulled himself away from the crack and hauled himself up on to the bulging sacks to see better.

In horror, Saker leapt upwards to grab his ankle before he'd crawled out of reach. He yanked as silently as he could, trying to draw the young man backwards. What in all the world was he trying to do: get them both hanged?

The lascar kicked, but Saker was below him, well away from his flailing foot. Infuriated, the young man turned back and slashed with his dagger. Saker released his hold before the blade connected and the lascar wormed his way out of reach, heading across the sacks towards the merchants.

And the Pontifect thought *he* was reckless? He was a model of circumspect decorum compared to this idiot of a tar. At that moment, he could have cheerfully murdered the fellow. Instead, he slipped down to the floor. Stepping over the shattered cask of turmeric, he headed through the maze of cargo towards the back wall of the warehouse and his dangling rope.

Kesleer was saying, "...but Regal Vilmar is a jackdaw, hoarding pretty things. He'll love the idea that King Edwyn will have to watch and fume while Ardronese court women clamour after goods like these, at our price. Huge profits for Lowmian merchants ..."

Every nerve in Saker's body told him that in a moment, the relative quiet of the warehouse would vanish. These men would react violently when they realised their secret meeting had been overheard. What if they were armed with pistols, those new-fangled wheel-lock ones that didn't need a naked flame to ignite the powder? If he climbed up on the bale to seize the end of his climbing rope, he'd be visible to anyone who looked his way. Worth it, or not?

The Pontifect's words echoed in his ears. *You're a spy, not a one-man army. In Va's name, try subtlety, Saker Rampion!*

Best to wait until the lascar was seen, then escape in the ensuing confusion. No sooner had he made that decision than a child's voice echoed through the warehouse. "Papa! Papa! Someone's been here. There's a broken barrel and yellow footprints! Come see."

He winced.

The fifth person. A child. At a guess, Uthen Kesleer's ten-year-old son, Dannis.

He had no choice now. He hauled himself up the wall of bales, gripping with his knees and digging his fingertips into the burlap for purchase. Behind him, chairs scraped, enraged voices shouted. Kesleer called out the boy's name, but it sounded as if he wasn't sure where the lad was in the maze of aisles.

And then, a gasp behind him, just as he pulled himself on to the topmost bale. Lying flat, he looked back over the edge.

He'd never seen Dannis Kesleer, but this had to be him. He was dressed in black, a miniature merchant, with silver buckles on his shoes and belt, his broad white collar trimmed with lace.

They stared at each other. He hesitated, reluctant to use force to stop the boy yelling for his father. But Dannis was silent, staring. Not at Saker's face, but at the medallion around his neck. It had fallen free through his torn shirt and now dangled over the edge of the bale. His cleric's emblem, the oak leaf within a circle. His immediate thought was that the lad would not recognise it, for it was the symbol of an Ardronese witan, not a Lowmian one. Ardrone and Lowmeer might share the same Va-Faith, but there were differences in the way they practised it. The oak leaf was not used in Lowmeer.

Beyond Dannis, he caught a glimpse of the lascar fumbling among the papers on the table on the other side of the warehouse. Their gazes met as the man found and snatched up what appeared to be a wooden rod. The merchants had scattered and were nowhere to be seen.

Saker looked back at the boy to find that Dannis Kesleer knew the oak symbol after all. He was making the customary bow given to all clergy, with both hands clasped under his chin. Saker smiled down on him and raised a conspiratorial forefinger to his lips in a sign of silence. Briefly he thought of directing the lad's attention to the lascar to make his own escape easier, but dismissed the thought. Instead, he made a gesture of benediction. Obediently, the lad laid his hand over his heart in acceptance. Then he turned and walked away.

Saker let out the breath he'd been holding, but his heart refused to stop thudding. He leapt for the rope and clawed his way up. The skin between his shoulder blades tingled as he imagined lead shot ploughing into his back. He scrambled on to the beam and hauled the rope up behind him, frantic.

How can they miss seeing me?

But the merchants were still shouting at one another, their voices coming from all over the warehouse as they looked for Kesleer's son. No one looked up.

Kneeling on the beam, he untied the rope with fumbling fingers, his mouth dry. A movement low on the opposite wall near the desks caught his attention.

The lascar was on top of the ledger shelving. Even as he watched, the youth began to climb. Saker froze. Va's teeth, how was he doing that? He knew sailors could climb rigging in the roughest of seas, but that wall was sheer, built of rough wood planks, and all the man had were his bare toes and fingers. And his dagger. He was carrying the stolen wooden rod too, which he'd shoved down the front of his shirt so that the top of it poked up over his shoulder. Even that didn't seem to faze him.

That must be the bambu they were talking about.

Fortunately for the lascar, that corner was deeply shadowed and so he remained unseen. Incredibly, he paused to look at Saker, who was keeping an eye on him as he slid back the loose shingles where he'd entered the warehouse. Their gazes met, and the lascar removed the bambu and waved it, grinning hugely, as if to say, *"Look what I found!"*

Saker winced, convinced the overconfident tar would plummet to the floor, or be seen by the traders. Yet his luck appeared to hold. He scrambled up to the top of the wall where he pushed open the ventilation shutter. The gap would be just wide enough for him to squeeze through, but the morning light now slanted in to illuminate him.

Va favours the bold, Saker thought. Still, on the other side there was a sheer wall dropping straight on to a narrow walkway along the canal, and near certainty of being seen by the outside guards.

Saker pushed his rope through the hole he'd made and prepared to wriggle out. Out of the corner of his eye, he saw one of the merchants rush past the table. His action scattered papers and something else lying there, something wispy. Gold-coloured filaments fluttered in the air, as bright as sparks. Yelling, the man pointed a pistol at the lascar, and pulled the trigger. The noise was deafening.

Looking over his shoulder, Saker saw the unharmed sailor one last time through the opening of the shutter. He was outside the warehouse, hanging on to a beam of the overhang. He made some sort of hand gesture just before he swung up on to the top of the roof, as agile as a squirrel.

Saker thought it was a wave of farewell, but then he saw the flash of a dagger blade flying through the air.

Not at any of the men below, *but at him.*

Impossibly, it spiralled through the air, its point always facing his way. It whirred noisily as it came, and the merchants below swivelled to follow its passage. Saker hurtled himself upwards on to the roof.

Something tugged at his trousers and scraped his leg. Grabbing up the rope and the coat he'd left there, he set off at a run up to the ridge of the warehouse roof. He heard doors crash open below, followed by shouts in the streets. He didn't stop.

He was already on the roof of the neighbouring warehouse when he heard the second pistol shot, followed almost immediately by the bang of an arquebus.

He didn't look back, but he did look down.

The wavy dagger was firmly stuck through his trousers below the knee, and his leg was stinging.